"Maybe I should fetch Doc Whitman to have a look at this."

"Nonsense. Not much he can do for this, and I've had worse."

Stubborn woman. "Let me at least run some cool water over it and have a look."

Mitch led Cora Beth toward the sink then extended her hand under the spigot. Holding her slender wrist, inhaling her cinnamon-and-honey scent, hearing that sudden catch in her breathing as the water hit her hand, he was suddenly sharply aware of her as a woman, a woman whose company he enjoyed perhaps a little more than he should.

He gave his head a mental shake. That kind of thinking was wrong for any number of reasons. Not the least of which was the solemn vow he'd made after Dinah's death to never marry. With God's help he'd made peace with that aspect of his future years ago.

Or thought

Winnie Griggs
and
Cheryl St.John

Second Chance Family
&
Marrying the Preacher's Daughter

LOVE INSPIRED
INSPIRATIONAL ROMANCE

LOVE INSPIRED®

INSPIRATIONAL ROMANCE

Recycling programs for this product may not exist in your area.

ISBN-13: 978-1-335-45474-4

Second Chance Family &
Marrying the Preacher's Daughter

Copyright © 2020 by Harlequin Books S.A.

Second Chance Family
First published in 2011. This edition published in 2020.
Copyright © 2011 by Winnie Griggs

Marrying the Preacher's Daughter
First published in 2011. This edition published in 2020.
Copyright © 2011 by Cheryl Ludwigs

This edition published by arrangement with Harlequin Books S.A.

For questions and comments about the quality of this book, please contact us at CustomerService@Harlequin.com.

Love Inspired
22 Adelaide St. West, 40th Floor
Toronto, Ontario M5H 4E3, Canada
www.Harlequin.com

Printed in U.S.A.

CONTENTS

Winnie Griggs is the multipublished, award-winning author of historical (and occasionally contemporary) romances that focus on small towns, big hearts and amazing grace. She is also a list maker and a lover of dragonflies, and holds an advanced degree in the art of procrastination. Winnie loves to hear from readers—you can connect with her on Facebook at Facebook.com/winniegriggs.author or email her at winnie@winniegriggs.com.

SECOND CHANCE FAMILY

Winnie Griggs

For my thoughts are not your thoughts,
neither are your ways my ways, saith the Lord.
For as the heavens are higher than the earth,
so are my ways higher than your ways,
and my thoughts than your thoughts.
—*Isaiah* 55:8–9

To my husband, Ronnie,
who supports me in all aspects of my life,
even when it's not such an easy thing to do.
God truly blessed me when He sent you into my life.

Chapter One

September 1893
Knotty Pine, Texas

"Hey, let me go! I ain't done nothing wrong."

Sheriff Mitchell Hammond wasn't buying that for a minute. The furtive way the boy had been sneaking out of the boardinghouse garden had guilt written all over it. In fact, Mitch's gut told him this kid was more than likely the culprit responsible for the rash of petty thefts that had plagued the town the past week or so. "Stop your squirming, son. I think maybe we need to talk about that bunch of carrots you have stuffed in your shirt."

"Them's my carrots."

The kid's voice had more than a touch of bluster to it.

Mitch tightened his hold on the boy's collar. "You don't say? Well, here comes Mrs. Collins now. Since she runs this boardinghouse and this here is her garden, why don't we see what she has to say about that."

Cora Beth Collins was hurrying toward them. Even in the early morning light, he could make out the concerned look on her oh-so-readable face, could tell that her honey-brown hair was pulled back in its usual tidy bun, could appreciate the way her crisply starched apron was tied around her trim waist.

Mitch frowned as he realized where his thoughts had strayed. He'd always considered Cora Beth a fine lady and a good friend. But lately he'd begun to feel something a little warmer than mere friendship when he caught sight of her.

And that was definitely *not* a good thing.

"What's all this commotion about?" Her breathless voice held an accusing tone that he was certain was aimed more at him than at the young scoundrel in his grasp.

Mitch tipped his hat with his free hand. "Morning, Cora Beth. Sorry if we disturbed you." He tilted his head toward his still-squirming captive. "I caught this boy raiding your garden."

Consternation flitted across her face and then she gave Mitch a challenging look. "It's not raiding if he has my permission."

He wasn't surprised by her quick defense of the boy. Cora Beth had the softest heart in town—she'd give up her last crust of bread if she thought someone else needed it more. Especially if that someone was a kid. But he also noted that she hadn't actually claimed to have given the kid permission. And he hadn't missed the surprise and relief that flashed across the boy's face— a dead giveaway that his captive hadn't expected her to back him up.

"And did he?" It would be interesting to see how she answered him—she was too honest to out-and-out lie, no matter how much she wanted to rise to the kid's defense.

But to his surprise, she looked him straight in the eye, her expression free of evasiveness. "Actually, he's been weeding the garden in exchange for whatever produce he can carry." Then she glanced back at the boy and gave him an encouraging smile. "And a fine job you've been doing of it, too, young man."

That gave Mitch pause. Had he been a little too quick to judgment with the kid?

The boy mumbled something that might have been a thank-you, then glared up at Mitch, renewing his efforts to get free. "See, I told you I wasn't stealing. So, you gonna let me go now, mister?"

But despite Cora Beth's staunch defense, Mitch wasn't quite ready to believe the boy was totally innocent. "It's sheriff, not mister. And hold still. I'm not through with you just yet."

"Go easy." Cora Beth put out a hand but stopped short of touching either of them. "He's just a boy, not some hardened criminal." Her expression softened as she turned to his captive. "What's your name?"

Mitch raised a brow. "Now that's mighty interesting. He works for you, but you didn't bother to learn his name."

Cora Beth's expression reflected a mix of guilt and bravado, but she refrained from responding.

Keeping his amusement in check, Mitch turned his attention back to the closemouthed youth. "The lady asked you for your name, son."

"Ethan." The boy dug a toe into the ground and his tone was surly, grudging.

"Got a last name to go with that?" Mitch asked.

No response other than a tightening of the lips.

Cora Beth placed a hand on her supposed-gardener's shoulder. "You know, my brother Danny is twelve years old. I'll bet you're just about the same age, maybe a little older."

"I'm eleven." The boy's suddenly straighter posture bespoke a pride that was no doubt due to the fact that she'd erred on the plus side.

Which, knowing Cora Beth, she'd likely done deliberately.

"Is that right?" she said. "Well then, you're a very *mature* eleven." She cocked her head to one side. "Have you had your breakfast yet?"

The boy shook his head, and his rebellious expression shifted to hunger for a flash before he guarded it once more.

From the looks of the kid, Mitch guessed it'd been a while since he'd had a decent meal. But he'd landed on the right doorstep, figuratively speaking, to take care of that. If there was one thing Cora Beth could do exceptionally well, it was cook.

Sure enough, she straightened and gave a nod toward her back porch. "Well, we're going to do something about that. You come on inside. I just took the biscuits from the oven and it won't take more than a few minutes to scramble up some eggs."

Ethan scowled up at Mitch. "I don't think the sheriff'll let me go."

Cora Beth tossed Mitch a look. "Well then, I guess we'll have to invite him to join us."

Mitch touched the brim of his hat, giving her an answering smile. "Now, how could I turn down such a gracious invitation?"

She placed a hand on the boy's shoulder, her gaze still locked on Mitch. "You can let go of him now. He's not going anywhere, at least not until he's had his breakfast." She gave Ethan a smile. "Are you?"

"No, ma'am."

Mitch repressed the urge to roll his eyes at the boy's overly docile tone. Cora Beth might trust him not to make a break for it but Mitch wasn't so gullible. Maybe because he had more experience with individuals who wore Ethan's hunted look. Likely as not, the kid would bolt at the first opportunity.

He kept a close eye on the boy as he let the two of them precede him. Stepping inside the large kitchen of the boardinghouse, Mitch removed his hat and hung it on a peg by the door. "Nothing like the smell of fresh baked biscuits to get a man's stomach to rumbling."

That earned him a smile from Cora Beth. "You menfolk take a seat at the table and I'll have your eggs and bacon cooked up quick as a cat's pounce."

Mitch smiled a thank-you before he pulled out a chair, careful to seat himself between the boy and the door. "You're in for a treat." He kept his tone friendly. "Mrs. Collins is the best cook in these parts."

"Smells good."

The boy seemed a little more relaxed now. Was he ready to answer a few questions? "You're not from around here, are you?"

"No."

The bitter edge to the boy's tone was unexpected. Mitch filed that impression away to mull over later and continued his questioning. "So where *are* you from?"

The boy shrugged, not meeting his gaze. "Here and there. We move around."

So he wasn't traveling alone. "Who all makes up that *we?*"

Ethan clamped his lips shut, then looked past Mitch. "Is there something I can do to help you, ma'am?"

Cora Beth smiled over her shoulder. "Why thank you, Ethan, but I have it all under control."

Mitch reclaimed the boy's attention. "I asked you who you were traveling with."

He saw Ethan's internal struggle play out on his face. "My pa likes to travel," he finally blurted out.

Something in the boy's demeanor gave Mitch the feeling that Ethan was holding something back. But before he could press further, Cora Beth looked over her shoulder again.

"Your mother doesn't travel with you as well?" she asked.

"My ma's dead." There was no heat in his answer this time—only a starkness of tone and expression.

The sounds of Cora Beth's utensils against the pans stopped. "Oh, Ethan—" her voice carried a caresslike sympathy "—I'm so sorry."

Ethan looked up to acknowledge her concern. "Thank you, ma'am. I miss her a lot."

Mitch, who'd lost his own mother at a young age, felt a tug of matching sympathy for the boy. But he couldn't let his feelings get in the way of his job. Learning what he could about the boy's situation—not feeling sorry for him—was the best way to help him. "And where is your pa right now?"

Ethan glanced back at the table. "Our camp is set up a couple miles outside of town."

Before Mitch could press further, Cora Beth set a

plate in front of each of them. "That's enough with the questions for now, Sheriff. Let the boy eat."

Ethan reached for a biscuit and scooped up a forkful of the scrambled eggs at the same time.

"Ethan." Cora Beth used that voice most mothers acquired instinctively, the one that was gentle yet un-compromisingly firm at the same time. "In this house we always give thanks before we eat."

Ethan tensed for a moment, rebellion tightening his jaw. But he set down his fork and gave her a pinched-faced apology. "Yes, ma'am. Sorry."

She touched his shoulder before taking a seat beside him. "I know you are." Then she turned her moss-green gaze toward Mitch. "Sheriff, would you say grace for us, please?"

He nodded and bowed his head, oddly touched that she had turned to him to perform that service. "Father, we thank You for this food and for the one who so gen-erously prepared it. We ask that You watch over us this day as we go about our business. And we also ask that You keep a special eye on this young man sharing the table with us since he seems to be in need of Your guid-ing hand. Amen."

Cora Beth and Ethan echoed his amen. Ethan sent him a glower as he looked up, but then dug into his food without comment.

Mitch frowned as Cora Beth stood and headed back toward the stove. "Aren't you going to join us?"

"The others will be down for breakfast soon. I've got several more plates of eggs to fix."

The "others" included Cora Beth's family—three daughters, a younger brother and an uncle—and her three regular boarders. He wondered what it would have been like to grow up with such a large extended family. His own parents had passed on when he was barely six and he'd been raised by his grandmother who didn't believe in socializing much outside of church. Thank goodness he'd had school to get him out of that oppressive house for a time.

"You go ahead and eat your fill." Cora Beth's words brought his straying thoughts back to the present. He glanced up to see that her smile was directed at Ethan. "There's plenty more if you're still hungry when you eat that up." Then she glanced Mitch's way. "That goes for you, too, Sheriff."

He studied her for a moment as she worked, then reluctantly returned his attention to his table companion. "Just where is this camp of yours?"

"Like I said, a couple of miles outside of town."

"I was looking for something a bit more specific."

"A couple of miles *south* of town."

Well, there was another way to get the answers he needed. "After breakfast, I think I'll give you a ride back to your camp."

The boy paused with his fork poised halfway to his mouth. This time he met Mitch's gaze head-on. "No need. I *like* walking."

"No doubt." Mitch gave him a broad, companionable grin. "I did my share of walking all over these parts when I was your age. Lots of interesting places to explore." He reached for his glass. "Still, I'd like to see this camp of yours for myself."

Ethan shoved the forkful of eggs into his mouth, his glower deepening.

"Besides, I like to meet the folks who spend time in Knotty Pine, welcome them to the area and get to know a little about them." He caught and held Ethan's glance. "I'd like to meet your pa. Seems strange that he would let you wander off so far on your own."

"Pa knows I can take care of myself."

Mitch let that one go unchallenged. "Is your pa planning to stick around Knotty Pine awhile?"

Ethan shrugged.

"Don't want to discuss that subject either?" Mitch planted his elbows on the table. "Then let's try a different one. Do you know anything about a shirt and sheet that went missing from Mrs. Johnson's clothesline Monday, or a pie that disappeared from Mrs. Evans's windowsill yesterday, or some damage inside Mrs. Oglesby's greenhouse?"

The boy's shoulders hunched but he didn't look up from his plate.

Mitch stabbed a forkful of eggs, trying to keep his irritation in check. The boy was looking guiltier by the second. The question was, had he been stealing out of mischief or genuine need? "You're about as forthcoming as a fence post, aren't you, boy? A person might think you aren't talking because you have something to hide."

That only earned Mitch a glare.

Time to be more direct. "Look, Ethan, I'm willing to listen to your side of things, but in order for me to do that you need to do some talking. So either you start answering my questions here and now or we can go down to the jailhouse to finish this conversation." There— direct but reasonable.

Cora Beth didn't seem to agree. She plopped down a platter of sizzling bacon on the table with a little more force than absolutely necessary. "I know you have a job to do, Sheriff, but Ethan's not a criminal—he's just a boy. No need to scare him like that."

That drew Ethan's shoulders back and slapped an indignant frown on his face. "I'm *not* scared."

Mitch locked gazes with the boy. "Then answer my questions."

Ethan licked his lips, then tilted his jaw defiantly. "We're not planning on settling here. Probably be moving on today or tomorrow."

Not the question he'd been referring to, but Mitch decided it was a start. "Where are y'all headed?"

Ethan shrugged again. He seemed to be fond of that gesture. "Wherever I—we can find work."

Interesting slip. "What kind of work are you looking for?"

Instead of answering, Ethan grabbed his glass of milk and began gulping it.

"Don't you know?"

The boy set down his glass with enough energy to make the liquid slosh wildly. "Course I know. Thing is, my pa can do just about anything. Mostly, though, he does carpentry work."

Mitch leaned back, giving the boy a challenging look. "Well, in that case maybe he *should* consider sticking around here for a while. I reckon Knotty Pine could use a good carpenter."

"That's right," Cora Beth added brightly. "Why I was just telling Mrs. Plunkett the other day that some of the railings on the front porch need replacing. But now that school's started back up, my brother Danny's too busy and Uncle Grover's not up to that kind of work anymore. I'd be glad to hire your father to do the job for me."

Ethan's expression took on a trapped look as he

stared back down at his plate. "I'll sure enough tell him, ma'am. But I think he's not really interested in settling down hereabouts."

The kid's answers took on a different tone when he responded to Cora Beth. She had a knack for dealing with kids, no doubt about it.

A sudden cry from Cora Beth followed by the clattering of a dropped spoon had Mitch out of his chair and across the room in a heartbeat. "What is it?"

Cora Beth clutched her left hand against her chest. "I'm such a ninny, I burned my hand on the skillet." Her tone was light, but her attempt at a smile had more than a touch of grimace to it.

"Let me see." Mitch gently tugged on her injured hand, cradling it in his own as if it were a baby bird.

"It's nothing, really." But her strained expression belied her words.

"Now, aren't you the one who always says talk like that is more foolish than brave?"

Cora Beth gave a shaky laugh. "No fair turning my words back on me." She tried to draw her hand away. "I need to finish—"

"Breakfast will keep." He made quick work of moving the skillet away from the heat, then frowned as he studied the angry red streak on the side of her left hand. "Maybe I should fetch Doc Whitman to have a look at this."

"Nonsense. Not much he can do for this and I've had worse."

Stubborn woman. "Let me at least run some cool water over it and have a better look."

He led her toward the sink, then extended her hand under the spigot. Holding her slender wrist, inhaling her cinnamon and honey scent, hearing that sudden catch in her breathing as the water hit her hand—he was suddenly sharply aware of her as a woman, a woman whose company he enjoyed perhaps a little more than he should.

He gave his head a mental shake. That kind of thinking was wrong for any number of reasons. He'd made a solemn vow after Dinah's death, a vow to never marry. It had been a bitter pill to swallow, but when he'd been faced with the reality and consequences of his own shortcomings, it had been his only choice. It hadn't been easy, but he'd finally made his peace with that aspect of his future a long time ago. Or thought he had.

Lately, he wasn't so sure.

"See—" Cora Beth's words drew his thoughts back to the present "—it's not so bad. You're making a fuss for nothing."

"What I *see* is that this burn of yours is going to make a very nasty blister."

Ethan appeared next to them, holding the crock of butter. "My ma used to say that butter was good for a burn."

The smile Cora Beth gave the boy seemed softer and more genuine than the one she'd attempted earlier. "Thank you, Ethan. My mother used to say the same thing."

With a nod, Ethan set the crock on the counter beside them and returned to the table.

While Mitch was slathering butter over Cora Beth's burn, carefully telling himself that she was no different from any other citizen in town, the door to the hall opened. Cora Beth's younger brother Danny stepped inside, then stopped as he took in the scene before him.

"What's going on? Why's the sheriff here? You okay, Cora Beth?"

"Your sister burned her hand on the skillet," Mitch answered.

Danny quickly crossed the room. "Is it hurt bad? Are you gonna have to get Sadie to come in and help again?"

Cora Beth laughed. "Don't be silly. It's just a little burn. I'll be right as rain in no time."

Danny glanced Mitch's way. "Then why are you here?"

"Nothing to do with your sister. I caught—" Mitch looked around, scanning the room. His jaw tightened as he realized he'd been outfoxed by an eleven-year-old boy. "Hang it all, the kid's slipped out on me."

Chapter Two

Cora Beth felt guiltily relieved that Ethan had gotten away. She admired Sheriff Hammond's integrity and sense of duty, of course, but sometimes a gentler hand was required, especially when youngsters were involved.

She stared at the door, wondering how Ethan had managed to slip out without either of them noticing. "I hope he's going to be okay."

"Who?" Danny stared at her, then at the sheriff.

"A kid I found prowling around outside." The sheriff's drawl was roughened by an edge of irritation.

"He was *not* prowling," Cora Beth insisted. "He knew he was welcome to that little bit of produce he harvested." She turned to her brother. "His name is Ethan and he's about your age. Sheriff Hammond spotted him over by the garden and thought he was up to mischief." She shot a stern look Mitch's way. "But the sheriff was mistaken. So I invited them both in for breakfast while we tried to get it all straightened out."

Her would-be-doctor shook his head. "And he repaid you by running off without so much as a thank-you."

"Not true. He thanked me very nicely when I invited him in."

Danny's brows drew down as he tried to follow their conversation. "I never heard of any kid named Ethan around these parts."

The sheriff nodded as if Danny had come down on his side. "Exactly."

Oh for goodness' sake. She deliberately turned away from Mitch and toward Danny. "He and his family aren't from Knotty Pine, they're just passing through. And I think it falls to us as good Christian folk to be neighborly and welcoming while they're here. Including—" she gave Mitch a sideways glance "—making certain they have enough to eat."

She raised her good hand to forestall whatever grousing the sheriff seemed primed to offer. "Now, the sun's up and school'll be starting before you know it. Danny, please make sure the girls are awake and about, then tend to your chores. I've got to finish getting breakfast ready before everyone comes down looking for something to eat."

"Before you do that," the sheriff interjected with a glance toward Danny, "fetch me something I can use to bandage your sister's hand, would you?"

With a nod, Danny left the room.

Silence descended and suddenly Cora Beth was acutely aware that the sheriff was still holding her hand. Feeling her cheeks warm as if she were a schoolgirl rather than a matron of twenty-seven, she drew away and turned toward the stove. "I should get back to my cooking." She was pleased to find her voice was matter-of-fact.

"That can wait a few more minutes." Sheriff Hammond took her elbow and guided her to the table. "At least let me bandage that hand first."

Cora Beth nodded and wordlessly allowed him to pull out her chair.

Did the silence seem as awkward to him as it did to her? Goodness, what was *wrong* with her?

She was actually relieved when Danny returned. He handed some strips of cloth to Mitch, swiped a crisp slice of bacon from the platter on the table, then gave a wave and headed back out to the hall again.

Mitch quickly unrolled the cloth. "Now, let's see about getting you taken care of."

Cora Beth studied the slight wave in his dark brown hair as he wrapped the cloth around her palm. The tickle of warmth in her chest no doubt came from the novelty of having someone tending to her for a change. She loved her family dearly, and loved taking care of them, but every once in a while she liked to feel she wasn't just a mother or a caretaker.

"Do you think Ethan's going to be okay?" she asked.

"More'n likely." He paused his ministrations and gave her a long look. "You do realize he's probably a thief?"

Why couldn't he stop thinking like a sheriff for just a few minutes? "If he's a thief it's only because he's desperate. Did you see how thin he was? And those bruises on his arms?"

He went back to bandaging her hand, but not before she caught a flash of something unreadable flicker in his expression. "I saw. Looks like he's had a rough time of it." He tied off the bandage and sat back, meeting her gaze head-on. "That's one reason why I need to find out who or what he's running from and why. I know you feel sorry for him, and yes he's just a kid, but my job is to uphold the law and to protect the citizens of this town."

He seemed to hesitate just a heartbeat before continuing. "And I figure the 'upholding the law' part of my job includes figuring out who is responsible for the boy and making sure they take that responsibility seriously."

Cora Beth smiled. She shouldn't have doubted Mitch—he *did* care about Ethan's welfare. "Of course."

"That's assuming he wasn't lying about traveling with his pa."

Had he always had that suspicious nature or had his job made him that way? "Why ever would he lie about a thing like that?" she asked.

"He could be a runaway."

"A runaway. Oh my goodness, do you think he's in some sort of trouble?"

Mitch shrugged. "Don't know. But I aim to try and find out."

"If he did lie about traveling with his father—oh, Mitch, he could be an orphan. What if he doesn't have anyone to look out for him?"

"One way or the other, he needs to be under the care of an adult. If there's no one to take him in, I'll see about getting him into an orphanage." He must have read something in her expression, because he gave her a sympathetic look. "I'm sorry if you don't like hearing that, but there are worse things out there for an orphan than being institutionalized."

What did he mean by that? Then Cora Beth bit her lip. She'd almost forgotten that Mitch himself had been orphaned young, though he'd had a grandmother to take him in. But still, why would he say—

Then she remembered some oblique comments about

his grandmother. From all accounts, Opal Todd had not been an easy woman. But Cora Beth wasn't sure exactly what that had meant for Mitch as he was growing up.

"You know as well as I do," he continued, obviously unaware of her thoughts, "running around the countryside, stealing for his meals, is no way for any kid to live. The next time he gets caught raiding a garden, the owner might not be as understanding as you were."

It was hard to argue with that kind of logic. Still, an orphanage...

She straightened. "Do you think he'll be back?" If only she could speak to Ethan again, perhaps get him to trust her.

Mitch gave her that crooked grin of his. "After getting a taste of your cooking, he'd be crazy not to." Then he sobered. "If he *does* come back, though, I want your word that you'll let me know right away."

Cora Beth hesitated. Mitch obviously made Ethan skittish. It would be so much easier to get the boy to relax if—

"I mean it." His I'm-the-lawman-around-here tone was back. "I can see you like the kid, but we don't know anything about him. You need to trust me to handle this my way."

She gave a reluctant nod. "All right. I promise." And truly she did trust his intentions, if not his methods.

She pushed back from the table and stood.

He followed. "Don't know if you noticed, but he slipped a couple of biscuits in his shirt when he thought no one was watching."

The man didn't miss much. A requirement of his job, she supposed. But more importantly, he'd seen what

Ethan did and hadn't called his hand on it. Mitch was more sympathetic than he'd have her believe.

"He's welcome to them," she said. "Poor boy was probably worried about where his next meal's coming from." Then she tilted her head to one side and studied him. "You weren't really going to arrest Ethan, were you?"

"Depends on just how much mischief he's been up to and what his motives were. Right now I'm more concerned with finding him and getting to the bottom of his situation."

"What do you mean?"

"Whether you want to believe it or not, there's the possibility that he's a troublemaker on the run, in which case I aim to see he faces whatever he has coming to him. He's young enough so that, if we can make him learn he has to bear the consequences of his actions now, it might set him on the straight and narrow going forward."

"True, as long as we temper those consequences with mercy."

"That depends." He gave her a long, steady look. "Sometimes the greater mercy is disguised as discipline. Of course, if he *is* running from trouble, it could be that it's not of his own making. That's a whole different story and, depending on what kind of trouble it is, he might need a lawman in his corner to straighten things out."

She hadn't thought of that. "He'd be lucky to have you at his side."

He ignored her compliment. "Then again, he could have been straight with us about traveling through here with his pa. In which case I'd sure like to have a word or two with the man to make certain he understands his responsibilities as a parent."

Cora Beth had no trouble at all picturing Mitch leading that conversation. "You left out one possibility—that he's an orphan trying to make it on his own."

"If that's the case, then I aim to see he finds a new home, one way or the other." He tugged on the cuff of his sleeve. "The point is, a kid on his own like that is trouble, any way you slice it."

She thought about Danny. What would have happened to him if her folks hadn't been willing to take him in when his own folks died? "Ethan's just a boy."

"Don't go feeling too sorry for him just yet. I still haven't ruled out the troublemaker scenario."

She held her bandaged hand to her chest. "I don't believe that for one minute, and I don't think you do, either." When he didn't dispute her statement she softened her voice. "He's a good boy at heart, I know it."

Mitch shook his head. "Now how on earth can you know that? He stole those carrots from your garden. And I'd stake my badge that he's behind a half dozen other thefts that have taken place around here lately."

"I told you, he didn't steal anything from me. He earned those vegetables by pulling weeds."

Mitch raised a brow. "You mean he really did that?"

She stiffened. "Mitchell Hammond, did you think I was *lying* to you?"

He rubbed the back of his neck and shifted slightly. "Not lying exactly, just maybe stretching things a bit."

"Well, I'll have you know it was the gospel truth."

He crossed his arms. "You want to tell me how you hired that kid without even knowing his name?"

It was her turn to shift a bit. "When I went out to

the garden yesterday, I found someone had pulled all the weeds from the row of pole beans. And it was well done—not some halfhearted, higgledy-piggledy job. I figured the few scraggly tomatoes that were missing were fair payment to whomever did the work." She refused to let the expression on Mitch's face make her feel guilty. "I left a note on the gate saying so in case whomever it was came back."

"Well, it sure would have been helpful if you'd said something to me about it yesterday."

There was no need for him to get so riled up. "I didn't figure it was anything I needed to bring a lawman in on."

"Hang it all, it's my job to know all the comings and goings around here. How can I keep a proper eye on Knotty Pine if my own townsfolk are hiding things from me?"

She decided to ignore his question—it was probably rhetorical anyway. "The point is, he didn't just *take* my vegetables—he did his best to earn them. I wouldn't be the least bit surprised if you went back to whomever claims they were robbed and find some kind of payment was left for them, as well."

"Even if that were true, it's still stealing if the owner didn't agree to the trade. Rita Evans was mighty upset about her cherry pie going missing—seems she'd made it as a treat for Alfred's birthday. Not to mention how livid Mayor Oglesby's wife was over the damage done inside that glass plant house of hers. Not only were several pots tipped over but it seems one of her prize plants was missing."

Cora Beth smothered a groan. "Oh my goodness—please don't tell me it was her orchid." Nelda Oglesby was downright fanatical about that plant. When she'd first received it, she'd spent almost all of the social hour at the Ladies' Auxiliary meeting going on and on about how beautiful and delicate the plant was, how much cosseting it needed and how much special care had been required to get it shipped to Knotty Pine from whatever exotic place it had come from. And the members of the committee had been given weekly updates ever since.

Mitch raised a brow. "I do believe that was the name she mentioned—about twenty times."

"Oh dear. Poor Ethan. If he's the culprit, she won't forgive him easily."

"Poor *Ethan.* He's not the one who had to listen to a tirade on just how special that plant was and how particularly heinous a crime it was to steal it. You'd think the blooming thing was sprouting diamonds and rubies, the way she carried on."

A smile tugged at Cora Beth's lips. "I believe listening to citizen complaints is part of your job, too, sheriff."

He glowered at her. "I take back my comment about your softheartedness. You are one hard woman."

Cora Beth chuckled outright at that, enjoying the teasing. "So what are you planning to do now?"

"Well, right this minute I'm going to help you get breakfast on the table." Mitch rolled up his sleeves as he moved toward the stove. "How many more eggs do we need to scramble?"

Surely he wasn't serious? "Oh, no, you don't have to—"

"No arguments or I *will* go fetch the doctor."

Her lips twitched. "Mighty high-handed of you."

His grin was unrepentant. "Comes with being a lawman."

"Do you even know how to cook?"

He shot her an aggrieved look. "I may not be able to set as fine a table as you set, Cora Beth Collins, but I can certainly scramble eggs and fry up bacon. Just show me how much is left to be done."

Before she could comply, Uncle Grover stepped into the kitchen. "Danny told me you had an accident. Are you all right?"

His obvious worry touched her. "I'm fine, Uncle Grover. Danny shouldn't have worried you."

"Nonsense, Danny did just as he should." He waved a hand toward Mitch. "And I may not be as spry as the sheriff over there, but I'm here to help."

Just what she needed, another man trying to do her job. "That's very sweet of you, Uncle Grover, but—"

"I'm finishing up the cooking," Mitch interrupted. "Why don't you find me some platters to dish it up on?"

The older gentleman smiled as he pushed his spectacles up higher on his nose. "Of course."

When had she lost command of her own kitchen? It seemed her place had been temporarily usurped by one determined lawman.

She watched Mitch crack several eggs into a bowl and then stir them up with a great deal of vigor. He looked surprisingly at home. Her late husband had been a dear man and hard worker, but he'd never willingly gone near a cookstove except to serve up his plate.

Her three daughters came skittering into the kitchen, seven-year-old Audrey in the lead. "Mama, are you okay?"

"I'm fine, girls." She adjusted five-year-old Pippa's

pinafore, then checked twin Lottie's hair ribbon. "Say hello to Sheriff Hammond."

"Hello, Sheriff Hammond." The greeting rang out in unison from all three.

"Good morning, girls. Don't you all look pretty this morning."

While Pippa and Lottie clamored to examine their mother's injury, Audrey approached Mitch. Cora Beth answered the twins' questions as she kept part of her attention focused on her more brash offspring.

"How come you're cooking breakfast?" Audrey asked.

Mitch smiled down at her. "Just helping out your mother."

"But I didn't know men could cook."

He pointed the spatula at her. "I cook my own meals all the time."

"Don't you have a mommy to cook for you?"

"Afraid not."

"Oh. Then you need a wife."

Cora Beth cleared her throat. "Okay, girls, time to get the table set."

"Yes, ma'am." They obediently moved toward the dining room, ready to tackle the morning chore.

Uncle Grover chuckled. "They're pretty wound up this morning. I'd better go supervise."

"Thanks, Uncle Grover." Cora Beth grabbed the dirty dishes from the table and headed for the sink. "Sorry about Audrey's stream of questions," she said over her shoulder to Mitch. "She hasn't quite figured out what's appropriate and what's not."

He smiled. "I like a girl who speaks her mind."

Nice to know. "Earlier, when I asked what you were going to do, I meant about Ethan."

"I know." Mitch didn't bother to turn around this time. "I'll take a ride and talk to some folks on the farms outside of town, see if anyone has spotted him, and look around for the camp he mentioned. Though to be honest I'm not even sure there *is* a camp."

Cora Beth had no doubt he would meticulously comb the area looking for Ethan. And he'd keep searching until he either found the boy or ran out of places to look.

Because Mitch Hammond was just that stubborn.

And just that caring.

He'd make a fine family man someday. The very thought caused a little flutter in Cora Beth's stomach, which she did her level best to ignore.

Chapter Three

"Knock, knock."

Cora Beth looked up from her clumsy attempts to polish the tea service to see a familiar petite form standing at her back door. "Sadie, hi. Come on in."

Sadie Reynolds stepped inside and removed her bonnet. "I saw Sheriff Hammond a little bit ago and he told me what happened to your hand."

Cora Beth rolled her eyes. "You mean he stopped in at your place and asked you to come by and check on me. That man can be worse than a mother hen sometimes."

Sadie grinned. "Especially when it comes to a certain boardinghouse proprietress."

Cora Beth ignored the warmth creeping into her cheeks as she shook her head. "Nonsense. He cares about everybody around here, you know that." Still, it had been mighty nice having him fuss over her this morning.

Sadie's mouth turned up in a smile. "True, but I think he favors a certain someone just a wee bit more than the others."

Sadie seemed to be having fun at her expense. "Don't be silly," Cora Beth said. "And he really shouldn't have worried you with this."

Sadie removed her bonnet and set it on the counter. "I guess he just figured since I helped you out around here once before, I could do it again."

Last spring Sadie had spent a couple of weeks at the boardinghouse to lend a hand when Cora Beth sprained her wrist. That's when Sadie had met Eli Reynolds, the man who would become her husband a few short weeks later.

"That was different," Cora Beth explained. "This is just a little burn, nothing worth making a fuss over. Not that I'm not happy to see you, but I'm perfectly capable of doing my own housework." She gave her friend a knowing look. "Besides, if Mitch knew your happy news I doubt if he'd have bothered you with this." Just last week Sadie had announced that she and Eli were expecting their first child. So far, they were only letting family in on the news. Cora Beth had been touched that Sadie considered her part of her extended family.

Sadie grinned. "You're probably right. Men can be so over-the-roof protective when it comes to dealing with women who are expecting. As if we were made out of glass." She laughed. "Eli won't even let me saddle my horse anymore."

Then she sent a pointed look toward Cora Beth's hands and turned the conversation back to her original topic. "Are you really going to try to handle that tea service one-handed?"

Cora Beth grimaced. She was holding down the creamer with her left forearm while she tried to polish with her right hand. "I'm managing."

"Of course you are." Sadie gave her a mock pout. "Are you sure you're not refusing my help because you're worried I'll botch it like I did last time I came to help."

"Fiddlesticks—you were a big help." At Sadie's skeptical expression, she grinned. "But I concede that your true talents lie elsewhere."

"That's a very polite way of putting it." Sadie crossed her arms. "Now, I know how very capable you are, but seeing as I'm already here and since the Ladies' Auxiliary is meeting in your parlor this afternoon, I insist that you put me to work. I might be all thumbs, but since you're having to polish that tea service one-handed I figure I can do near as good a job as you today."

Cora Beth gave in with a smile. "Have it your way. Grab a rag and help yourself."

As Sadie joined her at the table, Cora Beth nudged the silver polish toward her. "Did the sheriff tell you anything else about what happened this morning?"

"You mean about your sunrise prowler? Yes, he told me, though I suspect I didn't get the whole story. He did ask me to keep a lookout for the boy."

"The boy's name is Ethan and I'm not convinced he's motivated by anything other than necessity. He's only eleven, for goodness' sake, and the poor thing is thin as a twig."

Sadie held up her palms in mock surrender. "Okay, I'm convinced—he's a good kid."

Cora Beth smiled sheepishly, realizing she'd been a touch too vehement. "Sorry. But it's so frustrating not knowing what his situation is, not knowing if he even has enough to eat."

"Well, you can rest assured, unless he's hitched a

ride on a wagon headed out of town, the sheriff will find him."

Cora Beth fiddled with her locket. "The problem is, Ethan doesn't want to be found. Sheriff Hammond put the fear of the Almighty into him this morning."

"He was just doing his job."

"I know, and he's mighty good at it." Cora Beth didn't want Sadie to think she was being critical. "But sometimes a softer touch is required."

"Perhaps the sheriff just needs a good woman to set the example for him."

And there were plenty of single ladies in town willing to take on that job. Many a miss had set their cap for the good sheriff. Cora Beth made a noncommittal sound and moved toward the stove, hoping to turn the conversation to a different topic.

But Sadie wasn't to be deflected. "I often wonder why a man with as much to recommend him as Mitch never married. I mean, I know he's no hermit and he doesn't lack for partners at the town dances or invites to Sunday dinners. It almost seems like he goes out of his way, though, not to spend too much time with any one eligible lady."

Sadie had been in Knotty Pine less than a year, so she wasn't familiar with everyone's histories the way the locals were. And Cora Beth certainly didn't want to start digging it all up for her. "I'm sure Mitch has his reasons."

"But you'd think he'd want to settle down with a family of his own." She gave Cora Beth an arch look. "Goodness knows there's any number of young ladies around here who'd be tickled pink to receive an offer from him. After all, in case you haven't noticed, in ad-

dition to his other fine qualities, there's some who'd
consider him handsome to boot."

Oh yes, she'd noticed. But Cora Beth refused to be
baited so she held her peace as she opened the oven
door.

Sadie went back to her polishing, a musing look on
her face. "I just can't figure why a man like our sheriff
wouldn't have landed himself a wife by now."

Looked as if she would have to go into this a bit after
all. "Actually, he *was* engaged to be married, once."

Sadie sat back in her chair, polishing forgotten. "Oh
my goodness, he was? What happened?"

Cora Beth kept her back to her friend, taking her
time checking the batch of cookies. "Dinah, his fian-
cée, died a few days before the wedding. It was a freak
accident and poor Mitch was devastated." She remembered the horrible darkness that had seemed to envelop
him, the way he'd withdrawn into himself for a time.
"I don't think he's ever quite gotten over the loss," she
finally added.

"Poor Mitch. How awful for him." Sadie's voice softened in sympathy. "How long ago was this?"

Cora Beth finally turned to face her friend. "Nearly
ten years now."

"Ten years?" Sadie stared at her incredulously. "You
made it sound as if it were more recent. Ten years is
a very long time to grieve. It's past time he moved on
with his life."

Cora Beth winced at her friend's cavalier tone. "A
body doesn't ever stop truly grieving for a loved one.
I lost my Phillip five years ago and I still miss him."

"Oh, Cora Beth, I'm sorry." Sadie rose and gave her
a tight hug. "Of course you miss your husband," she

said as she stepped back. "But that doesn't mean you'd never marry again, does it? I mean, if the right man came along?"

Cora Beth thought about that for a moment. Would she? She'd loved Phillip dearly but he was gone now. And she'd really *liked* being married, having a help-meet at her side, someone to share her joys and burdens, someone to be a father to her daughters, someone to cherish and be cherished by in return. "If someone came along whom I loved and who loved me, then yes, I would marry again."

Sadie gave a satisfied nod as she took her seat again. "Quite right. And the same is likely true for Mitch. He may just need a push from the right woman to help him realize he should take a chance on love again."

Cora Beth wasn't so sure of that. A few years ago it had looked like Harriet Elkenberry would finally get him to take that walk down the aisle, but in the end she'd given up and gotten hitched to Roger Baker, with Mitch standing in as best man.

For all his popularity and friendliness, Mitch seemed quite happy with his bachelor status. Which, after all, was his business and no one else's.

Cora Beth glanced up to find Sadie studying her with a look that made her feel as if her friend could read her thoughts. But she was rescued from further unwanted discussion when the hall door swung open.

"Cora Beth, I—" Beulah Plunkett halted when she saw Cora Beth wasn't alone. "Oh, hello, Sadie." She turned back to Cora Beth. "Sorry for the interruption, I didn't know you had company."

Mrs. Plunkett, one of Cora Beth's three long-term boarders, was a tall, imposing woman with a hawk-like nose and a steel-gray bun that perfectly matched her no-nonsense personality and commanding voice. The starchy widow had rented rooms for herself and her daughter Honoria at the boardinghouse for over a dozen years. Cora Beth had learned a long time ago that beneath her severe, outspoken exterior, the woman had a heart of gold. She'd also suspected for a while now that Beulah Plunkett had a soft spot for Uncle Grover.

"You're not interrupting," she said waving the woman into the room. "Sadie and I were just indulging in a bit of idle chatter. Was there something you needed?"

"Mr. Collins told me about your little accident this morning."

Cora Beth hid a smile. Mrs. Plunkett was the only person in town who called Uncle Grover by his more formal appellation.

"It's unfortunate that you allowed yourself to lose focus on your task that way," she continued reprovingly. "But no doubt it was due to the distraction caused by your unexpected early morning visitors." She clasped her hands in front of her, which in no way detracted from her severe shoulders-back posture. "Since the Ladies' Auxiliary will be meeting here this afternoon, I thought I'd offer my services to help in getting everything ready." She cast a look Sadie's way. "However, I see that someone else was before me, so I will leave you ladies to your work."

Mrs. Plunkett, normally a stickler for protocol, rarely set foot in the boardinghouse kitchen and normally seemed more apt to give orders than take them so Cora Beth was truly touched by the offer of assistance.

She also sensed that Mrs. Plunkett was disappointed to not be needed.

"Oh, please don't go," she said impulsively.

Sadie exchanged a meaningful look with Cora Beth and set down her polishing rag. "Actually, if you don't mind taking my place here, I really should get back home."

Mrs. Plunkett moved toward the table. "Well, if you're certain you're not leaving on my account."

"Not at all." Sadie stood. "I promised Eli I would attend to the household accounts before he came home from the bank this afternoon."

Sadie gave Cora Beth a quick hug, then moved to the door. "Keep an eye on her, Mrs. Plunkett," she called back over her shoulder. "She shouldn't be doing too much with that hand." Then, with a final wave, Sadie was out the door.

When Cora Beth turned back to the table, Mrs. Plunkett was already busy polishing the creamer. Was she really just here to lend a hand, or was there something else on her mind? At any rate it looked like it was going to be up to her to initiate the conversation. "How is Honoria liking her new job?"

This past summer the townsfolk had decided Knotty Pine had outgrown its schoolhouse and had built an additional room onto the building. Which meant Mr. Saddler, the schoolteacher and another of Cora Beth's longtime boarders, needed some help. To everyone's surprise Honoria Plunkett, Beulah's daughter, had applied for the job. So, when the children of Knotty Pine had started back to school this fall, Mr. Saddler had taken the older children and Honoria had taken the younger group.

"She seems to be enjoying it very much," Mrs. Plunkett replied. "It has given her a reason to get out of the house and spend time with other folks besides her old mother. Between her hours at the schoolhouse and her time at home working on papers and planning lessons I barely see her at all anymore."

Ah, she was lonely. Cora Beth's heart went out to her. "Well, she appears to be doing a good job. My girls certainly enjoy having her for a teacher." Danny was in Mr. Saddler's class so he didn't share classroom time with the girls now. Ethan would be in there with him if he stayed here in Knotty Pine.

"I would expect nothing less of her."

Cora Beth hid a smile at that. "Yes, of course."

Mrs. Plunkett rubbed the creamer with increased vigor. "I was wondering, is Mr. Collins really your uncle?"

Interesting change of subject. "My late husband's uncle, actually."

"And he's been living with you for some time now?"

"Uncle Grover came to live with us when Audrey was still a baby, so I guess it's been nearly six years now. Before that, he lived up in Indiana." Where was all of this going?

"He's a widower, is he not?"

"Yes, though I never met his wife. She died before Phillip and I ever married. Unfortunately they were not blessed with children."

"But he has you and your girls."

Cora Beth smiled. "And we have him."

"I suppose you are wondering why I am prying into your family's personal life."

"I don't mind." Then she grinned. "But you're right, I did wonder."

Mrs. Plunkett allowed herself a smile, though her expression quickly returned to its normal schoolmarm severity. "I've reached a decision and I thought it only proper that I inform you of it."

"Oh?"

"I have decided to court Mr. Collins."

The outrageous declaration caught Cora Beth off guard. For the life of her she couldn't form a proper response.

Fortunately, Mrs. Plunkett didn't wait for one. "I realize that it is unorthodox," she continued. "But I have tried to let the gentleman know of my interest without being too forward, and he appears to remain oblivious. Since I am no longer in my prime, I have decided not to waste what years are left to me by being coy."

Cora Beth had trouble keeping her expression appropriately sober as she tried to picture Mrs. Plunkett being "coy."

"So, do I have your blessing?"

"Of course you do." Fascinated by this side of her normally staid boarder, Cora Beth joined her at the table. "May I ask how you intend to go about this courtship?"

"I intend to insert myself into his life at every given opportunity." She pursed her lips primly. "I am, however, open to suggestions."

"You know about his fascination with insects." Uncle Grover fancied himself an entomologist and had an extensive collection of specimens he had gathered himself.

"Yes, of course. One can't be around your uncle for any length of time and not be aware of his unusual hobby." She drew back her shoulders. "I'm afraid it quite put me off when I first met him. But I confess, if one pays proper attention to his discourse on the subject, his passion and knowledge of the subject make it all rather intriguing."

"Then how do you feel about hiking?"

"Hiking? I'm not at all certain that it is a suitable pastime for a genteel lady."

"That's unfortunate. Uncle Grover likes to explore the fields and wooded areas around here for new specimens. I'm sure it would make his treks more enjoyable if he had company."

"I see. And come to think of it, I do recall Dr. Whitman saying that vigorous walking is good for one's constitution. Perhaps I will rethink my stand on hiking."

"And if I might make another suggestion?"

"Please do."

"Everyone likes to feel useful, to feel needed. Perhaps if there was some project of your own that you could ask for his assistance with. Something of a long-term nature perhaps."

Mrs. Plunkett gave her a measured look. "A very sensible suggestion. I will have to think on that."

"Well then." Cora Beth stood. "I believe you've polished that creamer well enough. Thank you for your help."

"Thank you, my dear. We may need to have little chats like this more often."

"You're welcome in my kitchen any time."

Cora Beth smiled as the door closed behind Mrs. Plunkett. The woman had surprised her, but in a happy way. This little campaign of Mrs. Plunkett's, regardless of how it all worked out, would be good for both Mrs.

Plunkett and Uncle Grover. One could never have too much romance in life.

Even when it ended in tragedy, the way hers had. And the way Mitch's had.

Was she ready for another go at it herself? She'd told Sadie that perhaps, if the right man came along, she'd consider marrying again.

The thing of it was, when she thought about that "right man," one very specific image came to mind.

Dear Father, I know You already gave me one wonderful man to love and partner with in this life, but he was taken away from me so soon. I know You have Your reasons, and that those reasons are always perfect, but I sure would like a second chance at marriage, at finding a loving husband, a helpmate to share my joys and burdens with. I have a certain someone in mind, but I'm willing to follow Your will in this.

She thought a minute and then decided to add a postscript to her prayer. *If not a husband, then maybe just a little something to add a bit of excitement or a touch of the unexpected to my life.*

A smile teased at her lips. Wouldn't folks be surprised if they knew that no-nonsense, matter-of-fact Cora Beth Collins longed for excitement and romance in her life?

The question was, though, was she brave enough to help make it happen?

Chapter Four

Cora Beth placed the last of the tea cakes on the cart and nodded to Mrs. Plunkett. "That's everything."

The older woman raised a brow. "I should think so. You have enough here to feed half of Knotty Pine."

The business portion of the regular Wednesday afternoon meeting of the Knotty Pine Ladies' Auxiliary had adjourned and the group had moved into the visiting portion. Mrs. Plunkett had followed Cora Beth into the kitchen, insisting on helping her with the hostessing duties.

Now Cora Beth nodded absently in response to her comment. "I accidently doubled the recipe for the lemon bars and since some of the ladies don't like pecans, I made one batch of shortbread cookies with nuts and one without."

Truth was she'd been so distracted all day that it was downright surprising she had anything edible to serve at all. How was Mitch's search going? She'd hoped he'd ride back into town at lunchtime, but if he had, she'd missed him. Not that he was obliged to check in with her, of course. But surely he knew how anxious she was to hear whatever he'd discovered.

Was he still out there because he'd found some sign of Ethan that he was following? Ethan seemed a clever boy, but if anyone could track him down it would be Mitch. Hopefully the boy hadn't had time to get into any further mischief. Goodness knows the next person he ran into might decide to press charges, or worse.

Perhaps Mitch had already found the camp and maybe met Ethan's father. Or not. It was just so frustrating not knowing.

Heavenly Father, I know I've been calling on You a lot today, but please guide Mitch in his search, and please, please, watch over Ethan. Beneath that bravado, I can tell he's a scared little boy trying to make his way. He's taken a wrong path, somehow, and I'm afraid he might be in serious trouble. But You know all of that better than me. Just please let him realize he's not alone and help him to feel the comfort of Your presence. Amen.

Feeling a bit calmer, Cora Beth focused back on Mrs. Plunkett to find the woman studying her with an expectant look. Uh-oh, caught daydreaming again. "I'm sorry, did you say something?"

"I just asked you to open the door while I push the cart." She gave Cora Beth a probing look. "Is there something on your mind?"

Cora Beth nodded. "I just offered up a prayer for a friend in need."

Mrs. Plunkett nodded as if that settled matters. "Then you're helping your friend in the best way you can right now."

"I know. But I've never been very good at waiting."

"Patience is a virtue, my dear. You must learn to wait on the Good Lord's timing."

"Yes, ma'am." Feeling properly chastised, Cora Beth meekly followed her boarder down the hall and into the parlor.

Once Mrs. Plunkett had pushed the cart into the room, Cora Beth touched her arm. "Would you mind presiding over the teapot today?" She lifted her bandaged left hand. "I wouldn't want to risk making a mess of things."

"Of course, my dear, I would be honored."

Seeing the sparkle in the older woman's eye, Cora Beth was pleased she'd made the offer. She hadn't realized before how Mrs. Plunkett, without a home of her own as such, might have felt about not being able to play the role of hostess in these weekly gatherings. She'd have to see if she could find a way to work something out with her for future gatherings that wouldn't hurt her pride.

Then Cora Beth's smile wavered as she saw Nelda Oglesby approaching with a determined look on her face.

"I hear Sheriff Hammond caught a thief raiding your vegetable garden this morning." Nelda seemed to hold Cora Beth responsible for the presence of a thief in their midst.

Cora Beth pasted the smile back on her face and strove for a mild tone. "Actually, it was a misunderstanding. The boy he found was just doing some work for me."

Nelda didn't seem reassured. "Is that so? Then why is the sheriff searching high and low for that vagrant even as we speak?"

Alice Danvers and Ida Van Halsen, two of Nelda's closest friends, drifted over. Cora Beth tried not to feel ganged up on. "Because we're concerned the boy might be out on his own and need some help," she answered.

"On his own? Ah, a runaway is he?" Nelda gave a ladylike sniff. "Running from some kind of trouble of his own making no doubt. This probably isn't the first bit of hooliganism he's been up to. I hear several ladies here have experienced thefts this past week."

Other conversations had tapered off by this time and most of the ladies in the room were openly listening to the discussion about Ethan now. At that last comment, Patsy Johnson stepped forward to join them. "That's right. A couple of items from my laundry went missing on Monday."

Cora Beth raised a hand before anyone else could list their grievance. "But that doesn't mean Ethan is responsible. And besides, he's just a boy."

The mayor's wife drew herself up with a huff. "That's easy enough for you to say. After all, that little hooligan only took a few vegetables from you." Her voice took on a tone of genteel outrage. "But he stole my prize orchid. And he made a mess of my greenhouse in the process."

Ida tsked, patting Nelda's arm sympathetically. "After all the work you put into that beautiful plant. It must be such a heartache for you."

"I tell you, I could hardly take it in." Nelda had her hand over her heart. "I stepped into my greenhouse and I near swooned right there on the threshold. As I told Sheriff Hammond, anyone who would do such a terrible thing had to be a blackhearted scoundrel."

Cora Beth tried to reason with them once more. "But you can't be certain it was Ethan."

"That's right," Sadie added. "Perhaps some animal got inside and made that mess."

Nelda looked down her nose. "Only an animal of the two-legged variety would carry off a whole plant, pot an all. And, if not this Ethan, then who else could it be? Surely you don't think it was someone here in town."

Mrs. Plunkett handed a cup of tea to Sadie. "I hear you told Sheriff Hammond you thought it was the Colfax boy."

Ruby Colfax, Andy Colfax's mother, stiffened and Nelda had the grace to look embarrassed. "I was distraught. I didn't know what I was saying."

Ida patted her arm. "Of course you were. Anyone would be."

Sadie moved to stand beside Cora Beth. "I think we should leave this to Sheriff Hammond. I'm certain he'll get to the bottom of the matter and handle it in a way that is fair to all parties."

"He'd better. After all, we pay the man to handle crimes of this sort."

Was that intended as a slight to Mitch? "What we pay Sheriff Hammond to do is uphold the law," Cora Beth said firmly, "but as I'm sure anyone in this room can attest, he does so much more than that for this town." She gave Nelda a smile she hoped appeared reassuring. "And I have every confidence he'll get to the truth of the matter. Whatever that may be."

Determined to end this line of conversation, she turned and waved a hand toward the tea cart. "Now, please, everyone have some refreshments. I tried a new recipe for the shortbread cookies and I'd love to hear what you all think."

As the ladies complied, conversations turned to other topics and Cora Beth offered up another prayer—this time for courage for Ethan. Looks like he'd have some unpleasant music to face if Mitch succeeded in finding him.

And she was determined to see he didn't face it alone.

* * *

Mitch paused a moment as he stepped onto the back porch of the boardinghouse. Maybe he should have taken time to clean up a bit before stopping by. It had been a long, hot day and he had more than a little trail dust clinging to him. But he knew Cora Beth would be eager to hear any news he could bring her.

Then Cora Beth spied him through the screen door and took the decision out of his hands.

"Oh, Sheriff." Was her welcoming smile for him or for the report she was hoping for? "Don't just stand there, come in and tell me if you found out anything about Ethan."

Well that answered that. Removing his hat, Mitch opened the screen door but didn't enter. "I can talk from here. I don't want to track my dirt into your kitchen."

"Nonsense, that's what brooms are for. And you look like you could use a tall glass of lemonade. Get in here and let me pour some up for you."

Mitch stepped into the kitchen and hung his hat. "That sounds good." He moved closer. "How's the hand?"

"Barely remember I burned it." She reached inside the cupboard for a glass. "Well, don't keep me guessing. Did you find any sign of Ethan or his camp?"

He grabbed the pitcher before she could lift it. The woman sure didn't seem to be letting that burn slow her down any. "I spent most of the afternoon searching the likely places south of town and there wasn't hide nor hair of him to be found. I'm beginning to think he wasn't being exactly truthful when he told us where he'd pitched camp." Not that that surprised him, but he knew

Cora Beth had a lot of faith in the kid. Sure enough, she immediately rose to his defense.

"And who could blame him. He's just a boy. The poor thing was probably afraid you'd haul him in and put him in jail if you found him."

Her accusing tone stung. "Now, Cora Beth, you know good and well I—"

"Oh, I didn't say you'd do it." She handed him a glass, her expression softening. "But *he* doesn't know that. You can be mighty intimidating when you put your mind to it."

Did she disapprove? "The boy's been stealing things." He managed to keep the defensiveness from his tone. "Someone has to take him in hand before he gets into some real trouble."

She let out a soft sigh. "Sorry if I sounded critical— I know you're doing what you think is best for Ethan. And given time, he'll see that for himself."

"Like as not we'll never know. Chances are he's moved on."

He could see she didn't like that idea at all. "Surely he couldn't have gone far." She sat at the table and waved him to a seat across from her. "I'm worried about him. I keep wondering, what if Danny had found himself in that situation? I'd want someone with a good heart looking out for him."

He'd figured she'd make that comparison sooner or later. But Ethan wasn't Danny and she could get hurt if she started thinking that way. "I know you like to think the best of everyone, but you can't really be sure what kind of kid Ethan is. If you aren't careful, you're likely to get disappointed, or worse. Some things just aren't worth taking that risk over."

Her expressions softened. "Oh, Mitch, people are always worth taking those kinds of risks over."

There was no reasoning with her when she was like this. "Remember your promise to let me know if he comes back."

She met his gaze, worry etching a vertical line above her nose. "You wouldn't *really* put him in jail, would you?"

"Not unless I had no other choice. But, assuming I do find the boy, *something* will have to be done with him. As you admitted yourself, he's got no business living on his own."

"So you don't believe he's traveling with his dad?"

"It's possible." Just not very likely. "But if his pa is with him, why'd he let the kid roam lose at all hours of the night and day?"

"Maybe the man is ill or injured."

Or something a bit less innocent. No need to worry Cora Beth with that possibility though. "The sooner I find where he's holed up, the sooner we can get our questions answered."

He pondered a moment over whether or not to give her the other bit of news, then decided she needed to hear it. "I sent a telegram to the orphanage up at Casonville this morning and they've already responded. There's room for him there if that's what's needed."

"No."

He didn't like the decisiveness of her tone or the stubborn set to her jaw. "It's a well-run facility," he said, keeping his tone neutral. "From what I hear, they take real good care of the kids."

"Maybe so. But that's not the same as being part of a real family."

"Not everyone gets to be part of a real family." He should know. "Danny was lucky he had your folks to take him in. And Uncle Grover was lucky he had *you* to take him in. The orphanage is there to take care of those who aren't so lucky." He held up a hand to stop her response. "At any rate, I just contacted the orphanage as a precaution. He might not be an orphan at all."

"Which would mean he's a runaway."

Not necessarily. But again, there were some things he'd prefer not to point out to her.

She didn't seem to notice his lack of response. "What if he had a real good reason to run away? I mean, there's some folks who aren't fit to be parents. And there are worse dangers than the physical ones."

He noticed she'd cradled her burnt hand against her chest. Was she even aware she'd done it? "The law is clear that a minor belongs with his parents or guardian."

"Well, I think there should be some flexibility in the law where kids are concerned."

"Not if he isn't in mortal danger." He rubbed the back of his neck, uncomfortable with this line of talk. "Regardless of my personal feelings, I've sworn to uphold the law, and that's what I'm bound to do." No matter what it cost him personally.

"Of course. I'd never ask you to do otherwise."

He could tell she hadn't made peace with this. "Look, there's no sense in borrowing trouble. We don't even know that he *is* a runaway. I may stumble on him tomorrow, camped with his pa, just like he said. Or I may never see him again, which makes this whole conversation pointless."

Some of the tension seeped from her expression.

"You're probably right. But just so you know, before I let you put Ethan in an orphanage, I'll adopt him myself."

Cora Beth was normally a levelheaded woman. But when her much-too-soft heart was involved, common sense seemed to fly out the window. "You haven't been in that boy's company for more than thirty minutes and you don't know anything about him. What makes you think he's someone you'd want to take responsibility for, much less have sharing a house with your daughters?"

"Because I'm convinced he's a good kid who just needs someone to give him a chance, someone to believe in him." She took a deep breath. "But you're right, we need to stop going round and round this way. After all, it's in God's hands and we need to have faith that He will work it out for the best, whatever that is." She gave him a soft smile. "Would you pray with me for Ethan's well-being?"

"Of course." He watched her slide her hand across the table and after only a heartbeat, he took it in his own. Bowing his head, Mitch forced himself to focus on his prayer. "Almighty God, we ask that You keep a close watch on Ethan, that You keep him safe and lead him to those who can help him. And if that someone is not one of us, that You also give Mrs. Collins peace in the knowledge that You, who look after even the smallest of sparrows, will be watching over him. Amen."

Cora Beth echoed his amen, and he had a few moments to study her bowed head before she looked up to meet his gaze.

"Thank you." Both her words and smile were soft and intimate. It was almost as if she saw something special in him, something—

Abruptly he released her hand and pushed back his

chair. "Thank you for the lemonade, but I'll be on my way." He stood, rubbing the back of his neck again. "I need to tend to some paperwork before I make my nightly rounds."

He saw the puzzled surprise in her expression but was grateful that she left her question unvoiced.

"Thanks for stopping in to tell me what you found," she said instead. "And for praying with me."

With a nod he crossed the room in a few quick strides, retrieved his hat and made his exit. Once outside he paused and took in a few deep breaths.

Man, he had it bad. For a minute in there, when she'd given him that warm smile, he'd thought that there wasn't much he wouldn't do to earn another one like it from her.

Heavenly Father, I know these feelings I'm having about Cora Beth are inappropriate. We both know I'm not a till-death-do-us-part kind of man, no matter how much I wish I were. And a lady like Cora Beth deserves someone whose love for her will stand the test of time, someone who won't hurt her like my granddaddy did my grandmother. Or like what I almost did to Dinah before You took her. So please, help me to hold my distance and to not do anything to cause her distress.

He hadn't asked God for something for himself in a long time. The last time he'd done so, the result had been a disaster. Would God help him this time?

Trouble was, keeping his distance from Cora Beth was the last thing he wanted to do. Either way, he couldn't win.

Cora Beth watched as Mitch made his hasty exit. She hoped her earlier words hadn't upset him—she hadn't meant to be critical. Sometimes she needed to stop and think before speaking. Knotty Pine was blessed to have such a conscientious man as Mitch for their sheriff and next time she saw him, she'd make a point to tell him so.

She moved to the sink, where she could look out the window and watch him walk away. His stride was purposeful, confident and had just a touch of a masculine swagger. He looked solid. And dependable.

And alone.

Alone? Now where on earth had that thought come from? Mitch had lots of friends—of both the male and female persuasion. He was well respected and well liked by most everyone in Knotty Pine. He was welcomed everywhere and his standing as a bachelor was obviously through choice rather than lack of opportunity.

Yet ever since she'd had that conversation with Sadie this morning, she couldn't shake the thought that there was another layer to his long-term bachelor status. And now that the idea had insinuated itself into her thoughts, it was hard to shake it. He lived alone, had done so since his grandmother had passed on nine years ago. She herself couldn't imagine what it would be like not to be surrounded by family.

As if to punctuate that thought, the door burst open behind her and her three daughters shot into the room, clamoring for her attention. She smiled as she patiently listened to their excited chatter. What with these three, Danny and Uncle Grover, she was truly blessed to have such a warm and lively family. But there was always room for more.

Perhaps she would make a point to invite Mitch over to join them for supper occasionally.

After all, it was the neighborly thing to do.

* * *

Early the next morning, Cora Beth quickly descended the stairs, tying an apron around her waist as she went. She was up earlier than normal hoping that, despite what Mitch believed, Ethan would return. In fact, she'd throw a few extra eggs in the skillet, just in case.

Humming, she stepped into the kitchen, lit the lamp and headed for the stove. As soon as she stoked the fire she'd check the garden to see if—

A sudden urgent banging on the back door jerked her head around. "Coming." When she opened the door it was Ethan himself standing there, looking scared and more than a little worried.

She quickly pushed open the screen door. "What is it? Is something wrong?"

"It's Cissy, my little sister," he blurted out. "She's real bad sick and I don't know how to help her."

Oh mercy, he had a sister out there somewhere. "Where is she? Is she alone?"

"Scout is with her. He's a real good guard dog, but she needs someone who can do some healing. I wanted to bring her here, but she was too sick to walk and I knew I couldn't carry her this far."

The anguish in his face tore at her heart.

"I promised I wouldn't be gone long," he continued, "and that I'd bring someone who could help her get better. Please, ma'am, you got to come with me."

Cora Beth's mind was racing. The fact that he'd taken the chance to come to her for help was enough to convince her this was serious. And he hadn't mentioned anything about his dad—did that mean the children had no adult to help them? "Come on in and tell me what's wrong with her while I get a few things together."

"You don't understand. She's mighty sick. We gotta hurry—"

"I know, Ethan, and I promise I'll go as quickly as I can. But I need to gather a few things before I run off. And I want to get my brother to hitch up the buggy so we can reach her quicker and have a way to get her back to town if we need to." She laid a hand lightly on his shoulder. "Don't worry, Ethan, we're going to take care of your sister."

"Please hurry."

"I will." She needed something to distract him from his worry. "Do you know how to empty the ash box and stoke a stove properly?"

His brow drew down in a puzzled frown. "Yes, ma'am."

"Well, I'd appreciate it if you'd take care of that little chore for me while I go wake my brother. The kindling is here and the firewood is right out there on the porch."

With a nod, he moved to the stove.

She noted the heaviness in his slumped shoulders and her heart went out to the boy. At his age he should be going to school and playing with friends, not acting as sole provider for himself and a sibling. How ill was his sister? And how old was she? Please God, let it be one of those childhood ailments that seem more serious than they really are.

Cora Beth sent up a prayer for both children as she rushed up the stairs. She rapped on Danny's door, then stuck her head inside before he had a chance to respond. "Get dressed," she told her still-groggy brother. "I need you to take care of something for me."

"Now?"

"Right now."

Something in her tone must have caught his attention because Danny was suddenly alert and scrambling from his bed.

She rushed down the hall and tapped on another door. This time she waited for a response before she opened it. "Uncle Grover, something's come up and I could use your help downstairs right away."

As soon as she was satisfied he understood, she fetched a large carpetbag from her room and headed back to the kitchen, aware that every minute counted.

By the time she reentered the room, Ethan had the stove nicely stoked and ready for her—not that she'd be doing any cooking this morning. The boy looked as if he were standing on a hot griddle himself. The worry over his sister was stamped on his whole being.

"Thank you. Now, tell me what's wrong with your sister while I gather up some supplies."

"She was complaining about her stomach hurting when she went to bed last night. Then she woke up about an hour ago and her head was burning up and she was crying." The boy's concern for his sister was palpable. "Can we go *now?*"

"In just a few minutes. How old is your sister?"

"Seven."

So young—Audrey's age.

Danny came in still buttoning his shirt. "What's going—" His worried frown turned to man-of-the-house alertness when he spotted Ethan.

Before Cora Beth could say anything, Uncle Grover joined them, his sparse gray hair still spiky from sleep.

"Who's he?" Danny asked.

"This is Ethan." Cora Beth turned to their guest. "And Ethan, this is my brother Danny and the gentleman behind him is my Uncle Grover."

Ethan nodded to the new arrivals but didn't say anything.

"Fellows, Ethan needs our help. He and his sister are camping outside of town. His sister took sick last night and he's worried about her. She's the same age as Audrey and she's out there right now with only a dog for company."

She saw them both come to attention at that. "Danny, I need you to hitch up the horse and buggy as quick as you can and bring them here. Uncle Grover, would you please head over to Doc Whitman's and let him know his services may be needed shortly? Then go over to Sadie's and ask if she can spare Mrs. Dauber to come fix breakfast for the boarders this morning."

Danny nodded, gave Ethan one last measuring look, then headed for the front door.

"Don't you worry about anything here," Uncle Grover said. "You just see to that little girl. As soon as I take care of your errands I'll get the girls up and make certain they get to school on time."

"Thank you." Cora Beth patted the older gentleman's arm. "I knew I could count on you." Then she had a quick thought. "Mrs. Plunkett was very helpful to me yesterday. I'm sure she'd be willing to help you get things organized this morning, as well."

Uncle Grover looked a little surprised at her suggestion, but nodded. As he passed by Ethan, he gave the boy a reassuring smile. "Don't you worry, son. You're in good hands with Cora Beth. She's got three daughters of her own and knows all about tending to their hurts."

Bless him, Uncle Grover was a dear sweet man, even if he could be forgetful at times. She'd never once regretted taking him in, even after her husband died and she was worried about how she was going to make it.

She turned back to Ethan. "While we're waiting for the buggy, I'm going to gather up a few things I might need to make your sister—Cissy, was it?—more comfortable until the doctor can get a look at her. I'm sorry I haven't had a chance to start cooking breakfast this morning but there's some pie left over from last night's supper there on the counter. Feel free to serve yourself up a piece. And in the meantime, tell me just where this camp of yours is." Anything to keep his mind focused on something other than his worry.

While Ethan talked and ate, Cora Beth grabbed whatever herbs and powders she figured might be needed. She also gathered up a blanket, some clean strips of cloth and a flask of water, and stuffed them all into her carpetbag. Just as she finished, she heard the whinny of a horse.

Goodness, that was mighty quick, even for Danny. But she wasn't one to question the blessings sent her way. "Sounds like the buggy's here. Ready?"

Ethan didn't have to be told twice. He was up from the table and holding the kitchen door open for her before she'd finished her sentence. He reached the door ahead of her and threw it open.

Then he halted on the threshold.

As soon as she looked past his shoulder she saw why. There was no sign of the buggy, just a lone figure astride a horse, silhouetted in the shadowy predawn light.

She'd know that form anywhere. Mitch Hammond. And he didn't look happy.

Chapter Five

Mitch touched the brim of his hat, feeling a tad irritated at the guilty, caught-in-the-act expressions worn by the pair standing on the porch. Did they think he was here to confront Ethan when there was a little girl at risk? "Morning, Cora Beth, Ethan."

Cora Beth recovered quickly and placed a hand firmly in the boy's back, propelling him forward with her. "Good morning, Sheriff. What a welcome surprise."

He could almost believe she meant it. "I ran into your Uncle Grover on his way to Doc Whitman's place and he told me what was going on." Mitch dismounted and met the two of them at the steps. "Thought I'd see if I could lend a hand."

"As a mater of fact, you can." Cora Beth turned from him to Ethan, moving her hand to the boy's shoulder. "This is an answered prayer, Ethan. If you got up on that horse with Sheriff Hammond, the two of you could ride on ahead and be there to check on your sister in no time flat."

Mitch was as startled by her suggestion as Ethan

seemed to be. It wasn't that he didn't want to help, but he'd figured that helping meant escorting the two of them to the kids' camp, maybe driving the buggy and doing whatever heavy lifting might be required. He certainly didn't know anything about dealing with sick kids on his own. Surely a few extra minutes…

Ethan shot him a wary glance. "Maybe we should just wait on the buggy."

"The boy's right. I'll go help Danny—"

"Nonsense." The look Cora Beth gave him was schoolmarm stern. "There's a sick little girl out there who needs tending to, and even if Danny got the buggy here in the next minute or two, your horse can go cross-country and that's a lot faster."

That brought him up short. She was right of course. Whether he was good with kids or not wasn't the issue. Making sure that little girl got help of some sort as soon as possible *was*.

Cora Beth turned to Ethan. "And you need to go with him so your sister knows he's there to help and doesn't get frightened. I'll follow along in the buggy as soon as I can so we can bring her back to town more comfortably, but I think we'll all rest easier knowing someone is with her."

Mitch was already turning back to his horse. "If Ethan goes with me, how will you know the way?"

"He told me where it was earlier." She set the carpetbag down. "If I understood his directions, they're camping in the woods just past the Caster place, near Little Pine Creek. The sun'll be up in a few minutes so that won't be a problem. I can take the old creek trail to get there but I'm not sure how close to the camp itself I can get."

"You won't be able to see it from the trail." Ethan made it sound like that was a good thing. "I wanted to make sure no one would spot us."

Mitch nodded to himself as he mounted up. Definitely runaways.

Cora Beth gave the boy a reassuring smile. "Don't worry. Either I'll find you or you'll find me. God is looking out for us." Then she made shooing motions with her hands. "Well? Don't just stand there, there's a sick little girl waiting on you."

Mitch stared down at the boy, trying to gauge what he was thinking. "You ever rode double before?"

"Not since—" The boy swallowed. "Not in a long time."

"Well, looks like you're about to get reacquainted with the practice." Mitch reached down. "Let's go see about that sister of yours."

Ethan hesitated then squared his shoulders and took Mitch's hand. Once he was settled in the saddle behind Mitch, the boy cleared his throat. "There's something you ought to know about Cissy. She has a limp."

Cora Beth's brow drew down in concern. "She hurt her leg, too?"

"No." He shifted in his seat. "I mean, yes. Only it was years ago, back when she was just a baby. She can walk, and doesn't want folks babying her or anything, but her left leg doesn't work so good." His tone took on a defiant edge. "But that don't mean she ain't every bit as good as anyone else."

"Of course it doesn't." Cora Beth gave the boy that reassuring smile that could make a dying man feel he was going to be okay. "Now go on with Sheriff Hammond and see to your sister. I'll be there as quick as I can."

Mitch gathered the reins and looked down at Cora Beth. "You sure you'll be okay handling the buggy on your own?"

She put both fists on her hips. "Mitchell Fredrick Hammond, my dad owned a livery stable, remember? I learned how to handle a buggy before I started school. Now stop all this shilly-shallying around and go on with you."

Interesting how her face lit up when she was riled. "Yes, ma'am," he said with a tip of his hat. Then he turned the horse and headed east toward Little Pine Creek, setting a quick pace. The priority right now was getting to that little girl and making sure she was okay.

They rode in silence for a while, with Ethan sitting very stiffly in the saddle. The sky was brightening by the minute—soon it would be full daylight. Mitch let his passenger adjust to his perch and the horse's loping stride before he finally spoke. "I take it your pa isn't at that camp."

There was a long moment of silence. "No."

"Want to tell me what you and your sister are doing out in those woods without your parents?"

There was no hesitation this time. "No."

The boy's honest response drew a grudging smile from Mitch. But he was careful not to let it color his tone. "Tell me anyway." He didn't expect to get a lot of information, but this talk would give them both something to think about other than what might be happening with his sister right now.

"Our folks are dead."

The stark, matter-of-fact statement touched Mitch in a way a more self-pitying one would not have. "You got any other relatives?"

"None that want us."

This time Mitch winced. If that was true, it was no wonder the kid had such a big chip on his shoulder. It appeared that telegram to the orphanage hadn't been a wasted effort after all. How serious had Cora Beth been about taking Ethan in? Whatever her intentions, he knew the addition of a younger sister would strengthen rather than weaken her resolve.

"So, I guess this means you've been leaving your sister alone while you go out scavenging for supplies."

"Scout was with her." His tone was defensive. "And I made sure to only be gone a few hours each day."

"Who's Scout?"

"Our dog. He wouldn't let anything happen to Cissy."

"I see."

Another long silence, this time broken by Ethan. "I didn't like taking them things, you know. My ma taught me that it's wrong to steal and I did try to leave something in exchange." He squirmed a bit and then continued. "But I gave Ma my word before she died that I would watch over Cissy, no matter what. There weren't no other way I could see to do it."

The kid seemed to have his own brand of honor. "You could have just asked. There's lots of folks around here who would have been glad to help out."

"And there's folks who'd just as soon spit on you as look at you. I wasn't taking no chances after—" He halted, biting off the rest of what he'd been about to say.

The cynical, bitter words drew Mitch up short. What in the world had these kids been through and how long had it been going on? "After what?"

"Nothing." The words were mumbled, grudging. "We just wanted to be left alone, that's all."

There was definitely something the kid wasn't telling him. "So where exactly did y'all come from?"

Ethan hesitated for a moment, as if weighing the risks of revealing too much. "Back when both my folks were alive we lived near Howerton."

Howerton? That was almost fifty miles away. "How in the world did you two kids travel such a far piece on your own and end up in the woods outside of Knotty Pine?"

He felt the boy's shrug. "Same as anybody else, I reckon. Little bit of riding, little bit of walking."

There had to be more to it than that, but it was obvious he wasn't going to get much in the way of details. Not right now anyway.

"Can't we go any faster?"

"Homer's a good horse but he's carrying two of us." Mitch shared Ethan's sense of urgency, however, and nudged the horse to a slightly faster pace. "Where were you and your sister headed to?" Best to keep the boy talking.

"No place in particular. Anywhere I can take care of me and Cissy without folks trying to poke their noses into our business."

Another conversational dead end. Why was Ethan so set on he and his sister going it alone? What wasn't he saying?

This time Mitch let the silence draw out until they reached Little Pine Creek. "Where do we go from here?"

The boy pointed to the right. "Follow the creek for a little ways. I'll tell you when to head into the woods."

Mitch obediently turned the horse.

They'd only traveled a few minutes when Ethan motioned ahead to the left. "There's a pig trail just up there—hard to spot unless you're really looking for it."

"I see it." Though calling the barely visible gap in the trees a pig trail was giving it more credit than it deserved. It was going to be a tight squeeze getting the horse through the undergrowth. He led the animal up to the mouth of the trail then stopped. "How far is it to your camp?"

"Not far."

"Then I think we should walk from here." Leaving the horse here would also serve to let Cora Beth know where to wait if she arrived before they returned.

They quickly dismounted, and Mitch tethered the horse to a bush while Ethan watched impatiently. Mitch waved a hand toward the almost nonexistent trail. "Lead the way."

As if he were a hunting dog who'd slipped his leash, Ethan took off at a run.

Mitch matched his pace. *Please, Lord, let that little girl be okay.* He wished again that Cora Beth was here with them. Her quiet competence, compassion and maternal experience would serve the sick little girl much better than his inexperience with children.

"Cissy, I'm back!"

Almost before Ethan's words died out, the thicket opened up to a clearing the size of a large room. Mitch was relieved to hear a response to Ethan's hail—a good sign that things were not quite as dire as he'd feared.

Ethan's progress was momentarily hampered by the enthusiastic greetings of a gray and black spotted hound. Ethan gave the animal a perfunctory pat, with an absently uttered "Good boy, Scout" but his focus was obviously on the makeshift shelter the animal had been guarding.

The dog immediately gave way and turned a much less friendly eye toward Mitch.

Ethan disappeared inside the structure and Mitch could hear him speaking to his sister. As soon as he made a move to follow, however, the dog bared his teeth and let out a low, menacing growl.

Mitch halted. "Easy boy. I'm here to help."

Ethan stuck his head back out. "It's okay, Scout. Let him by."

The dog stopped growling but his suspicious gaze never wavered from Mitch.

"How's your sister?" Mitch asked as he approached, giving the animal a wide berth.

"She's really hot and still feeling sick."

The structure, built out of stout branches and a large sheet of canvas, looked like a cross between a tent and an open lean-to. Mitch had to bend almost double to get inside and it wasn't much better once he was in. Not only was the roof low, but there was barely room to contain the three of them. His eyes went immediately to the little girl lying on a blanket to one side. Even he could see she didn't look well. Her cheeks were flushed and she was drenched in sweat. As he watched, her shoulders fluttered in a shiver.

The little girl studied him with wide frightened eyes and her hand snaked out to grab her brother's.

Mitch tried to adopt a friendly tone. This would go easier if he could calm her fears before he tried to carry her out of here. "Well now, Ethan, you didn't tell me what a pretty little buttercup your sister is." He knelt down beside her. "Your name is Cissy, right?"

"It's really Cecilia," she said. Her voice sounded thready and her free hand plucked at her sheet. "But Cissy is easier."

"Well, Cissy, I'm Sheriff Hammond and I hear you're not feeling so good. Both your head and tummy hurt, do they?"

She nodded.

He rested his arm on his legs as he considered his next words. Cora Beth would know what to say. "You know, I've had my share of headaches and tummy aches and they're just not any fun at all," he said, feeling his way. Then he had an inspiration. He pulled a wax-paper-wrapped lemon drop out of his pocket. "I find when I'm feeling poorly one of these usually helps to make me feel a tiny bit better. Would you like to try one?"

Her eyes lit up at the sight of the treat. She shot a quick glance toward her brother, and at his nod she turned back to Mitch. "Yes, please. Lemon drops are my favorite but I haven't had one in a very long time."

"They're my favorite, too." He unwrapped the candy and handed it to her. "That's why I always have a few in my pocket."

He leaned back on his haunches again. "Did your brother tell you about the nice lady he met yesterday?"

"The one who gave him those biscuits and bacon for me?"

So that's why the boy had taken the extra. "That's the one. Well, she's headed this way with a buggy so we can take you where there's a doctor. You'll like her and Dr. Whitman. Between the two of them, they'll have you all fixed up in no time."

Her expression turned uncertain, and she glanced

back at her brother. "But, Ethan, we aren't supposed to go to town where folks can see us."

"Why's that?" Maybe the girl would be more forthcoming than her brother.

"Because *he* might—"

"Don't worry, Cissy," Ethan interjected. "We just need to see about getting you better right now. And Mrs. Collins is a real nice lady. She'll see nothing happens to us."

Now who was this "he" Cissy was afraid of? And what did Ethan mean by Cora Beth seeing nothing happened to them? Was someone after them? Well, they'd have to come through him to get to them. But now was not the time to start interrogating the boy again.

"The thing is," he explained to Cissy, "Mrs. Collins's buggy can't come here to your camp. So, if it's okay with you, I'm going to carry you out as far as the trail. And," he added quickly, "at the same time, you can protect me from that ferocious guard dog you have out there."

That drew a little giggle from the girl. "Scout isn't ferocious."

Mitch pretended surprise. "He isn't? I don't know, he seemed pretty ferocious to me. I'd feel a whole lot safer if you agreed to keep an eye on him for me. So is it a deal? If I carry you to the buggy, will you make sure your dog doesn't try to find out what my ankle tastes like?"

She giggled again and nodded. "It's a deal."

"Thanks. Now I'm gonna pick you up, Buttercup, real easy like." He scooped her up, sheet and all, frowning over how hot she was. The child was burning up. He was surprised, too, by how light she was. Too light, too fragile. He could understand why Ethan had resorted to stealing to care for her.

With a great deal of effort he managed to make his way out of the confined space without jostling her too much.

As soon as he straightened, Scout started growling, hackles raised, teeth bared. Ethan had been right about what an effective guard dog the animal was. Mitch gave Cissy an aggrieved look that was only partially feigned. "See what I mean?"

"It's okay, Scout," she coaxed. "Sheriff Hammond is a friend. He gave me a lemon drop." She said that as if it was the mark of his worth.

The animal stopped growling, but there was no doubt he was keeping an eye on Mitch.

Mitch turned to Ethan. "You need to gather up anything here you want because you might not be back for some time." Actually there was no *might* about it—he planned to make sure these two kids didn't live like this anymore. But no need to add to the boy's worries any more than necessary right now.

He saw the mutinous look on Ethan's face, then saw him glance at his sister. The boy's shoulders sagged and with a nod, he ducked back inside the structure.

Mitch used the time to study the small campsite. It was surprisingly well tended.

Someone had put quite a bit of effort into fixing the place up. Much of the area nearby had been cleared of the thickest of the brush. A small area off to one side of the lean-to, a safe distance away, had been cleared down to the bare dirt. In the center, a circle of stones and bed of ashes topped by a crudely constructed spit marked where the youthful squatters cooked their meals. There was a pile of twigs and small branches nearby, cut into firewood-size pieces. A low tree branch on the perimeter bore a change of clothes for each child, a sign that they were keeping up with everyday chores such as laundry.

Ethan really had done a remarkable job of creating a home for his sister.

The boy reappeared from the lean-to, carrying a small, lumpy tote sack that seemed barely a third full. He crossed the clearing to grab the clothes from the makeshift clothesline, then looked around as if lost.

Finally he squared his shoulders, turned back to Mitch and nodded. "Let's go." Without so much as a backward glance, the boy led the way up the trail to where they'd left the horse.

Mitch followed, with Scout bringing up the rear.

When they arrived back at the road, there was still no sign of Cora Beth and the buggy. Cissy was shivering again and her eyes were closed. The arm she'd draped around his neck had gone slack and she was shifting fretfully in his hold.

"My head hurts," she said in a pitiful whisper.

"I'm so sorry, Buttercup. Just hold on, our ride will be here soon." What did he do now?

"Ma used to sing lullabies to us when one of us got sick," Ethan said. "Cissy always liked that."

Sing? Mitch didn't know any lullabies. Then a long forgotten memory of his own mother singing him to sleep at night came to him. How had that song gone? He hummed for a few seconds, trying to capture more of the memory. Slowly the words came back to him, a few at a time.

Good night, happy dreams,
my sweet little one.
Close your eyes, go to sleep,

while I sing you this song.
The daylight has faded,
God's creatures now rest,
snuggle down my sweet child
In your own little nest.

Mitch was surprised to discover that the song, even with his stumbling rendition, really did seem to calm her a bit. He searched his memory for more of the words.

Good night, happy dreams,
my sweet little one.
You played and you laughed,
but now day is done.
We've said our prayers and
I've tucked you in tight.
Day is done, God is nigh,
time to wish you good-night.

Cora Beth scanned the tree line. Surely it wasn't much farther. Unless she'd gotten the directions wrong. *Heavenly Father, please don't let that be the case.*

A moment later the road turned and she sighed with relief when she saw the group waiting for her just up ahead. Then the unexpected sound of singing caught her attention. She couldn't catch the words from this distance, but the soft crooning was unmistakable. Mitch was singing a lullaby.

Mitch sat on the ground with a child cradled in his lap. Ethan stood nearby, a dog at his heels.

The family-like tableau tugged at her heart. She'd never seen Mitch so, well, so *fatherly* looking before. But it suited him.

He caught sight of her a moment later and the singing stopped. He got to his feet, taking obvious care not to jar his precious burden.

"Mrs. Collins is here, Buttercup," she heard him say. "You just hold on now. We're going to get you to the doctor and he'll fix you right up." But the worry in his voice told Cora Beth a different story.

She pulled on the reins, bringing the buggy to a halt and set the brake. "I came as fast as I could," she said as she hopped down. "How is she?"

Rather than answer directly, Mitch gave his head a little shake. "If you'll take her, I'll—"

"No." Cissy's tone was groggy and petulant. "I want Sheriff Lemon Drop to hold me."

Sheriff Lemon Drop? Cora Beth smiled as she saw Mitch's discomfort. His well-known predilection for the sweet treat had caught him out, it seemed.

"We talked about what a nice lady Mrs. Collins is, remember?" Mitch's tone was gentle but coaxing. "She's the lady who made those nice fluffy biscuits you mentioned. She's going to hold you while I drive the wagon—"

"No, I want you."

Cora Beth recognized that tone from experience. Tears were imminent if they didn't head this off quickly. "That's all right, Cissy. The sheriff can hold on to you while I drive the buggy."

She stroked the little girl's head. Poor thing, her forehead was burning up and her eyes were glassy.

Glancing up at Mitch, she gave him a reassuring smile. "Y'all hold on just a few minutes while I turn the buggy around."

"Maybe I should—"

Cora Beth shook her head. "It won't do to get her worked up right now. You're taking care of what's most important. I can handle the buggy."

She turned to Ethan. "As soon as I get the buggy turned, I need you to tie the sheriff's horse to the back. Think you can do that?"

Ethan was already headed toward the horse. "Yes, ma'am."

"Good."

Cora Beth climbed back up on the seat, glad to see the trail was wide enough to make turning the buggy a simple matter. Once she'd accomplished her task, she set the brake and climbed down again while Ethan took care of Mitch's horse.

Gently brushing Cissy's hair from her forehead, she gave the child her most reassuring smile. "Cissy, you need to let me hold you for just a little while so Sheriff Hammond can climb up in the buggy. I promise to let him have you back just as soon as he's settled in."

The little girl gave her a suspicious look. "Promise?"

Cora Beth traced an *X* across her chest. "Cross my heart."

Cissy looked up at Mitch and repeated her question. "Promise?"

"Absolutely."

Apparently satisfied, the child held out her arms for Cora Beth.

Mitch handed over the feather-light patient, gave Cora Beth a look she couldn't quite interpret, then climbed quickly into the wagon and reached back down.

"Here you go, sweetheart." Cora Beth gave the child a little squeeze before handing her up to Mitch. "Right back in the sheriff's arms where you'll be all safe and sound."

Seeing the way the little girl snuggled trustingly back into Mitch's arms was heartwarming. "You should slide over to the middle," she told Mitch. "Ethan and I will take the ends and help support you."

By this time Ethan had finished taking care of the horse and had fetched a cloth sack that he now tossed behind the seat.

Cora Beth glanced down at the dog. "There's no room for him in the buggy. Will he be all right?"

Ethan nodded, patting the dog's head. "Yes, ma'am. Scout's pretty fast. He'll follow along without any problem."

"Good. Then let's climb on up and we'll be off."

Ethan nodded. But before Cora Beth could boost herself up, he stopped her. "I know how to drive a buggy, ma'am. I can handle the reins so you can help the sheriff watch my sister, if you don't mind."

Cora Beth hesitated, not sure how adept the boy actually was. But her brother had handled larger carriages at a much younger age. And Ethan probably needed to feel as if he were doing something to help instead of just sitting around. She stepped back. "That would be mighty helpful, Ethan. Thank you."

She ignored Mitch's frown and moved around to the other side while Ethan scrambled up and took the reins. Once she indicated she was settled in, Ethan released the brake and set the horse in motion.

After a few minutes of observing the way the boy handled the reins, she gave a satisfied nod. Her faith had not been misplaced—he could handle a horse and buggy just fine. She relaxed and turned to Mitch and Cissy.

The child had fallen into a fitful sleep, stirring restlessly but keeping a hand against Mitch's chest. "I think you've made a lifelong friend, Sheriff Lemon Drop," she said quietly.

Mitch shifted, obviously uncomfortable with her words. "I gave her a piece of candy to ease her fears a bit," he said self-consciously. "She's a sweet kid," he added in a softer tone.

And you're a very sweet man. But saying that out loud would only serve to make him uncomfortable so she refrained and little else was said on the ride back.

When they reached town, Cora Beth directed Ethan to Doc Whitman's office. She was surprised to see children still straggling into the schoolhouse—it seemed so much later in the day than that.

Once Ethan set the brake, Mitch eased Cissy into Cora Beth's arms while he stepped down. She worried at how warm she was to the touch, how restless and fretful she acted even though she didn't open her eyes.

Mitch reached back up for the child and their gazes locked for a second. She read her own worry mirrored in his face. Then he turned to Ethan. "Make sure you help Mrs. Collins down." Then, without a backward glance, he strode quickly up the front walk. Doc Whitman, who'd obviously been on the lookout for them, held the door open.

As Ethan helped her down, Cora Beth could tell he was anxious to follow his sister inside. But there wouldn't be news or anything he could do for several minutes. "You saw the livery we passed when we came into town?" she asked him.

"Yes, ma'am." He nodded without taking his gaze off his sister.

"I need you to bring the buggy and Sheriff Hammond's horse there," she continued firmly. "The man who works there is named Freddy. Tell him I sent you. Then you can come back here and wait to see what the doctor has to say about Cissy."

Ethan didn't look happy, but with one last glance toward the clinic door, he obediently climbed back up and did as she'd directed.

When Cora Beth entered, Mitch was standing alone in Dr. Whitman's outer office, twisting his hat brim in his hand, looking every inch the worried father.

"Ethan's taking your horse and the buggy over to the livery." She glanced toward the closed door to the examining room. "Did Doc say anything?"

Mitch raked his fingers through his hair. "No, he's checking her out now."

"Is Lucy with him?" Doc Whitman's daughter often helped him out.

But Mitch shook his head. "Barney Waskom came by with word that Annielou's baby's coming. Lucy's tending her until Doc can get away."

Cora Beth moved to the door. "Then I'd better see if I can lend a hand." She checked for a moment as she passed him, reaching out to touch his sleeve. "Don't worry, Doc's going to take good care of her."

Chapter Six

Mitch watched Cora Beth disappear into the examining room. Just like back there in the woods, he felt useless, unable to help in any way that mattered.

Lord, please take care of that little girl.

He was almost relieved when Ethan burst through the outer door.

"How is she?" The boy stared at the examining room door as if, if he just tried hard enough, he could see through it.

"Doc Whitman hasn't come out yet. I'm sure he'll let us know as soon as he's able."

"Can I see her?"

"Not yet. Mrs. Collins is in there with Doc. We'd only crowd them if we went in." He searched his mind for something to distract the boy. "Where's Scout?"

"Sitting outside." Ethan finally glanced his way. "He won't bother nobody, promise."

"I'm sure—"

The examining room door swung open and Cora Beth stepped out. She wore an encouraging smile that eased Mitch's worse fears.

Ethan craned his neck, trying to look past her. "Is Cissy gonna be okay?"

"She's a very sick little girl, but the good news is Doc says she should be fine as a springtime robin in a couple of days. Assuming she gets proper care, that is."

Some of the tenseness eased from the boy's muscles. "Just tell me what I need to do."

Cora Beth placed a hand on his shoulder. "Your sister needs lots of bed rest and lots of nourishment to help her get better. And she won't get that out in the woods."

"I can see that she eats and rests," he said stubbornly.

"I have a better idea." Cora Beth gave him an encouraging smile. "I would really like for the two of you to stay at the boardinghouse with me."

It was an offer Mitch had expected her to make. But Ethan seemed reluctant.

Before the boy could say anything, however, she held up a hand. "It's admirable that you want to take care of things yourself, Ethan. But right now you need to think about what's best for Cissy. She'll recover a whole lot quicker if she has a comfortable, dry place to stay and plenty of nourishing food to eat. At least agree that you'll stay with me until she gets better."

The boy looked down at the floor. "I can't afford to pay you," he said gruffly. "And my pa always said a body shouldn't take charity as long as he can fend for himself."

Mitch raised a brow. So how did stealing fit into that picture?

But Cora Beth smiled in agreement. "Sounds like your pa was a practical, honorable man. But I'm not talking about charity. I'd expect you to do some chores around the place to earn your keep."

Ethan was silent for a moment, studying the floor as

if the answer were written there. Then he squared his shoulders and looked up. "If that's what's needed to get Cissy better again, then I reckon I can agree to that. You just tell me what needs doing and I'll take care of it."

"Agreed."

"But only until Cissy gets better. Then we need to be on our way."

Not if Mitch had his way. But before he or Cora Beth could say anything, Doc Whitman stepped out of the examining room.

"Hello, young man," he said when he spotted Ethan. "I suppose you must be this Ethan my patient has been calling for. You can go back there and sit with her for a while if you like."

Ethan didn't wait to be told twice. A moment later it was just the three adults in the outer office.

"Thank you for seeing to her, Dr. Whitman," Cora Beth said. "Please send me the bill."

He waved her words aside. "I'll have no talk of that. Just bake me up one of those special fruitcakes of yours next time you're in a baking mood and we'll call it even." He rolled down his sleeves. "Now excuse me while I get a powder that you can give her to help with her fever. Just mix it up with water and have her drink it twice a day until her fever is gone."

The doctor peered at her down the bridge of his nose. "And I notice you've got yourself a nasty looking burn on your hand. I'll get you some salve for that, as well."

"Thank you, but—"

He cut her off with a shake of his head. "Don't forget who the doctor is around here. Now, you're welcome to leave the little girl here for a bit, but you'll need to sit with her yourself. I'm heading over to the Waskom farm to help bring Barney and Annielou's new addition into the world."

"If it's okay to move her, I think we'll go ahead and bring Cissy over to my place. It'll be easier for me to keep an eye on her there." She turned to Mitch. "If you'll help me move her?"

"Of course. No farther than it is to your place, I can carry her there."

"Good." Dr. Whitman handed her the powders and the ointment. "Probably best to get her settled into a more comfortable bed, anyway. I'll plan to come by to check on her in the morning, but if you need me before then, just send someone to fetch me."

"Thank you, Dr. Whitman."

"You're welcome. Now I'm headed out. Just pull the door closed when you leave."

Mitch noted the smile Cora Beth gave Doc didn't reach her eyes and that her brow was still furrowed in worry. He gave her a probing look. As soon as they were alone, he voiced his question. "Is there something you didn't want to say in front of Ethan?"

"Oh, Mitch, that poor little girl."

His chest constricted at the sight of the pain in her eyes. Was Cissy's outlook worse than she'd made it sound?

"It's awful." Her voice almost broke. "The child's ankle," Cora Beth paused, swallowing hard. "There's an ugly welt, barely healed, that goes all around her left ankle. Mitch, I think someone *shackled* that child."

Mitch's gut tightened and his temper rose. What sort of low-down, miserable, slime-swilling toad would treat a little girl so harshly? If he knew who was responsible—

Seeing Cora Beth's stricken expression, he put a check

on his temper. She needed some reassurances right now. His arms itched to cradle her, to stroke her hair and soothe away some of the pain he saw in her eyes. But that would only trade one kind of concern on her part for another. So he settled, instead, for taking her hand. "Well, she's safe now. And I promise I'll make sure she stays that way."

He did his best to ignore what the approval and gratitude in her eyes did to his composure as he released her hand. "Now, let's get that little girl over to the boardinghouse before I make my morning rounds."

And part of those rounds would be a stop at the telegraph office so he could contact the marshal in Howerton. One way or the other, he aimed to get to the bottom of whatever or *whoever* had hurt those kids and sent them into hiding.

Cora Beth watched as Mitch gently lifted Cissy, sheet and all, from the examining table. He appeared more at ease with the child than he had earlier.

"She seems to be feeling better." Ethan looked at Cora Beth as if for confirmation of the hope expressed in his words.

"She's certainly less restless than before," Cora Beth answered. "And that's a good sign." She waved to the far side of the room. "If you'll gather up her shoes and socks we'll get her over to my place so we can make her more comfortable."

As they stepped out onto the sidewalk a few minutes later, Scout greeted Ethan with a friendly bark and wagging tail. Hmm, she hadn't considered the dog in the mix when she'd decided to take on the two kids. Not that it changed her mind any—she'd just have to adjust her plans. Hopefully he wasn't a house dog.

They'd only taken a few steps when a familiar figure came quickstepping up to them. "Cora Beth, what's going on? Is everything okay?"

Cora Beth blinked at the sudden appearance of her sister. "Josie, what on earth—"

"I just dropped Viola at the schoolhouse and Danny was telling the other kids some wild story about an early-morning adventure you had."

Cora Beth shot her sister a warning look. "Danny tends to exaggerate. And I can't stop to chat right now." She gave a slight nod toward Mitch and the child he was carrying.

Josie wasn't to be dissuaded. "Then I'll walk with you."

As her sister fell into step beside her, Cora Beth quickly made the introductions. "Josie, this is Ethan, and the little girl the sheriff is carrying is his sister, Cissy. Cissy's not feeling so well right now so the two of them are going to be staying with us at the boardinghouse for a while."

This time Josie took her cue and smiled down at the boy. "Hello, Ethan. I'm Cora Beth's sister, Josie. Glad to make your acquaintance."

Ethan nodded an acknowledgment and Josie turned to Mitch. "Hello, Sheriff. I take it you were part of my sister's adventure this morning?"

"Morning, Josie. How are things out at the ranch?"

Cora Beth hid a smile at the adept way Mitch dodged Josie's question.

Josie's raised brow indicated she'd noticed, as well. "Apparently not nearly as exciting as things are over at the boardinghouse." She glanced at the little girl who was shifting restlessly in Mitch's arms and her gaze softened. "Poor little thing. Is there anything I can do to help?"

Mitch looked past Josie and suddenly stiffened. Following his gaze, Cora Beth discovered why. The mayor's wife had spotted them and was headed their way, a determined look on her face. Cora Beth touched her sister's arm. "Josie, I promise to fill you in on the whole thing a little later, but right now I need to take you up on that offer of help."

"In what way?" Josie's voice held a note of suspicion.

"Nelda Oglesby is headed this way and I'd rather not have to answer her questions right now. Do you think you could distract her for me?"

Josie gave her a long look, then nodded. "Distract her how?"

"Ask her advice on something, anything. The latest fashions from back east or planting a flower garden would be good topics."

Josie made a face. "Not two of my favorite subjects."

Josie had always had a bit of the tomboy in her—Cora Beth supposed it came from all those years her sister was stuck running the livery to keep their family together. Her marriage to Sadie's brother Ry last year had softened her a little but her rough edges still peeked through from time to time.

With a martyred sigh, Josie nodded. "I'll do it, but you'll definitely owe me for this one."

"Thanks. I'll make sure I have a pot of coffee made and some pie sliced and ready when you come by."

"You'd better." Josie's frown plainly expressed her feelings of martyrdom. "And I'll be wanting the complete unabridged version of the story."

Nelda was almost upon them by this time. Josie pasted on a big smile and stepped forward to close the distance before Nelda could get any closer.

She unabashedly linked arms with the woman. "Nelda Oglesby, just the woman I need to see."

Nelda blinked, obviously caught off guard. "Yes, yes, nice to see you, too, Josie, but I must speak to the sheriff—"

"Oh, I'm sure that can wait." She waved a hand toward their party dismissively. "You can see them any time but I'm only going to be in town for a little while before I have to get back to the ranch. Besides, as you can see, the sheriff is busy right now."

"But—"

Josie continued on as if Nelda hadn't spoken. "Now, I've been told when it comes to flowers you are *the* authority in town, is that right?"

Nelda paused. "Well, it's true that I do know a bit on the subject." She patted her hair. "I suppose I could spare a few minutes. What did you have in mind?"

Josie gently tugged Nelda back the way she'd come. "I thought I might try adding plants along my front porch and I noticed the ones you have at your place are so pretty."

"My azaleas?"

"Is that what they are? Do you think we might go take a look and you can tell me..."

By that time the gap between them had widened significantly and Cora Beth let out a relieved breath. She met Mitch's glance from the corner of her eye and they shared a guilty smile, but neither said a word.

Their little procession was the object of several curious stares as they made their way to the boarding-house but they didn't pause for conversation—merely exchanged greetings and moved on with apologies.

A few minutes later Cora Beth led the way up the

boardinghouse steps. Before she could reach the front door it opened and Uncle Grover stepped out, holding the screen door wide for them. "I take it this is your little sister, Ethan. Poor thing, she looks in need of some special cosseting. But don't you worry, cosseting is Cora Beth's specialty. She'll have her in the pink of health in no time."

He turned to Cora Beth. "I thought you might be needing the downstairs room so Mrs. Plunkett and I have it all fixed up and ready for the little one."

"Bless you, Uncle Grover, I don't know what I'd do without you to help me."

Cora Beth hurried down the hall and opened the door to the downstairs bedchamber. Sure enough, there were fresh linens on the bed and the covers were turned down and ready for the patient.

"If you don't need me," Uncle Grover said, "I'll get back to the kitchen. Mrs. Plunkett sent Mrs. Dauber home right after breakfast and has been tidying up the kitchen for you." He seemed a bit bemused. "An amazingly efficient woman."

Cora Beth hid a smile. It seemed Mrs. Plunkett was already making progress with her campaign. "Thank her for me. Oh and, if you don't mind, ask her if she'd be so kind as to put a pot of water to heating on the stove so I can make a broth. Ask her to use the big stockpot."

When she turned back to the room, Mitch had already placed Cissy on the bed. The little girl opened her eyes and looked around.

"There you go." Mitch straightened. "Isn't that comfy? Mrs. Collins is going to take real good care of you and you'll be good as new before you know it."

"Aren't you going to stay with me, too?" Cissy's face puckered as if she were ready to set up a loud protest.

"Sorry, Buttercup, I have to get back to work. But I'll be back to check in on you this evening." He winked at her. "And I might just have a couple more lemon drops in my pocket by then. Would you like that?"

That seemed to mollify the little girl somewhat. "Uh-huh."

"I thought so. Now you get lots of rest and do just as Mrs. Collins says, okay?"

Cissy nodded and snuggled down deeper under the coverlet, closing her eyes.

Mitch stepped back, studying the child for a moment.

Cora Beth's heart was touched by the tender, protective look on his face.

When he turned to find her watching him, his expression shifted to a sheepish smile. Cora Beth decided to ease his discomfiture with a change of subject.

"I'm going to fetch her one of Audrey's clean nightgowns to help make her more comfortable." She was careful to keep her voice pitched low. "Then I'll fix a big pot of broth for when she wakes up again. Doc says it's important for her to get lots of food and liquids, and lots of rest."

Then she turned to Ethan. "There's a couple of vacant rooms upstairs. I'll make one of them up for you in a little bit, but if you want to keep an eye on your sister for a while, you can pull that chair over there up to the bed."

"Thank you, ma'am. But you don't need to fix me another room. I can sleep on the floor in here with Cissy just fine."

"Nonsense. There's no need for you to sleep on the floor when there are perfectly fine beds sitting unused—"

"No offense, ma'am, but I promised my ma I'd look out for Cissy and I don't think I can do that if I'm all the way up on a different floor."

To her surprise, Mitch nodded. "A man needs to stick by his word, and it's always important to protect those in your care." He placed a hand on the boy's shoulder. "But, Ethan, your sister is going to be well cared for here."

Ethan seemed to plant his feet more firmly. "Are you telling me I *can't* stay here?"

Cora Beth gave in. "Oh, very well, if you feel so strongly about it, you can stay in here with her, at least until your sister's feeling better. Then we'll discuss it again. But I'll have none of this sleeping on the floor nonsense—not in my house. There are several cots in the attic that I pull out when we get more boarders than expected. I'll fetch one down for you."

"You get that change of clothes," Mitch said. "I'll fetch the cot."

Fifteen minutes later Cora Beth had changed Cissy into fresh clothes, left Ethan to watch over his sister, and headed for the kitchen. And walked in on Mrs. Plunkett slicing corn from a cob and Uncle Grover chopping carrots.

"Oh, hello, my dear," Uncle Grover said. "I hope you don't mind, but Mrs. Plunkett thought it would be a good idea for us to get the broth started." He smiled approvingly at the apron-clad woman. "She seems to know how it is done."

"I don't mind at all—in fact, I'm grateful." She crossed the room and grabbed another of her aprons from a wall peg near the back door.

"How's the little girl doing?" Mrs. Plunkett asked.

"She's sleeping right now. Dr. Whitman thinks she'll be fine in a few days."

"That's good to hear." Mrs. Plunkett sliced the last few rows of kernels from the cob and moved toward the stove. "We've got corn, carrots and turnips in the pot now. Anything else you want to add?"

"That's a good start. And you two have done more than enough for me this morning. I can take it from here."

"Are you sure?" Uncle Grover finished the carrot he was working on and Mrs. Plunkett transferred the slices to the pot. "We don't mind helping."

"I'll be fine." She tied the apron strings behind her and gave Mrs. Plunkett a meaningful look before turning back to her uncle. "Besides, if I remember right, you mentioned last night that you wanted to go over to Fuller Pond today and look for damselflies."

"Is that right?" Mrs. Plunkett picked up her cue with admirable smoothness. "You know, when I was a girl I had quite an interest in botany. I even had a scrapbook where I pasted samples of different leaves and flowers and did the research to identify them."

"The mark of a true enthusiast as opposed to a mere hobbyist is the time they put into doing the research."

"Very true." She lifted her chin. "Actually I find my interest in the subject has revived. I imagine a location such as Fuller Pond would have quite a variety of plant samples to study."

"Why yes, I imagine it does."

Not to be deterred, Mrs. Plunkett tried a more direct approach. "It seems a fine day to begin my renewed studies. If your niece is certain she doesn't need my help, perhaps I could accompany you on your little expedition."

Uncle Grover nodded, looking slightly taken aback. "Why, yes, of course. I would be delighted to have a bit of company."

Cora Beth's amusement at the determination of the apparently love-struck Mrs. Plunkett faded once the two had left the room. As she raided her pantry for items to add to her stockpot, her mind kept replaying those awful scars she'd seen on Cissy's ankle. Did Ethan bear similar marks? What had happened to them and who was responsible? Should she ask Ethan about it or would that just push him to close himself off more?

"I've placed the cot in Cissy's room."

Cora Beth started. She'd been so lost in her own thoughts she hadn't heard Mitch step into the kitchen.

"Sorry. Didn't mean to startle you." He was holding his hat in his hands and looked uncharacteristically diffident.

"That's okay. It's what I get for woolgathering." She swiped the hair off her brow with the back of her hand. "Thank you for fetching the cot. I'll get the linens and make it up when I finish in here."

"I don't think Ethan is in any rush. He probably won't try to sleep until he's sure his sister is doing better."

Cora Beth nodded. "He's bound to be tired. I have a feeling that boy has been carrying a much-too-big burden for much too long."

"Give him time. He'll eventually learn to relax again." She nodded her agreement. Then she smiled, remembering the way Mitch had been with the children today—especially Cissy. "That little girl has sure taken a shine to you."

His smile was self-deprecating. "It was the lemon drops that did it."

She sincerely doubted that was all it was. "It seemed to me she was as fond of the man as the candy." She went back to chopping the greens. "That lullaby you sang to her was nice. Don't think I ever heard that one before."

Mitch rubbed the back of his neck. "It's one my ma used to sing to me. I'd almost forgotten it until Ethan said something about singing being a good way to calm her down." He smiled crookedly. "Funny what desperation will do for your memory."

"Well, it was sweet." She smiled at his grimace and then went back to work. "Did you learn anything more about their history?"

"The only information I got out of Ethan was that both their parents have passed on. And it doesn't sound like there are any other relatives in the picture. As soon as I leave here I'm going to send a telegram to the sheriff over in Howerton and see if he can shed some light on things."

He sounded confident and in control again. Then he absently slid the brim of his hat between his fingers. "Are you going to be all right here? Should I have someone stop in to lend a hand?"

"For goodness' sake, of course I'll be okay. What do you think happens when I have extra guests here at the boardinghouse?"

He raised his palms. "You handle it with your normal efficiency. But your hand is still burned and your guests don't normally include sick little girls."

"My hand is doing fine and I have three daughters of my own, remember? I've handled sick little girls before. Besides, Josie will be here soon, remember?"

He grinned. "But not necessarily in a mood to be helpful."

She returned his grin. "Josie is more than a match for Nelda."

As if to punctuate her assertion, Josie stepped through the hall door, with Sadie right on her heels. "Okay you two, after spending twenty minutes listening to Nelda expound on the relative merits of roses versus azaleas for showiness, I'm ready for that explanation I was promised. And I brought Sadie along so you only have to tell your story once."

Mitch nodded a greeting, then moved toward the door. "I believe your sister is more than capable of handling the explanations on her own. And since I wouldn't want to get in the way of any family talk, if you ladies will excuse me, I have morning rounds to take care of."

Cora Beth watched him leave with a raised brow. "It seems our sheriff would rather make his rounds than spend more time in my kitchen."

Josie grinned. "Don't worry, he's not getting off as easy as he thinks. When I left Nelda, she was ready to storm the sheriff's office and demand he give her an update on what progress he's made toward capturing some criminal who's apparently been vandalizing that fancy glass plant house of hers."

"Oh dear." Cora Beth stopped chopping for a moment. "Nelda's making much too much out of all this."

"Out of all *what?*" Josie's voice had a long-suffering tone to it.

Cora Beth waved her knife distractedly. "It's a rather long story. You sure you don't want to take care of your weekly marketing first and tend to this at lunch?"

"Positive. That's why I brought Sadie with me—reinforcements in case you try to renege on our agreement. Now, Cora Beth Wylie Collins, stop chopping those vegetables so you can tell us just what's been going on. I take it there's a connection between those kids you had with you at Doc Whitman's office and what's put that bee in Nelda's bonnet, but I couldn't make a lick of sense out of her ramblings and I sure as Sunday didn't want to encourage her to explain."

Cora Beth laughed outright at that.

"I tried to fill her in." Sadie had removed her bonnet and grabbed one of Cora Beth's clean aprons. "But she said she wanted to get it straight from the horse's mouth."

"How flattering." Cora Beth surrendered her knife to Sadie and took the already chopped vegetables and moved toward the stove. "All right, have it your way. I'm making a broth for my young patient. Don't worry, I can talk and cook at the same time. And you, little sister, know where I keep everything. You can start a fresh pot of coffee brewing."

Sadie frowned. "Patient?"

"Hush, Sadie." Josie grabbed the canister of coffee. "Let her start at the beginning."

Cora Beth sighed. "All right, but Sadie already knows part of this." She gave a quick rundown of all that had transpired since Ethan had burst into her life yesterday morning.

When she was done, Josie shook her head. "Those poor kids. I hope Mitch finds the rotten dung beetle who's responsible for their misery and tosses his sorry hide in jail. Anything I can do to help?"

"Anything *we* can do to help?" Sadie amended.

"Thanks, but not right now. They're going to stay here with me for the time being."

"And once Cissy gets better?" Josie asked.

Cora Beth shrugged, not ready to answer that question just yet.

Josie narrowed her eyes. "I know that look. You're planning to take them in, aren't you?"

"It's a little early to be thinking of that," Cora Beth answered mildly.

"Big sister, you're not fooling me for one second. Can you honestly say you haven't thought about it?"

"All right, *yes,* if you must know, I've thought about it. But that's all—I'm not *planning* anything. We don't even have the whole story yet. We may find they have other options we don't know about."

Sadie dumped her vegetables into the stockpot. "Well, regardless of what happens, it's a good thing you're doing, giving those kids a place to stay. Don't let Nelda, or anyone else for that matter, give you grief about it."

Josie grinned. "She's right. Giving you grief is my job." She pulled three coffee cups from the cupboard. "And don't forget, Ry can help if the kids need any kind of legal assistance."

Ry Lassiter, Josie's husband and Sadie's brother, was a lawyer who'd left a successful practice in Philadelphia to come to Knotty Pine and start a horse ranch. Though there wasn't much call for a lawyer in town, he still provided legal advice from time to time.

"Thanks. I'll let you know if it comes to that."

Josie took her cup of coffee and moved back to the table. "Now, if we're ready for a change of subject, I have some news to share."

"What kind of news?" Sadie asked.

But as Cora Beth watched the pink creep into her sister's cheeks, she instinctively knew what was coming next.

"Well, when Sadie's baby makes his or her appearance, there'll be a new cousin following close behind."

Cora Beth was already halfway across the room. And her own joy at the news was echoed by the squeal Sadie let out.

She gave her sister a hug. "Oh, Josie, I'm so happy for you. And you're going to make a wonderful mother."

Josie's expression was uncharacteristically uncertain. "Do you really think so?"

"Of course. You've been wonderful with Viola."

"But Viola was seven years old when she came into my life as Ry's ward. This is a baby we're talking about."

"A sweet, precious little baby. And you're going to be a marvelous mother. I promise."

Josie gave her a fierce hug, then laughed as Sadie tried to squeeze into their embrace.

Cora Beth backed away, letting the two of them have their moment.

Sadie hugged Josie then stepped back as well.

"This is marvelous. We can work on our layettes together." Sadie giggled. "Oh my goodness, that brother of mine must be over the moon excited."

Josie laughed. "And then some. But he's already trying to treat me like a helpless ninny. Tried to make me put off my trip to town today because he couldn't come with me. As if I suddenly can't handle a horse and buggy."

Sadie grimaced. "He and Eli will make quite a pair these next few months. Have you told Viola yet?"

Josie shook her head. "I remember you said you and Eli were going to wait until our trip to Hawk's Creek next week to tell his sister, Penny, so she could have time to get used to the idea away from her friends before letting the whole town in on it. That sounded like a good plan so Ry and I are waiting, as well."

Hawk's Creek was the Lassiter family ranch situated near Tyler, more than sixty miles northwest of Knotty Pine. The two families were taking a trip there to visit Ry and Sadie's brother Griff for his birthday.

Cora Beth moved back to the stove. "Looks like there'll be more than a birthday to celebrate when you all get together."

Sadie nodded. "Actually, this turned out to be great timing for the trip. It was all I could do to convince Eli it was perfectly okay for me to travel at this stage of things. Goodness knows what he'll be like in a few months."

While Josie and Sadie traded stories on how foolish their husbands were being, Cora Beth quietly went back to her cooking.

It was such a joy to know Josie and Sadie were getting ready to bring new lives into the world, new additions to their family. It was truly a blessing. But for some reason, hearing them laugh fondly about their husbands and share plans for the coming months of their pregnancies, left her feeling left out, restless. Which was silly. She'd had her shot at marriage and had three beautiful daughters to show for it.

And now God had put Ethan and Cissy into her keeping for a while. What more could she ask for?

Yet she did find herself longing for more. For someone to make her family complete. To make *her* feel complete.

Chapter Seven

Cora Beth studied the four faces staring back at her from their seats around the dining-room table. As soon as they'd come home from school, they'd clamored to find out all about her early morning adventure. Cora Beth knew Danny had had some misgivings about Ethan when they'd met, though she wasn't quite sure why, so she wanted to make certain she explained the situation properly so that they all accepted the newcomers in a warm, friendly manner.

She said a quick prayer, then took a deep breath. "I wanted to let you know about some special guests we'll have staying with us the next several days."

"Is it new boarders?" Pippa asked. "Does that mean Danny has to share a room with Uncle Grover again?"

"No, they're not regular borders. It's a young girl and boy. Their names are Ethan and Cissy. Cissy is the same age as Audrey, and Ethan is about Danny's age. The thing is, Cissy is really sick and they need a place to stay while she gets better."

"Don't their ma and pa want to take care of them?" Audrey asked.

"They don't have a ma and pa," Cora Beth explained. "And they're all alone."

"We don't have a pa, either." Audrey sounded melodramatically forlorn.

"I know. But you have me, and Uncle Grover, and Danny and your sisters. You also have Aunt JoJo and Uncle Ry and Viola. Ethan and Cissy don't have anyone. So, for now, I'd like us to take them in. What do you think?"

Audrey gave a vigorous nod. "We can be their family. I'll be their sister."

Lottie and Pippa echoed Audrey's sentiment almost in unison.

That left Danny. She studied his demeanor. Of all of them, he should have been sympathetic to the runaways' plight. Orphaned as a toddler when his folks were passing through Knotty Pine, he'd had no one else when her parents took him in. Of course he'd been so young when it happened, he probably had no memory of that time. "What are you thinking?" she asked him.

"I just think you ought to be careful is all. That Ethan looks like a troublemaker. Sheriff Hammond caught him stealing, didn't he? And I hear he took some other stuff around town, too."

How much had her brother heard? "Ethan's not a bad kid. He was only trying to take care of his sister. I don't think any of us really know what we'd stoop to if we were in similar situations." She held her brother's gaze. "Jesus forgave the thief on the cross when he repented. Don't you think Ethan deserves another chance, too?"

"I guess." Danny's tone was more grudging than gracious. "If he repented."

"Then we're agreed. We're going to do our best to make them feel at home while they're here."

"How long are they going to be here?" Danny asked.

"As long as it takes for Cissy to get better."

"Where are they?" This came from Audrey.

"They're going to stay in the downstairs bedchamber for now. That'll make it easier for me to check in on Cissy from time to time." She smiled. "Oh, and I misspoke—they're not *completely* alone in the world. They have their dog Scout with them."

"They have a dog?" Audrey hopped out of her seat, and Pippa and Lottie's eyes shone with excitement. Her girls had always wanted a pet but Cora Beth had been reluctant to have one around in case it put off potential boarders.

"They do. Scout is—"

The door swung open. "Mrs. Collins, Cissy is—" Ethan, holding a small pitcher, halted on the threshold when he realized Cora Beth wasn't alone. "Sorry," he said, starting to back out. "I'll come back when—"

"Nonsense." Cora Beth waved him over. "Come in and meet everyone."

Ethan stepped into the room with all the eagerness of a prisoner entering a cell. "Yes, ma'am."

"You've already met my brother Danny. This pigtailed imp is my oldest daughter Audrey. And these two look-alikes are Pippa and Lottie." She gave them all an encouraging smile. "Girls, this is Ethan."

Audrey had already popped up from her chair and crossed the room to meet the visitor halfway. "Hi." She stuck out a hand in a very grown-up gesture. "Welcome to our family."

Ethan gingerly took her hand and stared at her with a confused expression. "Excuse me?"

Audrey gave him a bright smile. "We decided, since you and your sister don't have a family, you can be part of ours, at least while you're staying here. And your dog, too."

Ethan glanced from Audrey to the rest of the group and then focused on Cora Beth. "You did?"

She nodded. "We all did."

"Ma says your sister is sick," Audrey added. "But don't you worry, Ma knows just how to make kids feel better."

By this time Pippa and Lottie had joined Audrey, and the girls had the poor boy nearly surrounded. "Can we see your dog?" one of them asked.

Cora Beth took mercy on Ethan and called the girls back to the table. "You all get to work on your lessons now and let Ethan be. You can meet Cissy when she's feeling a little better. And you can meet Scout when your work is done."

She turned to Ethan. "Was there something you needed?"

Ethan shook his head as if to clear it. "Yes, ma'am. Cissy drank the last of her water. I was going to refill the pitcher."

"You go right ahead. And I'll bring in another bowl of broth in just a bit."

A few minutes later, when Cora Beth stepped into the sickroom with a tray containing a bowl of the promised broth, she found Ethan sitting beside the bed, wiping his sister's forehead with a damp rag.

She offered the little girl a cheery smile. "Cissy, I brought you something to eat." Then she turned to

Ethan. "The family sits down to supper in about an hour. But I can fix you a bowl of broth to tide you over if you're hungry now."

Ethan shook his head. "I'd just as soon take my meals with Cissy if you don't mind."

Was he afraid he wouldn't be welcome? "But there's plenty of room at the table. I'll be glad to stay with Cissy while you eat if you're worried—"

"It ain't that." He drew his shoulders back. "You're an awful nice lady, and I sure do appreciate all you're doing for Cissy. But family should stick together, and no offense, ma'am, but nice as it was for your little girl to say what she did, Cissy is my family, not those folks out there."

Such a mature outlook for such a young boy. "I understand. But I hope you know that you would be truly welcome."

She set the tray on the bedside table and turned back to Cissy. "Now, how's the patient feeling? Ready for a bit of something to eat?"

"I'm not hungry." The child's tone was fretful, petulant.

"Why don't you try just a little," Cora Beth coaxed. "It'll help you get better quicker."

The child wiggled herself into a more upright position. "Is Sheriff Lemon Drop coming back?"

"He most certainly is. I think he's taken quite a shine to you."

That seemed to perk her up a bit. "Do you think he'll sing to me again?"

Cora Beth sat on the chair next to the bed and spooned up a bit of the broth. "Would you like him to?"

The child nodded. "He has a nice rumbly voice."

Cora Beth moved the spoon toward Cissy and the child opened her mouth automatically. "If you ask him, I know he'll be happy to sing for you."

A nice rumbly voice—yes, that was a good description. It was the kind of voice that resonated deep within a person. Deep and true, like the man himself.

Mitch stepped into Cora Beth's kitchen wishing he had better news for her and for those two kids. It had been a long day, and it wasn't over yet.

"So how did you fare with Josie and Sadie this morning?" It was cowardly to put off what he'd come here to say, but he wasn't in any hurry to give her the unsettling news.

"It went well. Told them all that I know about Ethan and Cissy, caught up on everyone's family news, had a nice little visit." She raised a brow. "How did you fare with Nelda?"

Mitch grimaced. "She's dead set on making someone pay, and pay dearly, for the loss of her precious plant."

A worry furrow creased her forehead. "Is she going to make trouble for Ethan?"

"I think I appeased her for now. But I'm afraid Ethan is going to have to eat quite a bit of crow."

That didn't seem to worry Cora Beth overmuch. "Eating crow is unpleasant, but can be good for one's character."

Time to quit procrastinating. "Thought you might like to know, I got a response to the telegram I sent to the sheriff over in Howerton."

She clasped her hands in front of her. "Oh?"

Ease into it. "Their last name is Prentiss."

"Prentiss." Her nose scrunched in concentration. "That sounds familiar."

"Remember about fifteen months back, Titus Brown returned from a trip with a wife and two kids?"

He saw the moment realization hit. Cora Beth sat down hard, her expression stricken. "Oh no." The words came out almost as a whisper.

"I'm afraid so. The wife was Janet Prentiss, a widow, and Ethan and Cissy are her two kids."

Titus Brown was well known in the area for his drinking, his foul mouth and even fouler temper. There wasn't a woman in these parts who would have anything to do with the man, much less marry him. It wasn't surprising that he'd gone off to where he wasn't known to find him a wife.

"That poor woman." Cora Beth placed her interlaced hands on the table. Her knuckles had turned white. "The Ladies' Auxiliary made several attempts to visit her and invite her to church and into some of our homes, but Titus wouldn't have it. Last time we tried, he met us at the door with a shotgun and told us that we were trespassing and to get off his property." She met his gaze. "But that was no excuse for giving up."

He'd known she'd react this way. "Don't go blaming yourself. Titus never was one to tolerate visitors." If there was any blame to be dished out, a wagonload should be piled high at his door. It was his job to protect the citizens of this community.

"Does this mean she's dead?"

"It fits with what Ethan told us. But I aim to find out for sure. I'm going to talk with Ethan this evening, then ride out to Titus's place in the morning. And this time he *will* talk to me."

She reached a hand across the table but stopped short of grabbing his. "Whatever that man says, you *can't* send those kids back to him, Mitch, you just can't."

Didn't she know him better than that? "I agree. But I'm pretty sure it won't come to that. I'd be mighty surprised if Titus took the time to go through a legal adoption. And if that's the case, he doesn't have any claim to them. They're wards of the state."

Some of her tension eased. "So what happens to them now?"

He held her gaze. "I think you already know the answer to that."

"The orphanage?" At his nod, she leaned forward. "No. We can't let that happen."

When had she started thinking of them as partners in this? And how exactly did he feel about that? "I don't see as we have much choice in the matter. Unless we can find a blood relation who wants to lay claim to them. And the sheriff in Howerton didn't seem to think there was much chance of that."

"But you don't have to do anything right away, do you? I mean, Cissy is sick and Ethan is half starved and they're both near about worn to a nub."

He wished he could give her the reassurances she wanted. "I won't do anything definite about their future accommodations until Cissy is better," he temporized. "But I'd like to speak to Ethan about what I've found out and see what he has to add."

She stood. "I'll get Uncle Grover to sit with Cissy and then ask Ethan to join us here in the kitchen."

Mitch watched her leave and then stood and paced the floor. He understood her concerns—he felt the same. He was the town sheriff, hang it all, he was supposed to protect the folks around here.

He'd made a few trips out to Titus's place in the months since he'd brought his new family home—it was the sheriff's job to check on everyone in the community occasionally, even those who didn't want to be checked up on. He hadn't seen the kids on any of his visits but he'd seen the new Mrs. Brown a time or two. She'd seemed nervous and withdrawn, but she hadn't given any indication anything was wrong, even when he'd asked. Of course Titus was always there, hovering around, telling Mitch they were fine and to get off his place and leave them alone.

Why hadn't he made more of an effort to check things out? He'd let Mrs. Brown down and now she was dead. He'd let those two kids down, as well. And there was no way he could come close to making it up to them, not with the terrible price they'd paid. It was something he'd have to live with for the rest of his days.

Five minutes later he was seated back at the table when Cora Beth escorted Ethan into the kitchen. The boy stared at him as if he were facing a firing squad. Another stab at Mitch's conscience.

"Don't worry, Ethan, you're not in any kind of trouble," Mitch said. "Have a seat, I just want to talk."

Ethan sat across the table from Mitch, perched on the edge of his chair. Cora Beth sat beside the boy.

Mitch decided it would be easier on all of them if he got right to the point. "I've been doing a little checking with the sheriff over in Howerton today and I've learned some things about you and your sister."

Ethan went very still. "What kind of things?"

"I've learned that your last name is Prentiss. That

your mother is Janet Prentiss. That she was married to Jonathan Prentiss, a carpenter who died rescuing a kid from a charging bull."

"My pa was a brave man," Ethan said proudly.

Mitch nodded. He could see a touch of that same courage in the boy, now that he knew a little more of his story. "I also learned that your ma married Titus Brown about a year and a half ago and the three of you moved here to live on his place."

Ethan stood, knocking his chair over in the process. "We're not going back there! Not ever. I promised Cissy I'd keep her safe. If you try to make us, I'll find a way for us to run away again."

Mitch tried to calm the boy. "Nobody's going to make you go back to Titus. You have my word."

Ethan didn't look convinced. In fact, he looked poised to run. "Does that mean you're gonna just let us go on our way when Cissy gets better?"

The boy was definitely no fool. "Let's just see about getting her well first." Mitch wasn't going to lie to him, but he didn't want to add more worries to the kid's already full plate. "There'll be time enough to worry about where you go next when the time comes."

Ethan's mouth pinched into a tight, distrustful line.

He couldn't blame the kid and there wasn't much more he could do to reassure him, either. Time to push this conversation in a different direction. "Tell me what happened to your mother."

Some of the tension leeched from Ethan, replaced by an air of loss. He stared down at the floor as his Adam's apple bobbed for a moment. "About three months ago she got real bad sick." His voice was thick but steady. "Titus wouldn't send for the doctor, no matter how much

I begged him to. He kept saying she was just trying to get out of doing all her chores. But my ma wasn't like that."

Cora Beth straightened the chair he'd knocked over. "I'm sure she wasn't," she said softly.

He nodded his acceptance of her sympathy. "She died a few weeks later. Titus just dug a hole on that little hill behind the house and buried her there. He wouldn't even send for the preacher."

Ethan's tone hardened, turned bitter. "Bad enough he wouldn't let her go to church on Sundays even though she begged him to, but it just weren't right not to have a preacher there at her graveside to speak to her passing. Cissy and I did the best we could to give her a proper burial service. Cissy picked the flowers and I made a cross out of two branches. We said a prayer together, but it wasn't special like if a preacher had said it."

Mitch mentally berated himself. How could he *not* have realized what was going on out there? That woman might still be alive today if he'd tried harder.

This time Cora Beth lightly touched Ethan's arm. "I'm so sorry there was no one around to help you and your sister get through that sad time. But you must know that God hears everyone's prayers and was as pleased with yours as He would have been with even the finest of preachers."

"If God hears everyone's prayers, how come He didn't help us when we begged Him to?"

Mitch winced at the bitter, jaded question. He knew exactly how the boy felt—he'd asked himself that very question when his own world had shattered.

But Cora Beth didn't flinch away from the question. "Oh, Ethan, don't ever doubt that He hears all our prayers, and that He loves us deeply. That doesn't mean He's going to keep the hard times away, but it does mean He's always right beside us to help us through them. You just have to remember that He knows things we don't, things we may never know or understand till we get to heaven ourselves. You just have to have faith, you have to believe that there is nothing that happens here on earth that He can't somehow turn into a blessing down the road."

Mitch studied her face as she spoke. Did she really believe that?

When Ethan didn't say anything, Cora Beth took his hand. "I'm sure your mother would have been very touched to learn that you loved her enough to do your best to give her a proper funeral, all on your own, especially given the conditions you were dealing with. Any mother would be."

"Thank you, ma'am." Ethan sat back down at the table, and glanced at the locket she wore around her neck.

"Ma had a real pretty silver locket, too. She wore it all the time—said it was a wedding present from my pa. Just before she died she gave it to Cissy—put it around her neck herself. But after Ma died, Titus took it. Said whatever Ma had was his now. We never saw it again."

Mitch felt his temper rising anew. What kind of sorry excuse for a human being would treat grieving kids that way? Which brought to mind another question. "Ethan, why does Cissy have that scar around her ankle?"

Ethan's face contorted. "It's all my fault."

Cora Beth brushed the hair from his forehead. "I very much doubt that."

"But it is. I didn't like the way Titus treated my ma,

and I kept telling her that we should leave him. I told her I'd find work and take care of her and Cissy. But Ma said I was too young for that and we didn't have anywhere else to go so we had to stay there."

Mitch hadn't thought he could feel any worse, but Ethan's words proved him wrong.

"After Ma died, I knew Cissy and me would be better off on our own so I told Titus that we were leaving. But he said we belonged to him, that he had paid good money to move us all to his place and he intended to get his money's worth."

Cora Beth's reaction to this was a sharp inhale.

"After Ma died, Titus said that Cissy had to stay to do the cooking and I had to keep helping with the fieldwork." Ethan's jaw tightened. "Since he knew I wouldn't leave without Cissy, and he needed me to work in the fields, he padlocked an iron shackle on her bad leg." Ethan's expression darkened even further. "Said it didn't matter since that leg wasn't much good for anything anyway."

Mitch felt his hands tighten into a fist as he thought about anyone treating that little girl so roughly.

"That doesn't make any of this your fault," Cora Beth protested.

There was a part of Mitch that wished Cora Beth were speaking to him, not Ethan.

Ethan continued as if she hadn't spoken. "Once a week, whenever he went into town for supplies and whiskey, he locked me in the root cellar just to make sure I didn't try to get her free while he was away."

The boy finally looked up and met Mitch's gaze, a hardened man-to-man kind of look. "I shouldn't have said anything to him about us leaving. I should have just up and done it when he wasn't looking. Then Cissy wouldn't have had to go through all that."

Mitch instinctively knew the boy wasn't ready to listen to anything that sounded like platitudes. "How did you manage to escape?"

"I used my work time to make my plans." Ethan's voice took on a more confident tone. "I worked with Beebob every chance I got, getting him used to me and used to carrying loads."

"Beebob?"

"Titus's plow mule. I knew we'd need a way for Cissy to ride since she can't walk too fast. Titus always took the horse and buckboard with him when he went to town, so Beebob was our best bet. He's a bit orncry, but I think that's because of the way Titus treated him. I fed him carrots and whatever I could find that I thought he'd like, brushed him extra careful with the curry comb, talked real gentle to him and after a while, he and I got to be good friends. Then I tried sitting on him whenever I knew Titus wasn't likely to see, just to get him used to having a rider."

Mitch had wondered how the two kids had managed to get so far from Titus's place in so short a time. And with so many supplies. "But how did you get out of the root cellar and Cissy out of her shackles?"

Ethan grinned for a split second before that hardened look came back. "Turns out the hinges on one of the root cellar doors could be lifted pretty easy. So after Titus left I'd come out and gather supplies, things I knew he probably wouldn't miss, and hide them down in that root cellar. Then I'd spend the rest of my time working to get Cissy free. I knew Titus would notice if I tampered with her shackles at all. But I figured he wouldn't notice if I worked away at the post that Cissy's shackles were secured to."

Clever kid.

"Titus always stayed in town until near dark, so when I knew it was closing on time for him to get back, I'd just clean up any sawdust and splinters I'd created, disguise my work as best I could and lock myself back in the cellar as if I'd never left."

"And Titus never noticed?"

Ethan snorted derisively. "He's not real smart and he never figured I could get out of the cellar. He only checked the lock where it was attached to Cissy's ankle—he never thought to look at the post. Though he did almost catch me once when he came home a little early. Lucky thing Scout started barking when Titus was still a ways off. I managed to slip out the back way and get in the cellar and put the door in place before he got close."

"But you did get the shackle off her."

"I grabbed a chisel and hammer before we left. First night out I made sure that thing came off and tossed it in the creek."

"What happened to the mule?" Mitch asked.

"We made camp that first night and when we got up the next morning he was gone." He rubbed the back of his neck. "Guess I didn't do a good enough job tethering him. Luckily I'd unloaded all our supplies. Anyway, that's why we were stuck here. I'd planned for Cissy and me to be far away from Knotty Pine by now."

"Where were you headed?"

"As far away from Titus as we could get."

"You were very brave and resourceful," Cora Beth

stated. "Your sister is very lucky to have you to look out for her."

Mitch stood and moved around the table. "Ethan, I'm sorry I didn't do more to check on your family. I can't change that now, but you have my word you won't have to go back to Titus's place." He held out his hand.

To Mitch's relief, after a moment, Ethan stood, extended his own hand and they shook. It almost felt as if the boy were forgiving him. But Mitch still didn't know if he could forgive himself.

"Ethan," Mitch cautioned, "your sister's not up for another of your daring escapes. She's safe here. You need to let her stay put and rest so she can get better. Understand?"

The boy nodded.

"Do I have your word on that?"

After a slight hesitation, Ethan nodded again. "Yes, sir."

Good enough.

Ethan turned to Cora Beth. "Whenever you want to set me some chores to do, ma'am, I'm ready."

She smiled. "Let's not worry about that just yet."

"No, ma'am, that wasn't the deal." There was a dignity and maturity about the boy that many a grown man would envy. "I aim to pay for me and Cissy's keep. If you don't have work for me, I'll find work elsewhere so I can pay you what's owed."

Mitch held his breath, hoping Cora Beth would understand the boy needed this.

And of course she did.

"Very well. First thing tomorrow morning you can get to work in the garden. There's a row of squash that needs weeding and then you can check the tomatoes and pick the ripe ones for me to pickle."

Cora Beth's answer seemed to satisfy the boy. "I'll go back now and stay with Cissy till then."

Ethan moved toward the hall door, paused and turned back to Mitch. "You gonna come in and see Cissy? She asked for you when she woke up a while ago."

It seemed he and Ethan had formed a truce of sorts. Mitch patted his shirt pocket. "Yep. I have her lemon drops right here. I just want to have a word with Mrs. Collins first."

As soon as they were alone, Cora Beth stood and started pacing. "I'm so angry I could spit nails. How could anyone treat kids that way? Mitch, that man should be locked up."

Mitch agreed. Too bad he couldn't do much about it. "I'm not sure there are any charges we can legally bring against Titus, but I promise you that he will *not* get his hands on those two kids again." That sorry excuse for a man would have to come through him to get to them.

She paused and her face seemed to crumple. "Oh, Mitch, what those kids have been through. It near breaks my heart."

He stood and put a comforting hand on her shoulder. "I know. It's hard to believe even Titus could be that cruel to a couple of kids."

She stepped closer. Almost of its own accord his hand slipped around her back until he was holding her in a one-armed embrace. She needed comforting. He was just being a friend, he told himself—that was all.

"I feel as if I let them down," she was saying as she kneaded her left hand with her right, "as if I should have done something to help them before it got this far.

At the very least I should have tried harder to befriend their mother."

He gave her shoulder a light squeeze and was unaccountably pleased when she leaned back into his arm. "This is *not* your fault," he said. "If you want to start passing blame around, dump a load of it at my door. As sheriff I should have been more vigilant in checking what was going on out there." He caught a whiff of cinnamon and honey, a sweet and spicy mix that seemed to be a part of her. He fought not to let it distract him. It wasn't easy—Cora Beth was truly a lovely woman, inside and out.

"No, don't—" She suddenly went still and then eased herself out of his hold. "I'm sorry." Her cheeks were prettily stained with pink. "You must think I'm being a goose."

"Not at all." His arm still tingled where she'd pressed against him, felt bereft without its sweet weight to support. "Hearing Ethan's story would upset anyone with a heart."

"Hand wringing doesn't do anyone any good. Those kids need more than my sympathy."

One thing about Cora Beth, her emotions always led to action. "You're already doing your part to help them. And even though we may not be able to change what's past, sure as night follows day we can make sure it doesn't happen again." Not on his watch at any rate.

"My biggest concern right now is what's going to become of them." She raised a hand, palm forward. "And don't you dare mention that orphanage again. They deserve something better than that."

This time he agreed. "I know. I'm just not sure what we can do about it." He felt strongly that he needed to do something to make amends for his inaction. Sending them off to an orphanage hardly qualified.

"How much time do we have to figure something out?" she asked.

"We can put off doing anything official until Cissy is fully recovered—maybe a week or so. And then there's the matter of having them declared wards of the state. The paperwork on that could take a bit more time."

She sat down again. "That's something. I'll be praying that the Good Lord shows me the answer."

Mitch had a pretty good idea how this was going to end up. But she was right—leave it in God's hands for now.

She gave him a sympathetic look. "I'll also be praying that things go as they should with your meeting with Titus tomorrow. I certainly don't envy you that encounter."

Despite the worry in her eyes, Mitch found his thoughts focused more on how sweet it had felt to hold Cora Beth than on what his meeting with Titus would be like.

He'd held her before. Whenever there was a town dance, he always made a point of claiming Cora Beth as his partner for several dances. But this had been different. This time she'd come to him. This time she'd drawn comfort from him.

This time she'd *needed* him.

Courting her was out of the question, of course. He wouldn't take the risk of hurting her the way he knew he could.

But maybe, as long as he kept firm control of his own treacherous feelings, he could be the friend she leaned on when she needed comfort or support.

Surely there was nothing wrong with that.

as well since, if I find you within twenty yards of either one of them, I'll haul your sorry carcass to jail, lock you up and throw away the key."

Titus's eyes narrowed. "I don't know what them two's been saying about me but you can't believe anything they say. They're a pair of mealy mouthed liars."

Mitch didn't bother to hide his sneer. "Unlike the fine, upstanding citizen you are."

"You ain't got no call to talk to me like that. And another thing. Them two are thieves to boot. They took my mule and a whole bunch of supplies and tools."

No more than they were entitled to as far as Mitch was concerned. "Tell me what happened to their mother."

Titus spat on the ground in front of him. "She was a puny, sniveling excuse for a wife. Always mewling about her kids. Then she up and died on me. Marrying that one was a waste of time and money."

Just concentrate on getting the information you need. "How'd she die?"

"How should I know? I ain't no doctor."

Mitch fought to keep his voice even. "I'll ask you again—how did she die?"

Titus let out a string of oaths. "That woman was always whining and complaining about some ailment or other. One day she took to her bed and refused to get up. Next thing I know she's stone-cold dead."

"Did you even once consider calling for Doc Whitman to look in on her?"

"Like I said, I didn't figure it was anything more serious than what she'd had before. Besides, doctors cost money."

With Titus, it always came down to what was best for Titus.

"I want them kids back." Titus glared belligerently. "You can't keep them from me, I'm their stepdad."

"Forget it, Titus. Unless you can produce adoption papers you have no legal claim to them. They're wards of the state now."

"Those kids owe me. They stole my mule and a hatchet and a bunch more of my stuff. It's only right they come back here and work it off."

Over his dead body. "You got a right to press charges if that's what you want to do." He kept his tone conversational but didn't bother trying to hide his contempt. "Come by my office whenever you get ready to file the paperwork. And when you do, we'll also talk about what charges might be filed against you on Cissy and Ethan's behalf."

A look of something akin to fear crossed Titus's expression, quickly followed by a chest-out posture that was pure bluster. "They got no claim against me."

"Don't they? The state of Texas looks harshly on folks who abuse kids."

"I never abused those kids. Just had 'em working for their keep is all, same as any real pa would do."

"Shall we put it to the test?"

Their gazes locked for several long moments. Titus was the first to look away. He crossed his arms over his chest. "Keep 'em then. They weren't much use to me anyway."

But Mitch wasn't quite through with him yet. "Ethan mentioned a locket that belonged to his mother. She promised it to Cissy, but it appears to have gone missing after she died."

"I sold it." The belligerence was back. "And don't you go telling me I had no right. I needed some way to pay for taking care of those two. Them and their mangy cur ate more in vittles than they worked off in chores."

Mitch seriously doubted that, but arguing wouldn't do any good. "Who'd you sell it to?"

"Danvers over at the mercantile." Titus spat on the ground again "Now if you're done asking me all these fool questions, I got chores to do. It's lots of work taking care of a place like this when you ain't got no help."

Mitch didn't waste words or time responding to that, simply turned his horse and rode away. Too bad he couldn't find some excuse to arrest the man. If ever a body needed locking up, it was Titus Brown.

Thirty minutes later he marched into the mercantile. He was relieved to see Horace Danvers didn't have any customers at the moment—he'd just as soon not have an audience for this little bit of business.

Horace leaned on the counter near his till. "What can I do for you today, Sheriff?"

"Titus came in here a while back and sold off a locket. You remember the piece?"

"Yep. Matter of fact, I still have it. It's right over here in the display case." Horace bent down and retrieved the keepsake. He laid it on the counter for Mitch's viewing. "Pretty little bauble, isn't it? I wondered how Titus came to have such a thing but he assured me it was his to sell."

No point debating that now. "How much do you want for it?

Horace's lips turned up in an arch smile. "You going courting, are you, Sheriff?"

"No," Mitch said, firmly repressing the sudden image of placing the locket around Cora Beth's neck, "and don't you go spreading any rumors to the contrary." Danvers had a marriageable-aged daughter and a matchmaking wife who loved to talk. The last thing he needed was a rumor flying around town.

Horace raised a hand in protest. "You know me, Sheriff, the soul of discretion."

Mitch decided to let it go at that and reached for his wallet.

Twenty minutes later he was seated in Cora Beth's kitchen, sipping on a cup of coffee. He seemed to be spending a lot of time there lately. "How's Cissy doing?"

"She had a rough night last night, poor darling. But her fever finally broke this morning and she's sleeping much easier now. Dr. Whitman stopped by to check on her and he thinks she's past the worst of it."

"Good to hear. And how about Ethan?"

"He never left her side last night. But bright and early this morning he headed out to the garden and spent the biggest part of it hard at work. That young man has a strong sense of duty. And more than his share of stubborn pride."

Mitch understood that. The boy probably felt pride was all he had left, that Titus had taken everything else. He'd learn in time that, with Cora Beth in his corner, he didn't have to constantly prove himself.

Cora Beth sighed. "I don't know what I'm going to do with him. He needs to be in school with the other children. Neither he nor Cissy have been to school since they moved to Knotty Pine. I only hope his mother was able to teach them at home."

Mitch imagined Titus had kept them much too busy to allow time for that.

"I saw Titus this morning."

Cora Beth stilled, apprehension drawing her jaw tight. "And?"

"I don't think he'll be bothering the children again."

Some of the tension slid from her shoulders. "Thank the good Lord for that." She smiled. "And thank you, too."

He shrugged. "Just doing my job." Better late than never.

She plopped her elbows on the table. "You can't fool me, Mitchell Hammond. I know it's much more than that."

The last thing he needed was for her to try to label him a hero. Especially considering he'd failed so tragically in this case. "I owed it to those kids."

He carried his coffee cup to the sink. "There's still the matter of all those items Ethan stole." He held up a hand to stop her protest. "I know he didn't think he had any other choice, though I still don't know why he thought he needed Nelda's blamed plant, but the fact of the matter is, in the eyes of the town, he's a thief."

To his surprise, she nodded. "You're right. And I think he feels bad about doing it."

"Feeling bad is a start, but it's not enough."

"What do you suggest?"

"You're the parent. If it was one of your girls or Danny who did that, what sort of punishment would you dole out?"

She stared at him for a minute and he could see her mind working to formulate an answer. Finally she sighed. "I'd make them face the consequences of their actions."

"I thought so."

"When do you want to talk to him?"

"No point putting it off."

She nodded. "He'll be in from the garden soon."

Mitch reached into his pocket and pulled out the wrapped packet he'd picked up at the mercantile. "When you have a moment, give him and Cissy this."

She stepped closer to have a look. "What is it?

He unwrapped the tiny parcel. "It's the locket that belonged to their mother."

"Oh, Mitch, I know how much this is going to mean to them. How in the world did you manage to talk Titus out of it?"

"Titus sold it to Danvers over at the mercantile a few weeks ago. Luckily, Danvers still had it."

Rather than taking the locket from him, she closed his fist around it. "I think it would be more appropriate if *you* gave it to them."

They stood there with her small hand closed over his, gazes locked. Mitch felt unable to move or look away. There was such warmth in her touch, such tenderness in her eyes. He didn't think anyone had ever made him feel so special before.

He wasn't sure how long they stood like that. The spell was finally broken by the sound of the back door opening. As Ethan stepped inside, Cora Beth quickly turned back to the sink and began rinsing out Mitch's coffee cup.

But not before he saw the color rise in her cheeks.

He could tell already that his plan to keep things between them on a friendship basis was going to be sorely tried.

Cora Beth vigorously scrubbed at the hapless coffee cup. She hoped neither Mitch nor Ethan had noticed the warmth blossoming in her cheeks. Goodness, what must Mitch think of her, holding on to his hand like some schoolgirl with an inappropriate case of puppy love? And this on top of the way she'd acted just yesterday. Goodness only knew how long she would have held on to his hand if Ethan hadn't walked in.

She heard Ethan acknowledge Mitch's presence with a quick hello, and she turned back around, hoping she looked sufficiently composed.

"I've got the row of tomatoes and cucumbers weeded. Looks like there'll be some ready to pick in the next day or so."

"Thank you." She nodded toward the hall door. "You can clean up over in the washroom, then come back in here. Sheriff Hammond and I need to speak to you."

Ethan looked from one to the other of them, a worried frown on his face. But he merely nodded and left the room without another word.

While they waited, Cora Beth dried the cup and set it carefully back in the cupboard. Neither she nor Mitch said a word. Was he thinking about what he had to say to Ethan? Or about what had just passed between them?

When Ethan returned, they all took seats at the table.

Mitch cleared his throat. "First, you should know, I went out to Titus's place today."

She saw Ethan's face pale. "You told him where we were?"

Mitch shook his head. "No, but I did tell him I'd found you two." He leaned forward, his expression open and earnest. "I made it quite clear that in the eyes of the law he had no claim to you or Cissy and that you two were under my protection for the time being. He shouldn't be bothering either of you again."

"Good to hear."

Cora Beth looked pointedly at Mitch. "I think you have something for Ethan and Cissy."

Something unreadable flickered in his expression. Then he reached back into his pocket. "That's right. I almost forgot."

Ethan craned his neck. "What is it?"

Mitch held the necklace by its chain, letting the locket dangle at Ethan's eye level. "I came across this over at the mercantile. Thought it might be the one you mentioned yesterday."

It was just like Mitch to downplay his efforts.

Ethan didn't make a move to take the locket, just stared at it as if he were a starving man and it was a steak. "That's my ma's locket." He finally looked up, meeting Mitch's glance. "I'll pay you back whatever it cost just as soon as I'm able."

There was a long pause and Cora Beth tried to send a mental message to Mitch. *Please don't dismiss Ethan's offer. He needs to know you take him seriously.*

Finally Mitch leaned back. "All right. I figure you can spend an hour sweeping and taking care of some other chores over at my office every day for the next two weeks. That ought to just about cover it."

Two weeks—good. That meant Mitch wasn't planning to send them away any time soon.

Ethan nodded. "Yes, sir. I reckon that sounds fair."

He extended his hand. "Well then, go ahead and take it."

But Ethan moved his hands to his lap. "No, sir. You hold on to it until I've worked it off. Won't feel right otherwise."

Cora Beth couldn't have been prouder of the boy if

he'd been her own son. She exchanged a quick glance with Mitch and his lips turned up for just a moment in a smile of understanding.

"I tell you what," he said to Ethan. "Why don't we ask Mrs. Collins here to hold it for us until you're ready to claim it? If she doesn't mind, that is."

"I'll be glad to." Cora Beth accepted the locket and set it on the table in front of her. "As soon as we're done here I'll place it in my jewelry box along with my mama's wedding band and my cameo brooch."

Deciding it wouldn't be right to make Mitch deliver the bad news, Cora Beth took a deep breath and stared directly into Ethan's eyes. "Speaking of paying off debts, Ethan, there's something else we need to discuss with you."

"Yes, ma'am. Do you have some more chores for me to do?"

"That's not it. We wanted to talk to you about those things you took from the folks around town."

The boy shifted, looking suddenly eleven years old again. "That was wrong I know, but I didn't know what else to do."

"I understand. But I think there are some folks that you at least owe an apology to."

His face paled, but he swallowed hard and nodded. "Yes, ma'am. As soon as Cissy gets—"

"I think today would be better," she said firmly. "No point putting off something like this. My Grammy Alma used to say, if you're dreading something you know you have to do, do it quick and be done with it. If you put it off, it'll just keep clawing at your insides and make you plumb miserable. Do you understand what she meant?"

Ethan had hung his head and was no longer meeting her gaze. "I suppose so."

Cora Beth looked at Mitch and he nodded, then leaned forward. "Okay, Ethan, we already know you took a shirt and sheet from Mrs. Johnson's clothesline, a pie from Mrs. Evans's windowsill and a potted plant from Mrs. Oglesby's greenhouse. Was there anything else?"

Ethan nodded and began to enumerate his thefts. "I took a few pieces of scrap lumber from somebody's woodpile, and I grabbed a couple more from an old shed that was falling down. I took a small pail and a handful of loose nails from someone else's back porch. I took two eggs from a chicken coop. Oh and I found almost a whole roll of twine out behind the mercantile and I took a broken board and a scoop of corn from a feed sack over at the livery."

Construction materials for his shelter and food for him and Cissy. But there were a few items Cora Beth couldn't figure out a purpose for. "I understand why you took most of these things," she said, "but can I ask why you took a plant from Mrs. Oglesby's greenhouse? I mean, it wasn't as if it were edible or useful."

"I know. But it was Cissy's birthday and I wanted to make the day special for her, like Ma used to do back when we lived in Howerton. That's why I took that cherry pie, too. After I took the pie I got to thinking that a fancy place like that big ole glass shed with the plants inside might have some special fruits or something. But it was just flowers."

His voice dripped with a young boy's disgust for such girly things. "Since I'd already broke in and Cissy liked pretty things, I reckoned that maybe nobody would miss it if I took just one. I mean there were so many and all, and I was careful to pick a small one. A raccoon followed me in, though. I caught just a glimpse of it and next thing I knew pots were falling over and there was a big old mess."

"I see." So much for Nelda's malicious prankster.

"And you're sure it wasn't you who knocked those plants over by accident?"

"Yes, sir. I was real careful."

Mitch believed him. "Do you think you can remember what houses you took all those things from?

"Yes, sir." He stared at Mitch as if prepared for the worst. "Are you going to put me in jail?"

"If you own up to what you did and offer to make restitution, I don't think that'll be necessary." He gave the boy one of those stern lawman looks he could do so well. "If you ever do anything like that again, though, it'll be a whole different story. Understand?"

"Yes, sir. It won't happen again."

"Good. Then I think you and I need to make some visits this afternoon."

Cora Beth stood. "Mind if I come along?" She figured it might be good if the townsfolk saw that Ethan had her support as well as Mitch's.

Mitch gave her a considering look. "That might be nice, Mrs. Collins. For Ethan," he added.

Cora Beth smiled. "I'll ask Uncle Grover or Mrs. Plunkett to sit with Cissy after lunch and then the three of us can make some house calls."

Chapter Nine

"Well, hello, Sheriff, Cora Beth. Is there something I can do for you?" Rita Evans stepped out on her front porch to greet them, a surprised but welcoming look on her face.

Cora Beth returned her smile, but decided to let Mitch do the talking.

"Hello, Rita." Mitch touched the brim of his hat in greeting. "We just wanted to talk to you for a few minutes if you've got the time."

"Certainly." Rita patted her soft white hair and stepped to one side. "Y'all come on inside and let me fix you up a glass of lemonade."

"No need for refreshments, this'll only take a few minutes."

"Well, suit yourself then." She allowed the screen door to close and looked from one to the other of them. "What can I do for you?" she asked again.

Cora Beth nudged Ethan to the forefront. "This is Ethan Prentiss. He and his sister Cecelia are staying over at the boardinghouse for a while. And he has something to say to you."

Rita gave him a friendly, grandmotherly smile. "Hello, young man. What was it you were wanting to tell me?"

Ethan's posture was fence-post stiff and his expression rigidly controlled. But he held up his head. "It was me who took your pie the other day, ma'am. I'm truly sorry and I'd like to make it right with you."

"Oh. I see." Rita looked from the boy to the adults, her smile fading to uncertainty. "I suppose you must have had a good reason."

"My reason don't matter none, ma'am. Stealing is stealing and it ain't right no matter what."

Cora Beth was proud that the boy wasn't making excuses for himself. It was a good sign that he truly regretted what he'd done.

"Well, of course but—

"Perhaps you have some chores that Ethan could take care of for you," Cora Beth prompted.

"Oh. Why yes." Rita took her cue and her flustered expression changed to something more businesslike. "As a matter of fact, I've been after Alfred to whitewash our front fence for a month now but he's just been so busy lately."

Ethan nodded. "I'll be glad to take care of it for you, ma'am. And don't you worry, I promise to do an extra special job. I can do it tomorrow morning if you like."

"Tomorrow will be fine. I already have the whitewash and brushes."

As they stepped back onto the sidewalk a few minutes later, Cora Beth gave Ethan an encouraging smile. "You did just fine. Are you ready for the next name on our list?"

* * *

Within two hours they had visited just about every one of Ethan's "victims." Most had taken it as well as Rita—a few were a bit more huffy—but all agreed to let Ethan repay them with chores, which meant he had quite enough to keep him busy for the next two weeks. Cora Beth had made careful note of each obligation.

"There's just one more stop we need to make," Mitch said.

Ethan shook his head. "Don't you mean two more? The livery owner and the lady with the glass plant house."

Cora Beth smiled. "I'm the livery owner. At least my family is."

The boy halted midstep, pausing for a heartbeat before continuing on. "Oh."

"I think an hour or so mucking out the horse stalls should more than cover the cost of one board and a scoop of corn."

"Yes, ma'am. So I guess now we go visit the lady with the plant house."

Mitch exchanged a look with Cora Beth. "That's right. Mrs. Oglesby. Before we knock on her door, though, you need to understand that she feels very strongly about her greenhouse and the plants she grows there. And apparently the plant you took was one of her favorites."

Ethan nodded gloomily. "You're trying to say she's going to be angry with me."

"Very likely."

Cora Beth gave him a sympathetic look. "Mrs. Oglesby tends to get a bit dramatic over things like this."

"You think she's going to yell at me?"

Cora Beth shook her head. "Oh, no, I doubt she'll actually yell." Though Ethan might prefer she had when it was all said and done.

Ethan squared his shoulders. "Well, I suppose I deserve whatever she wants to throw at me. Everyone else has been so nice, there was bound to be at least one person who wanted to give me what for." He gave them both a weak smile. "Like your Grammy Alma said, best to get it over and done with instead of worrying over it."

A few minutes later, they stood on Nelda's front porch, waiting for her to answer Mitch's knock.

When she opened the door her brows went up, but she offered them a neighborly smile. "Sheriff, Cora Beth, to what do I owe this unexpected visit?"

Cora Beth decided to take the lead on this one. "Mind if we speak to you for a few minutes, Nelda?"

"Of course." Nelda moved to let them in. Then she eyed Ethan suspiciously and stepped outside instead. "So, who is your young friend here?"

Cora Beth placed her hand at Ethan's back, not certain if she was offering support to Ethan or herself. "This is Ethan Prentiss. He has something to say to you."

"Does he, now." Nelda drew herself up to her full height. "Well, young man, out with it. What do you have to say to me?"

"I—" Ethan faltered, then straightened. "I'm the one who stole the plant from your glass shed."

Her eyes narrowed. "So you're the little thief, are you?" She turned to Mitch. "Well, Sheriff, I'm glad to see you've finally captured this criminal. What do you plan to do with him?"

Mitch crossed his arms. "Now, Nelda, hear him out. Ethan is here to make amends."

"Make amends? How can he possibly make amends for what he did?" She glared at Ethan. "And just what did you do with my prize orchid?"

"I gave it to my sister for her birthday."

"And did you tell her that you stole it? Is that how you honor your sister on her special day, with ill-gotten goods?"

"Please, ma'am, I'm awful sorry." Ethan sounded desperate. "If there's anything at all I can do—"

Nelda cut him off midsentence. "Where are your parents? They should be here with you, not Cora Beth."

"Ethan's parents are no longer with us," Cora Beth explained. "He and his sister are staying with me for the time being."

"Staying with you? This boy should be under lock and key so he doesn't prey on any more innocent folk while they sleep."

"Oh for goodness' sake, Nelda, he's just a boy." Cora Beth tried to hold on to her temper but the woman had perfected the art of making mountains out of molehills. "And he's trying to make things right."

"The bible tells us to 'withhold not correction from the child.' The only way for a wicked child like him to learn is to make sure he faces the consequences for his crimes."

How dare she call Ethan wicked? Cora Beth tilted her chin up. "It also tells us to forgive others as the Father forgave us."

Nelda drew herself up. "Of course I forgive him. I know my Christian duty as well as you do, Cora Beth Collins. But discipline is part of training up a child."

This was getting them nowhere.

Fortunately, Mitch stepped in. "What is it you want us to do?"

Nelda waved a hand. "He's outright confessed to being a thief. What does the *law* say you should do?"

Mitch stared her down. "I'm *not* going to lock up an eleven-year-old boy for stealing a plant to give to his seven-year-old sister for her birthday. Especially when he's willing to make restitution. Now, what do you think is a fair exchange? He can do chores around here if you like."

"I most certainly do *not* like." She stared at Ethan as if he were a hardened criminal. "I will not subject my daughters to his regrettable influence. Odine and Loretta are such delicate flowers themselves—"

"Very well, then, we'll find a way for him to earn some money. What is the replacement cost for that plant?"

Bless Mitch for keeping a level head.

"I'm not certain I can find another just like it. I labored over it for so long, took such care—"

"Nelda." Mitch's tone said he was reaching the limit of his patience.

"Oh, very well." She tossed her head majestically. "I suppose fifteen dollars would cover it."

Cora Beth blinked. "Fifteen dollars? For a *plant?*"

"It's a very special plant. You asked me my price and that is it."

"Agreed." Mitch put a hand at Ethan's back. "Now, if you'll excuse us, we'll be going."

None of them spoke as they strode down the walk to Nelda's front gate. Finally, as they stepped onto the sidewalk, Ethan broke the silence. "She sure was powerful angry."

"That she was." Mitch's tone was agreeable but firm. "But you *did* steal her plant."

Abashed, Ethan was quiet for several minutes. Then he kicked at a pebble. "It'll take me a long time to earn fifteen dollars, if I can even find a paying job. Do you think she's willing to wait?"

Mitch didn't turn his head. "I'll loan you the money. You can pay me back a little at a time."

Cora Beth smiled. Much as he tried to deny it, Mitch had a soft spot for these kids. "I'll hire you to help out at the stable," she added. Then she tapped the list. "Once you take care of all these other chores, that is."

There was another short silence, then Ethan looked from one to the other of them. "Why are you both being so nice to Cissy and me?"

Cora Beth found his question heartbreakingly sad. Had they really encountered so little kindness that he'd find this remarkable? "Ethan, I know you were treated poorly by Titus, but most folks around here aren't like that. They try to help others out when they can. Sheriff Hammond and I are glad to help you this way. And it's not like it's charity. You're paying for your keep by doing chores for me. And you're the one making things right with the folks around here. The sheriff and I just tagged along."

She placed a hand on his shoulder. "I'm very proud of how you handled yourself today. And more importantly, I know your mother would be very proud, as well."

Ethan's expression lightened and he stood a bit taller at that.

As they approached the boardinghouse, Cora Beth

quickened her steps. "It's just about time for school to let out. I need to start working on supper." She turned to Mitch. "You're welcome to join us for our meal this evening if you like."

"That's mighty tempting but I think I'll pass. I have some things that need my attention at the office and I have evening rounds to make. But I'd like to come by and check on Cissy a little later if that's okay."

The idea that his only reason for coming to visit was to check on the kids pricked at her pride. But she managed a smile. "You don't need to ask. You're welcome to stop in for a visit anytime."

With a touch of his hat brim, he took his leave.

As Cora Beth watched him walk away, she wondered what he would say if he knew that she sometimes daydreamed about having him court her. For a fleeting moment she toyed with the idea that she should borrow from Mrs. Plunkett's example and let her feeling show more.

But she quickly pushed that notion aside. After all, any number of other ladies—much more suitable than her—had done just that. If Mitch wasn't swayed by their efforts, what would make her think he'd be swayed by hers?

Still, as long as she kept her daydreams to herself, they would cause no harm.

Mitch walked down the hall of the boardinghouse, not sure why he felt slightly off balance this evening. He'd found Cora Beth on the front porch swing, taking care of some mending in the fading evening light. Rather than pausing to chat with him as he'd expected, though, she'd smiled, waved him on with a quick *you know the way* and gone back to her sewing.

Shaking off the vaguely dissatisfied feeling, he entered Cissy's room to find not one but four little girls there, playing with a set of rag dolls.

Dealing with one little girl was one thing, but four—

Audrey spied him first. "Oh, hello, Sheriff Hammond."

"Hi, Audrey, ladies. Don't you girls look as bright as a springtime garden." He turned to Cissy. "Glad to see you're feeling well enough to play today, Buttercup."

Cissy sat up straighter when she spotted Mitch. "I'm all better now but Audrey's mom says I have to stay in bed a little longer."

"That's right. We want to make sure you have all your strength back before you start running around with these two-legged whirlwinds."

"Why'd you call her 'Buttercup'?" Audrey asked. "Her name is Cissy."

"I know. But with her yellow hair and pink cheeks she reminds me of a buttercup."

"Oh." Audrey thought about that for a second. "Do I remind you of a flower?"

"You sure do. I think of you as a sweet pea. Pert and sassy."

Audrey turned to her sisters, preening. "Did you hear that? Sheriff Hammond thinks I'm like a sweet pea."

"What about us?" one of the twins asked.

Mitch had to think fast. He couldn't tell which twin was which and he didn't want to slight either of them. "Well, you," he said pointing to the one who'd spoke up, "remind me of a daisy because of how sweet and bright you are. And you," he said turning to the other twin, "remind me of a morning glory because you're quieter but your eyes are always sparkling like morning dew."

"Hear that, Pippa? I'm a morning glory."

Okay, he'd have to remember that—Pippa, daisy; Lottie, morning glory.

"Do you want to play with us?" Cissy asked. "We'll share our dolls."

"Thank you for the invitation but I'm afraid I can't stay long. I did bring you all something, though."

Cissy's eyes lit up. "What?"

"Lemon drops." He pulled the candy wrapped in wax paper from his pocket. "I have just enough here for you to each have a piece."

That earned him a chorus of "yes, please's" and "thank you's."

Once he'd handed out the last piece, he straightened. "Well, I'll leave you ladies to your dolls now. But I'll be back tomorrow to check on you again."

"Before you go," Cissy asked, "would you sing me that song again?"

Mitch felt his smile freeze. Singing out of desperation to a sick, fretful child in the middle of nowhere was one thing. But singing to four alert little girls was something else entirely. "But that's a lullaby and it's not time to go to sleep yet. I'm sure Audrey and her sisters would rather play with the dolls than hear me sing."

Her eyes widened like a forlorn puppy's. "Please?"

"We want to hear it, too," Audrey added.

The twins nodded. Mitch found himself the target of four pairs of pleading little-girl eyes and discovered he would rather face down a hardened criminal on a rampage. At least with someone like that he'd have a fighting chance.

"All right, you win." Taking a deep breath, he began to sing. *"Good night, happy dreams, my sweet little one. Close your eyes..."*

Cora Beth paused with her hand on the kitchen door and smiled as she heard the faint sounds of Mitch's singing coming from Cissy's room. The girls would be enjoying such special attention from him, she was sure. She stood there in the hall, letting the words wash over her, as well.

Mitch definitely had a way with the ladies, even the very young ones like the quartet he was with now. Part of his charm was that he made a lady feel special, worth looking out for. And he did it effortlessly, naturally and without being overbearing. More than likely, if you were to ask him, he'd deny he was doing anything out of the ordinary. Which made it all the more charming.

But it also meant any attention he was showing her was not to be taken too much to heart. Mitch was just being Mitch. He wasn't trying to single her out or make her feel in any way special.

Suddenly she wasn't quite so charmed. Truth be told, she *wanted* Mitch to see her as special. Was that wrong of her? And more to the point, was there any chance it would ever happen?

Chapter Ten

The next morning, Dr. Whitman arrived right after breakfast. Once he completed his examination of Cissy, Cora Beth stepped into the hall with him. "So, how is she?"

Before the physician could answer, Ethan popped into the hall from the kitchen. "Is she all better now?"

Dr. Whitman smiled reassuringly at the boy. "She's doing just fine." Then he turned back to Cora Beth. "In fact, if you'd like, you can let her get up for a while today. A bit of exercise will be good for her—just as long as you make certain she takes it easy and doesn't overdo it for the next few days."

"That's good to hear." Cora Beth turned to Ethan. "You can go back inside and check on her if you like."

With a nod he disappeared into Cissy's room.

"She'll be glad to hear the good news," she said. "I think she was getting tired of staring at those same four walls."

"Like I said, it's important that she takes it easy for the next day or two, and she'll be just fine. If anything comes up, though, you know where to find me."

"Are you sure I can't get you a cup of coffee and slice of pecan pie before you leave?"

"That's mighty tempting but no, thank you. I promised Mrs. Addison I'd check in on Billy this morning. Poor kid sprained his ankle when he fell out of a tree yesterday."

"Well, give Willa my best. And thank you again."

After she'd escorted the doctor to the front door, Cora Beth returned to Cissy's room to find the girl sitting up, her eyes sparkling with excitement. "Ethan says it's okay for me to get out of bed today."

"That's right. But you have to agree to go slowly and not tire yourself out. Can you do that?"

"Oh yes, ma'am."

"Good. Then I think a bath will be our first order of business this morning."

Cissy wrinkled her nose. "Do I have to?"

"Only if you want to get out of bed."

As Cora Beth escorted Cissy to the washroom she took note of the child's limp. "Does your leg heart you, sweetheart?"

"No, ma'am. I mean, sometimes, when the weather's damp or really cold or I been playing hard, it'll hurt some. But mostly it just doesn't work as good as my other leg."

"I see. Well, no doubt a nice warm bath will do it and you a load of good."

Once she'd taken her bath, Cissy was ready to explore the rest of the house. The child was self-conscious of her limp at first, but Cora Beth had already told the other members of her household what to expect, so it wasn't long before the four girls had their heads together, chattering and giggling over little-girl things.

For a while Ethan hovered over his sister like a biddy

hen protecting its chick, but after a bit, when he realized no one was going to make her feel uncomfortable, he relaxed. By midmorning he headed off to the Evans place to whitewash their fence. After that he was headed to the sheriff's office to start working off the money for the locket.

Danny worked at the livery on Saturday mornings so he was already gone. And Uncle Grover and Mrs. Plunkett had gone out on another field trip.

That left her and the four girls on their own.

"All right, girls, it's Saturday, and you know what that means."

"Baking day," her daughters said in unison.

"That's right, so get your aprons and head for the kitchen." Cora Beth usually got her daughters involved in helping her with her baking on Saturdays. It served to not only teach them skills they would need later in life, but gave her additional time to spend with them.

"Can I help, too?" Cissy asked.

"Are you sure you wouldn't rather just watch?"

"I'm sure. My ma taught me how to make stews and boil vegetables, but I never learned much about baking."

The reminder of what the child had been through caused Cora Beth to swallow hard and work to maintain her smile. "Well, come along then. I have an extra apron you can use."

Once everyone was gathered in the kitchen and Cora Beth had gotten out the basic supplies, the girls all stood around the table.

"All right, before we get started," Cora Beth said, "we need to explain to Cissy how this works."

Audrey raised her hand. "Can I do it?"

Cora Beth nodded her permission.

"We usually make nine pies," Audrey explained, "one for each day of the week and a couple of extras, just in case."

Cissy's eyes grew wide. "That's a lot of pies."

"We have a lot of people who live here." Audrey said this as if she were personally responsible. "Anyway, Mama lets each of us pick one kind of pie to make, and then we help her roll out the dough and put the filling in."

Audrey turned to Cora Beth. "Can Cissy pick a pie, too?"

"Of course."

"What's your favorite kind of pie?" Pippa asked.

"Apple."

"Mine, too," Lottie announced. "But I want to add in some blueberries."

"Mine is buttermilk," Audrey said with conviction. "At least this week it is."

"And I want a pecan," Pippa said. "Mixed with walnuts."

Sometimes her girls liked to get creative. "All right then. It sounds like we have an order for one apple pie, one apple pie with blueberries, one buttermilk pie and one pecan pie with walnuts. And how about we add two peach pies, two custard pies and a plain pecan pie to round out the week? What do you think?"

There were enthusiastic nods of approval all around.

Ten minutes later, each girl had an assigned task and, depending on her abilities, was sifting flour, whisking eggs, gathering filling ingredients or laying out pie tins. Cora Beth crossed the room to check on the oven temperature and glanced out the window as she passed by, the same as she'd done a half-dozen times this morning. Somehow she'd gotten used to Mitch paying visits every morning and every evening. But so far no sign of him yet today.

Just as she was turning around to the girls, though, she spotted a movement from the corner of her eye. Sure enough, Mitch was headed toward the back porch.

And suddenly her whole morning seemed just a tiny bit brighter.

Mitch stood in the doorway, surveying the kitchen full of females. "Well, well, looks like Miss Cissy is feeling lots better today."

Cissy stepped down from her stool and gave Mitch a hug around his knees. "Hi, Sheriff." Then she looked up at him, her flour-dusted face beaming. "I'm helping make pies."

Mitch was caught off guard by the demonstrative gesture. Uncertain how to react, he glanced up at Cora Beth for some hint.

When all he got was an amused smile, he looked back down at Cissy and gave her an awkward pat. "Good for you."

"We're all making pies," Audrey added. "I'm wishing the eggs."

"Whisking," Cora Beth corrected. She turned back to Mitch, that smile still teasing at her mouth. "Is there something we can do for you this morning?"

Cissy had returned to her task and Mitch cleared his throat, hoping to clear his head at the same time. "Just checking in to see how things are going. I saw Ethan over at the Evans place. Rita was plying him with lemonade."

She nodded. "I'm sure he's doing a good job for her.

He also plans to spend some time over at your office today."

"Good. I'll be ready for him." Ethan's prickliness he could handle much more easily than Cissy's adoration, or the smile it brought to Cora Beth's face.

"Do you want to help us make pies?" Cissy asked.

"I'm afraid I'm not much of a baker."

"You can share mine when it's done. I picked apple."

"Well now, that's mighty generous of you, but I'm sure Mrs. Collins here is planning to serve these with her fine suppers this week."

"Then you can come to supper, too." She turned to Cora Beth. "That would be okay, wouldn't it?"

He saw Cora Beth swallow a smile as she solemnly nodded her head. "That sounds like a fine idea."

"We'll see." Mitch stuffed his hat back on his head. It wouldn't do for him to start feeling like one of the family. "I gotta be going. Bye, ladies."

Cora Beth followed him out to the back porch. "It seems Cissy has a bad case of hero worship."

Mitch rubbed the back of his neck. "What do I do about it?"

"Enjoy it. And treat her affection with respect."

"But I'm nobody's hero." In fact he was far from it. If they only knew.

"You are a hero to her. She probably sees you as an adult version of her big brother." Cora Beth touched his sleeve. "It's a blessing you're the first man she came in contact with after what she experienced with Titus. You're exactly what she needs in her life right now."

Those words scared him worse than a charging stampede. "That's one heck of a responsibility."

"Which is why God gave it to you—the perfect man for the job."

As Mitch headed away, he mulled over her words. Him a hero? Ridiculous. Only a scarred little girl like Cissy could see him that way.

What about Cora Beth, though? Not that she really needed a hero. She was a strong woman—self-reliant, full of heart and solid as that huge oak that shaded her side lawn.

Just exactly the kind of woman that a man would slay dragons for.

At least *this* man would.

Mitch looked up from his desk when the door opened.

Ethan stood there, a closed-off expression on his face. "I'm here to start working for what I owe you for the locket."

"Good. There's a broom over there in the corner. You can start by sweeping out the place."

With a nod, Ethan went straight to work.

Mitch leaned back in his chair, tipping the front legs up slightly, and watched the boy work. For a while, the only sound was the swishing of the broom.

"I stopped by the boardinghouse earlier. Your sister's up and looking well."

"The doc says she's a lot better."

Another long silence. The boy sure wasn't much of a talker. "How are you liking it over at the boarding-house?"

Ethan shrugged. "It's okay. Mrs. Collins is a nice lady. And she treats us good."

Did the kid realize how lucky he was that he'd landed on her doorstep and not someone else's?

Ethan paused for a moment. "You reckon she'll let us stay there until I get everyone paid back? I mean, I can make it camping okay, but Cissy ain't as strong as I am."

"I don't think that'll be a problem. In fact, I believe she's counting on it."

Ethan nodded and went back to pushing the broom.

"I saw you over at the Evans place earlier. You been there this whole time?"

Ethan nodded. "Wanted to get it finished up today so I can move on to something else on Monday. The faster I get all these chores done, the faster I can get back to earning some traveling money for me and Cissy."

The kid still thought he was going to take Cissy and head out, just the two of them. "Ethan, I meant it when I said you have nothing to fear from Titus anymore. There's no need for you to keep running."

"Folks around here think I'm a thief and maybe worse. They're not going to give me a chance to prove different. Especially that Mrs. Oglesby—and I found out today she's the mayor's wife. I just think we'll be better off settling somewhere else."

"Not everyone feels that way. Mrs. Collins, for instance, told me how proud she is of the way you faced up to what you did. And I'm proud of the way you look out for your sister. There's others around here who'd be willing to give you the benefit of the doubt and let you prove yourself to them."

Ethan shrugged. "Still and all, starting over with a clean slate, with folks who don't already think the worst of me, just sounds like it would be better."

"And what if you run into folks in the next town who get the wrong idea about you? Are you going to move on again? Or if Cissy gets sick or hurt again—are you sure there'll be someone around who'll care as much about her as Mrs. Collins does?"

His chin jutted out. "We'll be okay."

"Ethan, at some point you have to put down roots and stand up for who you are and who you want to be. And you need to give Cissy a real home. That someplace could be right here." He'd pushed hard enough—time to back off. "Think on it anyway."

"I will. But I ain't making any promises."

What would happen when the boy realized the decision was not going to be his to make? Would he feel resigned? Relieved? Or betrayed?

Cora Beth sat on her front porch swing, an open book in her lap but her gaze was directed toward some unseen point past their front gate rather than at the pages. She absently reached down and scratched Scout's head and his tail thumped the porch floor in appreciation. She and the dog had become good friends these past few days.

It was Sunday afternoon, and they'd passed yet another hurdle with Ethan and Cissy—the pair had accompanied her family to church service that morning.

Cissy had walked in between her and Ethan and had held tightly to her hand as they walked down the aisle to their pew. But that was the only sign she gave of being self-conscious about her limp. And after the service Audrey had introduced her to several of her friends, including Loretta Oglesby. From what Cora Beth could see, Nelda's reservations didn't seem to be shared by her youngest daughter.

She'd noticed that Ethan stood off to the side by himself, hands stuffed in his pockets, a glower on his face and his gaze glued to Cissy. How long would it be before the boy learned to let down his guard and *be* a boy again?

After church they all had lunch at Sadie and Eli's house. Josie, Ry and Viola were there, as well. It was an opportunity for Ethan and Cissy to meet the rest of the family and for the adults to catch up with each other. Cora Beth surreptitiously kept an eye on the children, and she was dismayed to see Ethan again holding himself apart.

She had hoped that Danny would have been happy to have another boy by his side in the midst of all the girls, but he seemed to still distrust Ethan for some reason. She'd have to get to the bottom of that soon.

Very soon.

Because sometime between leaving Sadie's and their arrival back at the boardinghouse, Cora Beth had decided she was going to take in Ethan and Cissy on a permanent basis, and make them an official part of her family.

It was something she'd spent the last few days praying about, making sure this was the right choice for everyone—the two orphans, her own children, Danny, herself.

It wasn't just that she couldn't bear the idea of sending them to an orphanage anymore. Even if they had another place to go, another family who wanted to take them in, it would break her heart to lose them. Ethan and Cissy already felt as dear to her as her own children. So there was really no reason not to make the arrangement a permanent one. Sure, there were a few things that would need to be resolved, some issues to address, but with a bit of time and effort it would work out.

As soon as she'd made that decision a sweet peace had filled her. It wasn't going to be smooth sailing, she knew that, but it was the right choice. Already she couldn't imagine the household without them.

Would Ethan and Cissy be pleased? She was fairly certain Cissy would, but with Ethan it was hard to tell. He was so fiercely independent, so walled off. But, given his other choices, surely he would see this as his best option.

Her first thought was to tell Mitch, to discuss it with him and see what he thought. Not only was his advice down to earth and sound, she knew he would also offer her comfort and support.

But that was foolish, selfish, wholly inappropriate. She should tell her family first.

Heavenly Father, thank You for sending these children to me. Help me to be the kind of mother they need me to be, to make this a true home for them, to help them forget the terrible things that have happened to them. And most of all, give me the right words to say to them and to my family when I inform them of this decision. Open Ethan's and Danny's hearts especially to the rightness of this plan.

Scout barked, as if to add an amen to her prayer.

Chapter Eleven

"I have something I want to discuss with you."

Ethan and Cissy looked at her with equally solemn faces. But their expressions were quite different. Cissy just seemed puzzled. Ethan on the other hand looked braced for something terrible.

How sad that he always expected the worst. She would have to do her best to see that he learned to expect good from others.

Ethan looked at her straight on. "You've decided what you're going to do with us now that Cissy's better, haven't you?"

She smiled. "Let's just say I've decided what I'd like for us to do."

His hands were balled in a fist. "We're not going to any old orphanage if that's what you have in mind. They split up the boys and girls and I wouldn't be able to watch over Cissy."

Cissy, her expression suddenly stricken, snaked a hand out to capture her brother's, and her lower lip began to tremble.

So he'd thought through the possibilities already. "Oh, no, Ethan. That's not what I had in mind at all."

His shoulders drew back. "Then you're going to let us go on our way?"

But Cissy didn't seem as pleased as her brother with that plan. "Does that mean we have to sleep in the woods again, Ethan?"

Cora Beth didn't let the boy answer that one. "Oh, no, sweetheart, I have a much better idea." Cora Beth looked from one to the other of them. "I would like for you to both stay here with me and be part of our family."

"You would?" Cissy straightened, her smile splitting into that endearing gap-toothed grin.

"More than just about anything in the world."

The little girl turned to her brother. "Oh, please, can we, Ethan? I really like it here."

Rather than answering, Ethan turned to Cora Beth, his suspicion still very much in evidence. "What would we have to do in return? I can work hard at whatever chores you set me, but I won't have Cissy turned into a servant again."

"You don't understand, Ethan. I said you would be part of the *family,* not servants. What you'd be expected to do is to accept the responsibilities that go along with that. While I know I'd never be able to take the place of your real mother in your heart, you'd offer me the respect and obedience the same as you would her. And you'd have chores to do, just like Danny and the girls. And you'd be expected to go to school regularly and do your best to learn what Mr. Saddler and Miss Honoria try to teach you."

"That's all?"

"Other than being respectful and supportive of the

others, just as they will be to you, and accepting our love and friendship, yes, that's all."

"I won't be able to start school right away," Ethan said. "Not until I work off all my debts to everyone."

"Schooling is important and you've already missed too much. I think we should just plan on you taking up most of your Saturdays getting those chores done."

"But I promised the sheriff I'd work for him for two weeks."

"I believe an hour a day *after* school should cover it."

He didn't seem happy with that answer, but he nodded. "Yes, ma'am."

"Would Sheriff Hammond be part of our family, too?" Cissy asked.

It would be wonderful to be able to say yes. "No. But he would be a very good friend."

"Because he has another family?"

"No, I'm afraid Sheriff Hammond doesn't have any other family. He has his own house to live in, though, and his own work to do. But you'll still be able to see him often."

"Okay."

Cora Beth stood and held out a hand to each of them. "Now, let's go tell the others, shall we?"

Ten minutes later the three of them stood in the parlor with the rest of the family gathered around them. Audrey, Pippa and Lottie had plopped down on the settee, while Uncle Grover and Danny each claimed an armchair.

"I have something exciting to tell you," Cora Beth began. "I've just invited Ethan and Cissy to stay here with us permanently, and they've agreed. As of today, they are officially part of our family."

Everyone, with the exception of Danny, popped out of their seats immediately and came rushing over. Uncle Grover shook Ethan's hand and patted Cissy on the shoulder. "Wonderful news! Welcome to the family. The more the merrier, I always say."

Audrey gave Cissy an enthusiastic hug. "We can be twins, just like Pippa and Lottie," she said excitedly. Then she turned to Ethan. "Do you want to be twins with Danny?"

"Don't be silly," Danny interjected gruffly. "You can't be twins with someone unless you're born that way."

"Can too," Audrey insisted. "Can't we, Mama?"

Cora Beth frowned at her brother, then turned to Audrey. "Danny's right, you won't be twins by birth. But you can be twins of the spirit if you want to be." Why was Danny still so begrudging and suspicious of Ethan?

Satisfied, Audrey linked arms with Cissy. "Well, we want to be, don't we?"

Cissy nodded.

Once the initial hubbub had quieted down, Cora Beth waved everyone back to their seats. "All right, I know we're excited, but we should talk over what this means. Just like with any change, we're going to need to make a few adjustments to make this work. First off, the sleeping arrangements. Pippa and Lottie, I think you girls are big enough now to have a room all to yourselves. Audrey, we're going to move you to one of the extra guest rooms and you'll be sharing it with Cissy." She'd given that some thought because of Cissy's limp, but the girl had already tackled the stairs earlier when Audrey had taken her up to her room. Other than being a bit more deliberate in her steps and holding onto the banister, she hadn't seemed to have any problems. And Cora Beth had a hunch she'd rather be upstairs than isolated on the first floor.

Audrey gave Cissy's arm a squeeze. "See, just like twins."

Cora Beth turned to Danny, knowing he was not going to like this next part. "We'll put an extra bed in your room and Ethan can share it with you."

As she'd expected, Danny didn't look any too happy with that idea, but Cora Beth shot him a warning look and he kept his complaints to himself. A quick glance Ethan's way told her he was well aware that Danny was not going to be laying out the welcome mat.

"We're also going to redo the chore assignments. Cissy and Ethan, I expect you to lend a hand with getting the table cleared and dishes washed after every meal. And I also expect you to do your part to keep your rooms and the rest of the house neat and tidy."

She turned to Cissy. "You can help me and the girls with the household chores."

"Including the Saturday baking?"

"That's right." Then she turned to Ethan. "You can help with getting the firewood taken care of and the lamps filled and wicks trimmed. You can also lend a hand at the livery when needed—Danny can show you the ropes over there." Maybe getting them to work together would help ease some of the tension between them.

"I can handle what needs doing at the livery," Danny said.

"Be that as it may," Cora Beth said firmly, "I want Ethan to learn how to manage things there, too."

Danny didn't say anything else, but his eyes spoke volumes.

"All right, we'll figure the rest of this out as we go. For now, let's get the rooms rearranged so we can all get a good night's sleep tonight."

She waved her hands. "Boys, you help the girls move their furniture around, please. I'll be up to check on things in a little bit. I need to talk to our resident school-teachers for just a minute—Ethan and Cissy start school with you tomorrow morning."

As they started to disperse, she caught her brother's eye. "Danny, stay behind just a minute, please. I'd like to discuss something with you."

With a reluctant nod, Danny plopped down on the settee. After everyone else had gone, Cora Beth took a seat across from him. "Please tell me why you can't seem to get along with Ethan. Has he done something to deserve your distrust?"

"I just don't have much use for thieves and liars is all."

His tone, as much as his words, were full of anger. "Daniel Edward Atkins, I'm surprised at you."

"It's true, isn't it? I mean, he stole from half the families in town and everyone knows it. He even admitted it. How do you think it looks to my friends that we're treating him like he hasn't done anything wrong? And now I'm supposed to share a room with him?"

Cora Beth felt a stab of disappointment. "Danny, we can't control what others think, and we also can't let it control *us*. Yes, Ethan stole some things, but he was trying to provide for his little sister. It was the wrong way to go about it and he knows that now, but you can't fault him for *why* he did what he did. You also can't say that you've never done anything wrong yourself."

Danny's mouth was set in a stubborn line. "Stealing is stealing. I hear he lived with old Titus Brown for a while, and that he's turning out just like him."

Cora Beth felt her temper rise at that. "Whoever said that doesn't know what they're talking about." She held up a hand when he started to protest. "I mean they don't know the whole story. If they did, they'd probably think of him as a hero."

"Hero?"

She had tried to shield the children from the truth of what had happened, but perhaps that had been the wrong thing to do. "Titus treated both Ethan and Cissy very cruelly when they were with him. He never let them go to church or school. In fact, he never let them leave his farm. Titus stole the few items they had that were worth anything and sold them for whiskey. He forced them both to work from sunup to sundown, and he shackled Cissy with a leg iron so she and Ethan wouldn't run away. And still Ethan managed to get his sister safely away and keep them both alive for nearly two weeks out in the woods."

She held his gaze. "Now you tell me, what would you have done if it had been you and you had Audrey or one of the twins to protect?"

Danny swallowed hard. Then he rallied. "He could have just asked folks for help," he said defensively.

"True. But he wasn't used to folks being particularly kind to him. And he didn't want to take the chance of someone handing him and Cissy back over to Titus."

Danny didn't respond to that. He sat there, his posture and expression still defensive.

It was obvious he wasn't ready to listen to reason on this just yet. Did his friends' opinions mean that much to him? "Well, promise me you'll think about what I just said. And whether you like it or not, he's family now. I can't make you like him, but I do expect you to be civil to him. Understood?"

"Yes, ma'am."

Amazing how much displeasure and resistance he was able to pack into those two words.

She sighed. "All right, run along and help the others with setting up the rooms. I'll be up shortly."

As she went in search of the schoolteachers, she wished she could talk to Mitch, as well. Not only did she want to tell him about her decision to keep the children, but she would dearly love to get his opinion on how to handle this situation with Danny. Sometimes it was really hard to be both the father and the mother. Children, especially boys, needed a man in their lives. And she couldn't think of a better candidate than Mitchell Hammond.

Too bad he didn't seem interested in the job. Too bad for the boys—and too bad for her, as well.

Cora Beth had decided a long time ago that Monday was her least favorite day of the week. Of course, that was mainly because doing laundry was her least favorite chore.

It wasn't quite so bad in the summertime. Although the summer heat made the back-breaking work even more hot and sticky than usual, she at least had the children around to both lend a hand and make it a more sociable activity in the process. When school was in session, she was completely on her own.

As she hung the final pillowcase on the clothesline, though, she realized that she'd barely stopped humming all morning. Yesterday evening's decision to take in Cissy and Ethan still felt so right, so meant-to-be.

They'd headed off with the other children for school this morning, if not enthusiastically at least willingly. Ethan would be in Mr. Saddler's group of older children and Cissy would be in Honoria's younger group. Both teachers had assured Cora Beth last night that they'd keep an eye on their new students and do their best to help them fit in.

And to top things off, Danny had seemed just a tad less belligerent this morning. Maybe their little talk last night had had more of an impact than she'd thought.

She'd asked the children to keep an eye out for when Josie dropped Viola off, and to ask her to come by the boardinghouse before heading back to her place.

When she'd told Josie about her plans to make Ethan and Cissy part of the family, her sister had let out a whoop and given her a big hug. Then she laughed and said she'd already told Ry she figured there'd be two extra places set at the table from now on.

Cora Beth still hadn't seen Mitch since church service yesterday. Not that that was at all unusual. Up until Ethan burst into her life, Mitch had had no reason to stop by her place on any kind of regular basis. It was just that she'd gotten used to his twice-a-day visits this past week. She'd known it was only natural that things would go back to their normal routine in time—she just hadn't figured on it being this soon.

Cissy, of course, would miss seeing him every day.

Perhaps she'd stop by the sheriff's office later. After all, he seemed to feel he had as big a stake in securing a good future for Ethan and Cissy as she did. It was only right that she let him know about this turn of events.

A little corner of her mind hoped that her news became the cause for another of those hugs. She felt her face color at the thought, but so be it. Two friends could celebrate such a momentous decision without it meaning anything special, couldn't they?

Mitch approached the boardinghouse, wishing himself anywhere *but* here. At least when it came to this particular errand. He didn't like the idea of having to bring troubles to Cora Beth's doorstep.

He rounded the corner to the back of the boardinghouse and found Cora Beth approaching from the side yard with an empty laundry basket. Her face broke into a large, welcoming smile as soon as she saw him. Too bad that would disappear once he stated his business.

Sometimes he just didn't like this job.

"Why, hello," she said as the distance between them closed. "I was hoping you'd stop by this morning."

Any other day that would have been music to his ears. He noticed the becoming touch of pink in her cheeks—too much sun? "Were you now?" *Coward— just get to it.*

"Uh-huh. I have some wonderful news I wanted to share."

"Let me guess. You've decided to take Ethan and Cissy into your family permanently."

"You heard." She pursed her lips in a mock pout that somehow didn't detract from her sweet appearance.

He took the basket from her and let her precede him up the porch steps. "Audrey was proclaiming it to anyone who would listen on her way to school this morning."

Cora Beth's smile turned rueful. "That's my girl."

He reached past her and pulled open the screen door.

She turned, her face close enough that he could count the freckles on her nose. "Can I fix you a cup of coffee?"

He cleared his throat. "Uh, no, thank you."

She must have finally noticed something in his tone or expression. Her gaze sharpened. "What's wrong?"

"Nelda came to see me this morning."

She scrunched her nose. "That doesn't bode well for somebody. And since you're here, I assume that that somebody is me. What did I supposedly do?" She seemed more amused than worried.

"It's Ethan, actually."

That wiped the smile from her face. "Surely she's not still upset about that plant Ethan took? He's apologized and it's been paid for. I don't know what else he can do."

"No, it's something new. Someone broke into her greenhouse again last night and made quite a mess in there."

Cora Beth sat down with a plop. "And Nelda thinks Ethan had something to do with it?"

"She does."

Cora Beth folded her hands on the table. "He wouldn't do that. I mean, the first time he was just trying to make his sister's birthday into something special. He'd have no reason—"

He held up a hand. "You don't need to convince me. I said that's what Nelda believes, not that I believed it." He took a seat next to her. "The thing is, nothing was taken as far as Nelda could see. Someone just went in and knocked over some of her pots."

"Then Ethan definitely had nothing to do with it.

He's not malicious." She tucked a strand of hair back behind her ear. "So what happens now?"

"I'll talk to Ethan when he gets out of school this afternoon. I assume he's still planning to work off that money I loaned him."

She nodded. "And when he says he had nothing to do with it—then what?"

"I'm confident I'll be able to tell whether or not he's telling the truth." Mitch shrugged. "After that, it'll be her word against his. There's nothing to point to Ethan other than Nelda's suspicions."

"I just hate to have this air of distrust and suspicion hanging over him." Her eyes clouded. "He already feels so beaten down. I wish you didn't have to say anything to him about it."

"But I do have to. It's my job. And better he hear it from me than from someone else."

"I know. It's just that this is not going to help his self-confidence any, or make him feel as welcome in Knotty Pine as I'd hope he would."

Mitch placed a hand over hers, stilling her nervous fluttering. "Give it time. Once folks around here get to know him better, they'll learn to trust him. And making him a part of your family is definitely going to up his standing in the community."

"As I told Mrs. Plunkett the other day," she said dryly, "patience has never been my strong suit."

He gave her hand a last squeeze and then stood. "Trust me, we'll weather this just fine."

Ethan walked into the sheriff's office that afternoon and with a quick nod headed for the corner where the broom was kept.

"The sweeping can wait," Mitch said. "Have a seat, I want to talk to you."

Ethan eyed him warily, but did as he was told.

"I hear Mrs. Collins offered to take you and Cissy in. How do you feel about that?"

The boy nodded. "All right I guess. She's treated me and Cissy real nice these past few days. And Cissy needs a good place to stay and someone to treat her good."

"What about you? What do you need?"

"I don't need much. Just to be left alone."

"That sounds a mite lonely."

Ethan only shrugged.

The boy's walls were solid as granite. But if anyone could breach them it was Cora Beth.

Time to get down to that unpleasant bit of business. "Mrs. Oglesby came to see me today."

"The lady with the glass plant shed?"

"That's the one." He was watching Ethan closely but saw no sign of guilt or unease.

"Did she change her mind about me working for her? Because that's okay, I'll do whatever she thinks is fair."

"That's not it. It seems somebody broke into her greenhouse last night and made a mess of the place."

That got a rise out of him. "It wasn't me. I promise I didn't leave the boardinghouse at all after supper. You can check with Danny—we share a room now."

"I believe you. But I think you can understand why Mrs. Oglesby might think you had something to do with it."

Ethan looked down at his shoes. "Yes, sir. You gonna arrest me?"

"No. For now it's just her word against yours, so unless I get some proof convincing me otherwise, I'll assume you're innocent."

Ethan nodded, then glanced up and met his gaze. "Do you have to tell Mrs. Collins about this?"

He understood the boy's distress. He'd hate to disappoint Cora Beth, too. "Sorry, Ethan, she already knows. But don't worry—she doesn't think you did it. She jumped to your defense right away."

Ethan looked glumly down at the floor again. "I suppose everyone in town knows about it, too."

"I can't say for sure, but Mrs. Oglesby's not one to keep her grievances to herself." He couldn't leave it at that. The boy needed some encouragement. "Just hold your head up and don't give folks a reason to distrust you. You may not realize it but by confessing and working off your debts, you're making some friends here."

Ethan didn't look up. "If you say so. Can I get back to work now?"

"Just one more thing. You know Mrs. Collins is a special lady, don't you? The kind of person who always tries to see the best in folks."

That earned him an emphatic nod. "Yes, sir. I ain't never met anyone quite like her."

"I sure would hate to see someone, especially someone she cares a great deal for, betray that trust."

"I wouldn't do that, Sheriff, not even if somebody held a gun to my head."

Mitch hid a smile at the boy's dramatic assurances. "I believe you. Now, I've got work to do and you've got floors to sweep."

He hoped he'd handled that right. Had he been too easy on the boy? Too tough? How would Cora Beth have handled it? And how in the world did she manage to deal with these kinds of crises, day in and day out, with four youngsters—make that six youngsters now?

His considerable respect for her went up another notch. God had definitely handed those kids to the right woman.

He leaned back in his chair and stared absently at the ceiling. The right woman in so many ways. Amazing that she'd never remarried after Phillip passed. He would have thought some lucky man would have snatched her up by now. Sure, she came with a lot of family and other responsibilities, but if he were a marrying kind of man he wouldn't have let that hold him back. No sirree. The men in this town must be blind and lacking in common sense to have left such a fine woman unattached.

And for reasons he didn't care to explore, he was happy they had.

Cora Beth was in the front yard, weeding her flower beds while Scout lay at her heels, when the four girls came up the walkway, chattering like magpies. She was so pleased to see how quickly Cissy had become like a sister to her daughters. If only Danny and Ethan got along as well.

Scout offered slobbery greetings all around, eliciting giggles and mock protests that were music to her ears.

"Hello, girls, where's Danny?"

"He stayed behind to talk to some of his friends," Audrey said. "I think Charlie had a penny and was going to treat them to licorice whips over at the mercantile." She scrunched her nose indignantly. "He said no little kids allowed."

Cora Beth laughed. "Don't worry, you're going to

grow up fast enough. So, Cissy, how was your first day at school?"

"Miss Honoria is nice."

"Yes, she is."

"Did you know Cissy is a good draw-er?" Audrey asked. "She drew a little bird that looked just like the sparrow outside our classroom window."

"Did she now? How wonderful." Before she could say more, she caught sight of Danny marching quickly up the sidewalk, a thunderous expression on his face. What was wrong now?

He stopped in front of Cora Beth, his posture broomstick stiff. "I need to talk to you."

Cora Beth turned to the girls. "There's a cookie for each of you in the kitchen. Help yourselves and then get to work on your lessons."

After they'd departed Cora Beth climbed the porch steps and took a seat on the swing. She patted the spot next to her, but Danny remained standing. Not a good sign. "So, what do we need to talk about?"

"I was in the mercantile and I heard a couple of ladies talking about Ethan. Did you know he broke into Mrs. Oglesby's plant house again?"

She'd been afraid it had something to do with that. "It wasn't Ethan."

"How do you know? Just cause he denied it don't mean—"

"I haven't talked to him yet. But this wasn't a theft, it was an act of pure destruction, and I know he wouldn't do such a thing, any more than you would."

"Those ladies sure seem to think he was guilty."

"They don't know Ethan as well as we do. And Mrs. Oglesby's understandably upset by what happened and is ready to blame someone, whether she has proof or not."

She touched his arm briefly. "Danny, we talked about this last night. Ethan's not a bad kid. You need to give him the benefit of the doubt."

"Maybe he had a good reason for what he did before, but there's no excuse this time."

This was getting exasperating. "You're not listening to me. Ethan didn't do it."

"They always say where there's smoke there's fire and I sure see a lot of smoke circling around that Ethan. He's nothing but trouble."

"If so, then he's *our* trouble."

Danny folded his arms over his chest, stopping just short of huffing at her. "You're just too trusting."

"And you're not trusting enough." *Heavenly Father, please help me to get through to him.*

She took a deep breath. "Danny, we can't keep having this argument. If you won't trust Ethan, then trust me." She eyed him steadily. "At least promise me you'll pray about it."

"All right. But while I'm at it, I'm also gonna pray that God finds him another place to live." And after that shocking rejoinder, he spun around and headed inside.

Cora Beth found herself in a subdued mood the rest of the afternoon. The conversation with Danny kept playing over and over in her mind and she couldn't shake the feeling that she'd somehow failed him. Still, there had to be something more to his distrust of Ethan than what she could see on the surface.

When Ethan came home, she could tell Mitch had talked to him. The boy would hardly meet her gaze. She let him know that she hadn't believed Nelda's accusations for even a moment, but still Ethan remained quiet and aloof.

After supper, while she was seated in the family parlor working on a bit of mending, Ethan knocked on the door.

"Mrs. Collins, can I talk to you for a minute?"

Pleased that he was initiating a conversation, she lowered her mending to her lap and smiled a welcome. "Sure. Have a seat."

He remained standing and stuffed his hands in his pockets. "I hope you don't mind, but I went exploring up in your attic this afternoon."

"I don't mind at all. It's just filled with old bits of furniture and castoffs anyway. Did you see something you'd like to have?"

"Actually, I was looking at all the space you have up there. Almost half of the room has a high enough ceiling for a man to stand upright in and if you did a little rearranging, there'd be plenty of empty space."

"I suppose." Where was he going with this?

"I was wondering if, I mean, would it be all right, if I…" His words trailed off as if he wasn't quite sure he should continue.

"If you what, Ethan?"

He took a deep breath. "If I cleared me off a corner up there to turn into my own room?"

Oh dear. Had it come to this between him and Danny? "Mind if I ask why you don't want to stay in the room you're in now?"

"It's a fine room," he said a little too quickly, "and I sure do appreciate you fixing up an extra bed in there and all, but I kinda like the idea of having a place to myself. I won't take up much of your attic space, I promise, and I'll do all the rearranging myself."

Perhaps the two boys *did* need their own space. "I see. Well, if you're really certain that's what you want, you don't need to move into the attic. You could have the extra room at the end of the hall. It's kind of small, but—"

"No, ma'am. I know that's for when you have extra boarders and I wouldn't want to get in the way of that."

"You wouldn't be. We're used to doubling up when we have temporary guests—Danny moves in with Uncle Grover, or the girls move in with me. It gets a bit snug but we manage."

"Still, I'd feel better if you just let me fix up a place in the attic."

She could see he felt strongly about that. "All right. And help yourself to any of the furnishings you find there to set it up."

"Thank you. I'll get right to it."

"Would you like my help?"

"No, ma'am, I can handle it."

Once Ethan had rushed off to set up his room, Cora Beth slowly picked up her sewing and set back to work. Had she done the right thing by letting him have his way? Or would it have been better for her to make him stay in the room with Danny and hope the forced proximity would help them to eventually work out their differences?

More and more lately, as Danny moved into that shadow land between adolescence and manhood, her thoughts turned to Mitch. She wished she could discuss these things with him, to work through her fears and hopes and dreams—for the kids and, selfishly, for herself, as well. But she couldn't ask him to be any more involved than he already was.

Heavenly Father, please help me to make the right decisions regarding these children. And, if You could see Your way to helping me figure out what's got Danny so stirred up, I'd sure appreciate that, too.

Chapter Twelve

Alice Danvers, the hostess for this week's Wednesday afternoon meeting of the Ladies' Auxiliary, handed Cora Beth a cup of tea. "The little girl you had with you at church service—Cissy, was it? I noticed she walked with a limp. Did she injure herself?"

Cora Beth smiled as she took the cup. Thank goodness the meeting had been relatively short today. She really wanted to get back to her sewing. Both Cissy and Ethan were in desperate need of new clothing. "I'm afraid it's a permanent injury. Ethan says it happened when she was just a baby."

Alice's face softened in sympathy. "Oh, that poor little angel. Does it pain her much?"

"According to her, only when the weather is damp or she's been overexerting herself."

"Well I suppose that's a blessing of sorts."

Ida Van Halsen joined them. "Is it true those two are Titus Brown's stepkids?"

"Not anymore," Cora Beth said firmly. "Once their mother passed on, his claim to them ended."

"I'm sorry to hear about their mother passing, but it

was unfortunate that she brought two children to live under that man's roof in the first place." She gave Cora Beth an approving smile. "It's good of you to give them a more wholesome place to stay while the little girl gets better."

"Actually, Ethan and Cissy will be staying with me permanently."

Ida looked taken aback and even Alice paused in the process of pouring another cup of tea. Both women cast quick glances Nelda's way.

Ida cleared her throat and fiddled with the handle of her teacup. "Do you think that's wise? I mean, you don't *really* know anything about these children, do you? Maybe they have other kinfolk."

"Actually, Sheriff Hammond looked into that and it doesn't appear that they have anyone else." She sensed rather than saw Nelda walk up behind her. "As far as what I know about them, I know that they're good kids, that they've had to deal with a lot of tragedy and hard times in their short lives, and I know that I care for them a great deal."

Nelda moved forward to join the conversation. "You always did have a soft heart. But sometimes it's best to let your mind take precedence over your emotions. Otherwise you might be in for disappointment and heartache."

Did Nelda truly believe that? If so, Cora Beth felt sorry for her. "Some things are worth taking that risk over."

Mrs. Plunkett strolled up and served herself a tea cake. "Cora Beth, did everyone get off on the train okay this morning?"

Cora Beth turned to her with a smile, sending her

boarder a silent thank-you for the timely interruption. "Yes, but not without a lot of last minute scurrying. They're all very excited about visiting Hawk's Creek again." She gave the group of ladies a smile-with-me shake of her head. "If the looks on their faces were any indication, I'd guess the adults were looking forward to the trip every bit as much as the kids, if not more so."

Mrs. Plunkett lifted her cup. "Ah, the sign of a happy childhood is the eagerness to return to our home place once we grow older."

Cora Beth nodded, moving with her across the room as she did so. "From all indications, then, Ry and Sadie had a very happy childhood." And she intended to see that Ethan and Cissy built equally fond memories during what was left of theirs.

She found herself thinking of Mitch and wondering what kind of childhood memories he had. Like Ethan and Cissy, he'd been very young when he lost both parents—in fact, he'd already been orphaned and living with his grandmother when she'd started school and first got to know him.

Did he remember his parents? Had his grandmother been good to him despite what rumor said she was like on the outside?

Suddenly, she wanted answers to those questions. Would it be considered snooping for her to try to find out? Or merely the gentle probing of a friend who cared—deeply?

The next day, Cora Beth strolled up the walk to the boardinghouse, humming. She'd just finished her marketing and not even the strange, speculative looks she'd received from Alice Danvers had dampened her mood.

If folks were talking about her, let them. It was a gloriously lovely day, Ethan and Cissy seemed to be settling in well now that Ethan had moved into his attic room, and Mitch was still stopping by every day to check on how things were going.

She refused to think about why the idea of Mitch's visits added so much to her good mood—better just to savor the pleasant feelings while they lasted.

Scout ran up to meet her as she turned onto her front walk. "Hi, boy." She lifted the nearly overflowing basket she carried. "Sorry I can't pet you right now—hands full."

Scout seemed willing to forgive her for the slight, and trotted happily at her heels.

As she approached the house, she studied the honeysuckle vine growing on the trellis guarding one end of the front porch. It was getting too thick and raggedy looking. Trimming it back would give her a great excuse to spend more time out in the fresh air this afternoon.

Just as she reached the steps, Scout barked a greeting to someone behind her. She turned to find Mitch approaching. The day seemed suddenly brighter than before.

"Mitch, hi, I'm just back from doing my marketing. Come on in and I'll fix you a cup of coffee."

"Thanks, but I'll have to pass." He reached out and took the basket from her.

Her pleasure at seeing him quickly turned to concern. His usual easygoing demeanor was missing—instead, his expression was somber, controlled. Had Nelda filed another complaint? "What is it?"

"I need you to come with me to the mayor's office. Right now."

That sounded ominous. She bent down to stroke Scout's head with hands that shook slightly. "Why?"

"Nelda has called a meeting of the town council." His grim tone matched his expression.

The town council? "About what?" She caught her breath as a possible reason occurred to her. "Mitch, does she want to force you to arrest Ethan?"

She saw the muscles in his jaw tighten. "No. This goes deeper. She wants to discuss the suitability of your taking in Ethan and Cissy."

Cora Beth felt the blood drain from her face. "What do you mean? What business is it of hers or the town council?"

"You know Nelda—*everything* is her business."

Cora Beth, her mind spinning with all sorts of scary possibilities, was already heading for the front door. "If you don't mind, set that basket in the kitchen for me while I tell Uncle Grover where I'm going."

Please God, don't let them take those children from me. They are so precious to me. To send them to an orphanage would be heartbreaking for all of us. I promised to give them a home—they need me. And I need them.

Chapter Thirteen

The town council was composed of Archibald Oglesby, who was both the mayor and Nelda's husband; Horace Danvers from the mercantile; Hamilton Melton, who ran the hotel; and Alfred Evans, the town barber. She tried to guess how each would view Nelda's complaint.

Mayor Oglesby's leanings were pretty clear. Chances were high that he would side with his wife.

Alfred Evans was a bit harder to predict. Ethan had spent some time working at his place so hopefully that had given the barber an idea of what a hard worker the boy was. On the other hand, Ethan *had* been responsible for taking his birthday pie so that could still rankle with him a bit.

Horace Danvers was usually a fair man, but his wife Alice was a good friend of Nelda's and it was hard to say how much influence that would have over him.

As for Hamilton, she had no idea what he'd heard or how he felt about the whole matter.

By the time Cora Beth and Mitch arrived at the mayor's office she was a jangle of fears, nervous energy and determination. She and Mitch walked into the inner office to find the mayor and all three members of the town council seated along the wall behind the desk, facing the door. Nelda was there as well, seated in a chair facing the council. There was an empty chair beside her.

The men stood as she entered, and the mayor waved her to the empty chair. "Thank you for coming here on such short notice, Mrs. Collins. Please take a seat."

Cora Beth, mustering what composure she could, gave her most regal nod, and sat in the vacant chair. She sensed Mitch behind her, leaning against the wall near the door. He seemed a far distance away at the moment.

Once everyone had taken their seats, Cora Beth deliberately met each councilman's gaze in turn, holding it for a few heartbeats before moving to the next. Finally she asked, "Just what have I been summoned here for?"

Mayor Oglesby tugged on his lapels. "You're here because Nelda has raised some legitimate concerns about your plans to take in those two orphan kids. Since I'm certain we all agree that the welfare of such children is a matter not to be taken lightly, we thought it only fair that the town council listen to her concerns. And of course we also want to afford you the opportunity to respond to whatever she has to say."

He cleared his throat. "Since I could be deemed to have some bias in this matter, being as I am married to the complainant, I will merely be an observer to this discussion, not a participant." He nodded to the councilman to his right. "Mr. Danvers here will take the lead in my place."

Cora Beth clasped her hands in her lap, mostly to still their trembling. "I'm not certain I understand what concern it is of any of you just who I decide to take into my home, but I am prepared to listen."

Mr. Danvers frowned at that, then waved a hand. "Nelda, you have the floor."

"Thank you." She turned to Cora Beth with a smile that was sugary sweet. "First off, I want to say that it is very commendable of you to want to take in those two orphans. Your family has a history of taking in those less fortunates who seem to have no place else to go. No one here is questioning the purity of your motives."

Cora Beth gave a short nod to acknowledge the compliments, if that's what they were. She had no illusions, however, that there wouldn't be a "but" coming next.

"But, my dear, you already have so many responsibilities." Nelda began to enumerate them on her fingers. "You have three children of your own, a younger brother and elderly uncle who both look to you for support, you almost single-handedly run the boardinghouse, and since Josie got married and moved outside of town, you've taken on more responsibility for the livery, as well."

Cora Beth was determined to hold her temper. "I feel that I've been managing things quite well. As far as I know there haven't been any complaints from either livery customers or from my boarders."

Nelda waved a hand dismissively. "Be that as it may, you must admit that all of those responsibilities keep you quite busy. Even if these were two normal children, I don't see how you could manage the extra work involved." Her nostrils constricted as if she'd smelled something unpleasant. "But, as we all know, these are *not* normal children. The boy has troublesome behavioral issues that, if left unchecked, could prove detrimental to the community. And while we've yet to learn whether his sister has any of these unfortunate tendencies, the poor child is a cripple and that alone means she'll need more attention from whomever cares for her."

How dare she talk about Ethan and Cissy in those terms!

"I ask you," Nelda continued, "as a mother yourself, don't you think those two orphans deserve to be under the care of someone who'll be less distracted by other responsibilities and have the time to focus more closely on them and their needs?"

Cora Beth forced herself to speak deliberately. "First of all, I do not agree with your assessment of those children. Yes, Ethan did some things he shouldn't have before I took him in, but he was desperate. He's since apologized and he's doing his best to make amends. And he's given me his word he won't do such things again." She ignored Nelda's huff of disbelief. "And Cissy is a sweet child who doesn't demand or expect any special treatment."

Nelda raised her chin. "There's some in this town who are not as convinced as you that the boy has changed his criminal ways."

Mitch spoke up from the back of the room. "No one has come forward with any proof to the contrary."

Cora Beth shot him a quick smile, grateful for his support.

Nelda, however, seemed less than pleased.

Before the woman could say anything else, Cora Beth continued with her line of reasoning. "But all of that aside, is there someone else, someone with fewer *distractions,* who has stepped forward to take them in? If so, I'd like to speak to them." What would she do if Nelda said yes?

"It's my understanding that the orphanage at Cason-ville has already agreed to take them in. It seems the ideal solution on a number of levels."

This time the look Cora Beth shot Mitch had an accusing edge. Had he told Nelda about the orphanage? But he shook his head and she quickly turned back to Nelda, cutting her off before she could start listing the so-called advantages. "Surely none of you here honestly believes that those children would be better off in an orphanage than they would with me. No matter how good the caretakers there are, there is no way they'd have any more time to give the children individual attention than I would, regardless of my other responsibilities."

Again Nelda flashed that superior smile that made Cora Beth want to scream. "I know you have a soft spot for these orphans, my dear. But sometimes we only see the things we want to. The folks who operate the orphanage have experience in dealing with such children and undoubtedly have a love for what they do. One would assume they would do their best to find them good homes, homes with couples who would love them every bit as much as you do, perhaps more so if they are childless, and who would also have the advantage of being able to provide both a mother and a father to those children. Something, regrettably, you cannot do."

That last bit hit home. Cora Beth *couldn't* provide them with a father. But as far as anyone else loving them as much—

"Besides, you mustn't be selfish." Nelda clutched the handbag on her lap a little tighter. "This decision doesn't just affect you. I'm concerned, of course, about how a boy of such questionable character will fit into our community. It could have a tragic effect on our own dear children if they are allowed to associate freely with him. After all, he lived with Titus Brown for over a year.

One can only guess what kind of regrettable influence that horrid, unprincipled man had on him."

"Actually, Ethan found Titus's lifestyle as repugnant as you do, perhaps more so since he experienced it firsthand."

"Of course he would *say* that. And yes, the boy may seem fine to you now that things are easier for him. But how will he handle any troubles or frustrations that will come his way? Will he revert back to his criminal ways? No, as good as your intentions are, a boy like that needs the strong influence of a father, something you can't offer him."

Apparently, now that Nelda had found her weak spot she planned to keeping poking at it.

Cora Beth turned to the town council. "And what about all of you? Do you doubt my ability to raise these children?"

Horace Danvers spoke up. "It's not that we doubt you would give it your all, Cora Beth. But what Nelda is saying makes a lot of sense. And for you to take on such a responsibility might even affect the time you could devote to your own children."

This was getting more frustrating and insulting by the second. "I disagree. It is exactly *because* I have such a large family that this will work. They will have built-in playmates and peers to interact with. Uncle Grover will provide a grandfatherly influence. Living at the boardinghouse will provide them with a comfortable, loving home, as well as duties to help them grow into responsible adults."

Nelda shook her head. "That sounds all well and good, but that little crippled girl is going to require more than playmates—she's going to need some individual attention."

Cora Beth bit back an angry retort. How *dare* Nelda use that tone when speaking about Cissy?

Mitch had been doing his best to hold his tongue throughout this farce of a meeting, but he'd finally had enough. "Her name is Cissy," he said through clinched teeth.

Nelda cast a startled glance his way, obviously surprised by the interruption. "Yes, of course." She turned back to Cora Beth. "*Cissy* will need special attention. But the boy is another matter altogether. I shudder to think what might happen if his more reprehensible tendencies erupt. As I said, it might be different if there were a strong father figure, a man who could not only provide an upstanding example, but who had a firm hand when it came to—"

Mitch cut across her words again, tired of hearing her hammer Cora Beth with the same arguments over and over. "So your main objection is not some uncharitable grudge against the children?"

The mayor's wife drew herself up sharply. "Why I never! Of course not. I am definitely *not* the sort of person to bear grudges. I only—"

"Then it's that you don't think Mrs. Collins can handle this on her own, that the children need a firmer hand and a person with fewer distractions to watch over them. Do I have that right?"

"Exactly." Nelda's bearing spoke of righteous indignation. "Why, I feel for those poor orphaned children as much as the next person. I'm concerned for their welfare every bit as much as I am for the town's."

Mitch felt the stirrings of an idea. A totally outrageous idea. "Quite admirable. So if, say, a married couple could be found here in Knotty Pine who would be willing to take them in, and see that they were raised to be God-fearing and responsible, you'd have no objection?"

Cora Beth sat up straighter. What was Mitch doing? "But—"

He gave her a warning look, cutting off the rest of her protest. It stung to see the hurt in her gaze, but he'd explain later.

Nelda eyed him suspiciously. "I suppose. But it would need to be someone of strong character who understood exactly the gravity of the situation."

"Of course. Someone just like Mrs. Collins here, only married and with fewer encumbrances."

"Exactly. But as there is no one like that coming forth to volunteer, I'm afraid our next best option remains the orphanage."

That outrageous plan was taking clearer shape. It seemed doable. But he needed time to turn it over in his mind, look at it from all angles, run it by Cora Beth.

Mitch turned to the councilmen. "Gentlemen, I'm sure Mrs. Collins is understandably overwhelmed by what she's been put through here this morning. I think it only fair to give her a bit of time to reflect on it and try to come to terms with the situation before we make any hasty decisions."

The mayor frowned. "Sheriff, we're all busy men with other matters to attend to."

"Of course you are. But don't you reckon that when we're talking about splitting up a family, even one that's newly formed, it's worth a couple of hours' reflection before a firm decision is made?"

The men had the grace to look abashed at that.

But Nelda was staring at him with growing suspicion. "Sheriff, surely you don't think that in so short a time you can talk someone else into taking in those children. I assure you—"

"Mrs. Oglesby, surely *you* don't begrudge Mrs. Collins a few hours of time to gather her thoughts and try to come up with an alternate solution that will be acceptable to everyone, do you?"

"Of course not."

He turned to Cora Beth, eager to get her out of the room before she said something to sabotage his plan before he could even propose it. He needed to think. Was his far-fetched idea really worth pursuing? Would she buy into it? "Then, Mrs. Collins, might I suggest you take your leave now."

"But—"

Mitch grasped for whatever straw he could find to get her moving. "Perhaps a visit with Reverend Ludlow would help you settle things in your own mind. I'd be pleased to escort you there."

"Excellent idea," Mayor Oglesby said. "I'm sure the reverend would be able to offer you some sound counsel on this matter."

Mitch tried to communicate a mental *trust me* to her. "Then allow me to escort you to the parsonage. Gentlemen, Nelda, since it's nearly lunchtime, let's say we meet back up here at half past one."

Without waiting for a response, he took a firm hold of Cora Beth's elbow and led her from the room. He refused to meet her gaze until they were on the sidewalk. Once in the fresh air again he let out a long breath.

Cora Beth stopped dead in her tracks, forcing him

to stop with her. "Mitchell Hammond, I'm not sure exactly what that was all about in there, but—"

"I can explain, but not here in the middle of the public sidewalk." He gave her arm a gentle tug and she started walking again.

"I will have you know that, much as I respect Reverend Ludlow, nothing he has to say is going to change my mind. And I don't care what your duty to that badge tells you that you have to do, I am not giving up those children without a fight."

He smiled. "I'd expect nothing less."

She looked at him with a surprised expression and some of the fight seemed to leave her. In its place was a worried frown. "How will I be able to face Ethan and Cissy with this news after I promised them that they were part of the family now? You don't just break up families this way."

"I thought you weren't going to give up without a fight." He was itching to explain everything to her but not here.

"Can they legally take those children from me and put them in an orphanage?"

He winced. She wasn't going to like his answer. "The children are technically wards of the state. Theoretically, the council can lodge a complaint with the circuit judge that you are unable to care for them properly and the state would have no choice but to investigate. But I'm hoping it won't come to that."

"So what's this plan you have?"

"We're almost there."

She looked around and frowned. "I thought you were going to drag me to the parsonage. We're going the wrong way."

"We may want to speak to Reverend Ludlow later, but for right now, you and I need to talk. Alone."

"I agree. So where are you taking me?"

"I thought the church might be a good place to talk. There's usually not anyone there this time of day."

They didn't say another word until Mitch escorted her inside the church. He seated her in one of the pews, but remained standing himself. And suddenly, he wasn't sure he could go through with this.

He had to be crazy. Marriage. After all these years of denial and restraint, was it possible that this was his answer? But would Cora Beth go for it? He wasn't even sure he wanted her to. No, that was a lie. He suddenly wanted this more than anything.

God, I know I made a vow not to ever marry, but I hope You'll grant me this exception. I made that vow because I didn't want to make any promises to a woman that I couldn't keep. But, if Cora Beth agrees to my proposition, this will be a different kind of marriage. I plan to make good and certain Cora Beth knows I'm only offering friendship and support, not any romantic fairy tales. If I don't give her any promises of a forever-after love then I can't disappoint her if my feelings change once things are settled between us.

"Well, are you going to stand there fiddling with your hat brim or are you going to tell me what this plan of yours is?"

Mitch rubbed his jaw, trying to pull his thoughts together. "I have an idea to run by you."

"An idea for how I can hold on to the children?"

"Yes."

"Then let's hear it."

Again he hesitated.

"Don't worry," she said. "Whatever it is, I promise not to bite your head off. I know you're trying to help and I'm sorry I got so upset earlier." She swallowed, then lifted her chin. "Is it that you have another couple in mind to take them in? I plan to fight to keep them, but if it comes down to a choice between an orphanage and another family, then—"

"No, that's not my idea." He took a deep breath. "I'm still trying to work all this out in my own mind. I mean, it's going to sound crazy, but just hear me out."

"I'm listening."

"What if you could find a way to resolve all of Nelda's objections, to erase the reasons she gave the council to prove you unsuitable?"

"How would I do that? Short of getting married I mean." Then her eyes widened. She was suddenly very still, her expression guarded. "Please explain."

He took another deep breath and plunged ahead. "I guess what I'm saying is, what if you and I got married?"

Her face lit up in a brilliant smile. "You're proposing to me?"

He nodded, glad to see she was as taken with the plan as he was. "I know this is not the most traditional of proposals, but there's no time to do this proper."

"I don't care about traditional. But are you sure? I mean, it wouldn't be fair to force your hand if you don't really want to—"

"I'm most definitely sure. In fact, this is perfect for me. I've been resigned for some time to the fact that marriage wasn't for me. But I've been thinking lately that it might be nice to be part of a real family. This way, I get the family without all the romantic entanglements."

Like blowing out a lamp, the sparkle in her eyes

dimmed. "Oh, I see. So this would be strictly for the kids' sake."

Had she thought—

Mitch mentally berated himself for not explaining this more clearly from the get-go. He wasn't handling this well at all. "That's right. One of them in-name-only sorts." He rubbed the back of his neck, struggling to get the words right. "I mean the two of us suit well enough—at least I think we do. And I want those children to have a good home as much as you do, so we have a shared purpose. Even if we don't love each other, there's still plenty there to base a marriage on."

He decided, for both their sakes, he needed to be really clear on that point. "I want to be up front with you. I consider you a friend, one I respect a great deal, but I don't love you, at least not in the, uh, romance—or rather, romantic sense. And I can't promise that I ever will." Was he being completely honest with her? With himself? He wasn't sure anymore. Something about what he'd just said felt wrong.

Why didn't she say something?

"It's a generous offer," she finally said, "but I can't accept."

Mitch felt his chest constrict. He hadn't realized how badly he'd wanted her to accept until just this moment. "Mind if I ask why?"

She waved a hand then dropped it back into her lap. "Don't you see? This just wouldn't be fair to you. I mean, that 'romantic' kind of love you dismiss so easily is something very precious and not something to forego lightly. I had my taste of it with Phillip, but you, well, you need to hold out for it."

He ignored the stab of jealousy he felt at the mention of her former husband. "Cora Beth, you don't understand. I don't really think I'm capable of that kind of love. In fact, like I said, I was already resigned to the idea of never getting married. So you see, I won't be giving up on anything."

"Is it because of Dinah?" she asked softly. "Because of the depth of your feelings for her?"

"Yes." *But not in the way you think.* "I promise you, if you agree to this proposal, I will honor you and respect you and never give you any cause to regret marrying me."

He had to give it one last try. "I know it sounds crazy, but think of what this would mean to Ethan and Cissy. What it will mean if we *don't* go through with it. They've gotten under my skin and I don't like the idea of sending them to an orphanage any more than you do. If we got hitched, Nelda couldn't say they wouldn't have a father, and I could help lighten some of your load at the boardinghouse so it would give you more time to spend with the kids—*all* of the kids."

Her expression remained closed, unreadable. "*If* I accepted your offer," she finally said, "how exactly do you see this working?"

He felt hope flare up again. At least she was considering it now. "I suppose if I was going to be a proper father to the kids, I'd need to move into the boardinghouse. But, don't worry, we would maintain separate rooms." He saw her cheeks redden at that. A bit indelicate to speak of such things he supposed, but best to get it all out in the open as quickly and clearly as possible. That was the only way he could reconcile this plan with his vow. "What I'm saying is that you need have no fears that I'll impose on you in any manner that would make you uncomfortable."

"I see."

He wished he could figure out what she was think-ing. Had he shocked her? Insulted her? Or did she under-stand he was truly trying to help? Her face, normally so open and readable, was a complete blank at the moment.

Mitch had the distinct sense that he was doing this wrong. Completely wrong.

Cora Beth hoped her face didn't reflect the chaos her thoughts and emotions were in right now. Truth to tell, she wasn't quite sure *what* she was feeling at the moment. What Mitch was proposing was the answer to her problems, possibly a God-directed solution that she'd been praying for since she first learned what the council meeting was all about. This plan should cer-tainly satisfy all of Nelda's *stated* concerns.

And it had been so gallant and generous of him to make the offer. A lady couldn't ask for a more noble knight-errant to rescue her. But marriage! And one that both was and wasn't a true marriage. To a man who declared in no uncertain terms that he wouldn't—couldn't—offer her anything deeper than friendship.

The prideful part of her shrank from the knowledge that, if she agreed, everyone in town would know ex-actly why they were marrying—that it was purely a response to Nelda's attempt to wrest the children from her. Would they think this had been her idea? That she'd somehow twisted Mitch's arm into helping her?

And how dare he just assume she didn't want to hold out for a man who would love and cherish her the way a husband should? Did he think she was past such dreams and desires?

But it was true that neither her pride nor personal

yearnings were the most important thing here today. If doing this meant Ethan and Cissy could stay with her uncontested, then she would go through with it, pride be hanged.

She just wished—No! No point thinking that way.

She bowed her head and closed her eyes. *Heavenly Father, help me to be thankful for the blessings You send me, no matter what guise they wear. It's not what I'd hoped for when I'd dared to dream for a closer relationship with Mitch, but I also know You can take any situation and use it to carry out Your will in this world. And I just have to believe that it can't be Your will for Ethan and Cissy to go to that orphanage. So please bless what Mitch and I are about to do. And help me to do my best to make sure that he never, ever regrets making this offer.*

Finally she looked up and met Mitch's waiting gaze. "Very well, I accept."

She saw the flare of joy blaze in his eyes and felt a sharp pang that that joy was not a result of his love for her, but for the children.

What had she just gotten herself in to?

Forty-five minutes later, Cora Beth took the same seat she'd vacated nearly two hours earlier, but this time Mitch didn't hang back. He stood beside her, his presence offering silent support.

The time between her acceptance of his proposal and their arrival back here had passed in a bit of a fog. Mitch had escorted her back to the boardinghouse where she'd fixed them both a cold lunch. There'd been very little discussion between them—as Mitch had said when they left the church, there was no point in discussing any plans until they heard what the council had to say.

Which Cora Beth understood to mean if Nelda or the council found a hole in their plan, then he saw no point going through with the wedding. She didn't even want to imagine what that outcome would do to her pride.

As they were leaving the boardinghouse, he'd given her a searching look. "You're mighty quiet. Having second thoughts?"

Oh yes, she had plenty of those. But she was committed now, and she couldn't let the children, or Mitch, down. "Just a little anxious about facing the council again."

He gave her that smile that could melt her fears. "Just leave them to me. If it's all right with you, I'd like to do most of the talking."

How could she not feel something for a man like that?

"Well then." Horace Danvers' words brought her thoughts back to the present, "Let's get back down to business again. Mrs. Collins, now that you've had some time for reflection, do you have anything else to add to what was said earlier?"

"I believe Mrs. Collins and I have found a solution to the serious concerns that were raised this morning."

The group's gazes shifted from Cora Beth to Mitch, displaying various levels of surprise.

Horace turned back to her. "Mrs. Collins, is Sheriff Hammond speaking on your behalf?"

She held her stiff-backed pose, refusing to fidget. "Yes, he is."

Horace waved an impatient hand. "Then let's get on with it."

Mitch nodded. "If I remember correctly, Mrs. Oglesby's primary concern was that these children be put in the care of someone with a firm hand to deal with any disciplinary problems that might come up, someone with the time to care for their needs properly, and ideally someone with a home that includes both a mother and a father."

Nelda nodded. "That's correct. I only want what's best for both the children and the town."

Mitch raised a brow. "That's what we *all* want. And we have found the ideal solution." He smiled down at Cora Beth. "I'm pleased to announce that Mrs. Collins has agreed to do me the great honor of becoming my wife and to allow me to shoulder a portion of her responsibilities. We plan to get married in short order."

Cora Beth wondered what he meant by "short order." Surely they would wait at least until Josie and the others returned from Hawk's Creek. Pushing that thought aside as inconsequential for the moment, she glanced at the others in the room. Most of the men were leaning back in their seats, mouths agape, looking as stunned as if Mitch had announced he was going to the moon.

Nelda, on the other hand, had turned an alarming shade of red and looked ready to spit. "Are you mocking us, Sheriff?"

Mitch placed a hand on Cora Beth's shoulder and she could feel his warmth seep through the fabric of her dress. "I assure you that we are quite serious. I hope you all will agree that as her husband I am quite capable of providing the strong hand and fatherly influence you feel these children need."

"This is preposterous." Nelda looked from Mitch to Cora Beth, her eyes wide with disbelief. "Cora Beth, you can't get married just to keep from sending those kids—"

Mitch cut her off. "Mrs. Oglesby, I hope you're not presuming to now tell Mrs. Collins who she can marry and for what reasons."

Nelda straightened at that, getting herself back under control. "No, of course not, it's just—"

Mitch turned, dismissing her and facing the council. "Then, if you gentlemen have no further concerns on the matter of the disposition of Ethan and Cissy, I hope you will excuse Mrs. Collins and me. We have a lot of plans to make."

Cora Beth stood, more than ready to make her exit.

"Of course." Mayor Oglesby offered them both a relieved smile. No doubt he was glad to have the matter settled. "You have my congratulations," he said. "And we wish you both well with this new family you're building." He gave his wife a pointed look. "Don't we, Nelda?"

Nelda stood. "Yes. Of course. Congratulations to you both. Now, if you will excuse me, I have other matters to attend to." And with a swish of her skirts, she exited the room.

Cora Beth imagined Nelda scurrying off down the street to spread the word of their sudden engagement and the reason behind it. There was no telling what sort of light she would paint it in.

Dear Lord, forgive me for my not very charitable thoughts. I know I shouldn't judge and that everyone has their own struggles and faults, myself included. But there are times when I just want to give that woman a good shake.

When they stepped back on the sidewalk for the second time today, Cora Beth took a deep breath and turned to Mitch, feeling suddenly shy and awkward. What did they do now?

"I think that went about as well as could be expected," Mitch said, his voice perhaps a little too hearty.

"The children are safe, and that's what matters." She managed a weak smile. "I won't forget that I have you to thank for that. In case I didn't say it earlier, I am more grateful than I can ever say for what you're doing. I know this is a sacrifice for you." And that was the part that truly stung—the feeling that his hand had been forced by circumstances.

But his smile seemed free of regrets. "Not a sacrifice at all. I figure I'm getting the better end of this bargain and you're the one who had to bear the brunt of their inquisition."

Was it her imagination, or were the glances being cast their way on the sly side?

Mitch seemed to feel it, too. "I need to get back to work, but why don't I come by your place this evening and we can talk about what comes next?"

She nodded, and with a tip of his hat, Mitch headed down the sidewalk toward his office, his gait easy and unhurried.

As Cora Beth made her way back to the boarding-house, she couldn't shake the feeling that she was being watched from every doorway and window. Ridiculous, since Nelda hadn't had time to tell more than one or two folks. Still, she kept her chin up and her eyes focused straight ahead, and did her best to seem at ease while fighting the urge to lift her skirts and run.

Chapter Fourteen

Cora Beth stepped into her kitchen and looked around as if she'd never seen it before. Everything seemed suddenly different, foreign. But, regardless of how her whole world had just tipped on its axis, her day-to-day life had not changed—at least not yet. She still had responsibilities to her household. If she didn't get something on the stove soon, there'd be a lot of hungry folks at her table come suppertime.

She moved to the pantry and stood staring at the contents without really seeing anything. The children would be home soon. She'd tell them the news right away, of course. They should hear it from her before someone else told them. Would they be happy? She knew they liked Mitch, but how would they feel about him becoming part of the family, moving into the boardinghouse, taking on the role of father?

They'd already faced so many changes these past few days, would another one just be taken as a matter of course? Or be the final straw that got everyone up in arms?

Cora Beth moved to the table and sat down, her meal still unplanned. She'd need to choose her words carefully when she told them, paint this in the most positive light possible. The last thing she wanted was to make Ethan or Cissy feel they'd forced her and Mitch into this marriage.

She just hoped this wouldn't give Danny yet another excuse to lay a black mark at Ethan's door.

At least Cissy would be happy—it seems her wish to have Mitch be a part of their family was going to come true after all.

She felt a bubble of hysteria rise in her throat—whether it would erupt as laughter or a wail she wasn't quite sure, and she didn't want to find out. She swallowed hard, fighting to get herself back under control. What was wrong with her? This was a *good* thing.

Wasn't it?

She heard the door open behind her and straightened, trying to school her features into some semblance of normalcy. She didn't turn around but the sound of skirts swishing and the faint scent of lavender water told her it was Mrs. Plunkett.

Her heart sank—that woman saw way too much.

"There you are," Mrs. Plunkett said. "I looked for you earlier. I wanted to ask you something."

Cora Beth threw a smile over her shoulder, then moved toward the sink. "I'm sorry, I had some unexpected business to attend to."

Mrs. Plunkett quickly closed the distance between them. "My dear, what's the matter?"

So much for her abilities as an actor. She turned and leaned back against the counter, bracing her hands against it for support. "Was there something in particular you needed me for?"

"That can wait. You look as if you've just been given

a dose of bad news. Now sit yourself down here and tell me what's wrong."

Cora Beth slowly walked back to the table and took a seat. "Nothing's wrong. In fact you should congratulate me." She gave the woman a smile that she knew didn't ring true. "I'm getting married."

"I see. Isn't this rather sudden?"

"Aren't you going to ask me who I'm marrying?"

"I assume it's Sheriff Hammond, of course."

"You assume—"

"My dear, it's obvious you two were meant for each other. What I want to know is what finally brought him to his senses and why do you look like you've just received a death sentence?"

"It's not like that. I mean, this isn't, isn't a love match."

"Balderdash!"

"Truly." It seemed of utmost importance that she convince Mrs. Plunkett of the truth. "He only proposed to me to keep the town council from taking Ethan and Cissy from me."

"What nonsense is this? Why would the council want to—" She put up a hand. "No, don't tell me. Nelda Oglesby was behind this, wasn't she?"

"She was concerned that a widow with my responsibilities wouldn't be able to give them the attention they deserved," Cora Beth said, choosing her words carefully. "That's why Sheriff Hammond made the offer. It's a business arrangement, really, for the sake of the children."

Mrs. Plunkett studied her thoughtfully. "And that is how Sheriff Hammond couched his proposal?"

"Of course." Cora Beth reached in her pocket for a handkerchief. "As I said, this isn't a love match. We're both sensible adults who have a shared interest in seeing that Ethan and Cissy are well cared for."

"Well, I must say, you two have come up with a very practical solution to your dilemma." Mrs. Plunkett touched the brooch pinned to her bodice, a thoughtful expression on her face. "So when is this wedding to take place?"

Cora Beth wiped her nose, feigning a sneeze while she tried to pull herself together. "Everything happened so fast that we haven't worked out the details yet. Sheriff Hammond is coming by this evening so we can begin planning."

Mrs. Plunkett stood, giving her a probing look. "Well, you just let me know if there is anything I can do to help with the arrangements or the planning. I so enjoy a good wedding."

"Yes, of course. That's very kind of you to offer." Cora Beth stood as well, stuffing the handkerchief back in her pocket.

Before she could say anything else, the door opened and Uncle Grover stepped in. "I understand congratulations are in order," he said with a smile.

"You heard the news."

"Yes. Horace told me when I stopped by the mercantile to see if he had gotten in the new display case I ordered." He took her hands. "Are you happy, my dear?"

That was a good question. She wasn't *un*happy. "I am absolutely positive this is the right thing to do," she temporized.

He frowned. "Mitch is a good man—you couldn't ask for a finer husband. But if this is not what you want…"

Cora Beth gave his hands a squeeze. "Really, Uncle Grover, Mitch and I will get along wonderfully."

What was it Mitch had said, that they would "suit well enough"?

She freed her hands from his and turned to Mrs. Plunkett. "Oh, I almost forgot. What was it you wanted to see me about?"

The woman waved a hand dismissively. "Don't worry about that. It can wait for another time. As a matter of fact—" she turned to Uncle Grover "—perhaps *you* could help me with something."

Uncle Grover looked startled for a moment, then his gentlemanly instincts came to the fore. "Of course. What can I do for you?"

Mrs. Plunkett moved to the door. "Let's leave your niece to her work. We can discuss this in the parlor."

As the two moved into the hall, Cora Beth smiled. Mrs. Plunkett was definitely not letting any grass grow under her feet. Would there be another marriage in the family soon?

If so, she hoped it would have more going for it than being a "good business arrangement."

Mitch looked at the clock, alternately thinking that the hands were moving too slow and then too fast. School should have let out a few minutes ago. He'd been waiting for Ethan to arrive, wondering what he would say to the boy. He didn't have any illusions that Ethan wouldn't have already heard the news. Apparently everyone in town now knew that he and Cora Beth were planning to get hitched.

There'd been more traffic through his office this afternoon than in the entire month preceding. Some came by with pretenses of business, others out and out professing their curiosity. He certainly hoped they'd left Cora Beth alone. She'd seemed okay on the surface when he'd left her, but something about her smile had hinted at a certain fragility of spirit that had him a little worried.

The door opened, interrupting his thoughts, and Ethan stepped inside. As soon as Mitch saw his face he knew the boy had heard.

He tried to read Ethan's expression to gauge how he'd reacted, but Ethan headed directly for the corner where the broom was stored, never looking at Mitch.

"How was school today?" Mitch asked.

Ethan shrugged, pushing the broom with a bit more force than usual.

Okay, better get right to it. "I suppose you heard the big news."

A quick glance, a nod, and then back to sweeping.

"Well, what do you think?"

"They say neither one of you really wanted to get married but that you're having to do it because of me and Cissy. They say it's a shame you had to be saddled with so many unwanted burdens."

Mitch's temper rose at that. He wasn't getting *saddled* with anything he didn't want to take on. And it was nobody's business but his anyway. "I don't know who *they* are, but no one is making either one of us do anything."

The look Ethan shot him said he wasn't buying it.

Mitch reined in his temper and tried again. "Look, I like Mrs. Collins. And I like all of you kids. Getting to be part of a big family is going to be a new experience for me and it's one I'm looking forward to. So don't go thinking I'm making a big sacrifice here, because I'm not."

Ethan kept right on sweeping. "You sound just like

my ma before she married Titus. She did it 'cause of me and Cissy and look how that turned out."

So that's what had him so upset. "Ethan, Mrs. Collins and I are not your ma and Titus. We've known each other a long time and we know each other pretty well. We also know just what we're doing and why we're doing it." Or at least he hoped that was true. "This is a good thing—you'll see."

"Doesn't matter. Seems like whenever anybody does something 'for my own good,' it turns out bad."

The boy definitely had a problem seeing the bright side of anything. "Ethan, look at me."

Ethan stopped sweeping and did as he was told.

"You like Mrs. Collins, don't you?"

His expression immediately softened. "She's one of the nicest ladies I ever met. I'd do anything for her."

"I thought so. One thing you need to understand about Mrs. Collins is that she has a very strong spirit. As you've already learned, if she believes in you, she'll stand up for you against anything and anyone."

He leaned forward. "But she also has a very soft, tender heart. Granted this marriage plan of ours is a little unusual, but it's very important to her. That's because *you and Cissy* are important to her. So, don't make this difficult for her, okay?"

Ethan thought about it for a minute, then slowly nodded. "I still think it's a bad idea but I won't let Mrs. Collins know."

Mitch nodded approvingly. "I knew I could count on you."

Ethan went back to sweeping. "There's something you probably ought to know, though."

"What's that."

"Danny didn't look none too happy when he heard the news. And he took off like a shot for the boarding-house."

Cora Beth took a deep breath when she heard the front door open. The kids were home from school—time to tell them the news.

Danny came bursting through the kitchen door. "Is it true?" he demanded. "Are you and Sheriff Hammond getting married?"

Cora Beth mentally cringed. Why was he so upset? "Yes, it's true. Though I was hoping to be the one to break the news to you all."

"It's all over town—it's all anyone is talking about." She sincerely hoped he was exaggerating. And it was clear from his tone he did *not* think the marriage—or the gossip—was a good thing. "Well, it's nice that our neighbors take such an interest in us," she said mildly.

"You're doing this because of them, aren't you? Ethan and his sister, I mean. If they hadn't come here you wouldn't be having to do this."

"Daniel Edward Atkins, I'm getting really tired of hearing that kind of talk from you. Ethan and Cissy are part of our family now and you will treat them that way."

Danny set his lips in that rebellious thin line she was learning to hate.

She took a deep breath, tried to remember the sweet little boy he'd been not too long ago, and placed a hand on his shoulder. "Danny, I'm getting married. And whether you believe it or not, I *want* this. Can't you be happy for me?"

She could see the internal struggle play out in his

changing expression. Before either one of them could say anything more, though, the girls came rushing in. At least *they* hadn't abandoned the slower-moving Cissy.

"Mom, Danny wouldn't wait for us," Audrey complained.

"I was in a hurry, squirt." He shrugged off her hand but his tone and smile toward the girls was back to big-brother teasing. At least he didn't let his anger spill over to his sisters. Without a backward glance for Cora Beth, he left the room.

"Is it true?" Audrey asked, claiming Cora Beth's attention.

"If you mean am I going to marry Sheriff Hammond, then yes, it's true."

"That means he's going to be part of our family, doesn't it?" Cissy seemed pretty pleased by that idea.

"Yes, it does. Won't that be nice?"

"Is he going to live here?" Pippa asked.

"Yes, he is." She wasn't ready for them to start digging any deeper than that and quickly changed the subject. "All right, that's enough questions for now. There's a cookie for each of you on the counter and then you need to get to your lessons and afternoon chores."

Danny avoided her for the rest of the day.

Later that evening, Cora Beth opened the front door to find Mitch standing there, hat in hand.

"I hope I'm not interrupting anything."

"No, of course not. Supper's over and the evening chores are done. Come on in."

"I thought maybe we could talk out here on the porch. It's a nice evening."

"Of course. But first come in and say hello." She

pushed the door wider. "You're going to have to face them all eventually, and as Grammy Alma used to say—"

"Get it over with sooner rather than later." He gave her a stern look. "And just for the record, I'm a lawman. I've had to deal with thieves, bullies and drunken cowboys. I was *not* dreading facing these folks."

She didn't say anything, merely raised a brow in disbelief.

He grimaced good-naturedly. "All right, I wasn't dreading it *much*."

As Cora Beth had expected, Mitch had barely stepped across the threshold before nearly every member of her household came out to greet him. Only Ethan and Danny were absent. They'd both disappeared to their respective rooms once evening chores were done.

The four girls held back while the adults spoke, though Cora Beth could see they were barely containing themselves.

Mr. Saddler stepped forward first, pushing his spectacles up with his left hand while sticking out his right. "Let me offer my most sincere congratulations on your happy news, Sheriff. You're a very lucky man to have garnered the favor of so fine a woman as Mrs. Collins."

"Thank you. And I heartily agree."

Honoria merely smiled shyly and offered a soft congratulations to the mix.

Her mother was not so reticent. "Well, Sheriff," Mrs. Plunkett said, "I must say your news came as a most pleasant surprise. It's about time our Cora Beth here found a man worthy of her."

Not quite sure how to respond to that, Mitch merely smiled.

Uncle Grover gave him a surprisingly focused, assessing look. "Just see that you don't hurt our girl and you'll fit in here just fine."

Mitch nodded deferentially. "Yes, sir, you have my word."

The older man smiled, his expression returning to the jovial, slightly bemused look he normally wore. "In that case, welcome to the family."

Cissy tugged on Mitch's pant leg, apparently unable to remain quiet any longer. "Mrs. Collins says you're going to come live here with us. Are you really?"

He smiled down at her. "Mrs. Collins wouldn't lie to you, Buttercup."

"When are you going to move in?"

"Soon. Mrs. Collins and I are going to talk about that in a little bit."

Lottie tilted her head and clasped her hands behind her back. "What room are you gonna take?"

Time to break this up before the girls got too personal with their questions. "Enough with all these questions. Sheriff Hammond and I are going out on the front porch to talk."

"Can we come, too?" The question came from Audrey, naturally.

"No, right now we need to do some grown-up talking."

Uncle Grover stepped in. "Actually, Mrs. Plunkett was telling me just this afternoon about some new slides she got for her stereopticon. Why don't we see if she'll show them to us?"

"What's a steri-op-con?" Cissy asked, puzzled.

Mrs. Plunkett's brows rose and she placed a hand on her bosom. "You've never seen a stereopticon? Oh my dear, then we must get the slides out and show you how wonderful they are."

While Uncle Grover and Mrs. Plunkett herded all the children toward the main parlor, Cora Beth and Mitch made their escape to the front porch.

As Mitch pulled the door closed behind them, Cora Beth moved to the porch rail and looked out over the front lawn. Twilight was settling in and she could hear frogs harumphing in the distance. She rubbed her upper arms, not sure what to expect out of this meeting. Would they be awkward together now? She most desperately hoped not.

Pasting a smile on her face, she turned and took a seat on the porch swing. Mitch took her place at the rail, leaning a hip against it as he turned to face her.

He was the first to break the silence. "I guess we need to decide on a date for the wedding."

She nodded. "I hate to say this, but I won't feel the children are completely safe until we're married. I definitely want to wait until Josie and the others get back from Hawk's Creek, but I don't want to wait much longer than that."

"Of course. They'll be back on Saturday, right?"

Cora Beth nodded.

"Then how about a week from Saturday?"

Cora Beth's heart fluttered as she nodded. In a little over a week she'd be a married lady once more.

Mitch smiled. "That's settled then. We can go by and talk to Reverend Ludlow in the morning."

Trying to match his businesslike approach, Cora Beth lifted her chin. "Now, as for you moving in here, I've been trying to figure out the best way to make that work fairly for everyone. I mean, I know you're used to having a whole place to yourself, but space is at a premium here."

"Don't worry, I don't need a lot of space."

"Oh, I didn't mean I wanted to give your needs short shrift. Surely you need more than just a place to sleep. There's a small room we call the family parlor on the first floor. It's not as big as the parlor the boarders and guests use, but it's got plenty of windows to let in the light and it's a pleasant enough space. The family tends to congregate in the kitchen anyway, so it's hardly used at all. We could easily turn it into a study or office for you. If you had a desk or favorite chair you want to bring with you—"

"Cora Beth."

"Yes?"

"It's okay. Like I said, I don't need a lot of space. And other than a few personal items that'll fit in my bedchamber, I'm not attached to any of the furnishings in my old place. I plan to leave them there for whomever decides to buy the place."

"You're really selling your house?" It was the place he'd acquired when he got engaged to Dinah.

He shrugged. "Don't see any point in my holding on to it. Do you?"

"No, of course. I just—" Aware she was babbling, she took a deep breath and moved on. "As for sleeping accommodations, we've rearranged things a bit to make room for Ethan and Cissy, but there's still one vacant room upstairs and of course there's the downstairs bedchamber. You can look at them—"

"No need. I'll take the one downstairs."

"Don't you even want to take a look at the one upstairs?"

"I meant it when I said I don't need much space. And since my job as sheriff sometimes requires me to work late or have people calling on me at all hours, it'll be less disruptive if I'm on the first floor."

"If you're sure that's what you want, then that's fine. The downstairs room is probably larger anyway." She brushed an invisible speck of dust from her skirt. "About the wedding itself, under the circumstances I thought we'd keep it very simple."

"I'll leave that up to you, but simple is fine with me. If you need me to do anything, just let me know. Otherwise, you plan it and I'll show up and do my part."

Apparently the ceremony itself was not important to him. Why should it be? They were pledging their troth to each other, not their love. She wished that didn't sting quite so much, that she could be more pragmatic about it.

"I want you to know," Mitch said, "that even though this is going to be a name-only kind of marriage, I plan to pull my weight around here."

She smiled. "I have no doubt of that. I think being a father to six children is going to require more out of you than you imagine right now."

He grimaced. "I hope I'm up to that. But I was talking about the actual operations of the boardinghouse."

She frowned. This was her domain. "You already have a job—being sheriff. I've managed just fine all these years and I can continue taking care of things." Though, with her mother gone and Josie married and moved out, it had been a mite lonelier and more burdensome lately.

"I don't doubt your capabilities, and I don't claim to know anything about operating a boardinghouse, so you don't have to worry about me coming in and getting in your way. But I've been thinking that maybe there was just a kernel of truth in something Nelda said today."

She felt a little prick of defensiveness. "What was that?"

"She said that with all your responsibilities, you wouldn't have time to give the kids the attention they need."

How dare he! "But I—"

He raised a hand to cut off her protest. "I'm not saying the kids are being neglected. Far from it. You're a great mom to those kids. They don't lack for anything important, they've been raised to be respectful and God-fearing, and it's obvious they love you back. And it's plain that they know that you love them and you'd do just about anything for them, which is real important to a kid."

The way he said that made her wonder again what his life had been like in his grandmother's home.

"But you gotta admit that running this place is a lot of work," he continued. "It keeps you busy from cock's crow to owl's hoot."

Being busy wasn't a crime. "I enjoy running this place."

He gave her a skeptical look. "I'm sure you enjoy some parts of it, but you can't tell me you actually enjoy all the day-to-day work that goes into it. The cooking, cleaning, laundry—ah-ha!" He pointed a finger at her. "I saw that grimace. So laundry is your sore spot."

She laughed. "All right, so I'm not fond of doing laundry, but I can't let you—"

He quirked a brow. "Can't let me what? Take on the role of man of the house?"

"Somehow, I don't normally think of the man-of-the-house role as one that includes doing the wash." She had trouble picturing him wielding a paddle to stir a washtub full of wet laundry.

"You misunderstand me—I'm not being *that* noble. What I would like to do is hire someone to help out around here."

"Hire someone? Oh, Mitch, I don't know. That doesn't seem like a good use of money."

"And what else do I have to spend my money on? I mostly spend my sheriff's salary on groceries, stabling my horse and the little bit of upkeep my place needs. Moving in here is going to take care of most of that, which isn't going to do much for my standing as family breadwinner. If this marriage is going to work, I need to feel like I'm contributing to the household in a real way."

Ah, the male's need to be the provider. "I suppose I *could* use some help on laundry day." Actually, not having to tackle that wretched job alone was something she could quite happily get used to.

"Oh come now. I'm sure if you thought hard enough you could find tasks to keep a helper busy every day of the week."

"Then what would I do? Besides, there's not many folks available for full-time work of this sort."

"I have no doubt that you'd find plenty to keep you busy. And you'd be surprised who's available. In fact, Benny Thatcher's oldest kids, Hannah and Paul, have been trying to find odd jobs around town for several weeks now. I'm thinking Hannah might be a good one to talk to about the job."

Now he wasn't playing fair. The Thatcher family

had fallen on hard times this past year and were having trouble making ends meet. The Ladies' Auxiliary had put together several food baskets for them. If she turned her back on this opportunity to help them she'd feel like a wretch—and Mitch knew it. "I still plan to do most of the cooking," she said huffily.

He held up both palms. "You won't get any argument from me. I don't think there's a finer cook in the county and I'm looking forward to a steady diet of your meals after the wedding."

"Actually," Cora Beth said, "it might be a good idea if you start taking some of your meals here before the wedding. It'll give you a chance to ease into the routine around here, and it'll give the family and the boarders a chance to get to know you better before you actually move in."

"I reckon I can live with that." He grinned. "So, are you saying yes to hiring Hannah full-time?"

He was going to make her say it, was he? She let out a melodramatic sigh. "Yes, I suppose, for the sake of your fragile, manly pride, I will let you talk me into this."

Mitch repressed a smile at her saucy response and shook his head dolefully. "I can tell I'm going to have to keep on my toes around you."

She laughed, then quickly sobered. "By the way, thank you for whatever it was you said to Ethan this afternoon. By the time he made it home he seemed very accepting of the notion that we were getting married."

He decided against telling her about Ethan's first reaction—comparing their upcoming wedding to his mother's marriage to Titus. "He's a reasonable kid. A few words about it being what we both wanted was all it took." He gave her a probing look. "But I hear Danny didn't take it so well."

She shook her head. "Goodness, there really aren't any secrets in this town. Who'd you hear that from?"

"From Ethan."

"Oh." She nibbled on her lip for a moment, and he could tell something was worrying her.

Impulsively he moved to the swing and sat beside her. "Anything I can help with?"

"I don't know. Maybe. It's just, Danny hasn't been acting like himself lately and I can't figure out what's wrong with him."

"Tell me about it."

"He seems to have it in for Ethan. He believes every little word whispered against him, he seems to value his friends' opinions above mine and he wears a log-size chip on his shoulder whenever he and Ethan are forced together."

She waved a hand. "He's never been like this before. I mean, he's certainly no angel, but he's always been fair-minded and considerate of others."

"Danny's growing up. He's not a man yet but he's not a little boy anymore, either. That can really turn a kid on his ear sometimes."

"I understand that. I mean, I think I do. I don't have a lot of experience with adolescent boys. It was just me and Jo growing up for the most part. Danny didn't come into our lives until I was fifteen and I got married and moved out three and a half years later."

She frowned. "And that's another thing that has me confused about his attitude. Because of what happened to him, he of all the people in this household should have some sympathy for Ethan and Cissy's situation.

It just seems like there's something going on with him that I'm missing."

How much did she know about Danny's life outside the boardinghouse? "I reckon this might have something to do with the fact that he's sweet on Odine Oglesby." The stunned look on her face confirmed that she'd had no idea.

"Nelda's daughter? What—I mean, how— I mean, are you sure?"

"If you're wondering if anyone told me outright, no. But as sheriff I hear things. I also have a good view of the schoolyard from my office."

She sat back, a thoughtful look on her face. "So, what Odine's mother thinks has a big influence on Odine. And what Odine thinks—"

"—has a big influence on Danny," Mitch finished for her. Then he shrugged. "As far as what you do about it, sorry, that's outside my area of expertise."

"Don't apologize, this is quite helpful. At least now I know why he's acting the way he is."

There now, he liked it much better when she was wearing that soft smile rather than a worried frown. Before he could stop himself, he reached out to touch her arm.

For a second, he savored her soft skin, her warmth and her sweetness.

Their gazes locked and he saw her pupils widen and heard a little catch of breath. Was it his imagination or had she moved closer? What would she do if he leaned in to kiss her? A quick, best-friend kind of kiss, of course. They were engaged now after all. Tied to each other in a till-death-us-do-part partnership.

Wasn't that the kind of deal usually sealed with a kiss?

Chapter Fifteen

Cora Beth held her breath, waiting. Would he kiss her? If he was looking for permission, surely he would read it in her eyes.

They were isolated here. Even if the honeysuckle trellis hadn't screened them from the casual passerby, twilight had deepened to dusk while they'd talked and the moon was not yet up. The pool of diffused light coming from behind the dining-room curtain was enough light to see by, but it stopped short of spotlighting them.

Slowly, as if she were a bird that could be startled by a sudden movement, he reached up and caressed her cheek. She closed her eyes and leaned into the warmth of his hand—his large, rough, achingly gentle hand.

"Cora Honey." The whispered endearment was husky.

Cora Honey. So much nicer than Cora Beth.

"I think I'm gonna kiss you now."

Did he think she'd protest? Not a chance. She lifted her face, eager to meet him halfway.

And kiss her he did. Gentle at first, gentle and chaste. But just when she was feeling a stab of disappointment, it changed. His arm snaked around her back and he pulled her closer, deepening the kiss, making her heart race and her thoughts scatter. Being held in his arms like this felt wonderful, felt *right*.

When he finally pulled away, he looked as dazed as she felt. "That wasn't supposed to happen," he said bemusedly.

A smile tugged at her lips. "But it did."

He straightened and his expression turned to one of consternation, as if he were only just now aware that he'd spoken aloud. He popped up from the swing as if prodded from below and rubbed the back of his neck. "I'm sorry. I need to go. We'll talk some more tomorrow."

Was he apologizing for the kiss or because he had to leave? "Of course. And don't forget, I expect you to start taking your supper meals here."

"Yes, looking forward to it. Good night."

And with that he headed off, taking long, quick strides as if he couldn't get away fast enough.

Cora Beth moved to the porch rail and stared out into the night, a satisfied smile on her face.

She'd like to believe that if Mitch was upset it was because his own feelings had caught him unaware. There *had* been feelings behind that kiss, no matter how much he wanted to pretend there weren't. And knowing that gave her hope.

He might still have strong feelings about Dinah, and she might never take her place in his heart, but now she could believe that he just might have room there for both of them.

What in the world had he just done? Mitch raked his hand through his hair as he marched through town, wishing he had something he could vent his frustration on. Woe to any rowdy townsman who dared kick up a ruckus tonight.

He should have never given her that kiss, never allowed himself to enjoy it so much. It had been selfish and dangerous. He could only go through with this marriage if she went into it without looking for or expecting more than a purely business arrangement. If he let her believe he loved her, let her grow to love him and count on his love in return, it would only result in heartache and eventually bitterness.

And he couldn't, *wouldn't* do that to Cora Beth.

No, friendship was what he'd planned to settle for and it was what she needed to settle for, as well.

But, oh, how could he go back to thinking of her as just a friend after that kiss—that sweet, heart-stopping kiss that tasted of joy and sunshine and the spirit that was uniquely Cora Beth?

With a groan, Mitch picked up his pace knowing he'd keep himself out patrolling for quite some time tonight.

Chapter Sixteen

"Put away your mop and apron, we've got shopping to do."

Cora Beth, who'd been pleasantly daydreaming about her tête-à-tête with Mitch yesterday evening, looked up to find Mrs. Plunkett staring down at her with a frown. Had she mentioned shopping?

"I'm sorry, I did my shopping yesterday, before…" Before her whole world got turned on its head. "Well, before I met with the town council."

Which was just as well. Cora Beth wasn't particularly looking forward to her next visit to the mercantile. There's no telling exactly what Nelda had reported after the town council meeting yesterday, but she was sure it hadn't painted her in the most flattering of lights.

"We're not going shopping for you," Mrs. Plunkett said with exaggerated patience, "we're going shopping for *me*. I've decided I need a new dress for your wedding, and I want you to help me pick out the fabric."

Now why would she want her opinion on fashion? She'd never asked for it before. "Oh, you don't need me for that. Besides, I have all this cleaning to do—"

"It'll keep. I insist you accompany me."

This conversation was truly odd. What was going on? Cora Beth brushed the hair off her forehead with the back of her hand. "I'm sorry—" she strove for an equally firm tone "—but as I said, I'm in the middle of mopping my floors."

"Cora Beth Collins, you disappoint me. I've never before considered you a coward."

A coward? "I don't under—"

"You have to face everyone sooner or later. It won't get any easier by putting it off."

Cora Beth winced as she took in Mrs. Plunkett's version of her Grammy Alma's advice. And, much as she hated to admit it, it was still good advice. She'd been avoiding the moment when she'd have to face everyone, have to smile and accept their congratulations while wondering what they were thinking behind their smiles.

"Besides," Mrs. Plunkett added, "I'd think a woman who was newly engaged to one of the most sought-after-bachelors in town would want to flaunt it a bit, no matter what the circumstances surrounding that engagement."

Cora Beth leaned on her mop as she thought about that for a moment. Mrs. Plunkett was right. There was no way she was going to give anyone the impression she was embarrassed to be marrying Mitch, regardless of the circumstances.

She propped the mop against the corner and untied her apron. So what if Mitch's proposal had lacked a more traditional romantic element? He'd come to her rescue when she had needed him most, just like a true storybook hero, and that was romantic enough for her.

"As a matter of fact," she said as she placed her apron back on its peg, "I think I'll see if I can find a nice bolt of fabric to make myself a new dress, too." She gave Mrs. Plunkett an apologetic look. "Would you mind terribly if I went alone? I think it will be better that way."

Mrs. Plunkett beamed approvingly. "Good for you. My shopping can quite easily wait until this afternoon.

Fifteen minutes later, Cora Beth stepped into the mercantile to find Alice Danvers assisting two other ladies with their purchases. Smiling a greeting, she nodded and moved unhurriedly toward the bolts of fabric near the rear of the store.

Before long, Alice came bustling up to offer assistance, just as she'd expected.

Taking a deep breath, she turned to the mercantile owner's wife with a smile. "Hi, Alice. I'm looking for some fabric for my wedding dress."

Mitch was feeling grumpy and out of sorts this morning. He hadn't slept well last night—in fact, he hadn't slept much at all. And today hadn't started off much better. He'd not only managed to burn his breakfast, but he'd nicked himself shaving, too—something he hadn't done since he was a knob-kneed adolescent just learning to wield a razor. Then he'd got to the office and found Jonas Pickering waiting for him, all set on lodging yet another complaint against one of his neighbors. This time he'd supposedly spotted the Lawton kid cutting across his property to get to the next farm over instead of using the road.

He hated dealing with bickering neighbors, especially when the complaints seemed so petty. But the law was the law and upholding it was his job.

With a sigh Mitch unfolded himself from his chair and grabbed his hat. He'd make the rounds here in town and then ride out to the Lawton place and deliver a lecture on the ramifications of trespassing.

When he passed by the mercantile, though, he paused. Was that Cora Beth inside? He propped up his boot on a nearby bench, pretending to clean something off his heel with a pocketknife while he gave himself a moment to think.

He'd planned to keep his distance today, to make sure that their next encounter had a businesslike feel to it so that what had passed between them last night could fade into the background where it belonged.

But he was very aware of the kind of speculations that had been circulating since their engagement became the talk of the town yesterday. It was one thing for some of the more brash townsfolk to make gibes to him, disguised as good-natured jesting, of course, but he didn't like the idea of Cora Beth facing that alone.

He wavered a moment, then, swallowing an oath, headed inside. Hopefully Cora Beth would take what he was about to do in the spirit with which it was intended.

As soon as he stepped inside, conversations stopped and he became the focus of every pair of eyes there. To be more precise, *they* became the focus of every pair of eyes there as the others looked from him to Cora Beth and back again. But he'd expected as much and made sure his smile didn't waver and that his glance never left Cora Beth. "There you are, sweetheart," he said as he approached. "Thought I saw you duck in here." He placed an arm around her shoulder and gave her a squeeze before stepping back.

She never blinked, just met his smile with one of her own. "I thought I'd treat myself to a new dress for the wedding."

"Sounds like a fine idea. But you're going to make a beautiful bride no matter what you're wearing."

Cora Beth laughed and gave his arm a playful pat. "Flatterer." Then she put her hands on two different bolts of fabric. "Now be serious. I can't decide between these two. This yellow is pretty the way it's sprinkled with those little blue flowers, but this green is such a rich color."

"Definitely the green," he said without hesitation. "It matches your eyes."

"The green it is then." She pulled out the bolt and handed it to Alice Danvers. "Would you cut me four yards, please?" After a moment she pulled out the yellow, as well. "Actually, I think I'll take some of this one, too, to make new dresses for the girls."

Then she turned to Mitch. "Was there a particular reason you tracked me down?"

Her eyes were dancing. The little minx, she was enjoying this bit of playacting. Why hadn't he seen this side of her before? "As a matter of fact, there was. I forgot to ask you last night what time you want me over for supper this evening."

"We eat promptly at six-thirty. But you're welcome to come early if you like."

"You can expect me around six then." He smiled and then threw in a wink for good measure. He had the satisfaction of watching her have to swallow a laugh. "I need to get back to work. See you this evening." He turned back to face the others in the store and tipped his hat. "Good day, folks. By the way, hope you can all make it to the wedding next Saturday."

He stepped out on the sidewalk and decided today wasn't such a bad day after all.

* * *

Cora Beth watched him go, a smile playing around the corners of her lips. If the townsfolk wanted to see how she was taking this wedding plan, they were going to get an eyeful right now.

As Alice cut the fabric and chattered on about what a pretty bride Cora Beth was going to make, and how the sheriff had certainly become rather *demonstrative* lately, Cora Beth was very glad she'd decided to take Mrs. Plunkett's advice.

She'd made her appearance and come out the better for it. The worst was now behind her and she could face the rest of the town with a smile on her lips. Let them talk behind her back if they wanted to, but no one would be able to say she was moping or dragging about.

And who would have guessed Mitch could get into the spirit of putting on a show so thoroughly? The man was a ham at heart!

And most definitely her hero.

Chapter Seventeen

By Saturday morning, the novelty of Mitch and Cora Beth's engagement had begun to wear off and things were getting back to normal, at least as far as the townsfolk were concerned.

For Cora Beth, however, things were anything *but* normal. She was working hard to get the boardinghouse ready for Mitch's arrival. She'd cleared the downstairs bedchamber—which tended to get treated like a storeroom most of the time—of any clutter, and scrubbed and polished every visible surface until the room fairly sparkled. Then she made new curtains for the windows and placed one of her best quilts on the bed.

First thing next week, between her regular chores, she planned to tackle the parlor and turn it into Mitch's office.

But it was more than just the preparations that had her feeling a bit on edge. She couldn't get that kiss, and what it might mean for the two of them, out of her mind. To her disappointment, Mitch had avoided all mention of it. And while he'd been very good about making certain everyone knew he was happy about the upcoming

nuptials when they were in public, when they were alone
he'd been equally careful to keep their interactions brief
and to the point. Even when he'd joined them for meals
at the boardinghouse, he'd spent more time interact-
ing with the children and Uncle Grover than with her.

But Cora Beth was not ready to give up. Now that
she'd seen the signs of a spark in his heart, she was determined to do her part to help that spark grow. More
than likely he was just feeling a touch of guilt at an
imagined disloyalty to Dinah's memory. There was a
time after Phillip's death that she'd felt the same. But,
as much as she'd loved him, she'd grown to realize
that God didn't want His people living in the past. He
wanted them to move forward, to be happy and fulfilled
and whole again. It was up to her to show Mitch that
that was true for him as well, that it wasn't an either-
or proposition. He could cherish the memories of his
lost love and still find room in his heart for a new love.

It would take time, but in this particular instance,
she wouldn't try to hurry things along. She would be
patient and wait on God's timing.

And this morning, the two of them were headed to
the train depot to meet the returning Reynolds and Lassiter families. She'd wanted to be certain Josie and the
others heard the news from her before anyone else told
them, and the only way to ensure that was to be there
when they stepped off the train. And it had only seemed
right for Mitch to be there, as well.

Assuming his role of proud fiancé, Mitch had tucked
her hand in the crook of his arm. It felt good to have him
act so solicitous, so protective. In fact, Cora Beth decided, if this was the only way she could get him to drop

the businesslike attitude, she'd have to come up with more excuses for them to be seen together in public.

They arrived at the depot just as the train whistle sounded in the distance. Before long, the train was coming to a noisy, soot-filled stop in front of the depot.

Josie was the first of the group to disembark and she hurried up to give Cora Beth a hug as soon as she spotted her.

"Hi! It's great to see you but you didn't have to come out here to meet us. I was planning to stop by your place before we headed out to the ranch."

Then she spotted Mitch and her expression sobered. "What is it? Has something happened? Are all the kids okay?"

"Relax, it's nothing like that." By this time the others had congregated around them and greetings were hastily exchanged.

Josie allowed them only a few minutes of chatter before she waved a hand impatiently. "Well then, if everyone's okay, to what do we owe the honor of this little welcome-home reception?"

Cora Beth could feel her cheeks warm. "Mitch and I have an announcement to make and we wanted you all to hear it from us first." As she spoke, Mitch moved up closer beside her, placing her hand on his arm and putting his over it.

Before she could say more, Josie's face broke into a broad smile and Sadie let out a little squeal of excitement.

Mitch grinned. "As you ladies seem to have guessed, Cora Beth here has done me the honor of agreeing to be my wife."

There were more squeals as Sadie and Josie vied

with each other to hug Cora Beth. Ry and Eli resorted to thumping Mitch on the back and pumping his hand. Penny and Viola stared at the adults as if they thought they'd gone a bit mad.

Finally Cora Beth straightened. "There's more we need to discuss with you, but why don't we do our talking at the boardinghouse instead of standing out here on the platform."

Ry looked at Eli with mock resignation. "We might as well. There's no way we're going to pry our wives away from Cora Beth anytime soon."

Cora Beth smiled her best bride-to-be smile.

As soon as they reached the boardinghouse, Penny and Viola went in search of the other children, which left Mitch and Cora Beth free to explain what had led to their sudden engagement.

"So you see," Cora Beth said once the story was out, "Mitch and I are entering into this arrangement as a purely business proposition, for the sake of the children. I wanted to give you the whole story because, unfortunately, the way events unfolded, it's been the subject of a lot of talk around town."

Sadie patted her hand. "I'm so sorry we weren't here to support you when this all came up. It must have been a difficult meeting to sit through."

"It was. But, thanks to Mitch's quick thinking, everything worked out for the best."

"I'm sure there are some legal ways to fight this," Ry said, "without you two having to go through with a marriage you don't want. Legal adoption for one. If you want me to look into filing the papers—"

Cora Beth held up a hand to stop him. "Thank you,

but something like that could take time, and there's no guarantee the judge who reviews the case would grant my request. No, I think this is the best plan. That is—" suddenly realizing it wasn't entirely her decision, she turned to Mitch "—unless you want to try that approach first?"

Mitch shook his head. "I'm fine with holding to the current plan. As I said at the time, I like those kids and like the idea of being part of their lives." He turned back to Ry. "But it might not hurt to look into filing for adoption after the wedding."

Pleasantly surprised, Cora Beth touched his arm briefly. "What a wonderful idea."

Ry nodded. "Good. I'll brush up on what'll be required so I'll be ready to help whenever you say the word."

Josie gave Mitch a broad smile. "Well, whatever the circumstances, welcome to our family." Then she looked around the table. "A lawyer, a banker and now a lawman—who would've guessed a year ago that today I'd find myself so well connected."

Ry stood. "Well, as much as I've enjoyed this visit, I need to check on how things are going at the stables. Ladybird was due to foal when we left." He bent down to take Josie's elbow and help her up. "And you've had a long day already. We need to get you home so you can rest."

"Well we don't have quite so dramatic a reason, but we need to get back home, as well," Eli said as he also stood. "I'm sure Sadie is also ready for some rest."

Josie and Sadie looked at each other and rolled their eyes. "Men."

Then Josie smiled at Sadie while she reached for Ry's

hand. "We might as well let Mitch in on our news. He's practically family now anyway."

"I agree," Sadie said as she, too, reached for her husband's hand. "Besides, now that the girls know it won't be a secret much longer."

Josie turned to Mitch. "Both Sadie and I are in the family way."

Mitch's face split in a wide grin. "Well now, don't that beat all. Congratulations, folks." He rose and pumped first Ry's hand and then Eli's hand. "Looks like cause for celebration all the way around."

Josie nodded. "This family's sure enough growing by leaps and bounds.

Sadie stood, and Eli's arm snaked around her petite frame. "We do have to head home," she said, "but we hope you'll all come by our place for lunch after church service tomorrow. That includes you, too, Mitch."

"I'd be honored."

Once the others had gone, Cora Beth led Mitch back to the kitchen. "Thank you for helping me break the news to them."

"It was my news, too."

"And come next Saturday, they'll be your family, too." She waved a hand. "Well, technically Eli and Sadie aren't family, but they're as close as no never mind to it."

He shook his head, a crooked smile tugging at his lips. "It's going to be strange to be part of such a large family. You're used to it so I guess it's nothing remarkable in your books. But for all those years it was just me and Granny Todd. Then, after she passed, it was just me."

She smiled. "From desert to flood, I guess. You may find yourself in the midst of more family than you can stand." Not that she'd trade off any one of them for all of King Solomon's gold. But would he find their numbers overwhelming?

Monday morning, just as Cora Beth was finishing up with the breakfast dishes, she heard someone on the back porch. Looking through the screen door, she saw Hannah Thatcher raise her hand to knock.

"Come on in," Cora Beth said as she dried her hands on her apron.

The girl stepped across the threshold, then stopped, as if unsure of her welcome. "Good morning, Mrs. Collins. I hope I'm not interrupting anything."

"No, no, come on in."

"Sheriff Hammond, he said I should come talk to you. He said you might have some work for me."

Cora Beth studied the girl, taking in her thin frame and well-worn dress. For all of that, though, she was neat and clean. Her straw-colored hair was pulled back in a tidy braid and her clothing was spotless.

"Have a seat and let's talk for a bit. Can I fix you a cup of coffee?"

"No thank you, ma'am." She sat but she didn't relax. She perched primly on the edge of her chair, as if ready to take off at the first sign of trouble.

"So then, tell me, what sort of work are you looking for?"

"I can do just about any chores you set me to, ma'am. I can clean and cook and do laundry. I can do mending and scrub floors and—"

Cora Beth smiled and held up a hand. "So you're willing to do whatever is required." She gave the girl a sympathetic smile. "Tell me, how are things at home?"

Hannah lifted her chin. "My folks are doing the best they can, ma'am, but it's been hard this year. What with Pa hurting his leg right at planting time and those wild pigs getting into the vegetable garden and making a terrible mess of things and then our milk cow up and dying a'sudden like, it's been just one thing after the other. Pa says if we can just make it through this winter, things'll be better come spring." She finally paused to take a breath. "Folks have been real nice, but Pa don't like taking no charity."

It was worse than she'd heard. The family really did need help.

Hannah apparently mistook her silence for hesitation. "There's no need to pay me with cash money," the girl said. "I can work for vittles to bring home for the table, if you rather."

Cora Beth wondered just how sparse the meals had been at the Thatcher place. There were seven other children in that family, ranging from three years old to Hannah here at sixteen.

"I'll tell you what," she said. "Today is laundry day. Why don't you work with me here today and then we'll see whether we want to make it a permanent arrangement or not."

Hannah sprang from her chair as if given a reprieve. "Yes, ma'am. I promise I'll do you a fine job."

The girl was as good as her word. She was a hard worker, taking direction well and never complaining. She was also surprisingly good company. After she got over her initial shyness, she chatted away about everything from the weather to the antics of her siblings.

She made friends with Scout, professing to like animals of all sorts. She tossed him the occasional stick but never let it get in the way of her work.

Once the last piece was hung on the line, Cora Beth led the way back into the kitchen. "Well, now that you've got a taste for how much work is involved in the upkeep of a boardinghouse, are you still interested in working here?"

"Oh yes, ma'am." She grinned. "That's not a whole lot more laundry than we have at my house on wash day."

"Well then, here is my proposal. I would like to have you work here five days a week. You'll be in charge of getting most of the laundry and cleaning done—I'll continue to handle the shopping and most of the cooking."

"Thank you, ma'am. I promise I'll do you a good job."

"I'm sure you will. But I'm not finished with my proposal. Your family's place is a fair piece out of town. To make things easier on both of us, I think it would be best if you take over one of the upstairs rooms and sleep here. You could, of course, go back to your home place on Friday evenings and return on Monday mornings if you like—that would be up to you since Saturdays and Sundays would be yours to do with as you please. Of course, you would take your meals with us whenever you were here. Oh, and we'll figure out a weekly wage that will be fair to both of us." She sat back and looked at Hannah expectantly. "How does all that sound?"

"It sounds mighty generous." She leaned forward, her expression hopeful. "But excuse me, did you say I could have a room here?"

"Yes. Though I'm afraid the room I have in mind isn't very big, but it's clean and well lighted."

"Oh, Mrs. Collins, with four sisters I ain't never had a room all to myself before. That sounds downright wonderful."

Cora Beth laughed. "I'm glad. But don't give me your answer just yet. I want you to go home and talk to your parents and pray about it, and we'll talk again tomorrow. And for the work you did today, would a slab of bacon and a couple of jars of peach preserves work?"

"Oh, my goodness, that's much too generous."

"Nonsense. You worked hard today, and we'll consider it a good faith offering for your folks."

"They'll be right pleased to have it."

"Now, there are a few rules we need to discuss. My boarders here expect to have their privacy respected. For that matter my family does, as well. You don't go into any of the bedchambers without knocking first. And I don't hold with gossips. You are not to speak of anything that goes on in this household to outsiders—not even your own family. Is that understood?"

She nodded hard enough to make her braid fly. "Oh yes, ma'am, Mrs. Collins. I wouldn't ever go doing anything like that, I promise."

"Good. Now then, do you have a way to get back home?"

"Pauly is doing some work for Mr. Ivers today and he has the wagon so I can ride home with him."

Cora Beth stood, intending to gather up the foodstuffs she'd promised Hannah. Before she'd crossed the room, though, Mitch appeared at the back door. He gave Scout a friendly scratch behind the ears, then came on inside. "Hi, ladies. Y'all work everything out?"

Hannah gave him a broad smile. "Oh yes, sir." Then she clasped her hands in front of her as if to contain her joy. "Mrs. Collins is going to let me have a room here all to myself."

"Is that right?"

Cora Beth smiled. "Nothing's settled yet. Hannah is going to talk to her parents tonight and get back with me in the morning."

"I'll be here bright and early."

Cora Beth laughed. "Wait until daylight." She handed the girl a sack with the bacon and produce. "And if your parents want to speak to me about our arrangements before making a decision, they are more than welcome to come by in the morning, as well."

"Yes, ma'am, I'll be sure to tell them that."

With a wave and a decided spring to her step, Hannah exited the kitchen.

"Well, what do you think? Today was laundry day, wasn't it?"

She laughed. "Okay, you were right, it was nice to have some help with that."

"So you think she'll work out? If not, you can look for someone more to your liking."

"Mitchell Hammond, you knew good and well that once I spoke to Hannah, I wouldn't be able to turn her down."

He grinned. "That thought did occur to me."

She rolled her eyes. But she was pleased—quite pleased—at how well her husband-to-be seemed to know her heart.

Chapter Eighteen

Mitch liked the way Cora Beth's eyes sparkled this morning. He was happy that his idea to hire Hannah seemed to be working out so well. Perhaps this marriage arrangement could benefit her in other ways besides allowing her to hold on to Ethan and Cissy. He liked the idea of lightening her load and making her happy.

"So, did you stop by just to check on how Hannah and I were getting along?" she asked.

"Uh, no. There was something I wanted to talk to you about. I was taking stock last night of what I needed to clear out of my place, and there's a couple of pieces I might want to bring with me."

"Of course. You're more than welcome to bring whatever you like from your place. What kind of pieces are they?"

"One is a hall stand. It's nothing fancy, but my pa made it for my mother and I kind of like it." He felt a little foolish for being sentimental over such a thing.

But Cora Beth wasn't looking at him as if she thought him foolish. "Well, of course you do. We can put it right next to the hall tree I already have in the entryway."

He tried to wave aside that idea. "Like I said, it's not very fancy—Pa wasn't much of a woodsmith, so it's okay if we just set it here by the back door or in a corner somewhere."

She shook her head indignantly. "Absolutely not." Then she grinned. "Besides, the way this family is growing, I have a feeling a second hall tree will come in handy."

Deciding not to argue further, he moved on. "The second piece is my mother's hope chest. It's a fine piece, made out of cedar and rosewood." He rubbed the back of his neck, wondering what she'd think of his idea. "I know you probably already have one of your own but I figure maybe someday one of the girls might like to have it."

Her expression softened and she touched his arm. "Oh, Mitch, what a lovely idea. I already promised my mother's to Audrey, so it would be a lovely gift for Cissy. In fact, we can bring Mother's down from the attic when you bring yours over and place them both in the girls' new room. But I warn you, we'll probably have to deal with a little jealous pouting from Pippa and Lottie."

He definitely didn't want to be responsible for something like that. "If it's gonna cause problems for you, I can—"

She laughed. "You're going to have to learn to deal with a lot worse than that if you're going to help me raise those kids." His face must have shown his momentary panic, because she sobered and smiled reassuringly. "Mitch, just because one of the kids gets to pouting is no reason to withhold something from one of the others. As these little squabbles come up we deal with them, treat them as learning opportunities, and move on. That's how kids learn to deal with the big disappointments later in life—by learning to deal with the smaller ones when they're young."

Was he really up for playing the role of father? "Sounds like there are going to be a lot of 'learning opportunities' in my future."

She patted his arm. "Don't worry, I think you'll get the hang of it soon enough." Then she crooked her finger. "Now if you have a minute, I'd like to show you how I plan to rearrange the parlor to make it into your office."

Talk about your stubborn women. "I told you that wasn't necessary. I don't need—"

"Nonsense. Every man needs a sanctuary of some sort. Consider it my wedding gift to you." She moved toward the hall, giving him no option but to follow.

As he went with her to the room in question, Mitch found himself understanding that there was a lot more to this complex woman than even he had realized.

And wouldn't it be a grand adventure getting to learn it all?

Tuesday morning, Hannah showed up right after breakfast, accompanied by her father. Once Cora Beth assured Mr. Thatcher that she had in fact offered Hannah a permanent job and a place to stay, he gave his blessing, admonished Hannah to be a good girl and work hard, then promised to return on Friday evening to pick her up and took his leave.

With Hannah on hand to do most of the chores, Cora Beth was free to work on other things.

Tuesday afternoon, she took advantage of her new-found freedom to catch up on her sewing. She already had a good start on her new dress, but finishing that and making four little-girl dresses before Saturday was a lot to tackle in a short period of time.

Deciding to take advantage of the pretty day and outdoor light, Cora Beth carried her sewing basket to the front porch and took a seat in the porch swing. Remembering the kiss she'd shared with Mitch in this very spot brought a smile to her lips and a longing to her heart. If she had her way, there'd be many more of those in her future.

She'd barely had time to make her first stitch when the front door opened and Mrs. Plunkett stepped out. "Mind if I join you?"

"Not at all. I'd enjoy the company."

Mrs. Plunkett sat in a nearby rocking chair, then eyed the yellow fabric in Cora Beth's lap. "I'm glad to see you finally had the good sense to hire someone to help you around here. The Thatcher girl seems to be a hard worker."

Cora Beth smiled. "Yes, she is. But actually, hiring her was Mitch's idea."

"Good for him. He's making a positive difference in your life already."

"Do you mind if I ask you something?" Cora Beth said impulsively.

"Not at all."

Cora Beth paused a moment, wondering if she should have acted on that impulse. Well, she'd already opened the door, might as well go through it. "Did you know Mitch's grandmother very well?"

"Opal Todd? I knew her, though I'm not sure I'd say

I knew her well. It was hard to get to know that one, especially in her later years."

"Can you tell me about her?" She met the woman's gaze head-on. "I promise I'm not just indulging in idle gossip. I'd like to learn a little more about the woman who raised Mitch."

Mrs. Plunkett nodded. "Opal was about six years older than me so we didn't spend a lot of time together growing up—six years difference can seem a pretty wide gap at that age. But I do remember her wedding. She married Jasper Todd, one of the handsomest men around at that time." She smiled at Cora Beth. "Mitch favors him a bit."

Then she turned serious again. "Anyway, I'm afraid things didn't work out well for them. Rumor had it that Opal was jealous more than was warranted and that Jasper was not the most understanding of men. Whatever the case, by the time Mitch's mama was nearing school age, Jasper decided to head out and try his luck in the California gold fields. He promised to send for Opal and little Rebecca when he was settled in, but that never happened."

"Did she ever find out what happened to him?"

"Not that I know of."

"How awful. That must have been very hard on her."

"It turned her into a bitter old woman. She cut off ties with just about everyone and kept to herself mostly. Just came into town to do her marketing and to attend church services. It's a wonder Rebecca and Mitch turned out as well as they did."

Poor Mitch. It was no wonder he didn't believe he could love someone—it seemed he'd grown up in a home where very little love existed.

Well, somehow Dinah had gotten through to him. And, God willing, she would, too.

The rest of the week passed in a blur. Josie popped in every morning after dropping off Viola at school. She helped with the sewing, handling the simple but time-consuming things like hemming, and leaving the more complex construction to her sister. She also informed Cora Beth that she planned to arrive bright and early on Saturday morning to help her get ready because "that's what sisters do."

On Wednesday, Cora Beth considered skipping the Ladies' Auxiliary meeting, but decided at the last minute not to, especially since Sadie was hosting this week.

On Thursday, it rained, and she saw Uncle Grover and Mrs. Plunkett bent over a chessboard in the parlor. Apparently they had found a common interest that they could indulge indoors.

And every evening she had Mitch's visits to look forward to. He usually arrived thirty minutes before suppertime and stayed until the dishes were done. He'd started moving some of his things into the house, as well. She went into the downstairs bedroom Thursday morning to add a starched cloth to the top of his dresser and paused on the threshold. It felt strange going inside now, almost as if she were intruding on him.

She looked around as she arranged the cloth, noting the little touches he'd added here and there. A trunk now guarded the foot of the bed. An old wooden chair with a leather seat sat in a corner, a pair of boots against the wall nearby. A leather-bound bible sat on the bedside table.

Nothing fancy, just serviceable, sturdy, honed furnishings. Like the man himself.

* * *

Mitch was a little late arriving at his office Friday morning. Not that he'd overslept. He'd moved the last of things, barring a few personal items, to the boardinghouse bright and early and stayed to have breakfast. Hard to believe that starting tomorrow that would be his home full-time.

Whistling, he locked up his desk and prepared to make his morning rounds. But before he could make his escape, the door opened and in walked Nelda Oglesby. And she didn't look happy.

"Sheriff Hammond," she said without preamble, "I demand that you do something about that boy."

Mitch swallowed a groan. Nelda's complaints were getting to be routine, which was not a good thing. "What seems to be the problem?"

She drew herself up. "My greenhouse has been ransacked again. It is an utter mess in there."

Again? Why in the world would anyone keep breaking into that place? Unless it was just to torment Nelda. "Was anything taken?"

"Not that I could tell, but that's not the point. And this is after I padlocked the door."

Padlock? Mitch remembered something Ethan had said about the time he slipped in and took the orchid for Cissy. Could it be… "Was the padlock broken?" he asked.

Nelda seemed unprepared for the question. "Why, no, I don't believe it was."

He reached for his hat. "If you don't mind, I'd like to have a look around the place."

She gave an approving nod. "Of course. I'm glad to see you're finally taking this seriously. Perhaps the sight of all that destruction will convince you of the severity of the crime."

Mitch kept his thoughts on *that* topic to himself. He merely opened the door and let her precede him out to the sidewalk.

Fifteen minutes later he was stooped down, examining the rich black soil that had spilled on the greenhouse floor.

"Do you see what I mean?" Nelda demanded. "This is pure spite and meanness."

Mitch didn't bother to look up. "I'm not so certain of that. It may just be clumsiness."

"Clumsiness? Sheriff, if you're not going to take this seriously after all—"

"Oh, I assure you I'm taking it very seriously." He stood and slowly made his way across the loam-scented building, keeping his eyes on the tracks in the debris.

"Whatever are you doing?"

"Trying to figure out where your late-night visitor entered from since he didn't come in the locked door."

"Oh." She seemed to think about that a moment. "Do you think he broke one of the glass panels?"

"Possibly, but more than likely he took advantage of a hole that was already there." He reached the far wall where a low table containing a number of pots and garden implements stood. He stooped and smiled. "There it is, the hole your intruder used to get in."

Nelda bent over and frowned. "But that's not big enough for a toddler to get through. Surely you're not trying to suggest a mere tot did this?"

"Of course not. Your intruder is a raccoon." He hated to admit it but he took some pleasure in making that announcement.

"A raccoon! But—"

"See these tracks here in the soil? They were made by a raccoon—a fairly large one, by the looks of it. And I remember Ethan mentioning he saw one in here the morning he took your orchid. He figured the critter followed him in but I'm guessing it was already inside when he arrived. No doubt that animal has been foraging around for any tasty bulbs and other morsels he could find."

She looked around fearfully. "Do you think he's still in here?"

"I doubt it. But you might want to ask the mayor to patch up that hole as soon as possible. Once that's taken care of, I don't think you'll need to worry about this sort of problem again." He dusted the dirt from his hands. "Now if you'll excuse me, I have rounds to make."

He tipped his hat and left, amused to see Nelda scurrying quickly after him. As soon as she was outside she slammed the door shut and replaced the padlock.

It would be interesting to see if Nelda shared the information about the raccoon as widely as she had the accusations against Ethan.

He would make certain, though, that everyone at the boardinghouse knew the whole story. Perhaps it would help ease some of the tension between Danny and Ethan. And even if it didn't, they were his family and they deserved to know.

His family—that had a nice ring to it.

Cora Beth sat on the porch swing, sewing. She just had a little more work to do on Pippa's dress and then everything would be ready for tomorrow.

Tomorrow. Her wedding day.

A smile crossed her lips every time she thought of it.

A welcoming bark from Scout let her know she had visitors. Looking up she saw Mitch and Ethan heading up the walk, with Mitch carrying a toolbox.

"Well, hello, you two. What are you up to?"

"Today is Ethan's last day of work for me, so I thought, rather than sweeping out my office again, I get him to doing something more meaningful."

"Such as?"

"Such as seeing what we could do about those porch rails you mentioned."

Goodness, he remembered that casual reference she'd made two weeks ago. "It's those three slats over near the end," she said pointing. "They're pretty loose and I think at least one of them is rotted off near the bottom."

"We'll have a look. I was thinking maybe Danny could lend a hand, too. You know where he might be?"

She nodded. "He's in the kitchen, working on his lessons. Want me to fetch him?"

"No need. I know the way." He turned to Ethan. "I'll be right back."

After he'd stepped inside, Cora Beth went back to stitching. "So your two weeks are up, are they?"

"Yes, ma'am."

"You going to miss working at the sheriff's office?"

He shrugged. "Sheriff Hammond was a fair boss."

"You know what else this means, don't you?"

"Ma'am?"

Had he forgotten why he was working for Mitch? "Now that you've worked the two weeks, that locket of your mother's is yours, free and clear. Do you think Cissy would like to wear it to the wedding tomorrow?"

He gave her a broad grin—for once, there were no

tinges of shadow. "Yes, ma'am, I think she'd be right proud to."

"Good. Then I'll fetch it for you to give to her as soon as you finish your work here."

The door opened and Mitch stepped out, followed by Danny. As soon as Danny caught sight of Ethan, he paused and his expression closed off. If Mitch noticed, he chose to ignore it.

"Okay, boys," he said, "while I take a look at these three slats, why don't you check out the rest of them to make sure we fix all of the problems at one time. Make sure you give 'em a tug to check for snug fits."

Both boys nodded, but Cora Beth noticed they stayed as far apart as possible while they worked.

Mitch, however, didn't seem to be paying any attention at all to the boys. "I think these two here just need another nail or two to secure them," he said cheerfully, "but you're right, this other one is going to need replacing."

"Is that a problem?" she asked.

"Not at all. I just need to get a piece of wood cut to fit and painted up to match. I'll take care of it early next week." He pulled a hammer and a couple nails out of his toolbox. "By the way, I got another visit from Nelda Oglesby this morning."

"Oh?" She could sense both boys' ears prick up.

Mitch positioned a nail against one of the slats and gave it a good whack. "Yep. Seems like she found signs of another intruder in her greenhouse." He kept his focus on the handiwork, seeming to merely be indulging in a bit of small talk to pass the time.

But there was an almost physical wave of tension coming from the boys.

"Odd thing was," Mitch continued, "she'd padlocked the door and the lock was still intact."

"That is odd." Cora Beth trusted Mitch. He obviously had a good reason for bringing this up here, in front of Ethan and Danny. "Did you find out how it was done?"

"Sure did." He gave the nail another whack, still not looking up. "Seems a raccoon has been getting in through a small hole in one of her panels."

"A raccoon!" It was all Cora Beth could do to keep from looking at the boys, but she managed to restrain herself.

"Uh-huh. That's why nothing had gone missing. The critter was just rummaging around for whatever tasty morsels he could find."

"Well now, doesn't that beat all. I imagine Nelda was surprised."

Mitch grabbed another nail. "Very. I don't think there'll be any more reports of break-ins to her greenhouse." Finishing with his handiwork, he finally straightened and looked at Ethan and Danny. "How we doing? Find any slats that need repair?"

As Mitch moved to examine the slats the boys wanted to show him, Cora Beth went back to her sewing. He'd delivered the news of Nelda Oglesby's intruder with just the right touch. The boys had heard the story, understood the implications and been left to draw their own conclusions. She couldn't have handled it better herself.

Yes, Mitch was going to make a very good father to these kids indeed.

Chapter Nineteen

Her wedding day dawned bright and beautiful. The crispness of early fall was in the air and from her bedroom window Cora Beth could see that several of the trees were just starting to turn lovely shades of yellow and orange.

"You make a beautiful bride." Josie stood behind her, fussily tying the sash of her dress. "I just wish Ma and Pa were still around to see this."

Cora Beth looked over her shoulder. "I have you here, and I like to think they're watching."

Josie gave Cora Beth's sash one last pat. "There— perfect." She stepped back and made a twirling motion with her hand. Cora Beth complied.

"Perfect," Josie repeated. "That color suits you. Mitch won't be able to take his eyes off of you."

"He's the one who picked out the fabric." She smiled, remembering their playacting in the mercantile that day.

"Did he now?" Josie gave her an amused look. "I always had a feeling you and Mitch would end up to-gether. Truth to tell, I'm surprised it took this long."

That pulled Cora Beth up short. It was one thing for

her to daydream, but she didn't want to mislead anyone. "You do remember that this is not a love match, don't you?"

"Oh, fiddlesticks." Josie smoothed her own dress. "You can't tell me you don't love that man. It's there in your eyes every time you look at him."

Did Mitch see it, too? Well, trying to deny that she loved him would be a lie, so she didn't. "It takes *two* people in love to make a love match."

"It's plain as day that man cares for you, whether he admits it or not. Just look at how he came to your rescue when you needed him most. How much more romantic can a man be?"

If only that were true. "You have it all wrong. He made it quite clear that he did this for the children, not for me. He's formed quite an attachment to them— Cissy especially."

Josie shook her head stubbornly. "She's not the only one he's formed an attachment to. You can't tell me there's not something there when you two are together. It's sure as Sunday obvious to everyone else."

"Think what you will, just don't go trying to make this something it's not. I'd like to think maybe it'll grow into something more, someday, but for now, it is what it is. In fact, Mitch went to great pains to let me know that he prefers it this way." She took a deep breath before delivering the argument clincher. "He plans to set up in the downstairs room."

"Oh." Josie was silent for a long moment. Then she gave Cora Beth a smile. "I predict that, before Christmas, that situation will most definitely change."

Cora Beth felt her cheeks grow warm and Josie laughed. Then her sister took pity on her and changed the subject as she reached for the bouquet of flowers sitting on Cora Beth's bed. "Now, Sadie sent over these flowers from her own garden—she and Penny arranged them together. She sends her love and says not to worry, Mrs. Dauber has the reception well in hand."

Sadie had insisted on hosting a reception for them immediately after the ceremony, complete with a light meal for whomever cared to attend. She declared that there was no way she'd let Cora Beth go home and tend to her own meal on her wedding day, new servant or not.

Josie handed her the flowers, then slid her arm through the crook of Cora Beth's elbow. "Now, everyone's waiting. Are you ready to get yourself over to the church and become Mrs. Mitchell Hammond?"

Was she? Cora Beth stared at her reflection in the vanity mirror across the room. Oh yes, she was most definitely ready.

Fifteen minutes later she stood in the back of the church, alone except for Uncle Grover and Honoria Plunkett, who stood ready to throw open the sanctuary doors for them at their signal.

Cora Beth adjusted Uncle Grover's bow tie. Then she paused. He was *Phillip's* Uncle Grover. How did he feel about her marrying again? "You know, it means the world to me to have you walk me down the aisle."

He beamed fondly at her. "It's my honor, my dear. You know you are like a daughter to me."

She gave the tie a final tug, then laid her hand lightly against his chest. "I hope you realize that this doesn't in any way diminish the love I had for Phillip."

He gave her hand a pat. "My dear, what you and Phillip had was very good, very good indeed. It was obvious how much you loved each other. You made him very happy during the time you had together, and the two of you produced three very precious children. Nothing can diminish that."

He held her gaze steadily. "But he's gone now and I know in my heart he'd want to see you get on with your life." He gave her hand a squeeze. "Be happy, my dear. Feel free to find joy in this new chapter of your life."

Cora Beth gave him a tight hug as she felt the sting of tears. She hadn't realized how very much she'd needed to hear those words. "Thank you," she whispered.

But it wouldn't do to walk down the aisle with red eyes. So she swallowed hard, thought of Mitch, and let the joy of her wedding day fill her heart.

"Ready?" he asked as she stepped back.

Straightening, she nodded. He offered her his arm, nodded to Honoria to open the door, and the organ began to play. Taking a deep breath, Cora Beth gave his arm a light squeeze and together they started down the aisle.

Mitch watched Cora Beth approach on the arm of her Uncle Grover. The realization that her beaming smile and luminous eyes were directed solely at him, that from this hour forward she would be his lawfully wedded wife nearly drove him to his knees.

Mitch stood there waiting on her, a proud smile on his face.

Thank You, God for giving me this opportunity to find some of the happiness I thought beyond my reach. Please give me the strength to not try to greedily grasp for more, to honor my commitment to her and to always be worthy of the trust she is putting in me here today.

When she reached the front of the church and Uncle

Grover transferred her hand to his arm, he felt ten feet tall. Then, staring into her eyes and seeing the look of happiness and trust there, he was humbled all over again.

The ceremony itself seemed to take forever and at the same time sped by. He barely took his gaze from hers the entire time. Before he knew it, they were repeating their vows and he was slipping his mother's gold wedding band on her finger.

When Reverend Ludlow informed him that he could kiss his bride, Mitch cupped her face in his hands and gently touched his lips to hers. It was all he could do to keep it short and chaste, but he was afraid if he did anything else, he'd once more get lost in her sweet response.

Then the ceremony was over and the two of them were surrounded by a flock of chattering little girls all trying to talk at the same time, and a circle of beaming adults.

As they faced their well-wishers, Mitch kept a tight hold of Cora Beth's hand, letting the reality of his newly married status sink in.

He'd done it! He'd gotten married and the sky hadn't fallen and no one had been hurt by it. And though it was an in-name-only arrangement, it came complete with children and an extended family and the most wonderful woman a man could ever want by his side. It was more than he'd dreamed possible and he told himself he couldn't be happier.

That little voice in his ear that asked for more was much too faint to pay any attention to at all.

Chapter Twenty

Cora Beth felt as if her face was frozen in a smile. Not that she wasn't happy—she was beyond happy. But this was her wedding day and she wanted to spend it with her husband, not accepting the well wishes of the scores of guests attending the reception on Sadie's back lawn. To say the wedding reception was well attended was an understatement—she hoped Sadie and Eli weren't being terribly put out by hosting this.

To be honest, she was very honored and touched that so many of her friends and neighbors had shown up to wish her and Mitch well. And it wasn't as if she and Mitch had other, more exciting plans for the day.

She excused herself from the conversation with Annielou Waskom and moved toward the table holding the punch bowl, trying to avoid making contact with anyone who might want to detain her and at the same time trying to spot Mitch. Ah—there he was, talking to Eli and Ry over by the pecan tree.

Deciding the bride had a right to speak to whomever she liked on her wedding day, she altered her course. Besides, as far as she could tell, she'd spoken to every-

one here at least once. Maybe it was time to gather up
the family and head home. And how wonderful that the
family now included Mitch.

As she approached the trio, Ry noticed her first. "Ah,
here she is, the lovely Mrs. Mitchell Hammond."

Mrs. Mitchell Hammond. She rather liked the sound
of that.

Mitch kissed her forehead and linked his arm in hers.
"So how are you enjoying your reception?"

Conscious of Eli's presence, she was careful to give
a big smile. "It's a lovely gathering. I can't believe so
many folks came out for it."

Eli laughed. "Even in the short time I've been here,
I've learned that you two are the best known and best
liked folks in these parts. Watching you get married and
wishing you well on your special day is something no
one wanted to miss."

Cora Beth smiled at the compliment, but she knew
there was more to it than that. The circumstances
around their engagement had made their wedding the
town's main event.

Josie and Sadie came up just then. "Glad to find everyone together," Josie said, "so we can give you a little wedding gift."

"Oh, but that's not—"

"Hush, sister of mine, and accept your gift like a
good girl."

"That's right," Sadie added. "This being your wedding day and all, we decided the two of you needed a
little time to yourselves."

"Oh, but that's not—"

Again, her protest was cut short, this time by Sadie.
"Nonsense. Now, we know you're not wanting a hon-

eymoon trip or anything, but you can't say no to a nice little buggy ride out in the countryside all on your own."

Now that did have a nice ring to it.

"And before you mention the children, Uncle Grover and Mrs. Plunkett have agreed to see that the young'uns make it back to the boardinghouse. They even said they'll keep an eye on them until y'all get back." Sadie linked arms with her husband. "Eli has the carriage already hitched and waiting out front."

"And," Josie inserted, "since you haven't taken much time out from being sociable, I made sure there was a picnic basket slipped behind the seat. Now you two just scoot. We'll make your regrets to the remaining guests."

Mitch quirked an eyebrow at her. "Looks like we've been given our marching orders."

Cora Beth pretended to consider the matter. "It wouldn't do to turn down a gift that so much thought went in to."

Josie shook her head at them. "Enough. Just go."

Once they'd settled into the buggy, Mitch picked up the reins, then turned to her. "Where would you like to go?"

"How about we just set out toward Dogwood Hill? I know the trees aren't in bloom but it's still pretty up there."

"Your wish is my command." With a flick of the reins and click of his tongue, Mitch set the horse in motion. They rode along in silence for a while, but it was an easy, companionable silence with no pressure to break it. Cora Beth allowed the jostle of the wagon to throw her shoulder against Mitch's from time to time, enjoying the physical contact.

When they reached the top of Dogwood Hill, Mitch pulled the wagon to a stop. "How's this?"

"Perfect."

Mitch hopped down, then came around to help her do the same. He placed his hands at her waist and swung her down, holding her for an extra few moments after her feet touched the ground. As they stood there, his hands at her waist, hers at his shoulders, she found herself wishing he'd kiss her again—not a chaste, almost brotherly kiss like they'd shared a few hours ago at the wedding, but an achingly sweet, powerfully claiming kiss of the sort they'd shared in her porch swing.

To her disappointment, however, he released her and turned to the buggy. "Here's the blanket Josie packed. Why don't you find us a nice spot to set up our picnic while I tether the horse and fetch the basket?"

Feeling slightly deflated, Cora Beth smiled and did as he asked.

By the time he was finished with the horse, she had the small blanket spread across a relatively flat patch of ground that was in more sunshine than shade.

Mitch set the basket in the middle of the blanket and plopped down beside it. "Let's see what kind of goodies she packed. I'm suddenly famished."

As Cora Beth started laying out the much-too-abundant foodstuffs, she suddenly sat back on her heels. "I just remembered, tomorrow is first Sunday."

This past summer Reverend Ludlow had implemented a new tradition among their congregation. The first Sunday of every month, weather permitting, everyone would gather for a picnic on the church grounds after the service. It had been a great success from the start. Nothing like a shared meal out in the sunshine to bring folks closer together.

Mitch grinned. "I think I can handle that. Nothing wrong with having picnics two days running. In fact a man could get used to that kind of bounty."

The meal was delicious, the conversation between them light and easy, and totally inconsequential. They laughed together over the antics of the squirrels in the trees and over nothing at all.

Hunger satisfied, Cora Beth leaned back on one arm. "Remind me to thank my scheming sister and equally scheming friend. This was a marvelous idea."

"I agree." Mitch lounged on one elbow. "I was feeling a bit hemmed in and crowded there at the reception."

Cora Beth laughed. "Sounds like a man used to living alone. You do realize it's not exactly a small household you've just made yourself a part of, don't you?"

"I think I can live with that."

A sudden gust of wind blew a leaf into Cora Beth's hair. Before she could remove it, Mitch sat up and scooted closer. "Here, allow me." He plucked the leaf from her hair, then teasingly wrapped a tendril around his finger. "Soft as thistledown," he mused.

Suddenly, their gazes locked and the very air around them seem charged, ready to crackle at the slightest movement from either of them. She heard his breath quicken, saw his gaze move to her lips.

Cora Beth held her breath, willing him to kiss her the way she'd wanted to be kissed all morning.

His hand swept the hair from her temple. "You know," he said huskily, "we made an important commitment today. I think maybe that kiss I gave you during the ceremony didn't quite live up to the seriousness of the occasion. Mind if I give it another shot?"

She lifted her hand to his face and stroked his faintly stubbly jawline. "I think that would be an absolutely marvelous idea."

The kiss, when it came, was everything she had longed for. He tasted of apple cider and lemon drops. The feel of his hands at the back of her neck—warm, strong, supportive—played a perfect counterpoint to the urgency of his mouth over hers. It felt so wonderful to be in his arms this way, to feel the beating of his heart against her own, to know that he wanted her with him every bit as much as she wanted him with her.

Finally he pulled away, but this time it was no abrupt withdrawal, no sudden distancing of himself. He simply gave her a smile, stroked her cheek gently with the back of his hand, and pulled her against him so she rested in the crook of his arm. "*Now* our wedding vows are properly sealed," he said with satisfaction.

Did he realize how much he'd revealed in that kiss? Was now the time to let him know how she felt? Or would it just spoil the moment?

Saying a quick prayer that she could find the right words, Cora Beth took the plunge before she lost her courage. "About our marriage arrangement, I think you ought to know that I've changed the terms."

"What do you mean?" There was more than just a question in his tone—there was caution, as well.

"I know we promised to keep it businesslike, but I can't do that." She turned in his hold so that she was facing him. "I love you, Mitch. I know you say you can't love me, but I hope in time perhaps you can learn to."

"Stop." He gave her shoulder a warning squeeze. "Don't ruin this."

"Ruin this? But—"

He pulled away, his expression hardening. "I mean it, Cora Beth—you're mistaken, you don't love me. I'm sorry if that kiss gave you the wrong impression but we're good friends, that's all. And that's all we're ever going to be."

Why was he so afraid of accepting her love? "Mitch, it's okay if you don't love me, but you're going to have to accept that I love you. I know your grandmother wasn't the most loving of examples, but that doesn't mean you aren't lovable. Trust me."

"My grandmother—" He swallowed whatever he'd been about to say under a bitter laugh. "You don't understand."

"Then tell me. Help me to understand."

He stood and jammed his hands in his pockets. "I made a vow a long time ago that I would never, ever get married. The *only* reason I broke that vow now was because we agreed to keep love out of it."

What a terrible promise to have to live with. "A long time ago? You mean after Dinah died."

"Yes." He frowned down at her, his frustration evident. "But not for the reason you think."

What was she supposed to think if he wouldn't explain himself? She stood so she faced him more directly. "Mitch, I still haven't heard an explanation—just more nonsensical assertions."

He stared at her a moment, then sighed and raked a hand through his hair. "All right. I guess you deserve the whole story." He picked up a small broken branch from the ground and started stripping leaves from it.

"According to my grandmother, my grandfather was the great love of her life. Her whole world centered around him when she was younger. And she swore that, in the beginning, he loved her just as deeply." He sent her a probing look. "I guess you know he eventually abandoned her and my mother when Ma was just a little kid."

Cora Beth nodded and he continued. "Well, since she figured *she* hadn't changed, then it had to be something else that turned him from her, caused him to abandon them so abruptly."

"I can see where she'd want to believe that."

He yanked another leaf from the branch. "What you probably didn't know is that apparently my grandfather's father did the same to his wife. Up and abandoned her with two little kids to care for. Though I take it there were some other unsavory actions laid at his door, as well."

He broke the stick in half and tossed it away. "Anyway, the whole time I was growing up, my grandmother swore it was something in the Todd men's blood, that they were bound to turn from those who loved them, no matter how deep their love might run in the beginning."

How could a woman say that to her own grandson? She put her hand on his arm. "Mitch, that's ridiculous. Such things aren't passed down from father to son."

Seeing the stubborn set of his jaw, she lifted her chin. "And even if they were, you're *not* a Todd, you're a Hammond, and I never heard tell of your father doing anything so dreadful to your mother."

He nodded, but there was resignation in the gesture. "That's what I kept telling Granny Todd. And kept telling *myself.* I was certain, no matter what she said, that I would never, ever do that to the woman I loved."

His jaw worked for a moment, then stilled. "I look quite a bit like my grandfather Todd, you know. Of course, I never met the man, but grandmother had a tin-type of him up on the mantle. She would tell me over and over that if I was like him on the outside, chances were I'd be like him on the inside. There were days when I wanted to fling that picture into the fireplace."

Cora Beth was finding it hard to summon up forgiveness for such a woman. "Mitch, no matter what your grandmother said, no matter what kind of men your grandfather and great-grandfather were, you're *not like that.* If you truly don't have any feelings for me, consider your feelings for Dinah. I remember how hard you took her death, how devastated you were after the accident. And look at the way you've held on to her memory all these years. Surely that's proof of your ability to hold to a lasting love."

He gave another bitter laugh. "And there you've hit on the heart of my great undoing. You see, I *didn't* hold true to that love. Those last few weeks before our wedding day, I found my feelings for Dinah changing, starting to cool. Oh, I still liked her well enough, I just couldn't see spending the rest of my life with her. It was my worst nightmare—my grandmother's predictions coming true."

Her heart went out to the young man he'd been, faced with so terrible a prospect and no family or close friend to turn to. "Oh, Mitch, I'm so sorry. But that's still not—"

He held up a hand to stop her. "Here's the really funny part. When I realized what was happening, I prayed about it. Prayed harder than I've ever prayed about anything before or since. I prayed that God would help me to feel that love again or, barring that, to help me find a way out of my commitment to Dinah without breaking her heart. And you remember how He answered me, don't you? Four days before the wedding she trips and breaks her neck. Just like that—" he snapped his fingers "—problem solved."

Cora Beth thought her heart would break as he revealed that final bit of his terrible burden. A burden he'd shouldered so unnecessarily. "You are *not* responsible for Dinah's accident. God doesn't work that way. God didn't plan that accident in answer to your prayers."

"That's exactly how it looked from where I stood."

"Then you were standing in the wrong place."

He touched her cheek, then pulled his hand back as if it had been burned. "Ever the stalwart defender of the downtrodden." A small tic near the left corner of his mouth jumped once, twice, and then was still. "If you're worried about my spiritual well-being, don't be. My faith isn't shaken. I still believe in God, I still believe that He is the Great Creator, the Sovereign, the One who loves us above all others."

He drew his shoulders back. "I simply believe, also, that He chose this method to show me the truth of who I am, to help me to make the difficult decision I had to make. I also thought, maybe wrongly, that this marriage arrangement with you was God-sent, that He was providing a means for me to have a small piece of the family life I wanted, without anyone getting hurt. Maybe I was wrong about that, too. Maybe this marriage idea came from my own selfish desires and isn't of God at all."

She wanted to stomp her feet at him, to shake him until his teeth rattled, to make him *really* listen to her.

"Mitch, for goodness' sake, listen to yourself. Saying God caused Dinah to die so He could teach you a lesson is the same as saying God abandoned Ethan and Cissy to Titus's cruelty because He wanted to teach *them* a lesson."

She took a deep breath and softened her voice. "Yes, bad things happen, and yes, God can use those things to teach us, to do His work, to eventually bring good to us or others, but He is never deliberately cruel to us. A loving God just doesn't do things that way."

"Apparently we see things differently."

"Mitch, you didn't force God's hand. Prayer is good, of course, and prayer is an effective means of communication and petition, but prayer doesn't change God. He doesn't grant us our heart's desire on a whim, and He never goes contrary to His own perfect will. His will *always* prevails, is always perfect, whether we understand it or not. Don't you see, by accepting blame for Dinah's death, you're claiming a power over God that you just don't have?"

He didn't say anything for a long moment. Other sounds seemed to be magnified—the sound of the horse chomping at the grass, the hum of insects, the trill of a bird.

And, as his expression closed off completely, the wrenching sound of her heart breaking.

Mitch stooped down and began stuffing things into the hamper. "I think we're both too tired to continue this discussion right now. Why don't we head back to town?"

It was all Cora Beth could do to keep tears of helplessness and frustration from flowing down her face.

Chapter Twenty-One

Cora Beth got very little sleep that night. Her mind kept going back to that conversation with Mitch, torturing her with things she should have said, arguments she should have made to help show Mitch how skewed his thinking was.

What a terrible burden for him to have lived with all these years—to believe not only that he was destined to eventually betray any woman he dared to love, but that he was responsible for Dinah's death. How had he borne it? And, more importantly, how could she help him see how very, very wrong those two deeply ingrained beliefs were?

From the looks of Mitch the next morning, it seemed he hadn't slept well, either. Oh, his smile was as friendly as ever, and he chatted easily with the girls, but she saw the weariness in his eyes and the way he avoided meeting her gaze.

Even the day seemed tired and weary. While it didn't appear that rain was imminent, the sky was shrouded in clouds and the air had a damp feel to it. Not the best of weather for a picnic, but maybe the day would improve as the sun had more time to do its work.

Danny was the first of the kids downstairs, already dressed in his Sunday best. "Don't forget it's first Sunday."

Was he thinking about spending time with Odine? "Don't worry, the picnic hamper's already packed."

Mitch was effortlessly drawn into their Sunday morning routine—almost as if he'd always been a part of it. He was even recruited by Audrey to help tie a hair ribbon when Cora Beth was occupied making sure Lottie got her shoes on the right feet.

They walked to church, Mitch carrying the big hamper, Cora Beth carrying a smaller basket, and the children between them.

And during that walk, all she could think about was how to set matters right between them. The problem was, she didn't want things to go back to the way they were before. She wanted a true marriage. And now that she knew what stood in the way of that, she was more determined than ever to break down those barriers.

During the church service, she found herself having trouble focusing on Reverend Ludlow's sermon. Finally, she bowed her head.

Heavenly Father, please forgive me for my wayward thoughts, but I am so heartbroken and need Your comfort and Your guidance. Thank You for showing me what is in Mitch's heart and what is walling him off from ever finding fulfillment and the love You intended for him to have. Now please, please, help me find a way to get through to him, to shatter that horrid wall and set the true Mitch free.

Raising her eyes again, she did feel a measure of peace that had been missing before. Settling more comfortably in her pew, she determinedly focused her attention on Reverend Ludlow's words.

* * *

As soon as Mitch stepped outside after the church service, he excused himself from Cora Beth and went to help the other men set up the picnic tables. The busier he kept, the better. He'd been doing entirely too much brooding since he and Cora Beth had left their private picnic yesterday afternoon.

Cora Beth's admonishments kept rattling around in his mind, refusing to leave him in peace.

Sawhorses and long boards were pulled from the back of a number of wagons and quickly converted into sturdy tables. As quickly as they were set up, the women would cover them with colorful cloths and begin to lay out the food. The meal was a community event with folks free to sample whatever items struck their fancy.

Blankets and quilts were spread out on the ground with lots of good-natured jostling for the prime spots. It wasn't long before the churchyard looked like one big, colorful, crazy quilt, with wide swaths of uncovered grass to form the green outline for the individual pieces.

While the adults visited and got everything ready, the children were left to run around and play with friends amid admonishments to not go very far off and to not ruin their Sunday clothes.

Mitch crossed the church lawn, greeting longtime neighbors and friends, but not pausing for long with any one group. He was looking for Cora Beth. Before, he'd always been a bit of a tumbleweed at these events, moving from spot to spot, receiving invitations to join this group or that, always careful not to pay too much attention to any one family. It felt good to know that this time he had a place where he belonged, a family who waited on him to complete their group.

He finally found Cora Beth. She'd spread two blankets side by side toward the back of the church property. He noticed the Oglesby family was close by. Had Danny and Odine orchestrated this or was it just coincidence?

She greeted him with a warm smile and he felt himself relaxing. They could get past their argument. She knew the worst about him now and didn't seem to hold it against him.

"There you are," she said. "I hope this spot is all right. It's not too crowded on this end of the grounds so I thought it would give our group a chance to spread out a bit."

"Looks fine to me. I saw one of the hands from Ry and Josie's place. He said to tell you they're not here because Josie's a little under the weather but it's nothing to get concerned about."

"I wondered when I didn't see the three of them. I figured it might be morning sickness kicking in."

For just a moment, Mitch allowed himself to think about what it might be like to have Cora Beth carrying his child. Then he ruthlessly wiped that thought from his mind. "I think all the food's set up and ready to serve." His voice was surprisingly steady. "You ready to fix a plate? I saw Suellen brought some of her corn fritters and I want to grab one before they're all gone."

She handed Mitch and the twins each a plate. "If you don't mind, you help Pippa and I'll help Lottie serve their plates." She glanced toward the large oak where several of the older children were gathered. "Danny, come get your plate." Then she looked around. "Now where did those other three get off to?"

"Don't worry, they won't have gone far." Mitch waved to the dozens of children chasing each other in the open area near the church building. "And they know the rules, first come, first served. Those corn fritters won't last forever."

She laughed. "Audrey understands that, but I guess Ethan and Cissy may just learn the hard way."

"It won't take but one time for them to learn."

Mitch found himself enjoying helping Pippa fill her plate, even when she spilled half of it and they had to go back through the line again. It felt good to have the girl look up to him, to trust him to help her make choices, and to take his hand when she needed help navigating the rough ground. Finally their plates were filled and the four of them headed back to the blanket. Danny had disappeared among the food tables early on.

"I still haven't seen Audrey, Cissy and Ethan," Cora Beth said worriedly.

"They're probably at the food tables by now," Mitch answered. "But I tell you what, I'll get you three ladies settled on the blankets and then I'll go look for them." He raised a brow at Pippa. "That is, if I can trust you to guard my plate until I get back."

Pippa giggled then nodded.

Mitch, Cora Beth and the twins had just reached the right pair of blankets near the Olgesby family when a muddy and soaking wet little girl came running to them from the far side of the field, crying hysterically.

Nelda scrambled up and rushed forward, her husband right behind her. "Loretta? What's the matter, what happened to you? Did someone push you in the water?"

"I f-f-fell." The girl pulled out of her mother's grasp and ran over to Mitch. "You gotta help them. The water's getting higher."

Mitch, his pulse quickening, handed his plate to Cora Beth and placed a hand on the girl's shoulder. "Help who,

Loretta?" But he feared he knew the answer already as he scanned the crowd, still unable to see his three.

"Audrey and Ethan."

He heard Cora Beth's quick intake of breath, felt his own heart thudding. But he had to keep his wits about him. "Where are they?"

"The ground just fell out from under us and we were falling and—" Her teeth were chattering so hard she could barely talk.

Resisting the urge to shake the answers from her, he asked again, "Where are they, Loretta?"

She pointed over her shoulder. "Over by the far corner of the Clowsen place."

Mitch took off at a run. Three agonizingly long minutes later he spotted Cissy, flat on the ground, peering into a large opening.

As soon as she spotted him, Cissy scrambled to her feet and he saw the tears streaming down her face. "Help them!" she screamed. "Help them get out of there!"

He took one look inside the hole and his insides turned to ice. The hole appeared to be about eight feet deep and six feet across. There was water inside, lots of water. It was up to Ethan's neck and it was obvious it was still rising. But the boy was gamely holding on to an unconscious Audrey, trying to keep her head above the water, as well.

"Hold on, Ethan, I'm coming in." Mitch eased over the edge and slid into the hole, doing his best not to splash or swamp them. The water was freezing cold—no wonder their lips were blue. As soon as he took Audrey, Ethan slumped and began to tremble. The boy was exhausted.

"She's hurt," Ethan said through chattering teeth. "I think she hit her head when she fell in."

By this time several other folks had gathered at the mouth of the hole, sending clods of dirt and grass tumbling into the water.

"Careful up there," Mitch called out. "I'm not sure how stable the ground around this hole is."

"You heard the man, everyone but you and you, get back," he heard Eli say.

"Eli, help Ethan out of here before the water gets over his head."

Was Cora Beth nearby? He'd rather not scare her but there was no help for it. "Audrey's hurt. You'll need to fix up a sling to haul us both out with."

He heard some muffled conversation from the crowd above and then Eli's face and shoulders appeared above the hole at ground level. He dangled his suit coat over the edge. "Here, Ethan, grab hold of the sleeve and we'll pull you out." Eli glanced at Audrey, then looked at Mitch with a worried frown. "Doc Whitman is right here and Horace is fetching a rope from his wagon. We'll have you out of there in no time." Then, with a grunt, he focused on pulling Ethan out.

Mitch stared down into the face of the much-too-pale, much-too-still Audrey, then cradled her snug against his chest. This normally vibrant chatterbox, this bright, mischievous, curious child, his sweet pea—she couldn't be extinguished this way.

Dear God, please, please, don't take this little girl, not yet, not like this. It would drive a stake through her mama's heart.

He swallowed hard against the thickness in his throat. *And even if Cora Beth is strong enough to withstand such a loss, I don't think I am.*

Ten eternally long minutes later Mitch was back on

solid ground, seated on the edge of the pit, his precious burden still cradled in his arms. He allowed Eli to take the child from his nearly numb arms and watched him place her on a blanket at Doc Whitman's feet. She hadn't wakened, hadn't stirred, hadn't made a sound.

Someone offered him a hand and he stood, scanning the crowd. A heartbeat later, he stepped toward the blanket where Audrey lay and caught Cora Beth as she tried to get to her injured daughter. "Let the doctor do his job," he said gently.

With a sob, she threw herself in his arms. He stood there, holding her close, stroking her back, sharing her worry and fears, praying with all his might that Audrey would be okay.

Someone threw a blanket over his shoulder and he was vaguely aware that the rest of the family stood nearby, but his whole world had narrowed down to Cora Beth and the still, small form on the blanket.

When Doc Whitman finally straightened, both he and Cora Beth braced themselves and he kept a tight hold of her shoulder. Whether it was to support her or himself, he wasn't certain.

"She's got quite a knot on her head."

"Is she going to be all right?"

"I wish I could tell you yes, but I'm afraid it's too early to tell. More than likely she has a concussion. Best thing right now is to get her home, get her into some dry clothes and into a warm bed, and keep a close eye on her." He eyed them both sympathetically. "I'm afraid the rest is up to the Good Lord."

Chapter Twenty-Two

Mitch stepped onto the front porch and pulled his shoulders back, trying to get the kinks out of his muscles.

It had been nearly six hours since they'd pulled Audrey from that hole and her condition was still unchanged. He leaned his elbows on the porch rail, clasping his hands in front of him.

He tried to take comfort in the fact that at least she hadn't gotten any worse. But that was cold comfort indeed.

Scout padded up and lay at his feet, muzzle to the ground. "You're worried, too, aren't you, boy?"

A few minutes later, Ethan stepped out and joined him. "Any word on Audrey?"

"No change."

"I wish I could have gotten her out of that hole faster."

"You did all you could, Ethan. You saved her life." He slid a hand into his pocket. "I never did get a chance to ask you exactly what happened out there."

Ethan reached down to pat his dog. "I was looking

for Cissy, to tell her it was time to eat. I saw the girls heading for the tree line and went after them. Then they all just kinda disappeared and I heard 'em screaming so I took off at a run. When I reached where they'd been, there was a big ole hole in the ground with them trapped inside."

A sink hole, just like he'd figured. "So you jumped in after them?"

Ethan shrugged. "I didn't have no rope or nothing to pull them out with and Audrey looked like she was hurt and the water started seeping in pretty fast."

"How'd you get Loretta and Cissy out?"

"Loretta's the tallest, so I made her climb up on my shoulders and pull herself up. Then Cissy did the same, with Loretta's help. Then I told Loretta to stop bawling and run and get you."

"Smart kid."

"Yeah." Danny stepped out on the porch. "And pretty brave, too."

Had the boy heard the whole story?

"You would have done the same," Ethan said. "I just happened to be the one who was there when it happened."

"Yeah, well, still, they would likely have all drowned if you hadn't done what you did." Danny shoved his hands in his pockets. "Audrey would have for sure."

Then Danny pulled his shoulders back. "I want to apologize for how I've been treating you since you moved in here. I was wrong to believe all those things folks said about you. It won't happen again." He scuffed the floor with his toe, then looked up. "And you can move back into my room if you like."

Ethan grinned. "Thanks. But I kinda like it where I am."

Danny returned his grin. "Yeah, you have a pretty good setup. I mean, a whole floor to yourself, and walls that you can move whenever you want to. I gotta admit, I was just a little bit jealous when I first saw it." He nodded his head toward the door. "Hey, you want to have a look at my set of tin soldiers?"

Ethan straightened. "Sure."

With that, the two boys disappeared inside the house.

Mitch was glad to see they'd finally gotten over their differences. It was just a shame it had taken a terrible accident to accomplish it.

He pushed away from the porch rail and headed back inside, determined to see that Cora Beth took a break.

Cora Beth looked up when he walked in the room, her face pale and strained. She gave him a smile that was a weak shadow of her usual bright one. "I think maybe she's breathing just the tiniest bit better."

Mitch could detect no difference, but nodded. "That's a good sign."

"If only she'd open her eyes."

"Cora, honey, I want you to go in the kitchen and get yourself something to eat. Sadie dropped off a basket of goodies from the picnic a while ago and Hannah is here and has some good broth simmering on the stove in case we need it."

"I'm not hungry."

He took her hand. "You need to eat and you need to rest. You're not going to be any good to Audrey if you make yourself ill."

"I'll be fine." She looked up at him with swollen,

despairing eyes. "I just can't leave her, not while she's so helpless."

He pulled a chair up next to the one she was seated in and put his arm around her shoulder, cradling her against his side. "All right. If you won't leave her, then rest here. I'll keep watch and I promise to alert you if there's even the slightest change."

"Promise?"

"You have my word."

"Then maybe, just for a few minutes…" She snuggled more deeply into his arm and closed her eyes. A few minutes later, Mitch heard the soft rhythm of her breathing that signaled she'd drifted to sleep.

She was so fragile, so vulnerable, so very special to him. Holding her this way, knowing that she trusted him to see to her child, to support her faithfully while she slept, was both humbling and exhilarating. It felt as if something in his chest had expanded almost beyond his ability to contain it. There was nothing in this world he wouldn't do for her or for her children. He'd never in his life felt like this before.

That thought stopped him, gave him pause. Was that true? What about the love he'd felt for Dinah, before it had faded? He probed his memory, trying to dig through the cobwebs of the passing years and remember how that had felt back then.

And then the truth came to him, blindingly clear.

What he'd felt for Dinah was a young man's infatuation with the *idea* of love, the idea of starting a family of his own and of escaping the gloom and emptiness of life in his grandmother's household. He hadn't fallen *out* of love with her, because he'd never really been *in* love with her to start with. And somehow, he'd sensed that back then. That's why he'd pulled away from the idea of marrying her.

Could that be true? Or was he just looking for a way to justify what he was feeling now? But the more he thought about it, the more he compared those long ago feelings with what he now felt for Cora Beth, the more convinced he became.

Because with Cora Beth, he was in love with the woman—the stubborn, hardworking, amazing woman whose heart was big enough to encompass this whole mismatched, boisterous family that she had drawn to herself, including her latest acquisition—him.

There was no desire to pull back, no second guessing his plan to spend a lifetime loving her.

Dear God, thank You for showing me the truth, and for helping me to find my way to this place. I promise You I will strive every day to be worthy of this wonderful second chance at having a loving family that You have given me. And, Dear Merciful God, if it be in Your will, please bring Audrey through this and back to us. But in all things, help me to remember that Your plan for our lives, though sometimes hard to understand, is always perfect and always meant for our good.

Chapter Twenty-Three

"Cora, honey, wake up."

Cora Beth fought against the layers of cotton swaddling her, keeping her from opening her eyes. Mitch's voice had been thick with emotion. What was wrong?

Suddenly remembering, she jerked herself fully awake. "What is it? Audrey—"

"Is awake and asking for you."

She turned from Mitch's beaming face to that of her daughter, blinking up at her from the bed that was too big for her. In the space of one heartbeat to the next, Cora Beth was out of her chair and clutching her daughter to her.

"You're squeezing too hard," Audrey complained.

A bubble of laughter, part hysteria, part relief, erupted from her. "I'm so sorry, baby," She eased her hold but couldn't stop touching her. "Mama's just so happy to see that you're okay."

"My head hurts."

Mitch gave Cora Beth's hand a squeeze, then tapped Audrey's nose. "Glad to have you back with us, sweet pea."

Then he turned to Cora Beth. "I'll send for Doc Whitman."

* * *

An hour later, Doc Whitman had pronounced Audrey clearly on the mend and she was sitting up in bed, thoroughly enjoying all the attention she was getting. Cora Beth finally felt comfortable leaving her in the care of Uncle Grover while she went in search of Mitch.

She found him standing on the front porch, looking at the stars studding the evening sky.

"How's she doing?" he asked over his shoulder.

"Much better. Uncle Grover's with her." Cora Beth moved beside him and felt a little thrill of pleasure when he put his arm around her as if it were the most natural thing in the world.

Don't read too much into this, she told herself. It's been an emotional day. He'll go back to normal by morning. "We can bring her upstairs to her room if you want yours back now," she offered.

He shook his head. "No point in disturbing her right now. I can sleep in a chair for one night." He finally looked down at her and traced the line of her cheek with a finger. "You look beat. Why don't you go inside and get some sleep. I'll stay up with her tonight."

She shivered at the tingle of his touch and he pulled her back into the crook of his arm.

"I'm not sleepy yet. Maybe a little later."

They stood there quietly for a while, then she finally looked up at him. "What were you thinking about before I came out here?"

"What a lucky man I am to have been given this second chance."

"Second chance?"

He turned to face her, his smile a warm caress. "At having a family. At finding love."

"Love?"

He smiled, no doubt at her dull-witted repetitions. "I was thinking of something else, too. I was thinking it might be a good idea to add another room or two to the back of the house."

"Sheriff Lemon Drop, whatever are you talking about?"

Mitch smiled at her use of Cissy's nickname for him. "You never know when you might need to make room for another boarder. And it might be nice to have our master bedroom on the first floor where we can have a little more privacy."

It took a heartbeat for his words to sink in. Then she pulled back to eye him better. Did he mean what it sounded like he meant?

His smile turned earnest. "That is, if you'll do me the honor of tossing out this businesslike nonsense and *truly* being my wife." He took her hands. "I'm through fighting this, Cora Beth—I was the worst kind of fool to even try. I love you, love you so much that the idea of ever leaving you is so painful I'd as soon pluck out my own heart with a rusty nail. If you tell me I'm not coming to my senses too late, you'll make me the happiest man alive and I'll spend the rest of our days together trying to make you just as happy."

Cora Beth launched herself into his arms and threw her own around his neck. "Mitch Hammond, you *are* a fool. As if I could ever stop loving you. Now hush all this silly talk and kiss me like you mean it."

And, with a joyous laugh that could be heard all through the boardinghouse, he did.

* * * * *

Cheryl St.John's love of reading began as a child. She wrote her own stories, designed covers and stapled them into books. She credits many hours of creating scenarios for her paper dolls and Barbies as the start of her fascination with fictional characters. Cheryl loves hearing from readers. Visit her website at cherylstjohn.net.

Books by Cheryl St.John

Love Inspired Historical

Cowboy Creek

Want Ad Wedding

Irish Brides

The Wedding Journey

The Preacher's Wife
To Be a Mother
"Mountain Rose"
Marrying the Preacher's Daughter
Colorado Courtship
"Winter of Dreams"

Visit the Author Profile page
at Harlequin.com for more titles.

MARRYING THE PREACHER'S DAUGHTER

Cheryl St.John

And all these blessings shall come on thee, and overtake thee, if thou shalt hearken unto the voice of the Lord thy God. Blessed shalt thou be in the city, and blessed shalt thou be in the field. Blessed shall be the fruit of thy body, and the fruit of thy ground, and the fruit of thy cattle, the increase of thy kine, and the flocks of thy sheep. Blessed shall be thy basket and thy store. Blessed shalt thou be when thou comest in, and blessed shalt thou be when thou goest out.

—*Deuteronomy* 28:2–6

This story is lovingly dedicated to the readers who so patiently waited for Elisabeth's story. I appreciate you!

Chapter One

Colorado
June, 1876

"Toss your guns down now!" a male voice shouted. "Hands in the air."

Elisabeth Hart couldn't see past the layers of netting on a woman's hat in front of her, but sounds of alarm rippled through the passengers who sat in the forward rows. The interior of the railcar was sweltering beneath the midday sun, and she blotted her eyes and forehead with her lace-trimmed handkerchief. What should have been a routine stop along the tracks to take on water had become life-threatening.

Thuds sounded as firearms hit the aisle. A man in a battered hat and wearing a faded bandanna over the lower half of his face came into view. Eyes darting from person to person, he snatched up the guns.

Another masked bandit appeared in the wake of the first. Sweat drenched the front of his dusty shirt. "Turn over all your cash and jewelry. Ladies' bags, too, and none of you gets shot."

Two more thieves held open gunnysacks and gathered the looted items.

Fear prickled at Elisabeth, but a maelstrom of rebellious anger made her tremble. How dreadful of these men to point guns and make demands. Every fiber of her being objected to their lack of concern for the safety of the passengers and the downright thievery.

She turned to the tall, quiet man who'd been sitting beside her on the aisle side of the bench seat since they'd left Morning Creek, noting the way his hat brim shaded piercing green eyes. He watched the gunman with intense concentration, but made no move to stop what was happening. "Aren't you going to *do something?*" she whispered.

The man cast her a glare that would have scorched a lesser woman. One eyebrow rose and he gave an almost imperceptible shake of his head.

"They're going to rob us," she insisted. "You still have your gun. I saw it inside your jacket when you leaned to lower the window earlier."

He focused on the man wielding the revolver, but spoke to her. "Can you count, lady? Just give 'em what they want so nobody gets hurt."

"But—"

Pausing beside them, the masked robber pointed his gun directly at her seat partner's chest. The man gave Elisabeth a pointed glare and calmly raised his hands in the air before looking up.

"Right in here," the robber said.

The seated man handed him a coin purse and tossed several silver dollars and his pocket watch into the bag.

The barrel of the gun swung to Elisabeth. "Lady?"

Elisabeth's temper and sensibilities flared, but fear

kept her silent. Her heart beat so frantically, she thought her chest might burst. She wanted to refuse, but didn't want anyone to get hurt. Begrudgingly, she forfeited her black velvet chatelaine pocket with the silver handle and removed the gold bracelet she'd received for her last birthday, dropping both into the burlap sack.

The robber pointed at her neck. "You got a chain under there."

She clapped her hand protectively over the plain gold ring that rested on a chain beneath her damp and wrinkled cotton shirtwaist. "This was my mother's!"

"Just give it to him," the green-eyed stranger cajoled in his maddeningly calm manner.

"Now just wait," Elisabeth argued with a glare. "You don't understand. This was my *mother's* wedding ring."

The stranger gave her a quelling look that singed her eyelashes. Passengers called out their displeasure and shouted for her to give up her jewelry same as they had.

The ring was all she had of her mother. Since she'd drowned, Elisabeth had worn it every day…and tried to fill the woman's shoes. The wedding band symbolized Elisabeth's childhood and her sacrifices. Parting with it would break her heart…but she didn't want to be the cause of anyone getting shot. What would her father have to say in this situation?

She closed her eyes. *Do not store up for yourselves treasures on earth, where moth and rust destroy, and where thieves break in and steal.* Her true treasures were in heaven. The ring wasn't as important as the lives at stake.

The robber leaned down close as if he meant to take the ring from her neck. She raised her hand to her throat to prevent him from touching her. She could do this on her own. He grabbed Elisabeth's collar and yanked so hard that she jerked forward and the top button popped off.

In that same second, a grim click sounded. The bandit paused dead still.

Elisabeth stared into his shining dark eyes, and the moment stretched into infinity. She could hear her blood pulsing through her veins, her breath panting from between her dry lips. Was this the day she was going to die and meet her Maker?

"Take your hands off the lady, or you're dead." From beside her, the stranger's low-timbered voice was calm, but laced with lethal intent. The hair on Elisabeth's neck stood up.

No one else was privy to the robber's predicament. The green-eyed man's gun was still concealed between the two men, the business end jammed up against the robber's belly. Elisabeth dared a glance and saw the stranger's other hand clamped over the man's wrist, keeping that revolver pointed toward the floor and protectively away from her.

What could only have been seconds, but seemed like an hour, passed with their ragged breaths loud and the tick of a pocket watch encroaching on her consciousness.

"We ain't got all day, Hank!" one of the other thieves shouted.

The robber leaning over her attempted to move, and pandemonium broke loose. A shot rang out and Elisabeth's rescuer grunted in pain. The robber tugged at Elisabeth's collar, and the man beside her fired his gun.

The stench of gunpowder stung her nose. Men

shouted. Women screamed. Elisabeth watched the events unfold in a haze of fear and disbelief.

The man who'd threatened Elisabeth crumpled, slumping sideways over the back of a seat. A horrifying crimson blotch spread across his shirtfront. She covered her mouth with her hand to keep from crying out.

The stranger leaped from his seat with his arm outstretched. "Get down!" he bellowed. A rapid succession of shots nearly deafened her. She cupped her hands over her ears, belatedly realizing he'd been ordering *her* to get down. Praying for safety for the other passengers, she folded herself onto the floor and knelt with her heart pounding. The shock of seeing that man shot and bleeding stole her breath.

Minutes passed with her thoughts in chaos. Would she see her family again? If the stranger protecting her had been shot, maybe other people were being killed or injured, and all because she'd delayed. She'd been going to give him the ring.

An eerie silence followed in the wake of the previous pandemonium, and it took a few minutes to comprehend what that could mean.

The sound of hesitant footsteps and voices told her the battle was over. She opened eyes she hadn't realized were squeezed shut, unfolded her body and peered over the seat in front of her.

One of the male passengers had picked up the gunnysacks and now doled possessions back to their owners. In numb silence, she accepted her monogrammed velvet pocket and gold bracelet from his outstretched hand while her mind struggled to comprehend what was going on around her. A conductor and several other railroad men stepped over prone bodies on the floor.

The sight made her stomach lurch. Elisabeth could only stare in numb disbelief.

One of the uniformed men made his way to the stranger who was seated on a bench with his back against the side of the railcar, his hand pressed to his ribs. "Find something for bandages!"

Spurred out of her frozen state of shock, Elisabeth straightened and stepped into the aisle. She raised her hem and, holding it in her teeth, tore a wide strip from her petticoat. "Here."

Others provided handkerchiefs and scarves, and the conductor handed over the wad of material for the fellow to press against the wound. "Sit tight," he said. "We'll get you to the doctor in Jackson Springs quick as we can."

Several men dragged the robbers' bodies to the back of the car, the dead men's boot heels painting shiny streaks of blood on the wooden floor. Her stomach roiled and she thought she might be sick.

"Are you all right?"

She swung her gaze to those green eyes, now dark with pain. "Y-yes, I'm fine."

Had he killed all of those men? He made a half-hearted attempt to sit a little straighter, but grimaced and stayed where he was.

He'd probably saved her life. Without a doubt he'd saved her from losing her precious ring. She perched on the edge of the seat beside his leg, and reached to replace his hand with hers, pressing the cloth against his cream-colored shirt, where it was soaked with blood that flowed from his side. "I'm Elisabeth Hart."

"Gabe Taggart," he replied.

"That was a very brave thing you did."

His expression slid into a scowl. "Didn't have much choice after the stupid thing you did."

Taken aback, she was at a loss for words. Before that horrible man had reached for her, she'd been prepared to hand over the ring. Now she felt foolish for ever hesitating.

Steam hissed and the train jerked into motion, picking up speed along the tracks. The stranger winced at the jerking movement. The woman who'd been sitting behind them made her way along the aisle in the rocking car. "Thank you for rescuing us," she said to Gabe.

Casting a disapproving scowl at Elisabeth, she returned to her seat. Elisabeth glanced at a few of the other occupants of the railcar and noted an assortment of scathing looks directed toward her. None of them understood the value she placed on the ring or the reason for her delay. She hadn't meant to endanger anyone.

Silently, she prayed for his life, asking God to forgive her for putting him at risk because of her selfish attachment to an earthly treasure. Out of habit, she reached into the jacket pocket of her traveling suit and rubbed a smooth flat stone between her fingers. The keepsake was one of several she'd picked up during her family's perilous journey to Colorado. The stones reminded her of the sacrifice and dedication that had brought them to a new state and a new life.

The train rocked and turned a bend. Several other passengers expressed their thanks to Gabe as the train neared its destination. When at last they reached Jackson Springs, the tale spread to the baggage men and the families waiting on the platform. Several men carefully loaded Gabe Taggart into the bed of a wagon and drove him away.

Grateful this particular chapter of her life was over and that Taggart would be getting medical attention now, Elisabeth released a pent-up breath and joined the others disembarking.

"Thank the Lord, you're safe."

Elisabeth turned with relief and embraced her stepmother, their bodies separated by the girth of Josie's growing belly beneath her pretty green day dress.

"What happened to that man?" her six-year-old half brother Phillip asked. He had shiny black hair like their father's and a sprinkling of freckles across his nose and cheeks.

"He prevented robbers from stealing our things," Elisabeth answered, trying to keep panic and guilt from her voice.

"Lis-bet, Lis-bet!" Peter and John, the three-year-old twins, jumped up and down waiting for her to greet them.

She picked up Peter first, kissing his cheek and ruffling his curly reddish hair. After setting him down, she reached for John. He kissed her cheek, leaving a suspiciously peppermint stickiness on her skin.

Josie turned and motioned forward a slender dark-haired young woman that Elisabeth had assumed was waiting for another passenger. "This is Kalli Tyler. She's my new helper. Your father thought I needed someone full-time, and I didn't argue. She's a godsend, truly. You two are going to get along well."

"I've heard all about you," Kalli said with a friendly dimpled smile. "Are you sure you're all right?"

"Yes, I'm fine." She kept her voice steady, but her insides quivered in the aftermath of that drama. She collected herself to study the other young woman.

As her father's assistant, the notary public and a tutor, Elisabeth did have her hands full. It was wise of Father and Josie to hire additional help. At seventeen and sixteen, her sisters, Abigail and Anna, were busy with school, studies and social activities, and their bustling household did need extra assistance to keep things running smoothly.

"I brought a wagon and Gilbert," Josie told her. "You had bags, and I'm not up to the walk."

"Of course," Elisabeth answered. "Phillip, help me find my bags, please."

She turned toward the pile where luggage was being stacked just as two men carried one of the robbers from the train on a stretcher. He'd been shot in the chest and his vest was drenched with dark glistening blood. The man was quite plainly dead.

Chapter Two

"Stop!" Stunned, Elisabeth grabbed her little brother and spun him away from the sight. "We'd better wait until the crowd thins out so we can find my satchels." Thankfully, the throng of onlookers had prevented Phillip from seeing what she'd just witnessed.

"I wanna see!" He wriggled, but she held him fast, staying behind him and keeping him faced the other way.

Josie had to give him a stern look before he stopped struggling. Finally, he leaned back against Elisabeth. Regret ate at her stoic confidence. Her ring definitely didn't seem as important as it had before. Especially if her hesitation had been the cause of these men's deaths. She swallowed hard.

At last the final body was removed and the crowd thinned. Phillip joined her in locating her satchel and another bag and carried the biggest one with both hands on the handle, the weight of the case banging against his shins.

A tanned hand reached to take the leather bag from him, and Elisabeth glanced up. "Gil!"

Her longtime friend was now a deputy. The silver star on his vest winked in the sunlight. He wore his hat cocked back, revealing his smiling blue eyes, and his familiarity was a comfort. "Heard there was some excitement," he said.

He hefted both bags into the back of the wagon, and while her family climbed onto the seat and over rails into the wagon bed, she gave him a friendly hug.

"You're trembling, Lis."

"I'm a little shaken up, I guess."

He was the only person ever allowed to call her by a shortened version of her name. At about sixteen, she'd stopped letting his teasing bother her, and thereafter it had become his habit. "I'm glad you weren't involved."

"Well, actually…"

"Actually what?"

She thought better of what she'd been about to reveal and pulled away. "Actually, I read an entire book in the two evenings I was in Morning Creek," she answered, avoiding her involvement.

"You're a wild one, you are," he said and helped her up to the bed beside her younger siblings and Kalli. Josie was on the springed seat, and he climbed up beside her. "I'm going to deliver you home, but I need to get right back and help with the paperwork and identifying the—uh—criminals."

Kalli occupied the boys by singing a nursery rhyme, and Elisabeth was grateful for the distraction she provided. Gil halted the team at the bottom of the hill, where the church sat beside a tiny empty parsonage.

Her father exited the church's side door and crossed the lawn, his black hair shining in the afternoon sun and a smile on his handsome face.

"Papa, there was robbers on the train!" Phillip called.

Samuel Hart's smile faltered and he studied Elisabeth with concern. "Are you all right?"

She jumped down to embrace him, and gave him a brief explanation.

"I'll head over to Dr. Barnes's to pray for the wounded hero," her father said. Elisabeth had expected nothing less of her father, a man of compassion and faith.

Gil led the team up the hill toward their home at the top of the tree-lined street. When the shrubbery and mature trees that surrounded their vast yard came into view, Elisabeth sighed with appreciation. Josie had been a wealthy widow when Father had married her, and her inheritances had supplied this dwelling where, in the years since, love had abounded and faith flourished.

While the others bustled around her, Elisabeth studied the asymmetrical house with its bay windows, balconies, stained glass, turrets, porches, brackets and ornamental masonry. The structure was two-storied, except for a third floor at the top of one pointed turret. That was the room where she and her sisters had spent hours reading and dreaming. She still used the space to relax and find a peaceful spot away from the boys.

Elisabeth exhaled with relief at being safely home.

She found her bags just inside her doorway where Gil had set them. She needed to unpack. Father would have duties piled up for her.

Sweat trickled along his spine, but the bandanna he'd tied around his head beneath his black cowboy hat kept perspiration from his eyes. Vision was critical when a keen eye meant the difference between life and death.

Gabe studied the cabin baking beneath the blistering sun. The man he'd been hunting for the past six weeks was holed up in there with a bottle of whiskey and a slug in his thigh. If he hadn't passed out from pain or bled to death, heat and starvation would drive him out eventually. Gabe rested his rifle against a bolder and reached for his canteen. Empty? He'd only just filled it. His throat was burning and dry; he needed water badly.

Heat more searing than the sun licked up his side. The dry grass around him was on fire! He jumped up to escape the flames and a shot rang out. His prey had exited the cabin and aimed another shot at Gabe, now standing and exposed.

Gabe reached for his rifle. It was gone, and in its place a coiled rattler lifted its head and shook its tail in warning.

Gabe jerked awake.

He lay drenched with sweat and his side throbbed. His tongue felt too big for his mouth. For a moment he didn't recognize the room, but then the train robbery and his subsequent ride to the doctor's home came back to him.

"He's one stubborn fellow." Vaguely, Gabe remembered the doctor removing the bullet from his side, but now instead of a blood-spattered apron, the man was wearing a clean white shirt and tie.

"Heavy, too." The black-haired fellow beside him threaded his hair back from his forehead and stared down.

Grimacing, Gabe raised up on one elbow.

"No more getting out of this bed," the doctor ordered and poured a glass of water from a nearby pitcher. He had silver hair at his temples, but was probably only ten years older than Gabe.

That's right. He'd made a foolhardy attempt to use the outhouse on his own. Gabe gulped down four glasses of the cool liquid before he lay back. "How long was I out?"

"You blacked out when I removed the bullet yesterday. It cracked your rib, but traveled a ways. Now stay put or I'll tie you to this bed. Good thing the reverend came along or I'd never have gotten you back in here."

Reverend? "Am I dying?"

"You're not dying," Matthew Barnes assured him. "You're just weak from losing so much blood. You need to rest and build up your strength."

"Why'd you call the preacher?"

"He didn't call me." The man offered his hand. "I'm Samuel Hart. My daughter was on the train yesterday. She's one of the passengers you saved from being robbed. She told me all about the incident."

"Hart," he said with a scowl. "The blonde?"

"That's Elisabeth."

Gabe groaned. "She had a strong aversion to parting with her neck chain."

Samuel Hart nodded. "She's worn the ring on that chain ever since my first wife died."

Gabe glanced around the room, finally noting there was another man lying on a cot several feet away. He looked to be sleeping or unconscious. "What's wrong with him?"

"Snake bite," Dr. Barnes replied. "Just got here an hour or so ago."

Gabe turned his attention back to the preacher. "If the doc didn't call you, why are you here?"

"I came yesterday, too, though you never woke up. I prayed for you and came back to see how you're doing."

Gabe couldn't recall anyone praying over him before. "I hurt like I've been dragged behind a team of horses."

The man in the other bed moaned, and the doctor moved to attend to him.

"Well, thank God you're alive," the preacher said.

Gabe studied him again and attempted to sit up, but pain lanced through his side and took his breath away. He rested a hand over the bandages. "I've been shot before, but it never hurt like this."

"Cracked ribs hurt more than a wound," the doctor said. "But you can't take a chance on opening that hole or letting it get infected."

"I can't stay here," Gabe objected. For one thing, if any of the train robbers' friends had heard of him being shot, the first place they'd search would be the doctor's. "I have business to see to."

"Where do you plan to go?" the doc asked him. "You need close supervision for at least a week or better."

"Looks like you've got your hands full with the snake-bit fella," Gabe replied.

"You can come home with me," the preacher said.

Gabe gave him a sidelong look.

"I have a big house full of women who can help me look out for you."

"I do have to head out this afternoon and make calls," the doc advised. "Plus look after this fella. You'd likely get better care at the Harts'."

Gabe hated to admit it, but the thought of moving more than his toes made him sweat. He'd pulled through a lot worse than this, though. "All right. The preacher's house it is."

Chapter Three

Elisabeth returned from the clothesline with a basket of her clean folded clothing in time to hear a commotion coming from the front hall.

"Not there!" a man shouted. "Don't grab me there, for pity's sake!"

She didn't recognize the voice, but then her father's more calming words reached her. "We'll have you settled in just a minute, Mr. Taggart."

Taggart? She entered the enormous sunlit foyer from the back hallway, stopped and stared.

Her father and Gil supported the tall man, one on each side, and Dr. Barnes followed, carrying his bag in one hand, a carton in the other.

"Just a little farther," Sam coaxed.

"Any farther and you might as well just shoot me again," the man growled. Sweat beaded on his forehead and his swarthy face had turned pasty white. A steep set of narrow stairs led from the street up to the house, and he'd just maneuvered them with a bullet wound.

Sam glanced up. "Elisabeth, bring cold water and wash rags to the bedroom on the south corner."

"But that's…" At her father's stern look, she let her voice trail off. *Next to mine*. What was he thinking? "Yes, sir."

She set down her basket and hurried to the kitchen. Her father had brought that man here! To their home! She cringed in mortification. Now she'd be forced to face him—*and* her shame.

Minutes later, she climbed the stairs with a pitcher and toweling. She traveled the now-silent corridor and paused outside the closed door. From inside, she heard rustles and a couple of grunts.

The door opened and her father gestured for her to enter.

Gil stood just inside the room, and she met his interested gaze. "Looks like Mr. Taggart's going to be your guest for a while," he said.

Reluctantly, she followed her father inside.

They had removed the man's clothing and tucked a sheet up around his waist and over part of his chest. His ribs were bound, the white wrapping a stark contrast against dark skin that held scars from previous injuries. Who *was* this man?

"You did just fine," Dr. Barnes said, standing over him. "The wound isn't bleeding." He turned and took the pitcher from Elisabeth, poured water into the bowl and got a cloth wet. "The Harts will take care of you. They're good people."

Gabe took the wet rag from the doctor and wiped his perspiring face.

Dr. Barnes set a bottle on the bureau. "He gets two teaspoons every six hours for pain. It'll help him sleep. Give him a dose now."

"You'll be in charge of his medicine, Elisabeth," her father directed.

"Me-e?" She hadn't meant to squeak.

"You're the most meticulous," he replied.

She nodded her obedient consent, but kept the disagreeable man she'd hoped never to see again under her observation. He didn't appear any more pleased with the situation than she, which was a comfort.

"I'll check on you tomorrow," the doc told him.

Gil glanced from the stranger to Elisabeth with a crooked grin and headed downstairs, followed by the doctor.

"Elisabeth will see to your needs," Sam told Gabe. "And I'll be back at suppertime."

He progressed into the hall, and she followed, not wanting to be left alone with their patient. The other two men headed downstairs. "What am I supposed to do with him?" she whispered to her father.

"Give him his medicine and something to drink. Let him sleep. If he gets hungry, bring him a meal." He took a step toward the stairs, but stopped and met her gaze. "Oh, and you might try thanking him for saving your mother's wedding ring."

He turned and walked away.

Her heart picked up speed and, as though the pressure would calm her pulse, she flattened her palm against her waist. She took a deep breath and released it. Slowly, she turned back to the room and entered, lowering the hand to her side. The Taggart fellow leveled that piercing green gaze on her, but his demeanor was blessedly less imposing minus his hat and shirt.

"Alone at last," he said.

Normally she prided herself on her calm demeanor, but this man managed to fluster her with every breath.

"Where did they put my gun?"

"You're not going to need your gun here," she assured him.

Grimacing, he attempted to lean forward, but grabbed his side through the sheet and bandage. "It's on that bureau." He pointed. "Bring it here."

Rather than argue with him, she stepped to the chest of drawers and picked up the surprisingly heavy tooled leather holster that sheathed the deadly looking weapon. He'd shot half a dozen bandits in the blink of an eye with this very gun. Holding it on both upturned palms, she carried it to him.

Meeting her eyes first, and making her even more uncomfortable with his stare, he took the belt from her. Yanking the gun from the its sheath, he swiftly opened the cylinder and fed bullets plucked from the belt into the chambers. After flipping the cylinder closed and sliding the gun under the pillow behind his head, he let the holster fall to the floor.

"I'll go fetch a spoon and a water glass." She couldn't get out of that room fast enough. Elisabeth stood in the kitchen longer than necessary, finding reasons to delay. What kind of man loaded a gun and stashed it under his pillow? What—or who—did he expect to shoot here? He hadn't been wearing a badge or a star, but just carrying a gun didn't make him a criminal. Her own father had worn a gun during their travels west and for months after arriving in Jackson Springs.

Finally, she returned and measured a dose from the liquid in the brown bottle. "Would you like a drink?"

"I'd love a drink, lady, but I'll settle for that water."

Grimacing, he rose on one elbow to take the glass and finish the water. "Thanks."

Noticing the sun arrowing through the shutters, she closed them and pulled the curtains closed over both windows, leaving the room dim.

"I never asked where you were headed." She wrung out the cloth and hung it on the towel bar attached to the washstand.

"Here."

"Oh." She came to stand beside the bed. "Do you have family in Jackson Springs?"

"I own some land," he replied. "I'm going to buy horses and build a house. Might buy a business or two."

"What type of business?"

"Depends on what's for sale."

She had to wonder if he had any skills or definite plans or if he'd just set off willy-nilly. "I see." She left and returned with a small brass bell. "Ring if you need anything."

Her father's suggestion burned. She reached to place a hand over the ring that lay under her bodice and, even though the room was only semi-lit, Gabe's astute perusal followed.

He had protected her from harm, saved her ring and had become injured in the process. Why did she have so much difficulty forming the words?

"Thank you, Mr. Taggart."

He curled his lip. "That wasn't so hard, was it?"

Irritating man. She spun and fled.

"He's wike Wyatt Eawp."

"Where's his six-shooter?" another child asked.

"Jimmy Fuller said he shot the robbers with a six-shooter."

Gabe rolled his woozy head toward the open door and caught sight of three little boys. They scattered like chicks in the wake of a bantam rooster, and Elisabeth Hart entered with a laden tray.

In disbelief, he blinked sleep from his eyes. "You have *kids?*"

Elisabeth frowned. "I'm barely twenty years old, Mr. Taggart." She set the tray on the bureau and opened the curtains, the thick blond braid hanging down her back swaying with her movements. She slid the window open wider. "Those are my young brothers."

He blinked at the glare of the late-afternoon light, but the breeze gusting in was most welcome. The sheet stuck to his skin and he plucked it loose. "Your father only mentioned daughters."

Gabe hadn't thought she looked old enough to have all those kids, but looks were often deceiving. She stepped close to arrange the pillows behind him. He sat forward with her scent, a combination of freshly ironed linen and meadow grass, enveloping him. He hadn't expected the alarming effect she had on his senses. He scratched his chin. "He said there was a house full of females."

"My sisters have come home from school, but they have lessons to complete. My stepmother needs her rest, so…" She snapped open a napkin and draped it over his chest. "You're stuck with me." She uncovered the plate of food and carried the bed tray to him. "I prepared a roast while you slept, along with potatoes and carrots. Beef will build up your strength."

Spotting the plate of food and the savory aroma of

meat and gravy made his belly rumble. At least she could cook. He picked up the fork in anticipation. "I haven't eaten anything that looked half this appetizin' in a long while."

"I'm not the cook my stepmother is, but I'm not half-bad. My skills lie in accounting and organization, but I can do most anything I set my mind to."

He took a bite and savored the taste of the tender roast. She could cook *well*. "You're used to getting your way."

She studied him and shrugged. "I see that things get done."

He ate several bites, then pointed at the nearby wooden chair with his fork. "Where were you returnin' from when we met?"

Stiffly, she seated herself. "Morning Creek. I'm the notary public for this county."

"Unusual job for a female." He couldn't say he was surprised. She seemed anything but usual, and her persnickety ways probably made her good with details.

"The position fell into my lap after an elderly parishioner passed away a year ago. The post required someone willing to travel to nearby towns once a month or so." She raised one shoulder in a delicate shrug. "The job sounded like a good way to do a bit of traveling. And it has been. Until yesterday." A frown formed between her pale eyebrows. "Nothing like the incident on the train has happened before."

Her perfect speech amused him. "So the body count's been low until now."

She averted her attention to the window, and he was almost sorry for the jibe. Almost. "Ruffle your tail feathers, don't I?"

She swung her attention back. "You're the first person I ever met who is deliberately antagonistic. Why do you do that?"

Her directness did surprise him. The females he'd known invariably played coy and solicitous. "I'm not the one who provoked a robber holding a loaded .45."

She lifted her chin to say, "I was going to give him the ring. I was ready to take it off and hand it over."

"So you say now."

Her blue eyes flashed with aggravation. "I'm not a liar, Mr. Taggart."

Amused, he set down his fork and reached for the cup of coffee. It was strong and black, the best he'd tasted in a long time.

She delved into the pocket of her apron, withdrew a timepiece and glanced at it. She stood. "It's time for your medicine."

And then he'd sleep again. He didn't like the vulnerability of being unconscious for hours at a time. He tested the pain by raising his arm, then glanced at the forested mountainside visible from the windows she'd opened. "This place looks to be set against a foothill," he said when she approached with the spoon and bottle of medicine. "Is there a main road close by?"

"No. Just the mountain behind us," she replied. "And a few homes farther down the hillside. Only one street leads up here." The Hart home stood silhouetted against the lush green pines and above most of the town, protected by the shadow of the mountain.

"I'll pass on the medicine this time." He reached for his coffee again, wincing at the pain that shot through his ribs. "And I'd be obliged if you'd run an errand on my behalf."

Her expression hinted at reluctance. "It's the least I can do. What's the task?"

"I need you to inquire about taxes on my land."

She set away the bottle of medicine. "You'll be settling here then."

"Jackson Springs strikes me as a quiet place."

"What did you do before?"

"Traveled." He set down his cup. "The roast was tasty. Thanks."

She picked up his tray. "That wasn't so hard, was it?"

"I'm grateful for the care, no matter how begrudgingly it's given."

She ignored that comment. "I'll visit the real estate office tomorrow. Is there anything else you need?"

He shook his head.

She headed for the door. "I'll check on you later."

Gabe reached to move a pillow from behind his back and winced. He lay back as gently as he could. The house was silent, save for a clock ticking somewhere.

He didn't like lying around, and neither did he cotton to having the Hart woman waiting on him. Besides the fact that he didn't like her seeing him this way, he had things to do. He needed to find a place to live before his sister, Irene, got here in another four weeks. That should have been plenty of time, but now...

He hadn't counted on this setback.

As far as anyone knew he was a businessman here to establish himself in a new community and settle into a normal life. So far nothing had gone according to plan, but he could get things back on track.

Without the pain medicine, he slept fitfully. At the sound of a feminine voice, he again woke with the damp sheets sticking to his skin and his head throbbing.

"I'm sorry to disturb you, but the marshal is here to see you." It was her. Still looking fresh and irritatingly healthy. Maybe it was the drugging effect of the medicine on his head, but the woman was downright pretty.

"Is there water in that bowl over there?" He attempted to sit and swing his legs over the side of the bed, but at the pain in his side, lay back against the pillows. "I need to wash up."

Elisabeth noted the full bowl and arranged toweling on the washstand, then turned back to him. "Can I help you?"

"Send one of the lads in."

She glanced toward the door and back at him with a look of concern. "The oldest is only six."

"He can fetch for me. Unless you want to stick around while I get my pants on."

She stared at him without flinching; he had to give her credit for that. But then with a swish of skirts and petticoats, she turned to where his satchel sat against a wall. As she leaned to grab the handles, her braid swung over her shoulder. She hoisted the bag onto the bench at the foot of the bed and opened it. "I'll get Phillip." She looked Gabe square in the eye. "And then I will stand right outside that door where I can hear everything."

"Suit yourself." What did she think he was going to do? Give the boy shooting lessons? "Stand right here if you want to."

She left the room with her back ramrod-straight and returned a few minutes later to usher in a handsome black-haired little fella with freckles. He surveyed Gabe with curious wide blue eyes.

"This is my brother, Phillip," Elisabeth said. "Phillip, Mr. Taggart needs help getting up and dressing. I'll be right out in the hall." She glanced from her brother to Gabe and backed out, leaving the door open a full twelve inches.

"Thanks for comin' to my rescue," Gabe told him. "Think you could help me stand without pullin' on my left arm?"

"Sure!" Phillip hopped right up on the bed and got behind Gabe to push him upward.

Gabe did his best not to grunt or groan. He'd eat dirt before he'd show weakness in front of the boy— or the woman listening outside the door. He wrapped the sheet around his waist and stood, making his way over to the bowl of water. His reflection in the mirror revealed several days' worth of whiskers on his cheeks and chin. He scratched at it and poured water into the basin. "Can you find the roll of toiletries in my bag there? I need my razor."

Phillip found the roll and carried the supplies to the stand, where a shaving brush and mug sat at the ready. Gabe used water and powder to make lather and dabbed it on his face.

"My papa gots a black beard, too."

Gabe gave an unintelligible reply as he drew the razor up his neck and chin.

"I'm getting one, too."

Gabe eyeballed him in the mirror. "Might be a year or two before you need to shave."

"I'm gonna grow stubble like you."

"Ladies like a stubble," he replied.

"Mr. Taggart," Elisabeth cautioned from the hallway.

"Tickles when you kiss 'em," he added.

Phillip pulled a face. "I'm not gonna kiss girls."

"Mr. Taggart!" she warned more loudly.

He washed, wet his hair and used his brush and comb. "Can you find me a clean shirt and trousers?"

Phillip set himself to the task. Then the boy leaped up to stand on the bench and held out the shirt so Gabe could ease into it. "Is it true you shot all those robbers who tried to steal ever'body's jewelry?"

Gabe paused in guiding his arm through the sleeve and looked at the child. "Sometimes takin' another man's life is the only choice. But it's never an easy choice and never something to be proud of."

"Did you ever shoot anyone before that?"

Gabe buttoned his shirt without reply. Phillip helped him don a clean pair of trousers. "Can you pick that up for me?" he asked, and the lad grabbed his holster from the floor and handed it to him. Gabe showed him how to hold it up so he could get it over one shoulder and around his ribs without touching the side that pained him. He took his Colt from under the pillow and slid it into the holster.

Phillip's eyes widened. "Is that the gun you used?"

"Yep. Has your pa taught you about guns?"

The boy nodded. "Yes, sir. I ain't apposed to touch one until I'm bigger. Not Papa's gun, either."

Gabe absorbed the information.

"You're a top-notch valet." He flipped him a coin.

Phillip caught it. "What's a valet?"

"A fellow who helps a gentleman get dressed. Can't say as I ever had the need before, but I'm fortunate you were here. I wouldn't have wanted to endanger your sister's sensibilities." Gabe leaned close and whispered, "She's a good cook, but she's prickly."

Phillip grinned.

"Are you decent?" Elisabeth called from the other

side of the door. She didn't like the sound of that man whispering to her brother.

The door whisked open and he stood in the opening in a clean, albeit wrinkled shirt, his dark hair combed into sleek waves. He wore the leather holster with his loaded gun tucked against his good side.

She'd never faced him standing before. He was a good foot taller than she was and filled the doorway with his imposing presence. One side of his mouth quirked up and her traitorous thoughts raced to his remarks about kissing ladies.

"I'll get the marshal," she said.

"No. I'll come down."

He was a stubborn one, that was for sure. "Phillip," she instructed. "Walk on Mr. Taggart's other side."

"I'd crush the boy if I fell on him," he scoffed. "Thanks for your help, Phil. Run along and come back tonight, all right?"

"All right!" The lad tossed a coin in the air and shot toward his room.

She accompanied their antagonistic guest to the parlor, where Roy Dalton waited. He shook Gabe's hand. "Taggart?" he asked.

Gabe turned to Elisabeth. "Thank you."

She blinked in surprise. She'd been promptly dismissed in her own home. She turned and left to find Josie and Abigail in the kitchen.

"Goodness, you fixed an entire meal while I napped," Josie said. "I had so much energy when I woke that I'm making pies. Abigail is helping me."

Elisabeth's younger sister had learned to bake and cook at Josie's side, and her desserts rivaled any that the ladies of the church produced.

"Did you remember that the Jacksons will be here for supper?" Abigail asked.

"I forgot." Elisabeth glanced at her stepmother. "Will there be enough food?"

"We'll serve your roast, and we can add more potatoes and carrots and maybe a slaw," Josie answered.

"Mr. Jackson likes roast beef," Abigail remarked. At seventeen, she thought Rhys Jackson's presence at dinner was exceedingly romantic. Elisabeth was far too practical to be caught up in such silly imaginings.

As the preacher, her father invited members from the congregation for dinner at least once a week. It had been Josie's desire to make a home where they could entertain and where their neighbors would feel welcome. The Jacksons ate with them more often than most other families. Beatrice was a widow, but a well-to-do widow, and her son Rhys worked at the bank. Elisabeth suspected that their recurring invitations had something to do with the fact that Rhys was an eligible, well-mannered bachelor.

Her father and Josie had never said they were impatient for her to marry and leave their home, so perhaps the new concern she'd been feeling was only her imagination. The house certainly wasn't too crowded for her to remain. In fact, bringing Kalli into their midst had added yet another person to the household and the dinner table. She wasn't a burden on her parents.

"Do you suppose Mr. Taggart and the marshal would care for a glass of lemonade?" Josie asked.

Elisabeth glanced at Josie's flour-covered hands as she shaped the piecrust and then gave her sister a hopeful look. Abigail sprinkled cinnamon on her sliced apples without looking up. "I'll pour them lemonade," she finally offered.

She set out two glasses. "Josie? Do you feel I contribute to the family?"

"Contribute?" Josie looked up. "You are an important part of this family, Elisabeth. Why would you ask such a question?"

She shrugged off her insecurity. "No reason. Forget I asked."

Sometime later, she carried a tray into the parlor and set it on the serving cart. The men's conversation ground to a halt. She set a frosty glass in front of each of them on a low table before the settee. Gabe looked decidedly out of place on the dainty piece of furniture.

"Miss Hart, will you join us, please?" Roy Dalton asked.

Surprised, she recovered her composure and seated herself on a chair opposite the marshal.

"Mr. Taggart isn't willing to accept the entire sum of the reward money."

Startled, she glanced at Gabe and back. "There is a reward?"

"Three of those fellas were wanted in several states for train robberies," he replied. "And two of them for murder."

"Oh, my." Clasping her hands together, she silently thanked God. They'd all come dangerously close to losing their lives. She remembered the verse in the Psalms that talked about God giving His angels charge over her, and knew it was so.

"Mr. Taggart claims he can't take all the credit for catching those men."

"Meaning that God had a hand in what happened?" She looked to Gabe, but he didn't reply.

The marshal was still holding his hat, and he turned it around by the brim. "Seems he's of the mind that you were the one responsible for insisting he do something about their apprehension."

"Oh, he is." She bored her gaze into Gabe's and then couldn't resist a glance at the gun he wore.

"Claims he would've handed over his valuables and let those good-for-nothin's go on their merry way if you hadn't started the ruckus."

Anger burned a fiery path to Elisabeth's cheeks, but she didn't look away.

"Mr. Taggart's a real generous and honest fella. Half the reward money is yours." The marshal took a fat envelope made from folded parchment from the settee cushion beside him and shoved it toward her. "This here's your share."

She held the packet in both hands before she realized what had just happened. "What is this?"

"Half the reward money, like I said," Roy replied.

Reward. For killing those men? Elisabeth dropped the envelope as though it was a poisonous snake. The seams of the envelope burst open and a stack of currency spread across the rug.

Blood money.

Chapter Four

"I don't want that!" Elisabeth sized up the marshal and then Gabe. "I'm not accepting money for those men's deaths."

"That's what reward money is," Roy replied. He knelt and scooped up the scattered bills and tucked them back in order and closed the paper over them. He extended the package. "It's your half."

"But I didn't do anything," she objected. "I didn't hold a gun."

"They'd have gotten clean away with everyone's purses and watches if you hadn't caused a ruckus," Gabe disagreed. "I gave the bandit mine." His gaze fell to the chain at her neck, though the ring was beneath her bodice like always. "Your kinship with your jewelry set the whole episode in motion. So half is yours."

"Well, I won't take it."

Gabe raised a brow and looked at Roy. "What happens to the money if she won't take it?"

The marshal pursed his lips and scratched his chin with a thumb. "Don't reckon I know. It's never happened before. Goes back in the city coffers, I guess."

"Shame all that cash goin' to waste," Gabe remarked. "Could've bought your brothers shoes or hired your father a hand or…" Gabe appeared thoughtful, then pleased with himself. "You could have taken a trip somewhere."

"My brothers have all the shoes they need, thank you, and I am my father's assistant." She paused, however, considering that a trip might have been nice. But that was vain and selfish thinking. She could have given the money to the church to provide help to those in need.

Could have? She still could. Elisabeth extended her palm. "I'll take it."

Seeming pleased not to have to deal with the money, Roy handed over the packet.

"I'll give it to the church," she decided.

"It's yours to do with as you see fit," Gabe said with a shrug.

"Well, that takes care of the business I came to do." Roy finished his lemonade and excused himself. She showed the sheriff to the door, then returned to the sitting room.

Elisabeth held the envelope to her chest. The Taggart fellow's face looked paler than it had been, and he'd set his mouth in a grim line. He was quite obviously in pain and too stubborn to say so. "You should've let me bring the marshal upstairs so you didn't have to dress and come down."

"I needed to move a bit." He stood, but swayed on his feet.

She tucked the money in her apron pocket and hurried to his side. "Lean on me."

"I can manage."

"I said lean on me, Mr. Taggart. If you fall flat on your face, I'll never get you up by myself."

He seemed to consider that as a distinct possibility and wrapped one solid arm across her shoulders.

With him butted up against her side, his imposing height and hard muscle were glaringly obvious. Now the possibility of him falling and crushing her became the issue. "Phillip!" she called.

A minute later, her brother skidded to a stop in front of them.

"Get on the other side of Mr. Taggart and do your best to help me get him to the banister where he can hold on."

Phillip eyed the holster, but ducked obediently under Gabe's other arm, and they managed their way to the front hall, where Gabe grabbed the banister and helped support his weight.

"Don't get behind us," Elisabeth warned. "Run ahead."

Phillip scampered up the stairs.

The farther they climbed, the more Gabe leaned his weight against her, until, at the top, she feared they'd both topple down the stairs. With Herculean effort, she used every ounce of her strength to keep him upright. "Come back and get his other side!" she called to Phillip.

The boy was a minimal help, though his face turned red from his efforts.

"Mr. Taggart, you're going to have to help or we're going to drop you in a heap right here," she huffed.

Lifting his head, he rose to the occasion with a grunt and they made it through the correct doorway and to the bed, where they dropped him unceremoniously.

He lay atop the blankets, his face white, his eyelashes lying against his cheeks.

"This is ridiculous," she said, straightening her skirts and her disheveled hair, while catching her breath. "You're taking your medicine and sleeping and not getting back out of bed until you're better able."

She poured a dose of the liquid painkiller, and with Phillip's help got it down Gabe's throat, then got him situated on the bed and closed the curtains.

"Is he dead?" Phillip asked.

"No, he's breathing," she answered, but paused to watch his chest rise and fall. "He's sleeping."

"He's sleeping in his clothes," the boy remarked. "And wearing his holster and gun."

"That's his own fault. He could have stayed put and he'd still be comfortable." Her hand went to the thick envelope in her apron pocket. Just having all that money on her person made her uncomfortable. She would give the ill-gotten gains to her father and let him use it to his discretion. She led Phillip out of the room. "We'll let him be."

She carried the money to Sam's study and left it in his top desk drawer, then hurried to the kitchen to help Josie with supper.

The Jacksons were again their guests at dinner that evening. Beatrice had been a widow for the past five years and occupied herself holding tea parties and peddling her son as a perspective husband. From all accounts it looked as though Elisabeth was her first choice. Beatrice raised a questioning brow at her now. "Elisabeth, we were quite concerned when we heard the news about the holdup and learned that you'd been on the train. How dreadful for you. Thank the good Lord you weren't injured."

"I'm thanking God for my safety," Elisabeth replied, not wanting to talk about the incident.

"Mr. Taggart saved Lis'beth," Phillip piped up. "And he saved all the people's watches and rings and money, too. Din't he, Lis'beth?" He sat with a slice of turnip forgotten on the tines of his fork, his expression serious. "He gots a big gun."

Beatrice's eyes widened. Rhys glanced from Phillip to Elisabeth.

Samuel Hart spoke up, saying, "We're all appreciative for Elisabeth's safe return home."

Josie returned to the dining room at that moment. Elisabeth took the refilled bowl of mashed potatoes and reached to set it in the middle of the table. Unconsciously, Josie spread her hand at the small of her back before taking her seat. Elisabeth glanced at Rhys at that moment, confused by the fleeting expression that darkened his features before quickly disappearing.

She'd gone to school with Rhys, though he'd finished ahead of her. He'd always been interested in the Harts and enjoyed coming to their home. He worked at the bank and knew much of the goings-on of the townspeople.

"Does your new position sit well with you, Miss Tyler?" Beatrice asked.

Kalli had been assigned a seat between Peter and John, where she sliced their meat and encouraged them to eat their vegetables. She glanced up. "Yes, ma'am. Quite well."

"Kalli is a perfect fit for our family," Josie added.

Elisabeth glanced at her sisters to note any reactions

to Josie's remark. Anna was absorbed in her meal, and Abigail was giving Rhys surreptitious glances. Neither seemed to think anything of Kalli's presence or the conversation.

Anna glanced up and smiled, and with a surge of affection, Elisabeth returned the smile. She dearly loved her sisters. They shared so much history, and wonderful memories of their mother.

Sam had brought Elisabeth and her sisters to Jackson Springs after their mother's death and his remarriage to Josie. Elisabeth had been filling the role of caregiver and nurturer and at first felt usurped by Josie's new position as her stepmother. But it hadn't been easy to resent a woman so kind and generous and who made her sisters happy. She and Josie had come to an understanding, and she had grown to love the woman dearly.

Still, even though their marriage and family had turned out well, Elisabeth sometimes questioned her father marrying for convenience. She was far from a romantic—in fact she was a painfully logical and practical person—yet Elisabeth had always imagined herself finding a love born of common interests, mutual needs and future plans. She wanted to marry for love and passion, not practicality.

Her father had never questioned Elisabeth's choice to assist him in his duties, appreciating in fact, that she took care of details and finances while he saw to the spiritual and emotional needs of his congregation. Still, it was the natural order of life for a man or woman to leave her father and mother and marry.

She had turned twenty on her last birthday. Most of the young ladies with whom she'd attended school were married and already had their own children. Elisabeth loved her young brothers and had spent a good share of time caring for them. Perhaps that was why she hadn't yet experienced a burning desire to have her own children.

Once she was married she'd undoubtedly feel different. Love changed everything. Zebediah Turner had called on her for a season. She'd been to his family's ranch with her father a time or two. When Zeb had kissed her after an ice cream social, their relationship had grown awkward. He hadn't called on her again, and he later married someone from Morning Creek.

Studying Rhys now, she wondered about the whole kissing thing. Maybe it just had to be the right person.

"How was school today?" Josie asked, looking to Abigail and Anna.

"I finished all my assignments in class," Abigail replied. "So I have no studies this evening. I'd like to make pies with those apples Mr. Stone gave Papa, if that's all right."

"No one around here ever objects to pie," Josie answered with a smile.

"I have arithmetic to finish," Anna said. "May I sit in your study with you, Papa?"

The sound of a bell tinkled from a distance. It took a second for Elisabeth to process the sound. She set down her fork. "Excuse me."

"Can I come help Mr. Taggart with you, Lis'beth?" Phillip asked.

Rhys set down his fork and studied her with a questioning look.

"Your sister can handle it," Sam said to Phillip. "Eat your turnips."

"The man is *here?*" Beatrice asked. "In your home?"

"He was injured defending my daughter and many passengers," Sam told her. "The least we could do was offer him a place to recuperate. My wife wanted this great big house so we could be a blessing to others. Over the years we've had a goodly amount of guests stay with us."

Beatrice blotted her lips with her napkin.

"He was sleeping the last time I checked on him," Elisabeth told Josie. "I imagine he's awake and hungry."

"I made him a plate," Josie answered. "It's in the warmer."

In the kitchen, Elisabeth readied a tray and carried it up the back stairs.

"I could've come down," Gabe said when he saw her. He had managed a sitting position with the pillows behind his shoulders.

"That didn't go so well last time." She set the tray on his lap. He was still fully dressed, boots and all.

"You knocked me out." Frowning, he picked up the fork and tasted the potatoes.

She stood at the foot of the bed. "You're easier to get along with that way."

"You're amusing, but it's not safe for me to be unconscious."

"And why is that?"

"Train robbers have friends. And relatives. If word got out that the man who shot their friends was staying here, they might come looking for me."

"Nothing will happen to you while you're in this home."

He raised a brow. "Didn't see any armed guards when I got here."

"Our shield and fortress isn't visible to the eye. Psalm

ninety-one assures us that God has given His angels charge over us to protect us in all our ways."

He looked at her as though she'd just told him she could fly. "In my experience the only sure thing is something I can see and feel."

He stabbed a bite of meat and chewed it.

"Your limited experience doesn't change the truth," she answered.

Gabe looked at the woman. Really studied her. She was as prickly as they came, opinionated and unafraid of speaking her mind—even if her head was full of foolishness. But she was something to look at, that was for sure.

He'd thought so ever since she'd walked down the aisle of that railcar, looking for an empty seat and finding only the one beside him. Her hair was the palest shade he'd ever set eyes upon outside a field of summer wheat. Tonight she didn't have it braided, but gathered away from her temples and trailing down her back like a schoolgirl's.

Her delicate features belied her bold statements and cutting barbs, a juxtaposition he rather enjoyed for its uniqueness.

She was slender, but not skinny, with curves in all the right places. She wore a burgundy-colored skirt with a flounce of some sort in the back. Her fitted ivory blouse was printed with flowers the same color as her skirt and the rounded neck opening revealed the chain that held her gold ring.

She caught him looking at it and brought her hand up to touch the piece of jewelry.

"Medicine wore off, and it was awfully quiet," he said.

"We were having dinner."

He imagined the whole family around a table. "You can go on back."

"Are you certain you don't mind? We do have guests."

"Any pretty young ladies?"

"No, Mr. Taggart. A widow and her son."

"A pretty widow woman?" he asked.

She frowned. "'Beauty is vain, but a woman that feareth the Lord, she shall be praised.'"

"From the Bible?"

She nodded.

"What about you? You're pretty."

Pink tinged her cheeks, the only indication that his question had affected her. "I prefer to be appreciated for my abilities."

"So, you know you're pretty?"

"You're impertinent, Mr. Taggart."

"No disrespect intended. Most ladies enjoy a compliment." He dug back into his meal. "Your father said he had a houseful of women, and seems they're all good cooks."

"Leave your tray on the end of the bed when you're finished." She turned and left the room.

He stared at the spot she'd vacated for a long moment. Her idealism stood firm in the safe cocoon of her protected world, but one of these days when faced with a reality she couldn't pray her way out of, Elisabeth Hart was in for a big disappointment.

For some reason he couldn't explain, he hoped he wasn't around to see it.

Chapter Five

The following morning, Gabe found a pitcher of water outside his door, carried and poured it into the bowl on the washstand. It irritated him that the wound in his side was so debilitating, even to the point of making it painful to raise his arm.

After washing and shaving, he dressed and opened the door. Minutes later, Elisabeth appeared. "My father has excused me from my duties for a few days in order to look after you." Her tone relayed her displeasure in the fact. She extended a piece of paper. "I got to the land office early. This is how much you owe."

She'd obviously seen the amount, since the paper wasn't folded or in an envelope. He glanced up, noting her almost pleased expression.

He cocked an eyebrow. "Guess that will take care of my share of the reward money." Did she think that was all he had to his name? He went to the bureau, took out his packet of money and counted it. He extended all but a few bills. "That'll cover the taxes."

She took the money.

"One more thing."

She met his gaze, and her eyes reminded him of a clear mountain lake.

"I'm going to need a place to live until I can build." It was probably going to be a few weeks before he could work much himself, but he could hire someone to get the house started.

"I'll see what I can do." She turned back toward the hall. "I'll bring your breakfast and then run your errands."

While he ate, a dark-haired woman tapped on the open door. "Mr. Taggart? I thought it was about time I came to introduce myself. I'm Josie Hart."

"Pleased to make your acquaintance, ma'am. You're a fine cook, and I thank you for lettin' me stay here."

"You're most welcome." She was a pretty woman with a friendly smile and the girth of an expected new life under her white apron. "I climb the stairs as few times as possible during the day, so I wanted to stop by now."

"Pleased you did."

"How is your injury?"

"More bother than I'd like, but I'll be fine."

"Elisabeth has gone downtown, so I'll be listening for your bell, and I'll have Phillip come if you ring."

"Shouldn't need anything, ma'am."

Elisabeth had mentioned her stepmother. That was why Elisabeth looked nothing like this woman…and why she set such store by that ring around her neck. Her own mother had died.

He knew what it was like to lose a parent. He'd lost both of his when he'd been sixteen and Irene barely ten. He'd tried working two jobs, but it had been no life for a little girl, so he'd hired on with a cattle drive and left his sister in the best place he could find.

It hadn't taken long for him to learn there was more money to be earned hunting bounties than punching cows. Before long Irene was in one of the best boarding schools in Pennsylvania and he was earning a name for himself.

Now nineteen, his sister had been after him to bring her to live with him. In order to do that, he needed to make a new start, make a home for her and leave his past behind.

Irene didn't know what he'd done all those years. He'd led her to believe he'd made enough herding cows to invest and create a tidy nest egg. She would never know the truth as long as he had his way. And he always had his way. He'd be the most respectable man she could ask for in a brother, and he'd see to it she found a husband worthy of her.

If it wasn't for this bullet hole in his side, he'd be buying lumber and roofing nails right this minute. The frustration of this setback ate at him. He wasn't used to relying on other people.

Especially not persnickety women.

He checked his revolver and tucked it into its holster against his side.

"My ma sent me for the tray."

Gabe turned at Phillip's voice.

Eyeing him, the boy picked up the meal tray. "I gotta go to school."

Gabe nodded and gave him a silent salute.

He shouldn't have been so blasted tired just from getting up and shaving, but winded, he lay back down. He'd been sleeping a short time when footsteps woke him.

Elisabeth was turning away to leave.

"I'm awake."

She stopped and turned back. She held a sheaf of papers. "This is your deed and your proof of taxes paid."

After handing it to him, she opened the curtains and the shutters so he could look over the papers. After a cursory glance, he set them down. "Appreciate it."

She looked away and then back. "There are homes for sale here and there. The boardinghouse has an opening. There's a room over the tailor's for rent."

"I need a little more room than that. A small house would do."

"Well, there is one small house. It's at the bottom of the hill, just down from here, and it's vacant."

"I'll take that then."

"Don't you want to see it first?"

"I can hire someone to clean it."

"That won't be necessary. The church owns it and takes care of the upkeep. I'll let my father know you'll be renting it."

"As soon as the doctor says I can be on my own, I'll move in. Maybe in a day or so."

The time couldn't pass quickly enough for Elisabeth. She wanted to send this man on his way and get back to her normal routine.

Two days later, Gabe stood at the open window, staring out at the mountainside behind the Hart home. The day was bright and the scent of pine lay heavily on the air. He squinted at the forested foothills that rose above the grouping of houses. From half a dozen clotheslines, laundry flapped under the sun.

"You must be restless by now."

He turned at the male voice to see Sam Hart just inside the doorway. "You could say that, yes, sir," he replied.

"Did Elisabeth mention we're having guests for dinner this evening?"

He shook his head. Elisabeth didn't speak to him any more than was necessary.

"Think you're up to joining us? I'm sure you need a different perspective."

"Don't want to horn in on your company."

"Nonsense. You're a new citizen to Jackson Springs. It's time you meet a few townsfolk and let them get to know you. My wife and I enjoy having additional guests at our table."

Gabe nodded. "All right, then."

That evening Phillip showed up to assist him in dressing, though Gabe was able to prepare on his own. The lad talked nonstop, telling Gabe about a litter of kittens born under their back porch and how he'd been taking scraps to the mother cat.

Gabe handled the stairs more easily than the last time he'd attempted the descent, and Phillip directed him to the sitting room.

Sam stood from where he'd been sitting on a sofa beside a matronly woman and greeted them. He thanked Phillip and made the introductions.

The stout woman offered her hand in greeting and he touched her fingers briefly, ruefully remembering how he'd asked Elisabeth if their guest was a pretty widow woman. "Mrs. Jackson."

Getting to his feet, her son gave Gabe the once-over. His brown hair had been cut short and oiled into order with a precise part just shy of the center of his head.

The lines from the teeth of his comb were visible. He wore shiny brown boots with a pinstriped brown suit. Not a bad-looking fellow. He extended a hand.

It came as no surprise to Gabe that Rhys Jackson didn't have any calluses on his palms. "Any connection to the town of Jackson Springs?" he asked.

"My father's father founded this town thirty-six years ago," Rhys answered.

He wasn't overly tall, but he was built sturdily, with wide shoulders and a broad chest. "Where are you from?" Rhys asked.

"Born in Illinois but traveled of late."

"What's your trade?" he asked.

"Worked in a machine shop for a spell," he replied. "I've made shingles and built bridges. Even mined salt for a time."

"Couldn't make up your mind?" Rhys asked.

Gabe picked up on the barb. "Like to keep my options open."

One of Elisabeth's sisters was seated on a bench near a window, and she studied Gabe curiously.

Sam glanced at her. "Have you met Anna?"

"I haven't."

"Anna is my youngest daughter—at least for the time being. Anna, meet Mr. Taggart."

"I'm pleased to make your acquaintance, sir," she said and rose to greet him with a little bow and a bashful nod.

"Your daughters are equally lovely," Gabe said to his host.

Anna's hair was paler than Elisabeth's, not as dense or wavy however, and her smile was warm and infectious. He guessed her to be about sixteen. She held a closed book, her index finger keeping her spot. Once the attention was turned away from her, she opened the book and apparently picked up where she'd left off. She seemed content and confident. Watching her made him think about his sister and wonder about the years of her childhood and youth, growing up at the academy and not with a family like this one. He'd never had experience with this kind of atmosphere before.

He'd always believed he'd made the best choice for her, and he still did.

He couldn't have provided her education or safe upbringing if he'd had to work in a mine or a factory. The few times he visited the school, he'd been impressed by the stability and routine. Irene had been given every opportunity that an education and a respectable background could provide.

Now she needed a husband with a good job and a secure future. Someone established and responsible.

He glanced at Rhys. At a break in the conversation, he asked, "What do you do, Mr. Jackson?"

"After his death, I took over my father's position as president of Rocky Mountain Savings and Trust."

"Banking," Gabe acknowledged with a nod.

Another fair-haired young lady came to announce it was time to take their places in the dining room, and he was introduced to Abigail.

"I've heard all about you from my little brothers," she told him with a twinkle in her eye. "Of course their descriptions are exciting and involve guns and robbers."

She was younger than Elisabeth, not quite as slender, but just as pretty. He had to wonder if Elisabeth would shine in the same way if she allowed herself a charming smile and the same exuberance.

They reached an enormous dining room with a long table suited to dinners such as this. The table itself had a covering made of fancy needlework, and atop it were platters and bowls holding a mound of mashed potatoes, mouthwatering sliced beef, a slaw and other vegetables. He'd never seen so much food outside a restaurant in his life.

Rhys seated his mother and took the chair beside her as though familiar with the arrangement. Gabe waited for instruction.

"Please, sit here," Josie said, standing behind an empty chair.

"Thank you, ma'am." He stood behind the chair she indicated, but waited until she sat to take his own seat.

Sam sat at the head of the table, his wife at his right and Mrs. Jackson on his left, putting Rhys directly across from Gabe. Josie was on Gabe's right.

Sam continued with introductions, and Gabe learned the twin to his left was John. Beside John sat their nanny, Miss Tyler, and then Peter. Phillip sat at the foot of the table, and along the other side were Abigail, Anna and beside Rhys, Elisabeth.

As the food was passed and he helped himself, he considered the seating arrangement. Were Elisabeth and Rhys courting? He couldn't picture her accompanying him for a buggy ride or a picnic, but then maybe it was only Gabe she behaved so poorly toward. He made a point to pay close attention to her interaction with the others.

She chatted with Anna on her right, and Anna told her about a dress one of her classmates had worn that day. Elisabeth lent her undivided attention to the description.

"We might want to spend a few days in Denver," Elisabeth suggested. "That shop where we found the periwinkle gabardine might have a similar lace."

She appeared sincerely interested in helping her sister create a dress like her friend's.

There was a loud rasp, like the turn of a doorbell, and Elisabeth stood, holding out her hand as though to stop Josie from standing. She dropped her napkin on the seat of her chair, reminding him he hadn't even unfolded his. "I'll get it," she said.

Gabe opened his napkin discreetly.

"Where are you from?" Josie asked from beside him.

"Born in Illinois," he replied.

"I'm from Nebraska. Sam found me there and brought me to Colorado."

"A divine appointment to be sure," Sam said with a fond smile directed at his wife.

Elisabeth returned. "It's a telegram for Mr. Taggart." She handed him the folded and sealed paper and went back to her seat.

Uncertain what to expect, Gabe opened the telegram. His examination shot directly to the sender. Irene Taggart.

Tired of waiting STOP Will arrive on the tenth STOP Cannot wait to see you STOP.

His food rested uncomfortably in his belly. He hadn't told his sister he'd been shot. The last time he'd contacted her he'd told her his arrival date in Jackson Springs and assured her he'd send for her when he had a home ready.

He didn't have a home ready.

"Bad news?" Sam asked, and Gabe realized everyone's attention had focused on him and the piece of paper he held.

"No. No, it's good news, actually." He folded the telegram and tucked it into his shirt pocket. "My sister will be arriving sooner than I'd expected."

"You have a *sister?*" Elisabeth asked, the first time she'd spoken to him since he'd entered the dining room.

"Is that so hard to believe?"

Sam looked at his daughter, and she attempted to cover her surprise. "I just never pictured you with a family."

"I wasn't hatched."

An uncomfortable silence settled on the gathering until Josie interrupted it with, "Do you have family other than your sister?"

"My folks died a long time ago," he answered. "Irene's been at boarding school in Chicago."

"How old is she?" Anna asked.

He thought a second. "Must be she's nineteen now."

The news that Gabe Taggart had a sister shouldn't have surprised Elisabeth, but it did. People weren't born in a vacuum, but if she'd been going to imagine his family, she'd have thought up scruffy-bearded brothers, not a sister at a boarding school.

"I own land nearby," he said, as though offering an explanation to the others. "I'd planned to have looked it over by now and started building a house, so I'm behind."

Rhys focused his attention on the other man. "Where is this land of yours?"

"From what I can tell, the piece is northwest of here,"

Gabe replied, then shrugged. "Doc won't let me ride, so I haven't seen it."

"Do you think you could tolerate a buggy ride?" Sam asked. "We could go look at it tomorrow."

Gabe smiled, his teeth white. "I'd be obliged, Reverend."

"Your sister is welcome to stay here with us," Josie offered.

Elisabeth couldn't quite pinpoint the look that crossed his features. He studied Josie for a moment before speaking. "That's generous of you, ma'am, but I've got a place for us to stay until I build a house."

"Oh, really?" Beatrice entered the conversation for the first time. "And where will that be?"

"Seems it's nearby from what Elisabeth tells me." He tore his gaze from Josie to glance at the older woman.

"The parsonage," Elisabeth explained. "Mr. Taggart has rented it."

"Well, that is close by," Josie said. "You'll be able to join us for dinner at least once a week, and I won't hear any different."

"I can't argue with an invitation like that." The smile he gave Elisabeth's stepmother softened his features. His green eyes actually sparkled with appreciation. Elisabeth experienced an odd feeling, like the falling sensation in a dream, and placed both hands on the tabletop to steady herself.

"This is the best meal I've eaten in months," Gabe said. "The Hart females sure know their way around a kitchen."

"I made rice pudding," Abigail added, quickly vying for his attention.

He raised his eyebrows in surprise and appreciation.

"It's still warm." Abigail glanced at her stepmother. "May I serve it now?"

"Just as soon as we clear away a few dishes," Josie replied.

Elisabeth slid out her chair with the backs of her knees and stood. "Abigail and I will clear the dishes. You stay seated."

Kalli got up. "I'll help."

In the kitchen, Abigail said to Kalli, "Mr. Taggart is handsome, don't you think?"

Kalli blushed. "Indeed," she agreed. "It's not fair that a man has eyelashes like that."

Elisabeth scraped plates and rinsed them in the pail in the sink before stacking them. Handsome? She supposed if he'd ever done anything but scowl at her, she'd have a different opinion of the man, but he hadn't smiled at her like he'd smiled at the others this evening. Not that she'd wanted him to. She'd never have imagined her stepmother and siblings to be so easily fooled.

On her next trip for more dishes, she deliberately looked at his eyelashes. He caught her stare, and she turned away in discomfit.

Abigail carried her bowl of steaming cinnamon-scented rice pudding to the table and Elisabeth placed a stack of painted china jelly dishes beside it. Abigail sat, so Elisabeth spooned pudding and carried the bowls around the table, placing them in front of the diners. When she reached Gabe, she stood as far away as possible and leaned in to set the dish before him.

He turned a curious glance upward. "Thank you."

"We don't need any bridges."

Elisabeth glanced up to discover Rhys speaking to Gabe.

"And there are no salt mines nearby. Will you be making shingles in Jackson Springs?"

She sensed a mocking edge, as though Rhys was belittling the other man's skills or perhaps even questioning his intent.

"Actually, I'm planning to invest," Gabe replied.

Rhys lifted his eyebrows. "As in stocks?"

"Perhaps. But I'm more interested in finding someone who needs capital to get a business started. I don't want to work the business, so as long as it's a sound principle. I'd be a silent partner. Meanwhile I'll buy a few horses and try my hand at ranching."

Gabe had Rhys's attention now. The man sat forward, ignoring the dessert placed before him to focus on Gabe. "And you have the capital to fund a venture such as that?"

It was a rude question, akin to asking the man how much money he had, but Rhys was a banker, and she supposed it was his nature to question.

"That I do, Mr. Jackson."

"Rhys. Call me Rhys."

Chapter Six

Elisabeth set down the last dish in front of Abigail with a thud. Well, if that didn't beat all. Her father had taken the man in, and between him and Josie they'd made certain Elisabeth saw to all his needs. Her little brothers thought he was a hero, Abigail and Kalli called him handsome, and now even Rhys had rallied around Gabe's camp because Gabe had money to put in his bank. None of them had seen his antagonistic side or experienced his cutting tone.

He never had a civil word to say to her, but he was all smiles and compliments around everyone else.

"I've never tasted rice pudding this good," he told Abigail, and she blushed to the pale blond roots of her hair. "In fact I don't know when I've ever eaten so well. Reverend, your wife and daughters are excellent cooks."

"That they are," Sam replied with a proud grin.

Elisabeth rolled her eyes. Abigail noted it and frowned at her.

A knock sounded at the door, and this time Sam raised a hand to the others. "I'll get this one."

When he returned, he gave his wife's shoulder an apologetic squeeze. "I'm needed at the Quinn place. Seems Ezra collapsed and the doc thinks it's his heart."

"Oh, my," Josie said. "Well, we'll pray for him right now. You hurry on."

"Girls, you look after Josie tonight," Sam said with a look at Abigail and Anna. And then he turned to Elisabeth. "I never know how these types of things will go, so if I shouldn't get back in time, Elisabeth, please take our guest to see his land tomorrow. Take Phillip along if you need another hand."

Her heart sank, but she nodded obediently. "Yes, sir."

As soon as Sam was gone, Josie reached across the table for Beatrice's hand and Gabe's on her left. She closed her eyes.

Gabe hadn't held a woman's hand in a good long time, and never while the woman prayed, so Josie's action caught him off guard. Decidedly uncomfortable, he waited to see what happened next.

"Elisabeth, please pray for Mr. Quinn," she said, surprising him even more.

But Elisabeth didn't hesitate. "Father God, we lift our friend Ezra Quinn to You and ask that You would touch him with Your healing hand. We believe Your Word that says Jesus took our infirmities and bore our sicknesses, so we thank You that Mr. Quinn is delivered and whole this night in Jesus's name."

"And we pray for Ezra's boy, Lester," Josie added. "Give him strength and comfort and provide for him from Your gracious bounty. Thank You, Lord," Josie said and the others chorused their amens before she released Gabe's hand.

Gabe didn't set much store by their faith, and he

sure didn't think any prayer was going to make a difference if the man had already had a heart attack and his number was up.

They finished their dessert without their former enthusiasm, and Elisabeth and her sisters cleaned up the table. Josie ushered Sam and the Jacksons into a large sitting room. Sam's ribs ached something fierce, but he remained seated on an overstuffed chair until Elisabeth finished her chores and joined them.

"Excuse me," he said to the others. "I'm going to go upstairs and lie down."

Beatrice and Rhys said their goodbyes, and he climbed the stairs, Elisabeth on his heels.

"Would you like your medicine?" she asked.

He shook his head. "I'll just lie down."

"Suit yourself."

"You don't have to take me anywhere tomorrow. I'm sure I can find a driver and a buggy."

"If my father doesn't return, I'll accompany you," she assured him. She lit the lamp on the bureau and turned down the covers on the bed. Picking up the empty pitcher, she headed for the door. "I'll bring fresh water as soon as I've heated more."

"Much obliged," he said with a nod. Once she was gone, he eased onto the bed and closed his eyes. He didn't like being indisposed, and he really didn't like being indebted to the ungracious Elisabeth Hart. Even if she did have the prettiest eyes this side of the Rio Grande. It had been plain from the start that she didn't want any part of him and was only seeing to his needs out of obedience to her father.

The sooner Gabe Taggart was out of here and on his own, the better.

* * *

He woke to the sounds of the family the following morning, shaved and dressed on his own, then found his way downstairs to the dining room where they'd eaten the night before.

The boys, seated in their same places, glanced up when he joined them. Anna sat on the other side of the table, but Abigail was missing.

"Is your ribs better?" Phillip asked.

"They must be," he replied. "But if this is better, I don't know how I got through the past couple of days."

"Grunting," Phillip replied with a serious nod.

"Guess I did my share of grunting," he agreed with a sheepish grin.

The twins giggled.

Elisabeth hesitated in the doorway, then hurried forward and set down the bowl she'd been carrying. "Good morning, Mr. Taggart."

Obviously a greeting for the children's sake, because she didn't normally speak to him like that. "Good morning, Miss Hart. Has your father returned?"

"He came home for a few hours while it was still dark, but headed back to the Quinns'." She served her young brothers cooked oats and drizzled maple syrup on top of each one's bowl. "I will be accompanying you this morning. Phillip will join us."

"I will?" the lad asked with a hopeful expression. "And not go to school?"

"That's right." She stroked his back through his overalls and shirt. "I suppose we should pack a lunch in case we're out at noon."

He looked up at her with twinkling eyes. "Can I help?"

"Of course you can."

"I wanna go, too!" Peter announced. He already wore a glob of oatmeal on his shirtfront.

"Me, too," chirped John. At least Gabe thought that was John. The two younger boys looked just alike, but if they were sitting on the same chairs as last night, he had them straight.

Their mother entered the room carrying a platter of buttered toasted bread in time to hear their pleas.

"You're staying with Mama this morning," she said and gave each of them a kiss on the forehead and wiped Peter's shirt with a damp towel. "I need your help kneading bread."

John held up a bent arm to show her his biceps muscle. "I can hewp you, Mama. I gots big muscles. See?"

Abigail joined them, breathlessly seating herself, taking a piece of toasted bread and spreading jam on it. "Are you ready, Anna?"

"I've been ready. You're the one who changed clothing three times." She stood and picked up a stack of books and a lunch pail from the sideboard before giving Josie a peck on the cheek. "Where's Kalli?"

"Hanging wash out back. Don't fret about me. Have a good day at school."

After the girls hurried out, Elisabeth sat and ate.

The routine and the scurrying were foreign to Gabe. He'd eaten alone and traveled by himself most of his life, sleeping in his bedroll under the stars or in stark hotel rooms. Hotel dining rooms served decent meals, but most of the time he bought food in cafes or saloons and on the trail ate whatever he could carry with him.

He sure wasn't used to females or the order and stability they created by their very natures. The Hart daughters were training to be wives and mothers like the one who'd just seated herself beside him. And now... he could even picture Elisabeth as a wife. She was efficient and hardworking, and she had a different side to her when she interacted with her family. Nurturing...loving.

The discovery was unexpected. And unwelcome.

Apparently he was the only one who brought out her defensiveness and sarcasm.

"Enjoy your ride," Josie said, once she'd finished eating. "Elisabeth, I prepared chopped chicken, and you're welcome to make sandwiches for your lunch. Phillip, I want to hear that you were on your best behavior today."

He hopped down from his chair and ran to give her an uninhibited hug. "Yes'm. I'll be Lis'beth's helper."

"Shall I go get a buggy and bring it up the hill?" Elisabeth was looking at Gabe. "Or do you think you can walk to the livery with me?"

He wouldn't admit in a hundred years that her bringing the buggy to him sounded like a good idea, so he assured her he could walk just fine.

Once everything was prepared, the three of them exited the house, and Gabe had his first real look at the neighborhood. The Harts' home sat at the top of a steep incline, nestled against the forested mountainside. The closest homes were farther down the hill, but none was as impressive as the three-storied beauty on the hill.

"That's the parsonage you've rented." At the bottom of the street, Elisabeth pointed out a tiny square white house that sat beside the church with only a lot separating the two.

"That's *it*?" he asked.

"If you recall, you never mentioned your sister to

me," she explained. "And I did ask if you wanted to see it first," she added. "Since you neglected to tell me about your sister, I assumed you would be the only one living there. Two people can manage just fine, though. There are two small bedrooms."

"I didn't know she was coming so soon," he said. "I hoped to have a house built before she got here."

"You know what they say about the plans of men," she said.

"No. Who said something about plans?"

She glanced at him. "Well, there are proverbs about the plans of men."

"Chinese proverbs?"

Her next glance indicated she questioned his sincerity. "The *book* of Proverbs, Mr. Taggart. It's in the Bible."

"I've heard of it. So what does it say?"

"Well…there's one that says a man's heart devises his way, but the Lord directs his steps."

"What does that mean?"

"I think it means that we can plan the way we want to live and the things we want to do, but only God can enable us to live it and do those things."

"Did that Confucius fellow write that?"

"No, Solomon wrote it."

"Is Solomon his first or last name?"

She turned to discover him studying her from beneath the brim of his hat. His attention was flattering in a way she didn't want to admit, but she suspected he was enjoying himself too much at her expense. "*King* Solomon, the wisest man who ever lived."

"Hmm. Suppose he ever took a day off from being so smart?"

He was baiting her, and she wasn't going to fall into another of his antagonistic traps. "If he had, he wouldn't have been near as wise, now would he?" She struggled to remember the initial subject. "The house is small, yes. But you'll manage just fine."

Phillip had brought along his harmonica, and from behind them came discordant sounds as he did his six-year-old's rendition of "Shoo Fly Don't Bother Me," stopping and starting to get the notes right.

Elisabeth couldn't resist a smile. Her brother's playing ended their conversation, which was just fine with her.

She followed Warren Burke's directions, which he'd given at the time they'd rented the buggy, and left the road to head across an open meadow. They neared a stream and she guided the horses to a stop.

Gabe pointed to a shallow section where rocks protruded above the water. "We can cross over there."

"I can't take the buggy across this water."

"It's just a little stream. Barely two feet deep right here."

She didn't have the same paralyzing fear that her younger sister Anna did, but all the same, Elisabeth didn't like crossing water. Just seeing the sun reflecting from the surface and glimpsing the small fish darting in a hollow against the bank made her heart thud against her breastbone.

It had been over seven years, but the memory of the day their wagon had tipped over in a rushing river was as fresh as if it had been only the day before. The water had been startlingly cold, sucking away her breath. Immediately her sodden skirts had made treading water impossible, and she'd swiftly been carried downstream.

Miraculously, she'd spotted a branch protruding over the water and grabbed for it successfully.

The branch had been solid and she'd had a death grip. Most likely she could have clung to it and survived even if her father had gone after her mother first. But Elisabeth's terrified screams had led him to her. She'd latched her arms around his neck and clung for dear life as he carried her up the bank to safety.

And then he'd left her beside her sisters and in the care of the other women of the wagon train to continue his search for her mother. The hunt had concluded with a devastating discovery.

"Here. Let me." Gabe took the reins from her fingers.

She released her hold, glad for the interruption of her thoughts.

He spoke softly to the horse, directing it down the gentle slope toward the water and encouraged it to proceed across the stream.

"Hold on!" Elisabeth called to her brother, then gripped the edge of the seat and didn't breathe while the buggy bounced over the rocky streambed and up the other side of the bank.

"That was fun!" Phillip shouted, leaning forward between them. "Can we do it again?"

"On the way back," Gabe replied.

Elisabeth released her pent-up breath and turned to gape at the man beside her. Wearing that irritatingly cocky grin, he dropped his gaze to her hand where she gripped his forearm.

It took her a full thirty seconds to distinguish the hard sinew beneath the fabric and release her hold. Embarrassment got a hold on her. She looked away.

Uncomfortably aware of the man beside her, she

concentrated on the landscape. The horse pulled the buggy up a slope until they sat perched on the grassy rim above a meadow. A startled antelope fled into the aspens growing along the opposite hillside.

"Did you see that deer?" Phillip asked, excitement lacing his voice.

"That was a pronghorn antelope," Gabe told him. "A female."

The sky appeared incredibly pale against the vibrant greens of the trees and the rocky slopes glittering in the distance.

Still holding the reins, Gabe led the horse forward and halted near a patch of graceful blue columbines. "Let's stretch our legs."

Gingerly, he eased to the ground, and then reached back for Elisabeth. While she took her time wondering how she could avoid touching him, Phillip wedged around her and jumped to the ground with a whoop. He picked up a dried buffalo pile and sent it sailing through the air. Seconds later, he was running through grass up to his knees, startling half a dozen grouse that took wing.

"You stay close by!" Elisabeth called. Begrudgingly she accepted Gabe's help. His hand was warm and strong, and she released it as soon as her feet touched the ground.

Gabe set off at a quick pace, his long legs covering ground until he climbed a rise and stood silhouetted against the sky. Phillip spotted him and ran to join him. Elisabeth took a more sedate stroll, skimming her fingertips across the delicate petals of the wildflowers. It had been too long since she'd taken time to enjoy nature's beauty or the summer air. It seemed she was always too occupied with work to set aside an afternoon for a ride.

The sun beat down from a cloudless sky, warming her arms and shoulders through her cotton blouse, and she was glad for her straw hat. On a current of air, an eagle soared high above the timberline, dipping toward the trees, then disappearing.

Phillip looked tiny in the distance, appearing even smaller beside the broad-shouldered man. Gabe reached out and ruffled the boy's hair, and she could imagine the stream of questions spilling from her little brother.

Gabe left him and walked toward her, his outline growing larger as he neared.

Notes from Phillip's harmonica reached her on the hot breeze. She smiled to herself.

Gabe removed his hat, threaded his fingers through his hair and replaced it. He was an imposing sight, square-jawed and lean, that ever-present weapon strapped to his side. "You packed us a lunch, did you?"

She blinked to orient herself. "Yes."

She walked back to the buggy and reached behind the seat for the covered basket and the quilt. "How are your ribs feeling?"

"Not perfect," he replied. "But I've had a lot worse days."

She found a place where the grass had been flattened by wind or rain and deftly spread the faded quilt, then set the basket on it. It took only a minute to set out the food and napkins. "Phillip!"

He was still playing his harmonica, turning in a circle as he did so.

A breeze caught the edge of the quilt as Gabe lowered himself to a sitting position, and they both reached for the edge at the same time. Her hand lay on the back of his longer than necessary, but instead of pulling away, she stared in fascination at her slender white fingers against his long tanned ones.

He turned his hand over, palm up, until he held her hand, and still she didn't move away. Her heart picked up a staccato beat that surprised her even more than the touch.

With his other hand, he reached to tug off her hat.

She looked up at him then.

Even shaded beneath the brim of his hat, his eyes were as green as she remembered, reminding her of the first time she'd seen them—and him—that day on the train.

"In the sun your hair shines like spun gold," he said, surveying her hair and face with glittering green eyes.

He was so close she could smell the pressed cotton of his shirt.

"It's not as pretty as Abigail's," she said. "Hers curls on the ends and has reddish streaks."

"Yours is by far the prettiest," he disagreed. "Prettiest I've ever seen." It was the nicest—and most confusing—thing he'd ever said to her.

Her gaze dropped unerringly to his lips, conjuring up the memory of him talking to Phillip about kissing girls.

"Wonderin' if it tickles, are you?"

He was outrageously bold and improper, and she should have straightened and immediately taken back her hand...but she didn't. Because that was *exactly* what she'd been wondering.

One side of his mouth inched up, and the mocking familiarity sat with her more easily than his uncharacteristic compliment.

She couldn't have changed what happened next if she'd seen it coming.

And she should have seen it coming.

Chapter Seven

But when Gabe leaned ever-so-slightly forward, she ignored the warning of her erratic heartbeat and did the same. Their lips met. This was no Zebediah Turner kiss.

She wasn't thinking about the sun overhead or the off-key notes of the harmonica or the jar of pickles waiting to be opened. She was thinking about Gabe Taggart's warm mouth against hers.

Her father always said courting was a prelude to marriage. Kissing was part of courting, but she had no intention of marrying this man. She shouldn't be kissing him. She took her sweet time calling a halt to the experience, however. She was, in fact, foolishly reluctant to miss any part of it.

Nobody had ever called her hair spun gold before. No one had ever made her heart flutter as though hundreds of butterflies fought to get out of her chest. It was shallow to succumb to his flattery, but with him she felt different. Not quite herself…someone infinitely more exciting and attractive than plain old Elisabeth, the preacher's daughter.

She'd done nothing besides butt heads with this man

since the first moment they'd met. She shouldn't find kissing him enjoyable. Elisabeth should have been offended…at the very least put off. The wisest and most prudent action called for moving away and putting an end to this appalling lapse in judgment while she still held a scrap of dignity intact.

"Look, Lis'beth! I ain't never seen a butterfly that color b'fore. What do you suppose it's called?"

Nudged back to her senses, Elisabeth straightened and withdrew her hand in one swift motion. Cheeks burning, she refused to raise her gaze, but reached for the wrapped sandwiches and purposefully kept the breathlessness from her voice to ask, "What color is it?"

Phillip dropped to his knees on the quilt, but thankfully his attention remained focused on the grassy meadow. "Black mostly, with white stripes and little white spots. See?"

She picked up her hat, plopped it back on her head and then peered in the direction he indicated. "I don't know much about butterflies."

"How 'bout you, Mr. Taggart?" the boy asked. "Do you know 'bout butterflies?"

"'Fraid not," he replied.

"We can get a picture book at the library, though," Elisabeth told her brother.

Phillip sat cross-legged and bit into a chicken-salad sandwich. "Did Mama make these?"

"Yes, she did."

Gabe picked up his sandwich. Out of habit, he pored over the meadow and surrounding tree line. Reassured that the three of them were alone, he unwrapped it and took a bite. Elisabeth's cheeks were still pink. Could be from the warmth of the sun, but he suspected the high color was more than that.

Kissing her caught him as unaware as he supposed it had had her. What foolishness was that? He hadn't come to Colorado looking for a woman. He already had Irene to look out for, and he didn't have the first idea how.

"Is your mama a good cook?" Phillip asked, snagging his attention.

"My mother's been gone a long time."

With a bread crumb on his chin, Phillip frowned. "Where'd she go?"

Not wanting to traumatize the lad, Gabe swung a questioning glance at Elisabeth. The Hart children seemed quite sheltered.

"Mr. Taggart means his mother is in heaven," she supplied.

Realization crossed the boy's features. "Ohh." He set down a triangular-shaped crust. "Lis'beth's first mama is in heaven, too. Isn't that so, Lis'beth?"

She nodded.

Phillip raised his eyebrows as an idea struck him. "Maybe they know each other!"

"Quite possibly," Elisabeth replied.

"An' Jesus is with 'em, isn't that right?"

She nodded. "That's right."

Gabe didn't hold much store by the whole idea of heaven. He said nothing, but Elisabeth finally raised her gaze to him as though guessing his skeptical thoughts.

"You do believe in heaven, don't you?" she asked.

He didn't want to have this discussion with her, but he shrugged. "I think people make up their own beliefs to get them through grief—or to justify their behavior.

Likely it feels better to think their loved ones are in a good place."

Her expression showed her shock. "Jesus said He was going ahead to the Father to prepare a place for us."

"Don't know anything about that," he replied. "Your mama makes good chicken salad, Phillip."

She was quiet the rest of the meal, and once they'd finished and she packed away the lunch items, Gabe stood and studied the land again. "Looks like a good spot for a house just over there." He pointed. "I could clear a few of those trees and leave the rest to shade the yard. Barn and corrals off that way."

"Will there be horses?" Phillip asked.

"Fine horses. And a few cows."

"What about chickens? Jimmy Fuller gots chickens at his place and he has to give 'em food and water every day. They make their own eggs!"

Gabe grinned. "A few chickens might be called for. Eggs make a fine breakfast."

"Maybe I can come help you sometimes. I'm gettin' bigger."

"That would be a fine idea, as long as your ma and pa say it's okay."

On the ride back, Phillip leaned against Elisabeth's side and slept. The house at the top of the hill was uncommonly silent when they arrived.

Gabe followed Elisabeth inside, Phillip at her side. She removed her hat and hung it on one of the pegs that lined the exterior foyer wall. He followed her example.

The twins sat at the top of the stairs, quietly playing with wooden horses.

With one hand on the banister, Elisabeth climbed the steps. "Where's Mama?"

"In her room," John answered. "Westing."

With a swish of skirts, she hurried past them and disappeared along the upper hallway.

Gabe perched on a lower stair and watched the boys. He'd never seen them so silent.

Within a few minutes, Elisabeth returned. "Are you feeling well enough to fetch Dr. Barnes?"

He straightened with a nod. "What's wrong?"

"Everything's fine," she replied in a calm tone. "We're just going to have a new brother or sister very soon."

He glanced at the twins, then back at her. "Where's your father?"

"He hasn't yet returned from the Quinns."

"Do you suppose the doctor is still out there, too?"

"I have no idea."

"Better tell me where their place is, just in case."

"You can take the buggy," she offered.

"I'll return the buggy and get a horse."

"Are you able to ride?"

Without a reply, he loped down the stairs and grabbed his hat. "Take care of your mama. I'll be back."

He was relieved to have a task. Glad to be away from the unknown and uncomfortable atmosphere of child birthing.

When Warren Burke heard the news about Mrs. Hart, the liveryman loaned Gabe one of his own horses. The sleek speckled mare was some sort of Russian trotter mixed with Arabian blood. The white spots on its dark gray flanks resembled stars.

The horse had a black forelock and a gray tail that faded to lighter hair on the tips. Gabe took a liking to the unusually colored animal right off.

His side already ached from the day's exertion, but he pushed past the discomfort to focus on the job that needed doing. He checked the doc's house first. Matthew Barnes's wife told him her husband was right there at home, sleeping after his long night's vigil.

"I'll wake him and send him over to the Harts'," she assured Gabe.

Relieved, Gabe rode out of town. The Quinn farm was about a half hour ride. According to the landmarks, it was set to the west of Gabe's land, so it was probable his land adjoined the Quinn property. Studying the terrain again, he thought of all the years of travel, all the nights in a bedroll under the stars and those spent in a hotel room. Those hard years had paid for a future, and he was finally going to get to enjoy it.

Ezra Quinn's golden wheat fields waved under the afternoon sun. Gabe was no farmer, but it looked to him that it wouldn't be long before the wheat needed harvesting.

He'd grow hay to feed his horses and dig a well so Irene didn't have to go far for water. He was looking forward to getting to know his sister, but it was likely she wouldn't be with him that long. He would find her a good husband and see that she was settled and happy.

He spotted smoke curling from a chimney. A young man met him as he rode close to a one-story house and dismounted, holding his side. "Never seen you before, mister."

The young man was in his twenties, dressed in plain dungarees and a cotton shirt.

"Gabe Taggart. I'm lookin' for Samuel Hart."

"You the fella who shot those train robbers?"

Gabe nodded. "Is the preacher here?"

"In the house." The back door complained with a loud squeak as he led Gabe into a kitchen humid from an iron kettle steaming on the stove. "Back here. I'm Lester Quinn."

"Pleasure." Gabe snatched off his hat and worked to silence his boot heels on the wooden floor of the hallway beyond the kitchen.

Lester motioned for him to enter a dim room off to the left. Sam and a woman sat on chairs on opposite sides of a bed that held a motionless bald man.

Sam looked up, and it took a moment for recognition to dawn in his face. "Mr. Taggart?"

"Your wife's having the baby soon," Gabe told him.

Gabe glanced at the sleeping man in the bed.

"You go on home to your wife, Reverend," the woman said. "There's nothing more we can do here. I figure if God hasn't heard our prayers by now, He's not going to."

"He's heard them, Nell," Sam assured her. He followed Gabe outside, where the young man had anticipated his departure and hitched Sam's horse and buggy.

"Thank you, Reverend," Lester said. "You bein' here helped my mama a lot."

"That's why I'm here," Sam told him. "You see to it your mother gets some rest now. Maybe once I'm gone, she'll lie down."

"Yes, sir, Reverend."

Gabe rode a generous distance ahead of Sam so the horse wouldn't kick up dirt in his face, and they held a hasty pace. Thoughts of that brown bottle of medicine and the tranquil sleep it could bring taunted him. Doc Barnes had advised him not to ride, but he'd been all-fired convinced a lazy trip would do him well. He hadn't planned on extended hours in the saddle, however. While the animal beneath him had a sure, easy gallop, regardless Gabe's cracked rib had weathered a beating.

The hill to the house was the longest stretch of the trip. At last the sight of the gabled and turreted home relieved his tension. He eased the horse to a halt and dismounted to take the buggy reins from Sam. "I'll return the rig," he told him. "You go on."

With a distracted thank-you, Sam hurried up the steep brick stairs that led to the gate and the yard beyond. Gabe routinely checked the ground and the area for anything out of the ordinary, then tied the horse to the back of the buggy and turned the rig to head down the hill. He'd pay the liveryman's helper to give him a ride back.

He reached Main Street just as a locomotive released steam from its engine a few blocks away. He checked the street in both directions and made his way toward the livery.

"Mr. Taggart!"

At the call, his instincts went on alert. He turned to discover a reed-thin young man waving at him from the front of the telegraph building. The fellow stepped out from the shade of the overhang into the sunlight, and Gabe flexed his fingers without tensing his body.

"I have a message for you."

Relieved at the harmless notice, Gabe relaxed and met him in the street.

"I been lookin' for you," the younger man said. "Your sister is waiting for you at Mrs. Rhodes's café. I told her I'd watch for you and give you her message."

"Did you say my sister is here?"

"Yes, sir, Mr. Taggart."

Confused, Gabe reached into his pocket for a coin and flipped it in the air. "Thanks."

"I'm Junie Pruitt, by the way. In case you should need any errands done. Deliver messages, carry supplies, anything like that. You can find me on Main Street in the morning, and later in the day you can pin notes on the wall at the barber shop. I check 'em regular like."

"Good to know." Looked like he wouldn't be taking the buggy back just yet. Gabe searched out the café.

Irene shouldn't have arrived for another couple weeks. How was he going to take care of her when he'd had someone taking care of him until now? He hadn't even looked at the house he'd rented, though Elisabeth had assured him it was clean.

Why hadn't he thought to ask Junie Pruitt to handle Irene's luggage? This was a fine kettle of fish.

He no more than made it through the doorway before a woman in a jade-green traveling suit stood from beside the table where she'd been seated. She wore a feathery little hat that matched her jacket. "Gabriel!"

Her hair was as dark as he remembered, near black like his, but the rest of her… She looked nothing like the little sister he remembered. The person who hurried toward him was a beautiful woman, a woman with curves in places little sisters didn't have curves. "Irene?"

She flung herself toward him and before he could protect himself, she had crushed herself against him in an exuberant hug. The pressure against his ribs took his breath away. He managed to hold back all but a grunt.

"What's this?" she asked, leaning back and peeling open his jacket. Her eyes widened at the sight of his revolver. "I've never seen so many guns in my life as on my trip west," she told him. "Seems everyone has a weapon." She gave him a curious glance. "Am I going to need a gun? A woman on the train showed me the pearl-handled derringer she carried in her unmentionables. It was quite attractive actually. I wouldn't mind one of those."

"I wasn't expecting you for two more weeks," he said.

"I was weary of staying at a hotel," she told him. "My welcome wore out at school. After graduation all the other girls my age left. I helped with the younger children, but I'm not really cut out for nursemaid duty." She pulled a face.

"Children take so much work, don't you know. They are always hungry or spilling something…and the babies? Well, we won't even go into that."

"Are your belongings at the station?"

"Yes. I paid a nice fellow to watch them for me while I came here to get out of the sun. I can't wait to bathe and change into fresh clothing. Is your place far?"

"Actually… I've been staying with the preacher's family. There was a mishap on the train the day I arrived, and I was injured."

"Gabriel!" she said, her eyes wide with concern. "Are you all right?"

"Fine. Couple of tender ribs is all. I do have a small place rented. We'll stay there temporarily while our house is built."

"You're building a house for us?"

He nodded and urged her toward the door. The few patrons in the café had been staring while they reunited.

"Where is it?"

"Not far from town, but the building hasn't started yet."

"We won't be living in town?"

"My land is to the southwest. Not far, I assure you. You can come to town whenever you like. Often."

"All right."

She didn't appear entirely convinced about the idea of living away from Jackson Springs. "You won't be cut off from friends or shops."

He guided her to the buggy and headed toward the station. "I was thinking more about wild animals and Indians," she said. "I've heard stories about the danger of leaving civilization behind."

"Any Indians out our way will be friendly."

"What about wolves and bears?"

"I've spent years on the trail, and I've never had a run-in with a bear."

"A wolf?"

"A time or two," he answered begrudgingly.

She gaped at him in obvious concern.

"Maybe I will teach you to use a rifle," he decided. It was better to teach her to use a gun safely and with confidence than to leave her unprotected. He would have work to do and couldn't watch her every minute.

At the station, Gabe paid the fellow watching Irene's trunks and valises to load them into the buggy. He supposed he could check the two of them into the hotel. Josie had generously offered that his sister could join him at the Harts', but now with the baby arriving today, he didn't want to add more work and additional complication to their lives.

Briefly, he explained that his hosts were in the middle of a family event. He stopped the buggy and gestured for Irene to climb the steep stairs ahead of him. At the top, he masked his grimace and fatigue to take her hand and lead her up the porch stairs and, with a tap on the door, into the house.

"Oh, there you are!"

He looked up in surprise to see Elisabeth and Abigail coming from the back hall. Elisabeth handed the covered tray she carried to Abigail, and the girl carried it up the stairs.

"How is Mrs. Hart?" he asked.

"She's just fine," Elisabeth answered. "And so is the baby."

"He came already?"

"She," she said with a smile. "Rachel." She turned to Irene with a questioning expression.

"This is my sister, Irene." He gestured to Elisabeth. "Elisabeth Hart."

"I had no idea you would be here so soon." Elisabeth surprised him by taking Irene's hand and offering her a warm smile. "Welcome to Jackson Springs and to our home. You must be exhausted."

"I am weary of the dust," his sister replied with a smile. "It's a pleasure to make your acquaintance, Mrs. Hart."

"Oh, no, just Miss, but you must call me Elisabeth. There are far too many Miss Harts around here to keep us all straight." She glanced at Gabe, then back. "We'll get your belongings carried up to a room for you. I'm guessing they're outside now? And meanwhile I'll run you a bath."

"I was gonna get my things and take Irene to a hotel," Gabe told her. "You folks have your plate full already without us adding to the workload."

"You know Josie would never allow that to happen,"

she replied. "You will both stay right here until we get you situated in the parsonage."

"The parsonage?" Irene asked.

"My father's the preacher," Elisabeth told her. "But when you see the house, you'll know why we never lived there. Not that it isn't clean or nice," she hastened to add. "Just that we're a big family, and the house is small."

Abigail came back downstairs at that moment, and Elisabeth made introductions. "My sister Abigail will show you back to the bathing chamber and get water for your bath while I see to having your things brought in."

Once the two young women were gone, Elisabeth turned to him. "You didn't tell her, did you?"

Chapter Eight

Only years of inflexible restraint kept him from revealing his panic at her question. What did she know? "What?"

"That you were shot."

His alarm subsided. "How did you know that?"

"Because you're standing there with pain written on every angle of your face, but she didn't show a fleck of concern. Had she known, she would've sent you to bed, like I'm doing right this minute."

He jerked a thumb over his shoulder toward the door. "But I—"

"No discussion. I'll see to the trunks and the buggy. Take the medicine on the bureau if you know what's good for you." She took his arm and guided him toward the stairs. "I'll settle your sister for a nap of her own, and you won't be missed."

Gabe took in her flushed face, the earnest concern in her blue eyes, and felt the warmth of her hand through his sleeve. Her tone and words were as brusque as ever. Yes, she was as sensible and practical as always, but for this moment genuine warmth was evidenced in her behavior as well, catching him more off guard than his sister's unexpected arrival.

His thoughts traveled unerringly to their kiss that afternoon. That had been a mistake. He'd intended to tease and see her reaction, be it disgust or shock, but he hadn't intended an honest-to-goodness kiss. Never in a thousand years had he expected her to lean in and kiss him back.

Even if he did have time or the inclination to take a wife in the future—and it for sure wouldn't be until after Irene was married off and his ranch was established—this woman with her talk of heaven and Jesus, along with her persnickety ways, wasn't suited to him.

His ribs hurt so bad he was sick to his stomach. He lent all his energy into making it up the stairs and to the bed without losing the contents of his stomach on her shoes.

He hated that she'd recognized his weakness. He wasn't accustomed to letting anyone see him less than strong and confident, but there was nothing he could do about it at the moment. He made it as far as the bed and half fell onto the quilt.

She reached for a boot and tugged it off, then the other. "Take off your gun," she ordered, and he complied. She took it from him, surprising him again, rolled the holster and tucked the gun and belt under his pillows. "Will you take the medicine?"

"Half a spoon," he conceded. She measured the dose and held it to his lips. He swallowed and collapsed back upon the pillows. "Thank you, Elisabeth."

"You're welcome." She slid the curtains shut, closing out the late afternoon sun.

He felt better already.

Before he was aware, she'd left the room, closing the door behind her.

* * *

Elisabeth and Abigail prepared and served a late supper. Their father took his seat, appearing weary, but joyful. He said a blessing over their meal, thanking God for the new life in their home and for Josie's recovery.

"Are you happy baby Rachel is a girl, Papa?" Phillip asked.

"I'm quite happy," Sam replied. "It was time we had another girl."

Kalli sliced ham for the twins and cut it into bite-size pieces. "She's sure a pretty little thing. I never knew babies were so tiny."

"You don't have any younger siblings?" Sam asked.

"No, Reverend," Kalli answered. I have two older brothers. The only babies I've seen are those at church, but they're so much bigger."

"You'll be surprised how quickly she will get bigger," Sam told her.

"Mr. Taggart's sister arrived this afternoon," Elisabeth said. "I've given her my room, so I'll be bunking with you until we get them settled down the street." She glanced at Anna.

"Isn't her arrival sooner than expected?" Sam asked.

Elisabeth explained with what little she knew.

"You did exactly what Josie would have," Sam told her. "Of course Irene and Mr. Taggart are welcome here until they can move to the parsonage."

"Where is she?" Anna asked.

Elisabeth explained that Irene had been exhausted from her travels. "I'll prepare plates for both of them and keep their food warm."

"I am blessed that my daughters are capable cooks and gracious hostesses," their father said with a smile for each of them. "You will make fine wives for three lucky young men."

"I might not get married, Papa," Anna said.

Her father and siblings studied her curiously.

"I want to study, like you," she said earnestly. "I want to be like my namesake in the Bible and do great things for God."

Sam appeared thoughtful for a moment before he spoke. "I am confident that all my children will accomplish great things for God," he said kindly. "Whether they are married or not."

At his words, Anna smiled and picked up her glass of milk.

Elisabeth looked upon her younger sister with fond appreciation. She'd begun to wonder whether or not a husband was in her own future. If the disappointing selection of possible mates she'd seen so far was any indication, she doubted she'd become a wife anytime soon. No one could measure up to her father.

A bright bit of burnt orange caught her attention at the doorway, and Elisabeth glanced up to find Irene standing hesitantly at the entrance to the room.

"Come in!" Elisabeth stood to usher her toward an empty chair. Picking up a plate and silverware from the extras on the sideboard, she set a place before her and handed her a napkin. "We've only just sat down."

Elisabeth made introductions. "Were you able to rest?"

"I had a pleasant nap, thank you. Where is my brother?"

"He's resting," she replied. "I'll keep a plate of food warm for him if he doesn't come down now."

Irene took the bowl of fried potatoes Kalli passed and

helped herself. "Is it common for him to sleep through supper?"

"He must've worn himself out riding today," Sam supplied. "He's only just been getting around a couple of days."

Irene's eyes widened.

"Josie and Elisabeth nursed him back to health," he added. "And fed him well, which I'm sure helped him recover."

"What happened exactly?" she asked. "All I know is he has tender ribs, but he didn't explain."

"Mr. Taggart shot the bandits what was robbing Lis'beth and the other people on the train," Phillip piped up.

Elisabeth's heart sank. She hadn't had time to prepare the children, but what would she have said anyway? She couldn't have encouraged them not to tell the truth. But Gabe hadn't wanted to upset his sister.

"That's how he got shot," Phillip supplied.

Color drained from Irene's face, and she set down the potato bowl with a thunk, sending her spoon flying, but unaware. "Shot? Gabriel was shot?"

"He's perfectly fine," Elisabeth assured her. "His rib deflected the bullet, but was cracked, so it's quite painful."

Irene stood, dropping her napkin beside her plate and abandoning her food before she'd taken a bite. "He said nothing."

"I'm sure he didn't want you to worry," Elisabeth replied.

The other young woman turned and left the dining room.

Not knowing whether or not to follow, Elisabeth

looked at her father for guidance. She didn't want to intrude on their family moment, but perhaps she could act as a buffer between the siblings. She wasn't sure why she cared.

At her father's shrug, she got up and followed, hurrying up the stairs.

Hearing Elisabeth's steps behind her, Irene paused in the upstairs hallway. "Which room is he in?"

Elisabeth moved past her and led the way to a closed door. "This one. He might still be sleeping."

Irene glanced at her, and then turned the knob and pushed open the door. The room was still dim and Gabe lay motionless upon the bed. She moved forward, and the floorboard under her foot creaked.

At the same split second, Gabe shot into motion, reaching beneath a pillow to produce his revolver, and aiming it at Irene with a deadly click.

Chapter Nine

Elisabeth's heart stopped momentarily before hammering against her ribs at the thundering speed of a locomotive. Irene stifled a cry. Pressing both hands against her midriff, she stood on her toes as though the position elevated her from harm.

"Irene!" he barked. "Don't ever sneak up on a man like that." He tucked the gun away and moved to a sitting position.

"You scared ten years off my life," she told him. "Who did you think had come into your room?"

Elisabeth was now wondering the same thing.

He ran a hand over his eyes. "You took me unaware, is all."

"Well, I was unaware, too," she said with an accusatory tone. "You neglected to tell me you'd been in a gunfight and were *shot*."

He glanced at Elisabeth, and she shook her head to say it hadn't been her who told. "It wasn't precisely like that," he denied.

The incident had been *exactly* like that, but Elisabeth kept her mouth shut.

"You shot men who were robbing the train?" his sister asked.

"Not until the situation turned dangerous and lives were at stake. Then I did the only thing I could."

"And one of them shot you?"

"I wasn't quite fast enough."

Elisabeth studied him in the dimness. Hadn't been fast enough? He'd felled half a dozen men in the time it took her to draw a breath!

"What if you'd been killed?" Irene asked, her voice breaking. "What if I'd arrived in Jackson Springs to *that* news?" She raised a hand to her brow and stood like that, half shielding her eyes from view. "What would I have done without you?"

"It was my fault," Elisabeth said then, surprising herself and apparently Gabe, because he turned toward her with his black brows in the air.

Irene turned to face her.

"When those men held up the train and asked for all of our valuables…" She touched her fingers to the ring under her bodice. "I hesitated. I didn't mean to put anyone in danger. It was instinct, a protective reaction to the possibility of losing my mother's ring." She looked at Gabe. "He warned me to hand over my belongings so no one got hurt, but I dragged my feet too long. If I'd simply complied, the bandits would have taken their booty and left us in peace."

"You can't know that for sure," Gabe interjected.

"But you said—"

"At the time going along peacefully seemed the reasonable thing," he said. "We have no way of knowing if they'd have shot passengers or not. Thieves are an unpredictable lot."

Elisabeth blinked. This day had been full of surprises. His summation was the extreme opposite of anything he'd said regarding the holdup until now. He'd blamed her for all the injuries, including his own. She didn't know how to react to the pardon. But perhaps his understanding was only for his sister's sake. Elisabeth didn't care why he'd changed his tune. Irene was a gently raised young woman, who had traveled all this way to unite with her brother. Elisabeth understood firsthand what it was like to leave behind everything familiar and comfortable and face the uncertainty of starting over.

She also knew what losing a mother was like, though Irene had lost both her parents, and Elisabeth had always had her sisters for company and comfort. This girl had only Gabe.

She looked at him. May the good Lord help her. Sensing the tension between brother and sister, Elisabeth changed the subject. "Dinner is on the table right now. May I bring you a plate?"

"I'll come down." Getting to his feet without placing a hand against his side must have taken gumption, or he truly was much better. "Just give me a few minutes to wash up." Anticipating her next words, he said, "The water from this morning is just fine. I'll be down shortly."

Dismissed, she and Irene walked out, and Elisabeth closed the door behind her.

"You lost your mother?" Irene asked.

"Seven years ago," she answered.

Irene blinked. "But all those small children…"

"My father remarried. Josie is resting right now. A brand-new baby sister was born just today."

"And you've all been so gracious, when you already have a house—and your hands—full."

"Josie loves it that way. She was the one who initially suggested you stay with us."

"I shall look forward to meeting her."

"You won't be disappointed." She walked ahead of Elisabeth to the top of the stairs. "I lost both of my parents at the same time. Gabriel saw to my care and education. I've been counting the days until I could leave boarding school. I can't wait to live in a real home and get to know my brother."

"I can attest that it's his priority to make a home for you. Having his plans thwarted did not rest well."

They returned to the dining room, where Gabe joined them within a few minutes. He sat next to his sister, and she looked over at him with adoration.

Sam inquired about Abigail's and Anna's day at school, and once they'd finished sharing the details of their day—before they'd been summoned home to meet their new sister—he asked the twins what they'd done. Kalli filled in missing details. Finally he glanced at Elisabeth, then over at Gabe. "And how was your ride? How does the land appear?"

"Fertile," Gabe replied. "There are trees and bushes everywhere, so there's underground water. We saw streams. Of course I haven't looked over all of the property, but it doesn't appear anyone's ever settled there, and if they have it's been in years past. There are meadows for hay and grassland for pastures. And a flat spot for a house and stables and corrals."

"If you grow grapes, they will have to be carried on a stick between two men," Elisabeth joked.

Gabe looked at her like she'd spoken another language. "That's absurd."

She stared at him pointedly. "Joshua and Caleb after they saw the promised land?"

"Who are Joshua and Caleb?"

She shared a look with her father. "Never mind."

"No, tell me. Are Joshua and Caleb ranchers or farmers?

"They were Israelites Moses sent ahead to spy out the promised land after the people had been freed from bondage in Egypt," Irene supplied, surprising Elisabeth. "They returned saying the land God gave them flowed with milk and honey and that the bunches of grapes were so huge, it took two men to carry them."

Gabe nodded. "I've heard of Moses."

"The lesson to be learned," Sam said, "is that the other ten spies reported they'd seen giants. They thought it looked too risky to take over the land. They allowed fear to cloud their judgment, and their fear spread to the people. They wanted to tuck tail and run. What those ten spies had was an eye problem."

"What do you mean, Papa?" Phillip asked.

"They were looking at the circumstances with their natural eyes and not eyes of faith. They said, 'We seemed like grasshoppers in our own eyes, and we looked the same to them.' But they were spies, sent to observe in secret. The giants didn't see them at all. Those men imagined their fears."

"Tell about Joshua and Caleb," Anna said, leaning forward over her plate.

"Joshua and Caleb had a different perspective," Sam said. "God had, after all, promised that land to them.

They gave Moses a good report about the lushness of the land."

"Maybe they hadn't seen the giants," Gabe suggested.

"Oh, they saw them all right. But they figured that if God had promised Canaan would be their home that those giants would either leave or be destroyed. They saw the same circumstances, but they saw them through God's promise and power. They said, 'Let's hurry on in there and take that land. We're well able to overcome and possess.'"

"What happened?" Gabe asked.

"All the people listened to the naysayers. They cried and complained and grumbled about Moses bringing them there and wished they had died in Egypt where they were slaves, and Joshua and Caleb couldn't talk them out of their fears. Even after God had parted the Red Sea for them and swallowed up the Egyptian army behind. Even though He dropped manna from the sky to feed them, still they didn't trust Him.

"So God said then that none of those over twenty years old would see the promised land. The ten spies died from a plague. The people wandered in the wilderness for forty years until the last person, besides Joshua and Caleb, who'd been over twenty had died. Joshua and Caleb were allowed to enter Canaan.

"After that Joshua fought a lot of battles, and he's the one who led his army to march around Jericho until the walls fell."

"Tell us that story, Papa," Phillip encouraged.

"Another time," his father replied in a kind voice. "We've all had a long day and can all use some rest."

"Do you really believe in giants?" Gabe said later to Elisabeth as she reached to serve him rice pudding.

"There are several accounts in the Bible," she said. "Goliath was most likely a descendant of those giants the Israelites saw."

After Kalli, Elisabeth and Abigail had cleared away supper and finished the dishes, they joined the others in the great room where Anna sat working on her arithmetic and Sam held a twin on each knee. "Let's go up now so you can see your mother and Rachel for a few minutes," he said to the boys. "Then it's time for bed."

The younger siblings obediently joined him, and Kalli followed to help them prepare for bed, leaving Elisabeth with the Taggarts.

"Would you care for a game of cribbage?" she asked. "Or you're welcome to any of the books in Father's library down the hall."

"I believe I will get a book," Irene replied and left the room.

"Your father tells those stories as if they're real," Gabe said.

Elisabeth cast him a look. "They are real."

He said nothing.

Irene returned, book in hand. "You father has a copy of *The Memoirs of Uncle Tom*. I've never read it, but I've always wanted to."

"Sounds familiar," Gabe commented.

"It's Josiah Henson's personal telling of his life story. This is the book on which Harriet Beecher Stowe based *Uncle Tom's Cabin,* the book that practically started the war between the states by exposing the truth about slavery."

"I've always admired her," Elisabeth said. "She was

a Christian lady. She met with Abraham Lincoln, you know."

"The female abolitionists are my role models," Irene told her with a nod. "By taking a stand for equality, they laid the groundwork for women's rights. I've heard Elizabeth Stanton and Matilda Joslyn Gage give speeches."

Gage looked at her with a brow cocked. "Where?"

"Our headmaster took all of us to Philadelphia for women's suffrage meetings whenever a speaker came through. This is an important year. While we're celebrating a hundred years of freedom, women still have fewer rights than their male counterparts. Did you realize that women do two-thirds of the work in our nation, but aren't even allowed the same legal privileges as men?"

"Which privileges are those?" he asked.

"Most importantly, the right to vote," she answered, sitting beside him. "This month the leaders of the suffrage movement are traveling in the states and territories, talking to the people. Women will be wearing black crepe on Independence Day to show their allegiance to the cause. In many cities and towns the women will the orators of the day." She turned to Elisabeth. "Why, I've attended so many meetings, *I* could give a speech!"

Gabe wanted to groan, but still absorbing this new information and a side of his sister he hadn't anticipated, he thought a moment before speaking. "It's all right for you to read your books and talk to us about this, but it might be better for everyone if you don't make your interest public."

Irene stared at him, disappointment in her expression, her stiff posture revealing anger.

Elisabeth cringed inwardly, waiting for her next words.

"Gabriel," Irene said in a controlled voice. "Are you going to tell me I can't stand up for what I believe?"

"No," he replied carefully. "I was just thinking how the single men would react to your passion for this cause. It might put them off."

"And why would I give a whit about what they think?"

"Because they're husband prospects."

This time she left the book on the sofa and stood. She took a step back as though he'd stung her. "It's your belief that I need a husband, therefore I should be compliant and pretend I'm someone I'm not in order to catch one?"

Elisabeth closed her eyes, feeling Irene's hurt. She wished she could leave the room, but could hardly get up and run now.

"I didn't say that."

"You did say that." His sister pursed her lips, and then with more composure added, "You want to marry me off so I'm not a bother."

"No, Irene. It's not like that at all."

"Because I can support myself, you know. You paid for an education most young women never get. I can keep accounts, and I am familiar with many tasks. I could apprentice at a trade or I could be a bookkeeper. I even know enough about herbs and tinctures to help a doctor."

"That wasn't at all what I meant."

"What do you think, Elisabeth?" Irene asked, turning toward her. "Do you think women are entitled to have opinions about their own futures?"

Elisabeth didn't want to get in the middle of the siblings' disagreement. Neither did she want to take a side, but she sympathized with Irene and the hurt she was obviously feeling. "I understand that your brother has concerns for your future, and he feels a responsibility toward you. It's plain that he loves you."

Gabe seemed satisfied with her answer…but she continued.

"I don't necessarily agree with hiding your beliefs under a bushel just to please a prospective husband. You couldn't live your whole life stifled in that manner. When your true viewpoint became apparent, the man might feel as though he'd been tricked."

"As he would have been." Irene turned to Gabe again. "And that is the life you'd have for me? Tricking a husband into marriage because who I really am isn't pleasing enough?"

He rubbed a palm down his face and cupped his jaw for a moment before dropping his hand. "The two of you have twisted my words into something I didn't intend."

"I can make my own decisions about my future," Irene said. "Without a man telling me what to do. You or any other man."

She turned on her heel and left the room.

Chapter Ten

Irene obviously hadn't wanted her brother to see her cry. Once she was gone, Elisabeth cast Gabe a tentative glance.

He looked as though he'd been shot again. "That wasn't what I intended."

"Her feelings are hurt," she told him. "She's only just arrived and you've told her you're planning to marry her off."

He shook his head. "No, I didn't say that."

"Not in those exact words, but you said it. It's plain she adores you. She's never had a family or a home. You're all she has, and if your main concern is for her to marry, she probably feels as though you don't want her with you."

"I do want her. I always wanted her. I was never able to take care of her, but I gave her the best education possible."

"Obviously. And now you don't want her to use it."

He sat forward with his elbows on his knees, head lowered, and laced his fingers in front of his eyes.

Elisabeth felt his pain as acutely as she'd felt Irene's.

She moved to sit beside him and placed her hand on his shoulder.

He started at the touch, but turned his head to look at her. The anguish in his eyes told of his deep love and lack of confidence. He was so brash and smug in all other ways, this unfamiliar glimpse of vulnerability tugged at her heart.

"She loves you very much, Gabe. You're her only family in the world. Maybe she just wants to feel important in your eyes and have value. I've always had Father and my sisters, so I can't imagine what it would be like to spend Christmas and holidays without them and the knowledge that I belong. She needs to belong. You can give her that. You just have to be open."

He nodded, but didn't speak.

"I understand that you only want the best for her. You want to see her happy and fulfilled, and in your eyes marriage would be that fulfillment for her. Isn't that so?"

He nodded again.

"Just say it to her like that. Tell her you only want her to be happy. And that you'll support her in any manner that will bring her joy."

He lowered his hands and straightened. Elisabeth's hand, still on his shoulder, trailed down his back in a manner meant to be comforting.

Instead, he reached to take her by her upper arm and guide her closer to him. Her breath caught in her throat.

She'd never seen him in this light—and she liked the evocative glimpse into his heart. There was something endearing about the man who clearly loved his sister, yet fumbled with how to communicate with her. He'd believed he'd done the best he could for Irene by placing her in a girls' academy, but what effect had the separation had on *him?* "Do you still believe you did the right thing for her by placing her in that school?"

"Sometimes I feel like I abandoned her, but it was because I wanted the best for her."

"Maybe she felt as though you abandoned her, too. Just ask."

"You make it sound easy."

"Nothing worthwhile is easy."

"Some things are," he replied.

Her gaze dropped to his mouth. Even though she knew the answer, she couldn't resist asking, "Like what?"

"Like kissing you." He leaned forward and covered her lips with his.

Elisabeth experienced a kind of giddy happiness she now associated with *this*—and with this man and the untried feelings his nearness and attention created. Gabe cupped her jaw, laced his fingers into her hair behind her ear and stroked his thumb over her cheekbone with aching gentleness.

The touch was so unlike anything she'd ever known or imagined, her breath caught in her throat. A realization flitted around her, daring her to take notice. There was something developing between them, something more than their initial butting of heads and his bold teasing. Her feelings about him had grown confusing, and she didn't like being uncertain about anything.

She had unconsciously moved her hand to his shoulder, and only now realized she was clinging to him a little too intensely. Embarrassed by her behavior, she drew back and sat away.

He studied her, but she let her gaze drop.

"Thanks," he said.

"For what?"

"For talking straight and pointing out what I'm too dense to figure out."

"That wasn't so hard, was it?" Again she turned his words back to him, and this time he grinned.

The fact that he'd been open to her suggestions touched her. Listening to advice seemed contrary to everything she'd learned about him until now, and the book of Proverbs came to mind. She remembered several verses about a man who sought counsel being wise. "You're not dense."

"Say it with more conviction."

She grinned. "You are not dense."

"I'll go talk to her. Which room?"

What he knew about talking to females he could've written on the palm of his hand. It didn't amount to much. He could stare a cold-blooded killer in the eye and not flinch. He was comfortable lying in wait for hours—sometimes days, without food and very little water—but he'd rather face off with a mama grizzly than see disillusionment or pain on his young sister's face. He was completely out of his element.

Elisabeth had made it all sound so simple. And maybe it was. But it sure wasn't comfortable.

He tapped on the door Elisabeth had pointed out.

"Who is it?" came the soft reply.

He would have opened the door to avoid the disruption in the hall since Mrs. Hart needed her rest, but his sister wasn't a child any longer. He couldn't just go barging in. "It's me," he said, holding his voice down.

A moment later, the door opened. He was thankful

she didn't intend to ignore him. She had changed into her nightdress and a pale blue wrapper. Her feet were bare on the patterned rug. He followed her into the room and glanced around.

He recognized the straw hat perched on a metal sculptured stand atop a wardrobe. The unique scent of fresh linen and meadow grass unmistakably defined the room as Elisabeth's. Until that moment he hadn't realized how profoundly the woman disturbed him, but here he was recognizing her scent, identifying her belongings and experiencing an uneasy pull on his senses.

He focused on his sister. "We didn't get off to a very good start."

She sat on a chair and pointed to another beside a table in a slant-ceilinged dormer before several windows. "It wasn't the best news I've had, hearing you can't wait to get me out from underfoot when I've only just arrived."

How had he botched things so badly? "You're not underfoot and you never could be. I want you with me. The whole reason I came here and the reason I want to build a house is for you. For us. So we can be a family."

The tears that formed in her eyes made his chest ache. "Then why all this talk of being amenable to please and catch a husband?"

"I just thought—you're of an age when young ladies look for husbands, so I figured…" He stopped and shook his head. "I just want you to be happy. No matter what that means."

"I'm going to have plenty of time for all that to happen," she said. "And I don't want a husband who doesn't love me for who I am. I'm vocal about women's rights."

"I know that now."

"I wouldn't marry a man who opposed my convictions. If I marry, the man will have the same values and beliefs I do."

He didn't hold out for a man like that to turn up in Jackson Springs. He didn't need to voice his doubts, however. He was prepared to share a home with her forever. "Irene," he said.

She studied him.

"I never would have placed you in that school if I hadn't thought it was the best—and safest—place for you. I couldn't have paid for your education and the things you needed if I hadn't been able to travel."

"I believe you." She picked at a thread on the sleeve of her wrapper. "But I often wished you'd taken me with you. I'd have lived anywhere just to have been together."

The path he'd chosen had made that impossible. He'd spent over ten years chasing outlaws and staying alive by his wits and his skill with a gun. What he'd earned had been more than enough to fund boarding school; he'd lain by savings that would give them both a chance to start over. "What I did all those years was for us," he said. "For a future."

"Whenever you visited and I asked to come with you, you always said it wasn't possible. But you never told me what you did," she said. "And I guess I don't want to know if it was illegal."

She didn't know him. If he'd been in her place he'd have had plenty of doubts and suspicions…as well as questions. He didn't take her trust lightly. "It wasn't."

She folded her hands. "Good."

"Do you remember our parents?"

"Barely," she said. "I remember a big rocking chair by the fire, and Mother rocking me when I was small.

I can picture our father in his white shirt and tie, and I recall him buying me licorice from a row of jars in a mercantile. What did he do?"

"He worked at the courthouse," Gabe replied.

"And they were killed by a horse and wagon?"

He nodded. "I was in school when the sheriff came for me. He took me to the undertaker's. That's where I last saw them. Mother had left you with a friend while the two of 'em went to lunch. Our house was in town and I suppose they did that on occasion. A team got startled in front of the livery and ran wild down the street. Smashed the wagon right up on the boardwalk and into the front of the building where they were sitting near the window."

"I vaguely remember staying with one family after another after that," she said.

He nodded. "Until I quit school and took a job at the livery so we could be together. Had a little room over the seamstress's shop."

"That must've been hard for you."

"Harder for you, probably. You were alone a lot. I couldn't take care of you by myself, feed you proper."

"I'm sorry," she said.

"For what?"

"That you had to quit school to take care of me."

"I was old enough," he told her. "No hardship. I just wanted you to have more than I could give you. So I saved enough to board you with a family, joined a drive and sent back everything I earned that first time. A couple years later I had enough to send you to the academy."

"Thank you, Gabriel."

"You don't owe me any thanks."

"I do. You took care of me."

"You're not obligated. It was my duty."

"You were just a boy yourself."

He shrugged. "We're here now."

"Can we start over?" she asked. "Fresh?"

Relieved, he nodded. "I'd like that."

She got up and knelt at his feet, where she laid her head on his knee. The warmth of her tears wet the fabric covering his leg. Hesitantly, he touched her hair and bent to place a kiss against her head. She looked up at him then, and her lashes glistened. "Thank you for bringing me here."

It took a minute for him to speak around the lump in his throat. "It's what I always wanted. I was just waiting for the time to be right."

She smiled.

"The house will be serviceable and you'll be comfortable," he told her. "But don't expect it to be like this one." He glanced around the room.

"This place is something else, isn't it? And the Harts are such generous people. Elisabeth is sleeping with her sister tonight so I can have this room."

"They're good people," he replied.

"So she nursed you for the past week?" she asked.

He nodded. "Somewhat begrudgingly, to be sure."

"I can hardly believe that."

"We didn't get off to a good start."

"And now?"

He thought over their relationship. "She's tolerating me."

"I think she more than tolerates you."

"What do you mean?"

"When she thinks no one is looking—when you're

not looking—she casts telling glances your way. And *you…*" Wearing a teasing smile, she gathered her robe around her legs and pushed to her feet. "The looks you give her say more than 'please pass the mashed potatoes.'"

He had no reply. He didn't know what he thought about Elisabeth, and he didn't want to examine his feelings. The notion that anyone else had glimpsed his confusing attraction to her didn't sit well. He stood. "I'd better go so you can get some rest."

"Good night, Gabriel." She stepped against him and laid her head against his chest. "Everything's going to be grand now that we're together."

He returned her hug. One of his concerns had been set to rest. Irene didn't intend to pressure him to tell her how or where he'd made his living up until now. And if she did learn somehow, he was relatively certain she wouldn't be appalled or fault-finding. Still, he didn't want to risk losing her esteem.

Three gas lamps lit the long hallway, and in their glow, he spotted Elisabeth perched on a bench beneath a window. Behind her the night sky was dark and the moon filtered through the swaying branches of a tree. She'd freed her hair from its braid and the shiny mass hung down her back in ripples.

He strode toward her and she got to her feet.

"I don't mean to be intrusive, but I can't help wondering how it went," she whispered.

"Don't want to wake your family," he replied.

She glanced aside and then gestured. "Up here."

He followed her to what appeared as another room, but instead the door led up a narrow set of stairs to another door, which she opened and entered through. She lit a lamp, illuminating a tiny square room furnished with undersize chairs, enormous pillows and bookcases filled with books and dolls.

She closed the door. "This has always been a hide-away for we three sisters," she said. "The boys aren't allowed. I still come here when the household is chaotic and I want to be alone." She took a seat on one of the chairs and gestured for him to join her. "The few times my father's been in here, he used the cushions."

He had his doubts about the spindly little chairs holding his weight, so Gabe seated himself and hoped he could get back up without embarrassing himself. "I said the same things to Irene that I said to you."

"And she forgave you and you made up."

"More or less." He looked toward a window. "Thanks to you and your insight."

"It wasn't all that difficult to recognize her feelings. Or yours."

He faced her. "What am I feeling now?"

Chapter Eleven

She shrugged and a long skein of hair fell forward over her shoulder. "Relief? Regret maybe."

"Thank you for giving up your room so Irene could sleep in there."

"I don't mind sleeping with Anna. She thinks it's great fun when we have a lot of company and share rooms." She sat with her hands in the pockets of her robe and a clicking sound came from the one on the right.

Curious, Gabe glanced at her lap.

She withdrew her hand to show him what she held: three small smooth stones. He frowned in puzzlement.

"I have a collection of stones," she explained. "I gathered them along riverbanks and on the prairies as we traveled west with our wagon train. At first I just liked them and thought it would be fun to save mementos from along the trail." She held her hand open and studied the three rocks. "They've become reminders of the sacrifice we made to come here…of losing my mother. They remind me that the decisions we make have everlasting repercussions."

He understood that. He'd chosen to hunt down wanted men. He was good at it, and the bounties had been more than he could have made any other way. At the time it had seemed like the best choice...but now he had to live with the lives that had been changed—and lost—along the way. Now he had to keep his past a secret from civilized people like these.

"You get those out and look at them often?"

"I have a few with me all the time," she replied with a sheepish glance through her lashes. "These have been in the pocket of my wrapper."

"Imagine they're a good reminder to think before you do somethin' you'll regret." Though he doubted she needed the rocks. She seemed pretty set on doing what was right as a way of life.

She stared at the trio of stones in her palm for a long minute, and at last took a deep breath. She extended her hand. "Pick one."

He gave her a curious glance. Was this some sort of game?

"Go ahead," she coaxed. "Take one."

He plucked one with an interesting smooth divot from her hand. "Now what?"

"Now put it in your pocket. It's yours."

The gesture caught him off guard. The rocks obviously held great sentiment. "Thank you. Irene's the only one who's ever given me a gift."

She tilted her head to ask, "Are you poking fun at me? It wasn't a gold watch."

"Not at all." His voice was low. As a child his sister had drawn him pictures and once, in subsequent years, had sewn him a shirt that was too small. He still had it, though.

He closed his hand over the warm stone.

She pushed to her feet. "I have a notary job in the judge's chambers at the courthouse early tomorrow, so I'd better get some sleep."

"I'll be ordering lumber and getting supplies," he said. "Will Irene be all right staying here?"

"She can come with me," Elisabeth said. "She'll enjoy my meeting. The Tanners are adopting a little boy. This is only the second adoption I've witnessed, but it's a joyful event watching a family form. Last time I cried."

He grinned. "I'm sure she'll be glad to go with you. Do you have a key to the house we're moving into? I can have our things moved."

"It's in the carved teakwood box on the foyer table."

He had to stop at the bank to check on how his money transfer had progressed. He wanted to pay the Harts for food and lodging. Which gave him an idea for something to occupy Irene.

He held his side while he rose from the cushions.

They both reached for the doorknob at the same time, and her hand covered the back of his. She surprised him by not pulling hers away.

They stood like that, with his heart beating so hard he wondered if she could hear it and her shoulder touching his chest. Beneath his chin, her hair was as fragrant as he remembered. Without planning to, he raised his other hand to thread his fingers through the length of her cool silken hair.

Without preamble, she turned and was in his arms, her face raised to his expectantly.

She smelled better than a meadow full of wildflowers on a spring day. Better than fresh linens and new mown hay. Her own unique scent clung to her and filled his senses.

He still held the stone. The stone that was supposed to remind him of the consequences of choices. What could come of holding this young woman in his arms? What lasting ramifications would result from kissing her...from allowing himself these moments of sweet affection?

They were as far apart in experience and points of view as a mountain peak and a gorge. She was pure and filled with hope and promise, and he was a cynic who'd seen the worst of people and looked for trouble behind every tree. She'd been raised in the lap of a kind and God-fearing family, while he'd lived a solitary existence on guts and sheer determination. She possessed a stalwart faith he couldn't comprehend. Gabe, on the other hand, figured if there was a God up there, he'd done nothing to deserve any special consideration.

The stone was practically burning his hand.

Her eyes were as blue as the wildflowers down Texas way.

He dropped the rock into his pocket and placed that hand on her shoulder, trapping silken hair in his gentle hold.

The way she looked at him showed she was as uncertain about whatever it was that had been developing between them as he was, but she showed no fear or hesitation. If she had, he couldn't have taken her in his embrace and kissed her the way he did, with the joy of discovery and never-before-known wonder beating in his heart.

Had she shown any reluctance or resisted he'd have backed away and forgotten the idea, but she didn't. She seemed every bit as curious as he to examine the new and mystifying feelings.

He probably liked kissing her too much. He was certain he wasn't on her list of eligible men, and she...well he had too many other problems to take care of without adding this one to the list.

Didn't he?

The following morning, Irene had telegrams to send. "I'm contacting the governor of the Colorado Territory as well as the administrator of the Christian Women's Liberty Union. There's no reason why one of the spokespersons can't be here on Independence Day. It will add another dimension to the celebration."

"You know who to contact to make an arrangement like that?" Elisabeth asked.

"When in doubt, go to the top," she replied.

After Elisabeth checked her timepiece brooch, they headed for the courthouse.

"I admire your job," Irene told her. "Are there other women notaries?"

"I'm sure there are," Elisabeth replied. "If not many, the most likely deterrent is the travel. I take the train, and up until this last time it has been safe."

"How did it happen?" Irene asked. "I never heard all the details about the train robbery, and I want to know."

Elisabeth shared her account, not sparing the uncomfortable truth regarding her reluctance to part with her mother's ring and how it escalated the situation.

"I understand your attachment," Irene told her. "I have only a few things that belonged to my mother, and I would never part with them. Not even at gunpoint." They paused on a corner. "How did your mother die?"

She rarely spoke of that day. On occasion when one of Elisabeth's sisters brought it up, they talked about their fear and grief. But Elisabeth harbored more than grief. It was her fault their father hadn't gone in search of his wife when they'd been cast into the river. Elisabeth had been so terrified, that even though she'd been able to reach an overhanging branch and cling to it for dear life, she'd screamed in terror for help until her father had come for her.

If he'd gone for her mother first, they'd both have been saved.

She shared the story without those disturbing details, however.

"I wasn't as old as you when my mother died," Irene said. "But still I've missed her my whole life. I wasn't right there when it happened, either. I can't imagine how difficult her death has been for you."

"Thank you," Elisabeth said. By then they'd reached their destination, and she'd talked about the subject more than enough.

Half an hour later, Elisabeth and Irene left the courthouse with buoyant spirits. "Shall we stop at the café for tea and biscuits?" Elisabeth asked. "It's not exactly like the teahouses in Denver, but regardless, the tea is good."

"I would like that."

Penelope Berry greeted them. Irene balked at taking the table in front of the window, so they took seats in the back of the room. Elisabeth had never had close friends her own age. Her younger sisters had always kept her company, and she'd never questioned her friendless situation because she was content. Her classmates had been silly creatures, chattering about the boys and their dresses and hair, while Elisabeth had turned her focus squarely on her studies.

She'd never taken an interest in what she considered the foolish ways of other females. That's why her enjoyment of Irene's company puzzled her. But as far as she'd seen, Irene wasn't silly or obsessed with her hair or clothing. She had an enviable education, a fluent vocabulary and a knowledge of history and society that Elisabeth admired.

She had liked Irene from the first, and the more she got to know her, the more impressed she was. She'd never seen the need for a friend, never sought a companion or prayed for friends, but God seemed to have anticipated her needs and sent Irene anyway.

She still didn't hold as much appreciation for Gabe's presence in Jackson Springs as she did his sister's, but she now suspected that his arrival and the land he owned had been determined by God's hand and wisdom.

"I have prayed for Gabriel for many years," Irene mentioned now. "For his safety, of course, but also that God would lead him to a time and a place where we could be a family. Now God has answered my prayers and brought us here."

Elisabeth had discovered that many people never mentioned God in their everyday conversations, but those who had a personal relationship with Him spoke of Him as naturally as they spoke of their friends and family. At the confirmation of Irene's faith, her fondness for the other woman grew yet again. *Thank You, Lord. Thank You for a friend.*

She hadn't realized how much time had passed or that other customers were now filling the café and ordering lunch. "I would suggest we stay to eat, but I want to get home and see to my stepmother."

They paid and headed for the door. Just as they stepped out onto the boardwalk, Rhys Jackson greeted them. "Good day, Elisabeth." He glanced at Irene and removed his bowler. "Afternoon, miss."

"Rhys, this is Irene Taggart. Irene, this is a good friend of our family, Rhys Jackson."

"How do you do?" he said with avid appreciation shining in his eyes. "It's a pleasure to make your acquaintance." His expression barely faltered. Irene wouldn't have noticed the new interest Elisabeth recognized. "Taggart, you say?"

"Have you met my brother?"

His eyes lit up. "Indeed I have. And to what does Jackson Springs owe the pleasure of your visit?"

"Oh, I'm not visiting, Mr. Jackson. I'm now a resident. As we speak, Gabriel is seeing to building us a home nearby."

"In town?"

"About three quarters of a mile to the northwest," Elisabeth supplied. "A handsome parcel of land with meadows and a stream flowing from the mountains. Gabe has already selected the location for the house."

"Indeed. Well, welcome to Jackson Springs, Miss Taggart. Good day, Elisabeth."

As soon as he'd entered the café, Irene asked, "Jackson?"

Elisabeth nodded. "His grandfather founded our community and many of the businesses. Rhys and his mother own the bank."

"The people are certainly friendly. I think I'm going to like it here."

Stepping off the boardwalk, they headed for home.

* * *

Elisabeth found her stepmother sitting in a chair in her bedroom, the loosely wrapped infant in her arms.

"How are the two of you?" Elisabeth asked.

"We're doing well," Josie replied.

"What can I do for you?"

"I'd really love to take a bath and wash my hair," Josie replied hopefully. "I didn't want to ask Kalli to care for the baby. She has her hands full with the twins, and besides… I don't know that she has experience with one so small."

"Rachel and I would love to get acquainted while you bathe. Just let me go heat water and fill the tub. I'll be right back."

Nearly half an hour later, she returned for the baby who was now awake.

"She just nursed, so she should be all right until I return."

"Don't worry about us." Elisabeth took the tiny warm bundle into her arms and beheld her with affection. It never failed to astound her how perfectly a baby was created and how incredibly tiny and helpless they were. Rachel had straight dark hair that stood off the top of her head and fell forward onto her forehead. It was silky to the touch, and when Elisabeth ran a fingertip down her cheek, she was struck anew by the incredible softness of the baby's skin.

She'd been fourteen when Phillip had been born, seventeen when the twins arrived, yet even as a girl she'd felt this stirring awe and fathomless love for each of her younger siblings. Elisabeth touched her lips to the baby's forehead and inhaled her newborn scent.

In coloring, Rachel took after Elisabeth's father, like

the twins. Seeing who a child would resemble particularly fascinated Elisabeth. Each child was a glorious and unique gift, created in a wondrous way. For the first time she wondered what it would be like to have her own child, to hold a baby she'd carried inside her…to recognize hair and features of a husband.

Unexpectedly a picture of Gabe flashed in her mind's eye.

Chapter Twelve

Gabe had hair as dark as her father's...he was tall... handsome. Any child he fathered would be as pretty as this one—what was she doing?

Elisabeth had to corral those thoughts and focus on something more appropriate—and logical. She took a seat in the rocker and hummed until Josie returned, dressed and with damp hair.

How are our guests faring?" she asked. "I was disappointed I missed Gabe's sister's arrival. Your father told me about dinner."

"It was lively," she answered. "I really like her. She's smart and she doesn't carry on about fashion and social functions like most of the young women I know. Gabe is having their things moved into the parsonage today, though. I was thinking that while Rachel sleeps, I'll go down and help Irene get settled."

"Rachel won't sleep but a couple of hours at a time just yet," Josie told her. "And when she's awake each time she'll only want me." She smiled. "So you go ahead and we'll do just fine. You don't have to wait on me. Your father walks up the hill and checks on us every few hours. He wanted to stay home, but I told him definitely not." She smiled. "He has a tendency to hover."

"He's a wonderful father," Elisabeth said.

Her stepmother agreed. "And a wonderful husband." Josie opened the window wider and stood in a shaft of sunlight so her hair would dry more quickly. "I still remember the first time I met all of you. My heart went out to you over your loss, and Sam was so sad and blamed himself for your mother's death. He loved her so much... his love was plain in everything he said and did—and in what he didn't say or do. I yearned for a love like that. For acceptance. I never thought I'd have it for myself. And I never dreamed he would be able to love again... to love me."

"He loves you very much," Elisabeth said. "It took me a while to understand love has no limits. We aren't created to love only a certain number of people and then our love's used up. Loving you didn't mean he didn't love my mother and it didn't take anything away from her. He wasn't loving you *instead* of her."

Josie turned to look at her, and tears escaped over her lower lids to her cheek. She brushed them away quickly.

"I didn't mean to make you cry."

Josie emitted a little laugh that sounded like a sob. "Everything is going to make me cry for a few weeks. It's okay."

She took Rachel from Elisabeth and placed her in her cradle.

"I am only just beginning to see something else," Elisabeth said.

"What's that?"

"I always thought your marriage was convenient.

Father married you because he needed a wife and we needed a mother."

"I was so happy to have a family that I could have accepted that," she replied.

"But he *loves* you, doesn't he?" She studied her stepmother. "I mean it started out like that and love developed. Fondness, appreciation, all that. But it didn't stop there. I don't know what I'm trying to say."

"I do." Josie came to stand in front of her. "We fell *in* love."

Elisabeth nodded. "Yes."

"Couples have had arranged marriages since Bible times—not so much arranged as bargained for and given in trade. I have to wonder how many of those ended as well as ours. I fancied myself in love with my first husband before I married him, and I lived a lonely existence as his wife."

"Were you brokenhearted when he died?"

"I was brokenhearted while he was still alive," she answered.

"How can a person know if it's going to turn out badly?"

"You can't, sweetie. You just have to ask the good Lord to send you the right one and then trust Him."

"I know that if I do marry, I want a man just like Father."

Josie touched her cheek. "He is indeed a very good example of a loving husband and kind father. That's a pretty tall order."

"Not too big for God," Elisabeth replied. "He did it for you."

Josie smiled. "Indeed He did." She gave Elisabeth a gentle hug. "You run along and help Irene now."

Elisabeth gave her a smile and enjoyed looking at Rachel one more time. "My new sister sure is pretty."

Josie got tears in her eyes again and shooed her off.

That afternoon, Elisabeth assisted Irene in arranging the furniture in the tiny little house to her liking, unpacking and storing away Irene's belongings and shopping for food. Once the items were all put away, Irene looked around the kitchen. "I guess I'd better think of what I'll prepare Gabriel for supper."

"I had planned for you to eat with us," Elisabeth said. "You can get more practice before doing it all yourself. I don't know how much help I'll be advising you on your cooking. I've never had less than five or six people to prepare for, and it's often more than that. Maybe Josie can give you advice."

Everything was finished then, except Gabe's saddle bags, a valise and a wooden crate, which stood untouched against a wall in the tiny room he would be using. The two women stood staring at them.

"Do you want to unpack his things?" Elisabeth asked finally.

Irene glanced at her and then back. She shook her head.

The thought of going through Gabe's personal belongings didn't sit well with Elisabeth, either, so Irene's head shake brought her relief.

An hour later, they were back up the hill.

For the next few days Gabe stayed busy locating carpenters and having the materials delivered to the site of the Taggarts' future home. Irene accompanied Elisabeth and assisted her in the church office, which made the chores go more quickly and gave Elisabeth more time at the house with Josie and the baby.

"I can't trail you everywhere you go forever," Irene said thoughtfully on Friday afternoon. "I graduated several weeks ago, of course, but before that I was used to attending classes and studying. Right now there's not all that much for me to do while Gabriel is working. The house is tiny and doesn't take much upkeep. I don't fancy standing in the kitchen baking."

"You could certainly continue a study that interests you," Elisabeth suggested. "You've been a big help to me with my father's research. History, perhaps, or a Bible course. I know many subjects interest you, but is there anything you'd like to pursue? Do you paint or write poetry?"

"I am interested in government," she answered. "For example I've spoken with a few people lately, regarding the fact that this territory hasn't achieved statehood. It's a subject close to many citizens' hearts. Perhaps I could learn the steps that have been taken and petition the president."

Her idea, as lofty as it seemed to Elisabeth, was indeed a good one. Unlike Irene's eagerness for women to have the right to vote, this cause would garner support.

"Are there any women on the town council...or on the board of governors of the territory?"

"I couldn't say for certain, but it's not likely," Elisabeth replied.

"I've contacted several of my acquaintances, and I'm relatively positive we'll have a well-known suffragette here to make a speech on Independence Day. I'm quite persuasive."

Elisabeth had never been one to make waves, so she

admired Irene for her unflagging zeal and for not being afraid to state her beliefs or to take a stand for them. Elisabeth believed women deserved as many rights as their male counterparts, as well. She needed to follow Irene's example and not be too timid to do the right thing if the time ever arose.

"I admire you," she told her new friend. "And I think you're going to be a positive addition to Jackson Springs whatever you decide to do."

The Stellings had been invited for dinner well in advance of Rachel's arrival, and Josie insisted they continue with their plans. She trusted her stepdaughters and Irene to plan and prepare the meal, and she joined the others in the dining room, Rachel in her arms.

Sam had cleaned up the small crib that fit at the end of the room and became a fixture in their dining whenever they had a new baby. Elisabeth had washed fresh bedding and affixed a rag doll Anna had offered to the side. Josie smiled with delight when she saw the bed, and after Arlene and her daughters had admired Rachel's silky hair and tiny fingers, she gently laid her down.

Josie made appropriate introductions before taking her seat beside her husband, introducing their dear friends to the Taggarts. "When the Harts had first arrived in Jackson Springs, the Stellings were some of our first friends," she explained. "Chess and Arlene helped us make the adjustment to our new home. Elisabeth and Gilbert studied together and have been friends. And Abigail and Anna took right to Libby and Patience and have been chums ever since."

"Gilbert is our deputy marshal," Sam mentioned for Irene's benefit. Gabe had already met him.

"You're kind to call it studying together, Mrs. Hart," Gil said with a grin. "Truth is Lis tutored me so I could pass my English classes. I still can't tell you when to use lay, lie or laid."

Gabe took a bowl of mashed potatoes Irene passed to him, but his focus had been snared by the information about the deputy and his friendship with Elisabeth. Gil sat directly across from Gabe, with Elisabeth at his side. He observed as they took portions of food and interacted.

"Did you make these creamed carrots?" Gil asked.

"Are they still your favorites?"

He grinned. "Yes."

"Then I made them."

They shared a quiet laugh.

Gabe finally noticed Libby waiting for the mashed potatoes and handed her the bowl. "Abby and Anna told us all about how you prevented those robbers from getting their mama's ring," she said to him. "Elisabeth sets great store by that ring, so I know how much she appreciated you coming to her rescue like that. It was a very brave thing you did."

Uncomfortable with the subject, he decided explanations would only draw more attention. He was at a loss for a reply, and she was waiting. "Miss Hart does favor that ring."

"Do you have anything special that belonged to your mother?" she asked.

"Well…" He thought a few seconds. "I have a tintype of my parents on their wedding day. And some books…and a silver comb and brush set I've been saving for Irene. Guess she can have it now that she's not at school."

"You never mentioned that, Gabriel," Irene said from his other side. "Where are they? When can I see them?"

"They're in those crates in my room. Station delivered them a couple days ago. Had 'em stored all these years."

"You'll have to sort all that out yourself," she said. "Elisabeth and I didn't touch your things."

"I wouldn't have cared." He glanced at Elisabeth. "But I can take care of it."

Gil's parents, seated at Sam's right side and across from Josie, were engaged in a conversation with their hosts. Patience, Anna and Abigail held their own quiet conversation, which left Libby free to ask him more questions.

Gil glanced over a couple of times, and he and Elisabeth shared a look. It wasn't until that moment that Gabe realized Libby had been flirting with him all along, engaging him in conversation and showing avid interest.

"How old is Libby?" he whispered to his sister when no one else was paying attention.

"She's out of school, so maybe eighteen?" She gave him a curious look. "Why?"

He simply tilted his head to indicate he was merely curious and tasted the creamed carrots.

"Josie tells me you're building a house," Arlene Stelling said to Gabe.

He glanced from Gil to his mother beside him. "The work will get underway next week," he told her.

"Gil has mentioned getting a house of his own," she said. "Do you want one that's all ready to move into or will you build a new place?"

Gil shrugged. "I don't know. I don't need a very big place or anything special."

"You'll have a wife one of these days," his mother reminded him. "Maybe you do need something special."

"I guess I'll figure that out when it happens."

Elisabeth didn't blush or glance at him as though that idea held any significance for her. She asked Kalli to pass the bread, which had ended up on the far end of the table by the boys.

"Are there many homes available?" Irene asked.

"There must be enough to keep Thomas Payne in business," Sam replied. "He handles local real estate."

"Daisy Martin and her family moved to Denver," Abigail said. "They had a nice house on Spencer Street. The brick one with the porch and the foliage that grows up the chimney."

"That house is empty?" Gil asked. "I remember going to birthday parties there when we were kids. Remember, Lis?"

Elisabeth nodded. "It has a great big kitchen. Mrs. Martin had it painted bright yellow."

Gil's expression showed interest. "Maybe I'll visit Tom and ask to see the place."

"My schedule is open," Irene said with a grin. "I'm available to go with you."

Several sets of eyes turned to Irene.

"If you'd like company, that is," she added. "I was just thinking… I'm free and all. I could give you a woman's perspective."

Gil's parents deliberately surveyed their plates. Elisabeth locked gazes with Josie for the briefest of moments. Gabe turned to look at Irene beside him. Her cheeks were flushed, and she wore a hesitant smile. Now *she* was flirting! Right in plain sight of everyone at the dinner table.

Gil returned her smile with a hesitation, but interest. "That would be nice," he said finally. "I'll talk to Tom and let you know." Then he glanced aside, as though he didn't want anyone to get the wrong idea. "Anyone else want to come along?"

No one took him up on the offer.

"Lis?" he asked, looking directly at her.

"It would depend on my schedule," she replied. "If I don't have an appointment, I can join you."

After they'd finished eating, Sam asked Abigail and Anna to clean up the dishes. Elisabeth and Patience joined them. Josie directed the others into the great room.

"Remember when we were the ones doing the dishes?" Arlene took Rachel from Josie's arms. "Now we have all these grown children."

"Children are a blessing from the Lord," Josie agreed.

Gabe got his first good look at the baby as Arlene uncovered her scrawny legs and held her for Chess to see. "Can you remember when our babies were this tiny?"

"At that size I was scared to death of 'em," the man replied. "Still am."

"The girls keep a checkerboard in that side table drawer," Gil said to Irene. "How is your game?"

She gave him a warning look. "I have skills that will amaze you."

Obviously familiar with the room and comfortable helping himself as though he'd done it a hundred times, Gil found the board and disks and set up the game on the side table, then arranged chairs for the two of them on either side.

Libby took a chair across from where Gabe sat on a divan. "If their game doesn't last too long, perhaps you'd like to play."

Chapter Thirteen

"I don't know how."

Her eyebrows shot up. "You've never played checkers?"

"Nope."

"I can teach you."

If this was what civilized people did after dinner, he guessed he might as well learn. "Okay." And realizing polite conversation was expected, he came up with a question. "Do you…are you involved in any studies?"

"Studies. Like school? No, I graduated two years ago. I now work for Opal Zimmerman, the dressmaker."

"Oh. Do a lot of women need dresses?"

"All women need dresses. Some more than others. Coats, too. I only just made my first coat. It's in the window at the shop if you should walk past."

"I'll have a look."

"Appears you're healing," Chess said then, taking the seat beside him. "Feeling better, are you?"

"Much better," Gabe replied, relieved to have another person join the conversation. "I've been riding, and it's getting easier."

"I broke ribs once, and you couldn't have made me get on a horse," Chess told him.

"He didn't have any trouble coming to the dinner table, though," his wife remarked, eliciting a laugh from those nearby.

"Well, this one's cracked, so it's probably not as painful," Gabe said in the man's defense.

Chess gestured to Gabe and tilted his head at his wife. "You see?" He grinned. "At any rate it's good to see you doing well. Last Sunday you were still lying abed, but I reckon we'll see you at church day after next."

"Church?" Gabe glanced from the man to his hosts, who were smiling encouragement. He'd been taken in by the minister's family. Of course they'd expect him to come to church. "Well, I—"

"We're looking forward to services," Irene said. "If we ever attended church together before, I was too young to remember. I can't wait to meet more residents of Jackson Springs, especially if they're all as nice as those I've met so far." She gave Gil another meaningful glance.

Elisabeth entered the room in time to pick up on the topic. "Father is an inspiring preacher. He plans his sermons for days, sometimes weeks in advance, and delivers them with conviction and compassion."

Sam caught her hand. "Elisabeth is my right hand. She sees to all the tasks that would keep my attention from preparing lessons or seeing to the spiritual needs of the congregation."

"Don't glorify straightening hymnals and baking communion bread."

Sam looked straight at Gabe. "She's humble. She

does a great deal of research for me, finding scriptures I need and locating details of history and Bible interpretation in my library. She used to do all the cleaning and preparing of communion, too, but now she delegates those jobs. She even counts the tithes and offerings and makes the bank deposit each week. And she often accompanies me to visit the sick and elderly."

Gabe had never even thought about all the work that went into being a preacher. He'd seen how much Elisabeth did in this home, what with sharing meal preparations and changing bedding. In addition she managed to fit in her notary duties.

She was of an age to marry. Considering all her attributes, it was a wonder no man had offered for her yet. Perhaps the idea of marriage didn't appeal to her.

He studied Irene and Gil at their checker game. Why hadn't Gil proposed to her? Why hadn't the banker? Maybe one of them had and she'd turned him down. Elisabeth seemed as headstrong as his sister.

"Each one of my children is a blessing," Sam assured them. "Each unique and special in his or her own way."

"And now you have yet another blessing," Arlene Stelling said with a warm smile.

"My cup runneth over." Sam looked directly at his wife as he said the last.

More than once Gabe had picked up on the looks that passed between them. They shared something special. Something unfamiliar in his experience. As unfamiliar as attending church. He didn't want to let on to Irene that he hadn't set foot inside a church since their parents' funerals. She took God as seriously as these others did, and he didn't want to appear the only heathen in their midst.

An hour later, Elisabeth got up. "I'll set dessert and coffee out on the sideboard in the dining room. Once I have it ready, you can eat in there or bring your plates and cups in here." She turned directly to John and Peter, who had arranged their blocks into corrals for their toy horses. "That doesn't include you boys. You will eat at your usual places."

She glanced around and Gabe figured she was looking for help. A couple of the girls had only returned from finishing supper dishes and cleanup a few minutes ago, and Irene was still occupied at the checkerboard.

"I'll help," Gabe said.

His offer caught her by surprise. "You?"

"I have two hands."

"Of course. All right then, thank you."

In the kitchen, she heated the coffee she'd made earlier and pointed to a cupboard. "The dessert plates are in there."

He opened it and figured the smaller ones were dessert plates. "How many?"

"All of them."

He lifted them out. "Dining room?"

"On the sideboard please."

He delivered them and returned. "Are you disturbed about Irene making friends with your deputy?"

"Not at all, and he's not *my* deputy."

"But there's something between the two of you, isn't there?"

She uncovered two baking dishes that held something with a golden crust. "Something like what?" She glanced up. Her expression changed to one of surprise. "Do you mean…romantic? Goodness, no. Gilbert and I are friends, and that's the extent of it. I have never considered him in any other way."

"What about him? Maybe he has designs on you, but he doesn't let on."

She shook her head. "No," she said firmly. "It's not like that. We've always had an easy, comfortable association. Anything else would ruin that. Huh-uh. If you had any inkling that he took a romantic interest in me, how would you account for the rapt attention he's been paying your sister all evening?"

"You noticed?"

"It would be difficult not to notice. They've been making eyes at each other and *smiling*." She gave an impression of a silly smile.

"I was afraid of that."

"Of what?"

"He isn't the sort I'd want to see her involved with."

She stopped in the middle of reaching for a china sugar bowl. "Why ever not?" she asked as though he'd personally insulted her. "Gilbert's a trustworthy and honest person. He's a deputy, for goodness' sake. What does that say about his character? He's kind to his sisters and good to his parents and he's a very loyal friend. He attends church every Sunday, unless he's on duty at the jail, and he's not hard to look at. He's rather handsome actually."

"I'm sure he is all of those things you say," he told her. "It's the deputy part that bothers me. If she was to marry him—and I'm not saying that after one evening and a checker game she's going to marry him—but if she did…a lawman's job is dangerous. I wouldn't choose a lawman for her."

She poured fresh cream into a small pitcher that

matched the sugar bowl. "Well, it's not up to you, now is it?"

He should have guessed she wouldn't see the subject from his perspective. He'd be hard-pressed to think of anything they'd agreed upon yet. "That Jackson fellow," he said. "Now he has a safe job at the bank. Unless of course...*he's* the one you have your sights set on."

"Again," she said, "if you start pressing her toward marriage or a husband she doesn't select for herself, you will push her away." She placed a handful of forks on the tray beside the cream and sugar. "And just how many more men can you imagine pairing me with?"

"He does have designs on you," Gabe said. "I saw it."

"I've never encouraged him." She hadn't denied Jackson's attraction to her, only her encouragement. "You flatter me if you think every man in town finds me irresistible."

Odd, the relief he'd experienced at her denial on both counts. "I can only think you have discouraged them because of your desire for independence, because you'd make any one of them a good wife."

She had picked up the tray, but she paused with it hovering inches over the table. "If God shows me a man He wants me to marry, I'll consider it then."

"How will you know?"

She looked down. "Can we finish this conversation later? I need to set out dessert before the boys have to go to bed."

"We don't have to talk about it at all if you don't want to."

She met his eyes briefly and headed for the dining room.

He appreciated her advice regarding his sister. She

understood females far better than he did. The last thing he wanted was to offend Irene again, but if she took a shine to the deputy, he was going to have a rough time keeping his nose out of it. For now, he would stay in the background and see what happened. Except...

"If she goes to see the house with the deputy, go along, will you, please?"

Her eyes held humor when she looked at him. "It was the *please* that got me. Yes. I will accompany her."

"Thanks." He held up a hand before she could say it. "No, that wasn't hard at all. Thank you. See?"

Her laugh melted something inside him.

Later that night after they'd arrived at the tiny house and Irene had gone to her room, he pried lids from the crates. Minutes later she opened her door to his knock.

"I found these for you."

Her gaze dropped to the silver-handled comb, brush and mirror he held. Tears welled in her eyes. "Oh, Gabriel."

"They're tarnished."

"I'll polish them." She accepted the set, carried them into her room and placed them on the bureau before turning back.

"Thank you for saving them for me all this time." She wrapped her arms around his neck and hugged him soundly. "I prayed for this time to come. I prayed that God would keep you safe all those years, and He did. Even if we never got a bigger house, even if we lived here forever, I'd be content."

If there was a God, Gabe figured he was on the bottom of the list as far as prayers went, so his safety had to have been purely by coincidence and sheer wit. "We're getting a bigger house."

* * *

Before the service began Sunday morning, Elisabeth was tying Peter's shoe for the third time when the hum of conversation faded out, and the sanctuary grew unusually quiet. She glanced up, noting heads turning toward the rear of the building. Conversation buzzed again, this time with excitement.

"That's him, the man who saved the whole car full of people from the robbers."

"The Taggart fellow is more handsome than I expected."

"Is that his wife?"

"No, I heard his sister has joined him."

Elisabeth got to her feet and helped Peter get situated with the rest of family in the two front rows. She turned then, spotting Gabe and Irene as half a dozen people greeted them just inside the doors. Though it was a warm morning, Gabe wore a dark jacket over his white shirt and string tie. He held his hat in both hands, worrying the brim in a circle, his discomfort evident. She hurried to extricate the two of them from the gathering, showed him where to hang his hat, and ushered them to the join the rest of the Harts.

Just as they took their seats, the strains of the first hymn came from the organ as Constance Graham opened the service with *A Mighty Fortress Is Our God* and the choir led the singing. Voices rose around them, the various sopranos and baritones blending into a joyful chorus of praise. Elisabeth's father stood at the podium, his smile showing his pleasure at the sizeable turnout that morning.

About halfway through the last song, the doors at the rear of the sanctuary burst open.

Music and song came to an abrupt halt.

"There's trouble over at Doc Barnes's place!" the out-of-breath man in the doorway shouted. "A bunch o' rowdy good-for-nuthins are holding him at gunpoint! The marshal needs a few guns."

Heart pounding, Elisabeth scanned the room. The Stellings sat on the opposite side, a few rows back. Gil wasn't with them. "Oh, dear Lord," she whispered.

Gil's cousin, Will York, shot out of his seat and immediately ran for the door. Dan Larken, another deputy, made his way past his concerned-looking wife and son seated on the pew, and his father, Victor, joined him. Warren Burke, the livery owner, stood, too. Rhys remained seated beside Beatrice.

Behind Elisabeth, Irene said, "No," and Elisabeth turned as Gabe rose to his full stature and stepped into the aisle. "Please, be careful," Irene pleaded.

He nodded and calmly made his way to the rack on the back wall, grabbed his hat and left the church.

"Let's pray," Sam said from the front. Church members exchanged looks, and then bowed their heads in prayer. "Lord, watch over our brave men, stand watch over Dr. and Mrs. Barnes and all the citizens of Jackson Springs. Protect them, Lord. Just as we sang only moments ago, You, Lord God, are their refuge and fortress. Because these good men have made You Lord of their lives, no evil shall befall them or an accident overtake them. Lord, give Your angels charge over each one this day to keep them in all their ways. We put our trust and confidence in You and ask these things in Jesus's name. Amen."

"Amen," the people echoed.

At that moment Elisabeth's concern was that Gabe

had never made God Lord of his life, so she added softly, "And Lord, please protect Gabe. Keep him safe so he can one day make You his Lord and King. Satisfy him with long life as the scripture says."

The unrest in her chest eased after she'd prayed that. She was concerned for Gil, but as a believer he was probably praying right that very moment. He'd faced similar situations in the past. He was prepared for danger.

The way Gabe had avoided a confrontation on the train that day made her surprised that he'd so willingly joined the other men at Dr. Barnes's.

"Let's break up into small groups and continue to pray," Sam suggested. The people did as he asked, forming circles and petitioning and thanking God for the safety of those who'd gone to help and those who were directly involved.

As they prayed, the sounds of gunfire reached them.

At the noise, Melissa Larken cried softly, and Josie handed Elisabeth the baby so she could comfort her. Instead of showing distress, Irene gathered all the children and took them up front near the organ, where she sat and played songs to which they could sing along. Elisabeth listened with appreciation.

Across the aisle and over several lowered heads, she met Arlene and Chess's eyes and gave them an encouraging smile. Gil knew how to take care of himself.

The door opened and closed, and she assumed someone had gone to check on the situation. A few minutes later, Karl Stone entered the building and spoke privately to Sam.

Sam glanced from face to face before saying solemnly, "Dr. Barnes has been shot. The report doesn't sound good."

Kathryn DeSmet, the schoolteacher, wept softly. Abigail and Anna hurried to her side and comforted her. Josie carried Rachel over to stand beside Arlene. Arlene automatically reached for the baby and held her close, as though doing so was a comfort and a life affirmation.

Feeling helpless, but knowing how much more difficult this was for Irene, Elisabeth guided her to a private spot.

"I can't just sit here," Irene said.

"Praying is the best we can do for them right now," Elisabeth told her.

Irene shook her head, distress evident on her face. "No. I can't take this."

She shot up and ran for the door.

Chapter Fourteen

As the dark-haired young woman ran outside, Elisabeth cautioned softly, "Irene." And then more loudly, "Irene, wait!"

Instinctively, she followed, not surprised when her father joined her in pursuit.

Irene paused for a moment, and with relief, Elisabeth realized Irene didn't know which direction would take her to the doctor's home and office. A shot rang out just then, crumbling her momentary respite. Irene gathered her skirt hem and darted toward the sound.

"Irene, come back!" Elisabeth called.

Sam was faster than Elisabeth, whose skirts impeded her progress, but Irene was faster yet, taking the lead with unexpected agility.

A grayish haze accompanied the acrid smell of gunpowder hanging in the air as they neared the house where Matthew Barnes lived and worked. Several men, including Will York and Deputy Dan Larken, crouched behind water troughs and at the corners of buildings, their guns and attention directed at the doctor's home.

Elisabeth's heart hammered at the fear that Irene

was going to heedlessly run smack-dab into the center of the fray.

"Will!" her father shouted, catching the man's notice. "Stop her!"

Gil's lanky cousin shot out of his hiding place at the corner of the telegraph office and grabbed Irene around the waist.

She didn't have a chance to put up much of a fight, because at that moment another flurry of shots erupted from the house. Bullets splintered wood and kicked up jets of dust in the street. She emitted a shriek.

Sam halted and spun to grab Elisabeth's wrist and together they darted behind a building.

"Throw out your guns!" Elisabeth recognized Marshal Dalton's voice. "You're not getting out of there alive!"

"Neither are your friends," came the reply.

Elisabeth and her father moved around the back of the building which shielded them and crept up the other side so they were farther away from the fray, but could peer around the corner and watch from a closer perspective.

She spotted Gabe now, crouched behind an overturned wagon. Movement caught her eye and she discovered Gil on a rooftop, far enough behind the view from the doctor's front door and side window that no one in the house could see them. Her heart lurched. She tapped her father's shoulder and pointed. He looked where she'd directed and caught his breath.

The door to the doctor's house opened slowly inward. A patch of bright blue appeared, and as the form emerged into the sunlight, Elisabeth recognized Donetta

Barnes. A man held her from behind, using her as a shield. Even from this distance, her terror was evident.

"Why is that man doing this?" Elisabeth asked around the thickness in her throat.

"Father God, keep Mrs. Barnes safe in Jesus's name," was his only reply.

Elisabeth echoed her father's prayer and leaned against him.

"Let her go!" Marshal Dalton called.

"Let us get to our horses and she might live," came the reply.

As the first man cleared the doorway and stepped off the boardwalk with his hostage, another armed man appeared behind him, holding up a third stranger who was bandaged around the waist and shoulder, his bloody shirt gaping open. The two of them were easy targets for the men in wait in every direction, but if one of them took a shot, they risked Donetta's life.

Where was Dr. Barnes? Already dead inside?

It seemed a hopeless situation either way. If someone shot the easy targets, the first man would shoot Donetta. If they held their fire and let the men escape, it was likely they'd take her along and get rid of her once she was no longer useful.

"Let her go."

Elisabeth had been so involved in her thoughts, she hadn't noticed the tall figure who now walked directly into the street, right out in the open, boldly challenging the man who held Dr. Barnes's wife in front of him. The barrel of the man's gun swung to point at Gabe.

Elisabeth's heart lurched into her throat. She was going to be sick. *Gabe!*

"What are you doing?" came Irene's distraught cry. "Gabriel, get back!"

He showed no sign that he'd heard her plea.

"I'll shoot her!" the man threatened.

"This is the last time I'm tellin' you to let her go," was Gabe's reply.

Donetta closed her eyes and remained rigid and silent in his hold. No doubt she was praying, and Elisabeth joined her by petitioning God softly enough for only her father to overhear.

All that passed were seconds, but the intense danger of the situation seemed to stretch those moments into infinity. Elisabeth couldn't imagine a good outcome. She refused to entertain visions of Gabe or Donetta shot and bleeding in the street.

The man inched away from the doctor's house, dragging Donetta with him.

More quickly than she'd have believed possible, Gabe grabbed the gun from the holster against his side and fired.

A single shot rang out and the sound volleyed against the buildings.

Both Donetta and the man holding her slumped to the ground.

Irene's scream was louder than the gunfire.

The man who'd still been standing in the doorway dropped his bandaged friend in a heap. He fired wildly at Gabe. A store window shattered. He spun and darted around the corner of the house.

Gabe ran after him.

Others moved out from behind cover with their weapons aimed at the man lying still on the ground. Donetta was sobbing, her hand at the side of her face.

Elisabeth and Sam ran toward her.

As they neared, Sam stopped her with an upheld palm. "Don't come any closer, Elisabeth."

She halted in her tracks.

Another man had joined her father, and together they extricated Donetta from the man's hold. "Where are you hit?" Sam asked.

If she was hurt badly, what would they do? Who knew what condition the doctor was in—or if he was alive at all?

"I don't think I'm hit," she said, but she wiped spattered blood from her face. Her hair was flecked with crimson.

"It's his blood," Marshal Dalton said to Sam.

Sam held Donetta steady and motioned for Elisabeth to come for her. Elisabeth couldn't resist a look at the man lying dead at their feet, and then wished she hadn't.

Donetta was trembling as Elisabeth wrapped her arm around her shoulders.

"Get her out of here," the marshal said. "We don't know if there are more inside or not."

"Three horses out back," Dan Larken told him from the corner of the house. "Accounts for these two." He gestured to the bandaged man lying in the doorway and the one Gabe had shot. "And the one he's following."

"Paul Jeffries and Voctor are watching the back, right?"

"Yeah, but there are wagons and stacks of crates. The man could hide anywhere."

"Sam, you watch this fellow. That 'un's dead. The rest of us will split up and surround the alley." He called, "Will! See if the doc's okay inside. Dan, cover him."

"I can't let go of this crazy woman," Will returned.

"You're preventin' us from doin' our jobs, little lady," the marshal hollered. "Stay put or I'll handcuff you to a lamppost."

Sam took off his belt, pinned the injured man's arms behind his back, and bound him.

Elisabeth led the sobbing woman to safety beside the building where Gabe's sister had wisely chosen to wait. Irene nearly swooned when she saw Donetta's face.

"She's not hurt," Elisabeth assured her.

"Gabe shot that man right out from behind her."

"Let's take her somewhere and clean her up."

Irene seemed to come to her senses. "Of course. What are the men doing now?"

"They're chasing that man who shot my Matthew," Donetta said. "Those swine held their guns on us and forced Matthew to tend to their friend. He had just finished wrapping his wounds when Ezra Quinn rang the bell and walked in the side door. Matthew moved toward me then, and that man shot him." Her voice broke, and she continued with a sob, "He's lying in there bleeding right now."

"The others are seeing to him," Elisabeth told her.

"I should stay," the woman said. "There's no one else who would know how to treat a wound. I'm not a doctor, but I've watched him treat a lot of injuries, bullet wounds included."

"I think she's right," Irene said.

They stood nearly a block away now, the air and the sun drying the blood smears on Donetta's face and neck. The shoulder of her blue shirtwaist was speckled red. Elisabeth spotted a neighbor peering out the second-floor window of the room she rented over a store.

"Are you all right?" Elisabeth asked. "I could leave you here and go back to help with the doctor."

"I'm fine. I want to go help Matthew."

"All right then. But we'll wait far enough back to stay out of danger until they tell us we can go in."

The three of them took the spot Will and Dan had vacated and observed the front of the Barnes's home from there. After several minutes Deputy Dan rode up beside them on his horse. "You can go tend to the doc. Your pa and Paul are taking those two to jail. The rest of us are heading out."

"Where are you going?" Irene asked. "Where's my brother?"

"He was the first one to ride out," he answered. "Took one of those men's saddled horses."

He turned his horse's head and galloped down the street, the animal's hooves kicking up dust.

Donetta jumped up and ran toward her home. The other two women followed.

The men had moved the doctor to an examination table in his surgical office. Elisabeth took one look at the front of his shirt and then his ashen face and felt her heart drop.

Donetta calmly took a scalpel and sliced open the front of his shirt. Blood trickled from a neat hole in his chest.

"If the bullet hit his heart or an artery, trying to remove it would kill him. I don't know what I'm doing. If the bullet was somewhere else, I could do it. I don't know what to do."

"Stop the bleeding?" Elisabeth asked.

"He's been bleeding far too long," Donetta said, but she nodded. She packed the hole and applied pressure.

"I don't know what to do," she said again. Elisabeth shared her sense of helplessness.

"Is there a doctor in a nearby town?" Irene asked. "We could take him there."

"Not close." Irene bent to press her lips to her husband's forehead. "The trip would likely kill him."

"We could bring the other doctor here."

Donetta met Elisabeth's eyes. "It's worth a try."

Elisabeth shot out of the house and ran all the way back to the church.

Several members still remained and, seeing her, gathered around.

"Elisabeth, are you all right?" Josie asked in alarm.

Elisabeth glanced at her hands and her Sunday dress, realizing she had come in contact with Donetta and her husband both. "I'm fine. But Dr. Barnes is hurt badly. He needs another doctor, and needs him fast."

Two men offered to ride to a nearby town for help. They left seconds later.

"What can we do?" Arlene asked.

"All of your husbands and sons are just fine," she assured them and then explained what had happened and how a posse had gone after the man who'd shot Dr. Barnes. "Continue to pray for all of them."

"I'll come with you to stay with Donetta," Arlene said and accompanied Elisabeth back to the doctor's house. Sam had locked the prisoner in a cell and returned to pray for the doctor.

The day grew warm and the afternoon stretched endlessly.

The men who'd gone after the shooter returned first, and Junie Pruitt delivered the news. The man who'd shot

Dr. Barnes had returned to Jackson Springs draped over a saddle, shot to death by that Taggart fellow.

Elisabeth and Irene shared a look.

"That's two men he's killed today," Elisabeth said aloud.

"What would you have had him do?" Irene asked. "Your friend's life was in the balance." She glanced at Donetta. "Would you have wanted him to let that man ride off and get away with what he did to the doctor?"

Elisabeth shook her head. She didn't know what to think. She'd known what Gabe was capable of. She'd been there when he'd confronted half a dozen train robbers without blinking an eye. She should have read the signs then. But today, in the street…he'd shown no fear or hesitation. He'd walked directly up to a man who held a gun pointed at his chest, calmly told him to let go of the woman and then pulled his gun faster than the other man could fire. He'd shot that man right out from behind his hostage.

If she hadn't seen it with her own eyes, she wouldn't have believed such a feat was possible.

What kind of man took risks like that? What kind of man could draw and shoot as though he'd practiced his whole life for that moment?

The answer she hadn't wanted to face floated to the surface of her consciousness: *A gunfighter.*

Chapter Fifteen

Before dusk, Matthew Barnes took his last arduous breath. Donetta pressed her forehead against his and cried softly. Arlene rested her hand on the woman's shoulder to comfort her.

Tears ran down Elisabeth's cheeks, and Irene held her hand. Elisabeth wiped her face on her sleeve and stood. "Let's go ask a couple of Donetta's friends to stay with her."

The two of them exited the house and shared the devastating news with those waiting. Elisabeth located someone she knew would be a comfort and suggested the woman go on inside.

Irene learned her brother was at the marshal's office and grabbed Elisabeth's hand. "Come with me. Please."

Several men sat on the stairs and benches near the open door of the lawman's office and jail. Gabe extracted himself from their midst to join the approaching women. He looked at Elisabeth without expression, his green gaze flickering to her blood-smeared dress.

She took a shaky breath. "Dr. Barnes didn't make it."

The men behind him murmured and shook their

heads. Gil ran his hand down his face and moved to stand at the edge of the boardwalk and take stock of the tree-covered mountains.

"I never want you to do anything like that again," Irene rebuked in a low angry tone. "You could have been killed. Do you think you're invincible?"

"Not with this gunshot in my side," he replied.

"Why did you *do* that?" she questioned, her tone incredulous.

He glanced from his sister to Elisabeth. Without blinking, he answered, "It's what I do."

He untethered a horse from a nearby post and led it by the reins as they walked toward their street.

"I don't want you to take a chance like that again," Irene pleaded.

"Didn't mean to frighten you. You should've stayed put at the church. Your yellin' and carryin' on lost us one gun hand when we need him."

They stood in front of the church now. Irene turned toward their little house and walked away, leaving Gabe and Elisabeth standing. The horse snorted softly behind him, and he turned to run his knuckles over the animal's forehead and nose.

It wasn't full dark yet, but a light came on in the parsonage Irene had entered. The church beside it stood dark and silent.

"She was scared," Elisabeth said softly. "We all were. Maybe you should leave her alone for a little while."

He shifted his weight. "Want a ride up the hill?" he asked.

She glanced at the horse. "I haven't ridden much."

"I won't let you fall." He hoisted himself into the

saddle with a creak of leather and led the horse over to the set of steps where buggies unloaded. "Climb up."

"I don't think so." She turned and headed for home.

He followed, guiding the horse at a walk. "I'm sorry about the doc. He was a good man."

"Yes, he was."

"If there's a God, why would He let someone like that get killed?"

At that Elisabeth halted. She turned around to look up at him. "God isn't in the business of shooting people. He gave everybody free will. Free will to believe in Him or not. Free will to live for Him and do what's right or to carry guns and rob and lie and cheat. Those men chose a life without godly principles. Of course their behavior makes God sad, but He doesn't control people like puppets. We make our own choices."

"Not everyone who carries a gun lies and cheats."

"Not everyone who carries a gun kills people, either," she returned.

"Your own father has a gun. And he's a preacher."

"It's not for gunfights. It's for defense."

"Same thing."

She spun and started back up the hill.

"Your friend Gil is a deputy. You don't have a problem with that."

"But you do. You didn't want Irene getting involved with him. How hypocritical is that?"

"I don't want her to marry someone in a dangerous occupation is all. We were talkin' about you."

"Gilbert's a lawman. You're a...a gunfighter."

"I'm not a gunfighter."

"What then?"

He drew a deep breath. "Bounty hunter. But not any longer. You know I'm starting a ranch."

"Doesn't that sort of life follow you wherever you go?"

"Why don't you stop? I'll get down and we'll talk."

"We are talking."

He nudged the horse with his heels, got ahead of her and slid from the saddle to prevent her from getting past him. Gabe didn't know why it drove him crazy, but the fact that she wouldn't listen to his explanations or discuss this irritated him. He'd left one angry woman at home and was confronting another.

She leveled her gaze on him and placed her hands on her hips. "It's no business of mine what you did in the past or what you do now."

"If it makes no difference to you, why are you so mad?"

She dropped her hands to her sides. "I'm not mad. I'm...disappointed."

"I'll bet a lot of people disappoint you."

"Are you saying I'm judgmental?"

"No. Only that it's tough to live up to the standards you set for yourself and everybody else."

"They're God's standards, not mine."

He mulled that over a moment. "God doesn't want criminals brought to justice? What about that Joshua fellow your father told us the story about? He fought battles and won. What's so different about that?"

"I'm really tired, Gabe. I've had a bad day. I just want to go home."

Jaw set, he moved aside to let her pass.

She climbed the hill and he watched her reach the steep stairs that led up to the Harts' property. She didn't look back. At the top, she opened the iron gate and closed it behind her.

Why did he care what she thought of him?

He mounted his horse and led it down the hill at a gentle walk. He'd done the right thing. He'd gone after the man who'd killed Dr. Barnes and he'd caught him. That was the only justice he knew.

Most of the residents of Jackson Springs showed up for the funeral. With no family at her side, Donetta Barnes made a lonely figure in her black dress and hat. Friends and her husband's patients lent her support and sympathy.

Gabe sat with the Hart family during the church service, because Irene had immediately led him toward them. Victor Larken performed the eulogy, and then the people solemnly followed a black-draped horse and wagon along the streets to the cemetery on the outskirts of town. There Sam prayed and read from his Bible.

Gabe had witnessed more death than most people, though he hadn't attended a funeral since his parents'. Living and dying was the natural way of things.

"Let not your heart be troubled, Jesus said." Sam read, *"'Ye believe in God, believe also in me. In my Father's house are many mansions. If it were not so, I would have told you. I go to prepare a place for you. And if I go and prepare a place for you, I will come again and receive you unto myself, that where I am, there ye may be also.'"*

These people sure set store by their Bibles. Elisabeth talked about God as though He was a real person. His sister, too, he was learning, lived by the same principles and beliefs.

"'Verily, verily, I say unto you,'" Sam continued. *"'He that believeth on me, the works that I do shall he do also, and greater works than these shall he do, because I go unto my Father. And whatsoever ye shall ask in my name, that will I do, that the Father may be glorified in the Son. If ye shall ask any thing in my name I will do it. If ye love me, keep my commandments.'"*

Gabe had heard of the golden rule, of course, and of the ten commandments. He'd figured he'd broken most of them, so what was the use in thinking God had any special love for him?

"'He that hath my commandments, and keepeth them, he it is that loveth me, and he that loveth me shall be loved of my Father.'"

Yep, he was pretty much at the end of the line in God's opinion.

"'Peace I leave with you, my peace I give unto you, not as the world giveth, give I unto you. Let not your heart be troubled, neither let it be afraid.'"

Gabe was glad if those words gave the doctor's widow some comfort. She was a real nice lady and had been kind to him during his stay at her place. But he also hoped it helped knowing the man who had taken her husband wouldn't be hurting anyone else.

He glanced aside at Elisabeth. She wouldn't understand his logic. Since he'd met her his life had become more confusing and complicated. She questioned his way of thinking. What was worse, she made him question his own thinking. She challenged him to consider things outside his realm of knowledge or understanding.

He asked himself at every turn why he should care what she said or thought. That he spent hours lying awake, going over their conversations...and their kisses should have been some kind of clue, but he still hadn't faced the truth. He'd never backed away from a confrontation in his life, but right now he was hiding from something he didn't want to acknowledge.

He had strong feelings for Elisabeth Hart. However, the timing was all wrong. Their relationship was definitely all wrong. But those facts didn't stop the way he felt about her.

He wanted to be a man she admired.

It would never happen. How could he ever measure up to her standards or the people she admired?

After a final prayer, Sam picked up a handful of dirt and handed it to Mrs. Barnes. She tossed the dirt onto the lowered coffin. Friends followed suit, the clumps hitting the wooden box until several inches of soil silenced them.

Gabe was one of the last to grab dirt and toss it into the grave. After the women and most of the people had headed back to church for a meal, Gabe joined Dan and Gil in picking up shovels and finishing the work.

"The marshal said you hunted for bounty," Gil said.

"That's right."

"Does your sister know?"

"She does now."

"And Elisabeth?"

Gabe looked up. Dan wasn't paying any attention to their conversation, but Gil looked right at him.

Gil shrugged. "I've noticed something between the two of you is all."

"She thinks I'm lower'n a snake's belly."

"Give her some time."

"Don't know if I have enough time left. She's mighty fixed on her ideas."

"You, uh…you fancy her, do you?"

"Can't sleep half the night. Can't get her out of my head."

Gil rested a hand on his hip, pausing to rest on the handle of the shovel. "A woman like that can sure get a hold on a man's thinkin', can't she?"

Gabe agreed.

"Same thing your sister does to me."

Gabe stopped shoveling to look at him. "You asking my permission or something?"

"I'd like it if you weren't opposed."

"She's every bit as set on her notions as Elisabeth. Maybe more. She wants to make her own choices and decisions about her life. A lawman's job seems dangerous to me, but look what happened to this good doctor just minding his own business. Guess there's no telling who's safe and who isn't." He tucked the shovel handle under his arm to lift his hat away from his head and tie his handkerchief around his forehead, then settle the hat back on. "If it's her choice to let you come calling, I'm not going to stand in her way."

Gil gave a satisfied nod and they resumed their grim task.

Chapter Sixteen

In the days that passed, Gabe stayed busy overseeing the construction of the house. The Barnes woman stayed on his mind. He wondered off and on how she was getting along and whether or not she would stay. If she had family elsewhere, she might join them. He remembered how alone and lost she'd seemed the day of the funeral.

Irene was content to write in her journals, perform chores around the house and accompany Elisabeth when she had notary duties. He was glad for their friendship, because he wouldn't want her stuck in that tiny house all day long.

Everything had changed now that he had feelings for Elisabeth Hart. Living in Jackson Springs was going to be difficult when he'd see her and her family—and he would, since she and Irene had developed a close friendship. Was he doomed to spend his days regretting that he would never be the sort of man she could love or marry?

But he couldn't ask Irene to leave now, not so soon after arriving. Not when she was delighted to be here and making additional friends and feeling more at home every day.

On his way out of town early one morning, he shot a deer. After he dressed it, he took a portion of the meat to Mrs. Barnes and gave Josie the rest.

Irene hadn't caught on to cooking just yet, though she gave meals her best efforts. Some evenings they ate at the café, other nights Gabe prepared a quick meal, and when they were especially fortunate, the Harts invited them for supper. One of those evenings, the Stellings were guests as well, and Gil invited Irene to another game of checkers. Afterward, the two of them took a stroll through the gardens and sat on the porch.

He worked every day to accept this thing that was developing between his sister and the deputy. He wanted her to be happy, and if Gil made her happy, Gabe could deal with that.

Ironic how he'd always considered himself capable—invincible actually—in his line of work. He'd been solely responsible for Irene, and had something happened to him, she'd have been alone. Now in context, his concern that something could happen to the lawman was pretty hypocritical.

From all appearances his time with Irene was already running short. If she married Gil…if she married anyone…he'd be alone again. His concern was more like a father than a brother, he realized. But when it happened, he would let go.

The evening before the Independence Day celebration, Irene was beside herself with excitement when Junie Pruitt brought her a message. Jane Carter Lockhart had arrived on the train.

Irene asked Gabe to accompany her to the hotel,

where they met the famed suffragette and her husband. Gabe shook hands with the man. Funny, Gabe hadn't paid any attention to the fact that these prominent women had husbands. Attention was always focused on the woman, but he learned that Silas Lockhart campaigned right alongside his wife, petitioning for women to be able to vote in local and national elections.

The people of Jackson Springs had been preparing for the holiday for over a week, decorating the buildings along Main Street with banners and patriotic swags and constructing a platform. Even dealing with their sadness from the loss of their friend, the community moved on.

The following day Gabe stood on the boardwalk as Irene participated in the procession of decorated wagons, sharing a ride with Mr. and Mrs. Lockhart. Penelope Berry, the café owner, offered him a jar of lemonade and he enjoyed the parade from a good vantage point before returning the jar.

Abigail Hart spotted him and motioned for him to join their family. The boys greeted him as though he was one of them and Josie showed him how much the baby had grown.

Peter was sitting atop Sam's shoulders so he could see the goings-on, but John clung to his mother's skirt with a frown.

"Can I give you a seat?" Gabe asked.

Delighted, the boy raised his arms and Gabe lifted him to his shoulders. The minimal pain the effort took was well worth the boy's delight as he watched the parade. They all shouted and cheered for Irene when the wagon she perched on slowly passed by.

He and Elisabeth had barely spoken since the evening she'd learned of his true occupation. There was nothing he could say to change her opinion of him, nor could he change who he was or what he'd done.

As the family strolled toward the booths lining the street, she glanced up at John and offered Gabe a hesitant smile. "How is the house coming along?

"Frame's up. Two fireplaces are built. Roof goes on next."

"Sounds like everything's going well. How's your side?"

"Better. Hardly notice it anymore, unless I do something without thinkin'."

"Like picking up small children?"

He shot her a glance.

"I saw you wince when you picked up John."

"He's heavier than he looks."

She smiled.

John joined his brothers then to play games along the row of booths. Eventually the band played, announcing the speeches. Gabe and the Harts joined the crowd that surrounded the platform. The mayor spoke first, expounding on the United States' freedom and the basis of this centennial celebration. He introduced the governor of the territory who spoke of their ongoing pursuit for statehood. Andrew Johnson had turned down their requests for statehood, but another petition was currently before President Grant.

After much applause for that cause, the mayor introduced Rhys Jackson. Rhys spoke about the founding of their community and his grandfather's part in it. Eventually Irene was welcomed to the podium.

Gabe knew she'd been spending a lot of time writing, and he guessed he shouldn't have been surprised, but when she took the podium and didn't immediately introduce the visiting guest, he cocked his head. In a clear voice and with heartfelt enthusiasm evident, she spoke with knowledge and passion.

After meeting Silas Lockhart, Gabe had a more sympathetic view of the suffragettes and their cause. He caught Elisabeth watching his reactions. "I think I might be proud of her," he said.

Spotting Gil in the crowd, he wondered about his reaction to Irene and her cause. At the moment, she held the attention of nearly the entire town. The young man listened intently, but he also glanced at the nearby people's faces to gauge their reactions.

"Her passion for women's rights is contagious," Elisabeth said from beside Gabe. "I've noticed only a few grumblers in the crowd."

She drew her talk to a close and, with added excitement in her tone, Irene introduced Jane Carter Lockhart. The crowd applauded for the well-dressed woman. She wore a jaunty hat at an angle over her upswept dark curls.

She was indeed an impressive speaker. She incited the gathering to applaud after every high point in her talk. Finally, the band played and Mrs. Lockhart mingled with the townspeople, shaking hands and answering questions.

Abigail took Gabe's hand and led him to a sign-up table for the friendly competitions. "Will you be my partner at one of these? How about the three-legged race?"

"There's always the potato toss," the man at the table suggested.

"I can probably toss a potato," Gabe said.

"We need two more people for that," she told him. She glanced aside. "Elisabeth! Anna! Come join us."

The others joined them and Abigail signed them as a team. The competition began, and he discovered the snag he hadn't known about. Each person wore an apron and wasn't allowed to touch the potato with their hands. They had to use the apron to throw and catch.

"Never done this before?" Elisabeth asked as he watched.

"How can you tell? We haven't started yet."

"That frown on your face gives you away. What are you thinking?"

"I'm thinking…do people really *do this?*"

She grinned. "Some do."

He pretty much made a fool of himself, but only got hit in the shoulder with the vegetable once. In the end he and the Hart sisters took second place and congratulated each other.

Later they located the rest of the family and shared a picnic supper. As the sun lowered, ice cream makers were brought out and Gabe took a turn cranking.

Rhys Jackson spotted him. "I have a proposition for you."

"What's that?"

"I'll buy that land from you and give you one of the houses I own in town." He named a price.

Gabe mulled over the man's generous offer. What did the banker want with land so far from town? "No other spot of land you'd want?"

"I own the other pieces around that spread. Over the years I tried to find the owner of yours without any luck. If I had that section, my holdings would be joined."

"Well, you know I've taken a shine to that particular property. My house is underway. I'm not selling."

"I'll double my offer."

Taken aback, Gabe stared at him. There was something fishy about the man's insistence. "That's a tempting offer. Overly generous actually. Still not selling."

A muscle ticked in Rhys's jaw, and he thinned his lips into a straight line. "You won't get another offer like that."

"Don't want one."

The man gave him a sidelong look before moving away and joining a group of men.

Elisabeth approached with a long wooden spoon and stirred the ice cream. "That was odd."

"You heard?"

She nodded.

"Ever heard him mention looking for the owner of my land?"

"Never. Perhaps to my father."

He waited until she finished stirring and cranked again. "You're speaking to me again."

"It's rather difficult not to when my whole family thinks you're grand."

He thought a moment. "If me being around is a problem for you, Elisabeth, I'll back away and leave you be."

Her cheeks flushed pink. "That would be selfish of me. My family enjoys your company. And Irene is my friend. I don't want to make things more awkward."

"I enjoyed myself today," he said. "And I enjoyed spending time with you. Even the potato game."

"You looked awfully silly wearing the apron, but you were actually pretty good at the toss."

"Those rascals smart when they hit."

"Years past we've done it with eggs."

He raised his eyebrows. "Now that's just a waste of good eggs."

"But incentive to catch them," she replied with a laugh.

"Oh, I don't know. Not getting hit in the head with a flying potato is pretty good incentive to catch the spud. I'd still rather eat them any day."

"I've noticed."

He caught the teasing lilt to her tone. "You and your stepmother and sisters cook better than any of the cooks in the restaurants and cafés where I've eaten over the years. Only home cooking I ever had was when I was a boy. My mama was a good cook. I can still remember picking apples and her baking them into a golden-crusted pie."

"Josie taught us all to cook."

"Is she giving Irene any lessons?"

"Irene's catching on. She's a little impatient. Cooking and baking take time. You can't rush tender meat or creamy sauces. She's getting there."

"Her heart's not in it," he pointed out.

"It's not my life's ambition, either," she replied. "Some things we just do because we need to, and we might as well do a good job while we're at it."

He studied her in the fading light. Her thick blond braid hung over her shoulder, and her skin was pink from the sun and the activity. "What *is* your life's goal, Elisabeth?"

Chapter Seventeen

He'd surprised her, evident in the way she looked at him and then away. Finally she glanced back. "I'd like to use my skills in a manner that pleases God."

"Not cooking."

"Not especially. I had always wanted to go back to where I lived as a child, so after graduation I spent nearly a year back east. I studied bookkeeping."

"I didn't know that."

"I keep my father's ledgers for home and the church. I've also helped Josie with investments. She has her own money and it's set up in trust funds and stocks."

He wasn't going to ask how a young woman like Josie came by so much money, but the question nagged.

"Her father left her an inheritance, as did her first husband." Before he had a chance to consider, she explained. "She was a widow when we traveled through Nebraska and met her."

Gabe's impression of Josie Hart improved even more at the knowledge that she could have lived her life well-off and done as she pleased. Maybe traveled. Instead she'd chosen to raise a family and keep a house where the Harts could welcome friends and neighbors. What made some people so unselfish and others only out for what they could get?

"I was mean to her at first," Elisabeth admitted. "I resented her taking my mother's place in our family… and in my father's heart."

"That's understandable."

"I don't know. Abigail and Anna loved her right off. I held her at arm's length and found fault with everything she did and said."

"Maybe there's hope for me yet, huh?"

She looked him in the eye, her confusion evident. "There's no comparison."

"You're holding me at arm's length…and probably wishing your arms were longer," he said. "You don't approve of me."

"It's not the same."

"You're right. I'm sorry. What's the rest of your life goal?"

"I'm a little confused about the rest of it."

"What about children?"

"Perhaps one day. But not right now. I have plenty of children in my life."

"Not your own."

"Do you want children?" she asked.

"I suppose I do. Never thought all that much about it 'til lately, but bein' around your brothers and sisters started me thinking about family. I was so focused on setting by enough to take care of Irene and make a home for her that I didn't plan for kids of my own.

"Now I see that so much time has passed…she's already a young woman, and she'll likely be marrying and having her own family. I'm not pushing her or preventing her. She's making her own choices. It's the natural way of things should she decide she'd be happy with Gil. But then there I'd be with a big house and a ranch and no one to share it. So yeah, I guess I want kids."

He'd need a wife for that, but neither of them mentioned it.

She changed the subject entirely. "I suggested Irene join one of the footraces today, but she declined. Too undignified for a celebrity, I suppose."

"Irene?"

"Yes! You should have seen her the day of the shootings. When you left the church and she took out after you, neither Father or I could keep up with her."

"Junie Pruitt won one of the races," he said.

A couple strolled past the table where Gabe still cranked the ice cream. "Evenin', Miss Hart," the man greeted them. "Gabe."

"Evenin', Willis," Gabe replied. "You and the missus enjoyin' the celebration?"

"We've had an exhausting day, but we're staying for the fireworks." The two of them moved on.

The fellow had addressed her as Miss Hart, but Elisabeth hadn't recognized them. A lot of people knew her family because of her father's position. "Who was that?"

"Hand and his wife who work on Frank Evans's ranch."

"How do you know them?"

"I helped Willis load supplies at the mill one day. Later he showed up and lent a hand framing the house. His missus brought sandwiches and cookies for everyone that noon."

Elisabeth studied him with interest. Between her notary duties and her father's position, there weren't very many people she hadn't met at one time or another. All evening, she'd noticed him speaking to people she hadn't guessed he'd known.

"I guess it wouldn't have been proper for Mrs. Barnes to come to something like this so soon after the doc's death," he said.

"Probably not."

"And she's still dealing with her loss. Must be hard for her sitting at home with so much ruckus goin' on only a few blocks away."

"I'm sure you're right. After my mother died, it seemed wrong that life went on and people carried on with their activities, when it felt as though my life had ended."

He studied the cold confection in the freezer and stopped turning the crank. "Maybe we could take her a dish of ice cream."

Elisabeth looked at him with surprise and...an uncalled-for sense of pride. Her eyes stung at the thought of his acute thoughtfulness. She wouldn't have thought of the kind gesture. "That would be really nice, Gabe." She turned and waved to catch Arlene and Kalli's attention. The younger girl reached her first. "We're going to take some ice cream to Mrs. Barnes. Will you serve the children?"

Gabe scooped a generous portion of the dessert, and Elisabeth covered it with a red-and-white-checked napkin. "Let's hurry before it melts."

They walked the few blocks that took them away from the festivities. Seeing the doctor's home for the first time since that fateful day gave Elisabeth a sinking feeling in her stomach.

"Are you all right?" Gabe asked.

"I'm fine."

Donetta answered the door looking tired. Her dress was rumpled as though she'd slept in it. She gave each of them a once-over, followed by a tentative smile. Tucking strands of hair into the knot at the back of her head, she said, "I wasn't expecting anyone."

"We thought…well, that is, *Gabe* here thought… We brought you some ice cream."

"That's real thoughtful." Mrs. Barnes stepped back and gestured for them to enter the house.

Elisabeth handed her the bowl. "I'll get you a spoon so you can eat it before it melts." She hurried toward the kitchen.

When she returned Donetta had offered Gabe a chair in the tiny sitting room. Elisabeth handed the woman a spoon and sat beside her on the divan.

Gabe's gaze traveled to the doorway that led to the area where Dr. Barnes had treated patients.

Donetta tasted the ice cream. "This is a nice treat. People have been so kind. I have so much food I can't eat it all. And truthfully I'm not very hungry most days."

"People don't know what else to do," Elisabeth said. "And they want to help."

Mrs. Barnes glanced at Gabe. "I made a stew from the venison you brought me."

Elisabeth turned toward Gabe, who only nodded. He'd brought her meat?

"Is there anything else we can do?" he asked. "Bring wood?"

"I don't think so. I'll be moving whenever the town council finds a new doctor," she answered, and then added with a shrug, "I'm not sure just yet where I'll go."

"Seems I recall you're a fine cook," Gabe said. "You served some tasty meals when I was laid up here for a few days."

"I always cooked for Matthew and myself, of course. And I've taken meals to the jail for the past several years. I stopped doing that when one of those men responsible for Matthew's death was locked up in there."

"Think you could cook for eight or ten men?"

Elisabeth couldn't figure out what he was getting at.

"Oh, yes, easily," the woman replied.

"My sister's still learning," he told her. "But I don't expect she'll be ready to do justice to a real meal anytime soon. I'll need someone to cook for the hands. I'll have a room ready. Good-size one." He glanced around. "Probably fit in some of your favorite things."

"I don't need much," she said, her tone hopeful.

"Think about it."

"I can tell you right now it sounds like a perfect way for me to work and have somewhere to stay. We never had any children, and I don't have family."

Elisabeth slowly absorbed what had just happened. Gabe had been considering this, she suspected. He'd been thinking about Mrs. Barnes enough to wonder how she was faring on her first holiday without her husband. And he'd just found a solution for the woman's livelihood right in his own home. Just like that.

"Matthew told me you were a good man," Donetta said. "He was perceptive."

Elisabeth lowered her gaze to the bowl Donetta had placed on the nearby table and the remainder of melting ice cream.

"Thank you for helping me," she said.

"You'll be helping me out, Mrs. Barnes. You saved

me from searching to hire someone. And I already know you're a good cook. The house isn't finished yet," he added. "But it will be in a few weeks."

At that Elisabeth joined the conversation. "If a new doctor is hired, you can stay with us until Gabe's house is ready."

"I'm humbled by your generosity." She had tears in her eyes now. "Both of you."

Elisabeth, too, had been humbled by Gabe's kind consideration for the widowed woman.

A few minutes later, Donetta washed the bowl, and they said their goodbyes.

"Had you been planning that?" Elisabeth asked as they walked along Main Street, where gas lamps and paper lanterns lit the booths. Another platform had been built on a grassy area beyond the businesses, and a gathering of local musicians tuned up for an evening concert. Townspeople had spread quilts and blankets and were getting children settled.

"Planned I'd need a cook is all," Gabe replied.

"How did you know she'd accept your offer?"

"I didn't." He pointed. "There's your father."

She let him change the subject, and they joined the Harts, Irene among them now. Josie had taken the baby home so the two of them could rest in the quiet house.

Irene spread an extra quilt and showed them where they could sit.

John already slept, but Peter kept jumping up and walking toward another family, where he chattered to a redheaded little girl. Sam repeatedly snagged him back and sat him on the quilt. The last time, he gave him a stern warning to stay put. The boy pouted, but crawled into his father's lap and leaned his head against his chest. Within minutes he was asleep.

The band played a selection of patriotic tunes, and when the people knew the words, they sang along.

Gabe had given Elisabeth a lot more to think about. His concern for Mrs. Barnes had been completely unexpected.

She couldn't help that she felt deceived by him. He hadn't let on that he had hunted down men for a living. He'd been evasive about his past, and for good reason.

She reached into her skirt pocket, found two smooth stones, and rubbed her fingers over their surfaces. The fact that others, like her family—and even Irene—had taken the news of his bounty hunting in stride confused her even more. She hadn't been able to forget his question when he'd asked about Joshua and the battles he'd fought, wondering how that was any different.

Perhaps Joshua fighting for his land wasn't any different from protecting Mrs. Barnes, but both were far different from setting out to chase men for the rewards on their heads. How could she look aside?

The songs turned to popular tunes of the day and old familiar music.

She felt betrayed. Deceived, plainly and simply. When she tried to fall asleep at night, she nursed that hurt. She knew dwelling on it was wrong. She'd been working to put his past out of her mind. Her resentment was a protective shell. He recognized it. She needed it there. He wasn't a man she wanted to care for.

As the band finished and the first fireworks burst overhead, Gilbert located them and joined Irene where she sat. Though the sky was dark, the fireworks created bursts of light. Elisabeth sat close enough to notice when Gilbert reached over and took Irene's hand in his.

She glanced at Gabe. He had noticed, too, but he directed his attention back to the exploding colors above. He was a handsome man, no doubt about it. She studied his profile, the shape of his nose and chin...the mouth she knew was soft.

At memories of kissing him, her resentment softened more than she liked. Anger had been her defense, but it was getting more and more difficult to stay angry. Especially when he did something like he'd done that night in offering Mrs. Barnes a position and a home.

Even if she could put his past aside—and that was a big if—Gabe was nothing like the husband she wanted. She had expectations, and he didn't meet them. She embarrassed herself by allowing the attraction she felt and, admittedly, his kisses to veer her off her chosen path. She'd never questioned the qualities she held in esteem, still didn't. Gabe was not a man she would consider marrying.

Friendship was out of the question. She'd been friends with Gilbert for years, and their friendship was nothing like this crazy, emotionally exhausting relationship she had with Gabe. The two of them were definitely not friends.

Her head and her heart told her two different things. He might have good qualities, but Gabe didn't match up to her ideals. While fireworks burst against the black heavens and murmurs of appreciation and wonder echoed around her, she prayed for wisdom. *Lord, show me what You'd have me to do.*

She believed with all her heart that God answered prayer. She just hoped His answer came soon.

* * *

Elisabeth received a telegram requesting her services in a nearby town. She invited Irene to accompany her, but the other young woman declined. "Gil has invited me to dinner on Friday, and I need to get my good dresses aired and pressed. When do you leave?" she asked.

"Tomorrow morning."

"Will you please meet Gil with me this afternoon then? The real estate man is able to show him the Martin house at three."

Elisabeth agreed and accompanied Irene at the appropriate time. Gil and Mr. Payne were waiting on the porch when they hurried up the brick walk.

Gil greeted both of them, but his smile was for Irene. As long as she'd known him, Elisabeth had never seen him behave this way. He'd always been easygoing and polite, but he went out of his way to do things for Irene, to make her smile and to see to her comfort.

Mr. Payne let them in, and they strolled through the rooms. Eventually they reached the kitchen. "It's not yellow any longer," Gil said.

Elisabeth had noted that fact, too. "Look how big it is. And the stove comes with the house? It's a dandy."

"I don't know much about stoves," Irene commented. As the real estate man opened a pantry door and investigated, Irene said to Gil, "I'm sure someone would be able to cook fine meals in this kitchen and on this stove."

"Probably," he said.

"Now, I'm not much of a cook myself," she added.

Gilbert had said nothing about her cooking in this

kitchen, but Elisabeth picked up on what she assumed came as a veiled warning on Irene's part.

Gil slanted a meaningful glance at Elisabeth. She read his plea and walked toward the back door. "Mr. Payne, will you show me the yard and outbuildings, please?"

Thomas Payne joined her quickly. "Mrs. Martin kept a fine herb garden. I'm afraid it's sadly overgrown right now."

Out of doors, she listened to Mr. Payne rattle on about the good condition of the exterior of the home and the convenient washhouse out back. "I remember when your family moved here," he said to her. "You were just a girl when I took you and your stepmother to visit that big house on the hill. She fell in love with it right off. I couldn't believe my good fortune," he went on. "That beauty was priced head and shoulders above what most people could afford, and I figured it might take a long time to sell. But then you folks came along."

Elisabeth nodded, wondering what was going on inside while she stood out here with the real estate man.

"How is Mr. Taggart doing? I've seen him about town and he looks fit as a fiddle."

"He's good."

"Shame about Dr. Barnes, isn't it? Such a good man cut down in the prime of life. Can't help wondering what his missus will do now."

"I believe she has a job and a new home lined up."

"Well, isn't that good news? Glad to hear it."

The back door burst open, and Irene ran out, pulling Gilbert by the hand. "Elisabeth! You're the first to hear! Gil has asked me to marry him."

Elisabeth stared, surprised, though she shouldn't

have been. She pressed a hand to her breast. "Oh, my goodness. Well…well, did you say yes?"

Irene laughed. "Of course I said yes."

"That's wonderful. Congratulations!"

She gave both Irene and Gil a heartfelt hug.

"None of the females in all of Jackson Springs ever caught his eye," Elisabeth said, her hand on Gil's sleeve and her statement directed at Irene. "I guess it took God bringing you right to his doorstep for him to think of marriage."

"I am a good catch," Irene said and rested her hand on his shoulder. She studied Elisabeth. "And yes, he knows exactly what he's getting into. He's duly warned that I'm not much of a cook. Between his mother and Josie, I will learn. He agrees that women should be allowed the same rights as men, and he has no intention of trying to hush me."

"I was proud of you on Independence Day," he told her.

Irene looked from his earnest face to Elisabeth and gave her a broad smile.

Elisabeth was sincerely happy for her old friend and her newest one. On one hand her head spun with how quickly this had developed. On the other, she appreciated how certain both of them had been about their feelings and the other person. Would she ever feel that way?

Of course her thoughts went directly to Gabe. She couldn't help wondering how he would react to this development. Until now she'd been a buffer for much of his dealings with his sister. She prayed he was prepared for this and that he'd be happy for her. Elisabeth expected the best.

Gilbert turned to Mr. Payne. "We're buying this house."

* * *

The remainder of the day, while Irene spoke giddily of a wedding and a honeymoon trip, Elisabeth stewed about what would happen when Gabe learned of the engagement.

"Come for supper," Josie insisted. "Gil should be here, too."

"Oh, yes," Irene answered. "We need to tell people together." Her expression changed as though she'd only just thought of something. "We'll have to tell his parents."

"After school, I'll send Anna over with an invitation to supper," Josie supplied. "Or would you rather tell them privately?"

"I'd better ask Gil about that."

"Don't worry about how they'll receive the news," Josie told her. "Arlene is one of my dearest friends, and she has already expressed her fondness for you. She is well aware that her son is completely taken with you. She'll be delighted."

"Oh, I hope so."

Josie was probably right about the Stellings. Elisabeth just wasn't as confident of Gabe. "Do we have any apples?"

"There's a bushel in the root cellar," Josie replied.

"Irene, let's bake apple pies for dessert."

"I don't know how."

"I'll show you. You can peel and slice while I make the crusts."

As the supper hour neared, the women set the table and changed into clean dresses. Elisabeth took herself outdoors to cut flowers for centerpieces.

Gunshots not far away took her by surprise. At another volley of fire, she dropped the stems and stared toward the center of town, though of course she could see nothing from here.

A bell rang, probably the one in the firehouse yard, startling her further. Another joined the peals.

Kalli ran out into the yard, the twins and Phillip on her heels. Josie followed seconds later, carrying Rachel. Abigail and Anna, who'd been reading under a tree in the side yard, abandoned their books and slates and joined them.

Josie stopped beside Elisabeth, a furrow in her brow. "What's happening?"

"I don't know."

More gunfire erupted and then a string of firecrackers and another, as though it was the Fourth of July all over again.

"I guess we'd better go see," Josie said. She turned to the younger girls. "Take the boys' hands."

As a group, they hurried down the steep brick street. At the bottom of the hill the racket grew louder. Irene was standing outside the little house, a hand shading her eyes.

Sam stood in front of the church and motioned for them to join him.

A wagon lumbered past, harnesses jingling. Several men rode in the back, waving their hats and cheering.

Sam ran forward. "What's happened?"

"The president declared Colorado a state!" one of them shouted, and the others whooped and hollered. "We have statehood!"

The men continued down the brick street, cheering and shouting the news to all who came out of doors.

Gabe rode up just then. He'd heard the reports on his way back into town. His hair was damp with sweat.

"Let's go on into town and join those celebrating," Sam suggested.

"I'll catch up with you after I wash up," Gabe replied.

The entire length of Main Street was filled with joyous citizens. One group had joined hands and danced in a circle. Others laughed and several lit firecrackers. Victor Larken carried a drum out of his store and made a racket.

Shortly, Gabe joined them. Donetta Barnes had ventured into the throng and Arlene Stelling led her over to their gathering near the post office.

At last people started home for their meals, and Josie invited Donetta to join them for supper. The widow seemed pleased to be asked. The Stellings had a buggy, so they gave Donetta and Josie a ride while the rest walked up the incline.

Gil joined them, and once they arrived at the house, Elisabeth and Josie added another place setting.

"Thank You, Lord, for answering the prayers of the people of Colorado," Sam prayed. "Lord I pray that each person in our community is thankful to You this day. Hold the citizens of Jackson Springs safe." After he asked a blessing for the food, conversation broke out. Bowls passed and there was more mirth than usual.

The voices and laughter evoked a sense of belonging and peace within Elisabeth. Sometimes she wondered how different their lives would have been if her mother had lived. But God had seen her father's need—the need of her entire family—and sent them Josie. God could take any bad situation and turn it to His glory if only His children put their trust in Him.

That situation on the train had been bad. Through it, Gabe and Irene had been welcomed into this circle of friends and family. Gil may not have found Irene if Gabe hadn't been shot and come to stay with them. And…it was difficult to think on…was God using Gabe to turn Donetta Barnes's situation around? How could that be? Didn't a person have to be willing to let God work through them?

Once everyone had finished eating, she and Kalli carried in the pies. The golden crusts and warm cinnamon smells met with sounds of appreciation.

"I helped," Irene said and gave Gil a proud smile.

"Would you like to serve?" Josie asked.

Irene stood and walked to the end of the table where the pies sat and sliced them into neat wedges. Abigail held small plates and carried the servings around the table to serve the guests first.

Gabe looked at the generous piece of pie in front of him and raised his eyes to meet Elisabeth's. She'd been thinking of him when she'd asked Josie about the apples and made the filling. Somehow he knew. He gave her a half smile that inched up his lips on one side, which in turn loosed a dozen butterflies in her stomach.

Irene squeezed Elisabeth's hand on her way back to her chair. An eternity later, everyone had eaten and been served a cup of coffee or had their milk refilled.

Finally, and Elisabeth's heart jolted with expectation, Gil cleared his throat, pushed back his chair with his legs and stood. "I have something I'd like to share with you now."

The room grew unnaturally quiet. All eyes focused on him.

The sound of the clock in the foyer could be heard over the thick silence.

He reached for Irene's hand and she gave him an adoring smile. "I can't remember being this happy." He cleared his throat again. "I've asked Irene to marry me, and she's accepted."

Arlene reached for her husband with one hand and with the other dabbed tears with her napkin. Chess held her hand and patted it, nodding with pleasure.

Gil leaned to give Irene a peck on the cheek and a quick reassuring hug. She held both his hands, gazed into his eyes and then released him to go to her brother. At her approach, Gabe inched his chair back and stood to embrace her soundly.

She leaned back and gazed up at him. "Are you happy for me?"

"I am," he replied.

"I thought you might pitch a fit when you found out."

"You buttered me up with apple pie," he said and glanced at Elisabeth.

The others chuckled.

"And besides he came to me yesterday, and we had another talk."

Irene swatted his arm playfully, hugged him again and returned to her fiancé. "Why did you let me worry?"

"I didn't know you were worried." Gil turned toward his parents. "Oh. And I bought the Martin house."

More excitement broke out. People talked over each other in their rush to share their reactions to all the day's news.

Later, after the dishes were finished and the children were in bed, the Stellings visited with her parents in the great room. Elisabeth surveyed the rooms but didn't find Irene, Gil or Gabe. She checked out of doors and discovered Gabe perched on the porch stairs by himself.

She joined him, sitting nearby and lacing her fingers over her knees. "Are you all right?"

He gazed into the star-studded heavens. "I waited too long."

Chapter Eighteen

"Too long for what?"

"To call an end to a life of chasing outlaws. To bring Irene here and make a home for her. I left her alone all those years." His voice got thick with emotion. "A child raised by strangers." He stood and walked a few feet away. "And now she's making a family for herself with no help from me, and I'm the one who's going be alone. Fitting, I suppose, because I sure don't belong with these people."

"How can you think that?" she asked. "You've already made plenty of friends since you've been here. I haven't run across anyone who didn't like you or admire you or who didn't have something good to say about you."

He shrugged. "I read people. I'm adaptable."

"You accept people for who they are," she said. "Everything's cut and dried for you. Black and white. Simple."

"People aren't that hard to figure out."

She got up to stand beside him, and with a hand at

the small of her back, he led them across the yard in the darkness.

Turning to face her, he opened his palm, and in the moonlight she recognized the stone she had given him. "You said this represents choices. Everything has a consequence, good or bad. I thought I was doing the right thing for my sister. Looking back, maybe the best school in the east wasn't the best thing I could have done for her. Maybe just knowing someone's there for you and wants you is better than all the provision in the world."

"She knows you care for her and that you only want the best for her."

"No, she doesn't. How could she?"

"Because you provided for her in the way you believed was best. She loves you, Gabe, and she believes in you."

"She believed in me all those years I was gone, too," he pointed out.

Elisabeth closed his fingers over the stone and held his hand that way. "You can't change the past. None of us can change the choices we've already made. We can only choose to make better ones in the future."

"Is that what the stones do for you? Remind you to make better choices?"

"I hope so."

"And what choice have you ever made that was so bad? You do everything perfectly."

She let his words sink in. Absorbed them. "I'm the reason my mother died."

"Didn't she drown?"

She looked away, gathering her thoughts, her composure. "Yes, she drowned. Our wagon train had come to a river. It wasn't terribly deep, but the water was swollen and running swiftly. I still get a sinking feeling when I hear the sound of a river or a bubbling stream.

"I don't know how it happened or what caused us to tip, but one moment we were all seated on the bench or just behind it, and the next moment the wagon lurched sideways, throwing my mother and Abigail and me into the water.

"The current was strong. The water was so cold it took my breath away. I was terrified, screaming, trying to swim, but my skirts were heavy. The water carried me downstream and an eddy pushed me toward a craggy bank where a limb hung out over the water. I grabbed on to it and screamed for all I was worth. I think I screamed for my mother. I cried for my father and prayed he'd reach me before I could no longer hang on."

"You must've been terrified."

"I was terrified. But I was also relatively safe, secured as I was to land by that branch. It seemed like forever I clung there, screaming until I was hoarse. And then he came. His arms locked around me, and I let go, safely carried to shore.

"Father set me down beside Anna, who had been wrapped in a blanket by one of the women from the train. Abigail was standing and her teeth were chattering so hard I thought she'd break them. Someone brought me a blanket. Eventually I stopped crying.

"I looked at Abigail. She hadn't been crying, just watching the stretch of river beyond where we sat. 'Where's Mama?' I asked.

"'Papa's looking for her. The other men are looking for her, too.' Her lips were purple, but her face was white. I probably looked just the same." Elisabeth brought three warm stones from her pocket and looked at them. She raised her gaze to Gabe. "My mother had been carried downstream by the current. She hadn't been able to reach a branch like I had. She wasn't hanging on or safe like I had been.

"If he'd gone for her first and then come back for me—or let one of the other men fetch me—he knew I was safe—he could've reached her before it was too late."

"Did he find her body?"

She nodded. "We didn't even mark her grave. The wagons rolled right over the spot so it was indistinguishable. Like she'd never been there."

"You know they had to do that."

"I know."

"You're not responsible for her death, Elisabeth."

"Yes, I am."

"How old were you?"

"Twelve."

"How many twelve-year-olds wouldn't be frightened and calling out for help in the same situation? You had no way of knowing who was in more danger. That bank could've given way, and you'd have been buried under mud and water and not discovered. Currents like that are dangerous."

"I can't let go of the responsibility I feel," she said.

"Your expectations of yourself are unrealistic," he told her. "And so are your expectations of everyone else."

"Well, I don't think so."

"I know you don't. At least I know I'm not perfect, and I don't hope to be anytime soon."

She bristled. "I don't think I'm perfect."

"No. But you think you should be. Everyone else falls short, as well. You must wear yourself out being disappointed all the time. If something doesn't conform to your neat and tidy equation of the world, you dismiss it."

"You're just being mean now."

"Am I? Or am I being honest? You don't have a problem with telling the truth, do you?"

"How did this conversation get twisted around to be about me?" she asked. "We were talking about your sister." His accusations stung. She had shared her most private feelings with him, which she now regretted with all her heart.

"I'm traveling in the morning," she said. "I'm going to bed." With that, she turned and hurried back to the house.

Once everyone said their good-nights, Gabe ushered Irene home. She was happy, and he would never say or do anything to tarnish her tender feelings or discourage her from seeking the life she desired. After getting them both a pitcher of water, she wished him a goodnight and ducked into her tiny bedroom.

Gabe washed and lay atop the covers, staring at the shadows of the oaks dancing on the ceiling. Half an hour later, he got up and walked quietly out into the kitchen and dipped fresh water to drink. He lit a lantern and sat in one of the two chairs at the tiny table. A leather-bound book rested within reach. He pulled it toward him and opened it.

The pages were thinner than in most books, the text in columns. He recognized Irene's Bible and turned to a few of the pages marked with slips of paper.

Proverbs caught his attention and he read several,

then flipped back and found Psalms. He ran his finger over a few verses. If he hoped to gain any understanding, he'd better go to the beginning of this chapter.

There was a lot of talk of the law and the ungodly and heathen and kings. But as he read forward the writer cried out for God to save him and hear his cries.

In chapter seven, he lingered over the words of the psalmist. *The Lord shall judge the people. Judge me, O Lord, according to my righteousness, and according to mine integrity that is in me.*

Gabe sure didn't want to be judged on his actions or his decisions. It gave him some peace of mind to think that God would judge him according to his integrity. He knew right from wrong, and he had upheld what he believed was right by seeing that those who'd murdered and stolen came to justice. Whenever it had been possible, he'd brought that person back to sit in court before a judge. Killing had always been a last resort.

Further on he read that the heathen are sunk down in their own pits and the wicked are snared by the work of their own hands. Their choices to do wrong had caused those men he'd hunted their own fates.

He wanted to know more about that Joshua fellow Sam had talked about. How in this whole fat book of names and places would he ever hope to find the one?

On one of the first pages, he found a table of contents and ran his finger down the names of the chapters. Come to find out, Joshua had his own chapter.

Gabe extinguished the lantern and carried the book back to his room. Irene wouldn't mind if he borrowed it.

A couple of weeks later, Gabe stood inside the bank, securing a cashier's check.

"You've been having a lot of expenses," Rhys said, coming out of his office.

"Nothing comes free," Gabe replied.

"My offer still stands for the land."

"Still not interested. The house is almost finished. I'm heading for Durango to buy horses first thing in the morning."

"Got riders to help you with that?"

"Hired two cowboys a week ago. They're workin' out just fine." He tucked the check inside his vest pocket and left.

Elisabeth exited the courthouse after witnessing a legal transaction. Tying the ribbons of her bonnet under her chin, she spotted Gabe mounting his horse in front of the bank.

Since the night of Irene and Gil's announcement, he'd accepted Josie's invitations to dinner and had been cordial to Elisabeth, but they'd barely spoken. He was busy getting his ranch established, and she was…well, she was busy, too.

August drew to a close, and September was still warm, but the nights were cold. Elisabeth helped Josie launder bedding and quilts and hang them in the morning sun.

"I sense you're holding some things inside lately," her stepmother said to her. "You're not yourself."

Elisabeth waved the skirt of her wet apron in hopes of drying the fabric more quickly. "I've had a lot to think about."

"Do you want to talk about it?"

Elisabeth thought a moment. "I'm not ready."

"I understand you're a very private person, Elisabeth.

And your feelings run deep. But don't hold things in that your family could help you with."

Elisabeth nodded. She appreciated her stepmother's concern and her wise counsel, but she wasn't ready to voice her feelings.

"You know, my favorite place to go think has always been up the mountainside. Once you get about a third of the way up this incline behind the house, there's a deer trail that leads to the most beautiful scenery you can imagine. You can look over the treetops and streets of Jackson Springs and to the south, the valley and ridges." She glanced that direction now. "It seems silly, but I've never shared my place with anyone before. It's my refuge."

"Like our turret room," Elisabeth said.

"But more private because I've been the only one to ever go there. It's a good place to feel close to God and to think," she said. "In case you should ever want to walk up there and be alone, I just thought I'd let you know."

Josie's secret place intrigued her, and the idea of investigating it stayed with her. Once the laundry was dry and the beds made with fresh sheets and the winter quilts, Elisabeth changed her clothes, picked up her Bible and made her way up the mountainside. The deer trail was easy to find, and she followed it until she came out at the place Josie had described.

There was no mistaking the location. She could see for miles in one direction, and in the other look down at the tops of homes and see the square yards, outhouses and clotheslines. She recognized trees in rows that obviously lined streets. Smoke curled from chimneys, and she picked up the faint smells of burning wood and coal. Farther up, above the ridge, the aspens were turning gold.

She imagined Josie as a newcomer to this town, newly married to a man she barely knew, faced with three young girls who had lost their mother—one of them being downright rude to her—and could see how this vantage point had been a refuge. From here the entire world appeared small and insignificant. Elisabeth felt small, but also like a part of something bigger than herself and infinitely more important than her day-to-day concerns.

God cared about her every need, she never doubted that. But His majesty and power became very real when gazing upon the beauty and magnificence of His creation. A scripture came to mind, and she said aloud, "Who am I, Lord, that You are mindful of me?"

She sat on a flat outcropping of rock and opened her Bible to the Psalms, quickly turning pages. *When I consider the heavens and the work of Thy fingers, the moon and the stars, which Thou hast ordained, what is man that thou art mindful of him?*

She knew precisely how David had felt, awed as he was by God's magnificence. She read all of Psalm eight twice, and then traveled back to the preceding chapter and read. *Oh, Lord my God, in Thee do I put my trust: save me from all them that persecute me, and deliver me.* She read on. *Arise, Oh, Lord, in Thine anger, lift up thyself because of the rage of mine enemies, and awake for me to the judgment that Thou hast commanded.*

The Lord shall judge the people. Judge me, Oh, Lord, according to my righteousness, and according to mine integrity that is in me. Oh, let the wickedness of the wicked come to an end, but establish the just. For the righteous God trieth the hearts and reins. My defense is of God, which saveth the upright in heart. God judgeth the righteous, and God is angry with the wicked every day. If he turn not, he will whet his sword. He hath bent his bow and made it ready.... His mischief shall return upon his own head, and his violent dealing shall come down upon his own pate.

Elisabeth read these verses with a new perspective. Obviously God didn't approve of people who did wicked things, but these were strong words. Words of warning and judgment. God ordained his arrows against the persecutors! Men like Goliath who tormented the king's army? He had fallen to a young boy's stone. Men like the one who killed Dr. Barnes?

"Thank You for showing this to me, Lord." She read aloud the last verse in the Psalm. "'I will praise the Lord according to His righteousness, and will sing praise to the name of the Lord most high.'"

Even a preacher's daughter had to work things through on occasion. And yes, maybe she was as hard on herself as Gabe claimed. But much was expected of her—from God, from her father, from the community.

She'd been as disturbed by the fact that Gabe had hidden his profession from her as she'd been by the occupation itself. Looking at it from his point of view she could see where he'd wanted to start over and not carry the baggage of his past into a new life.

Humming a little, she admired the expanse of blue sky and the various green hues of the trees. Eventually she made her way back down the hillside. Instead of going into the house, she traveled down the street to the church and entered through the side door.

Pausing outside her father's office, she rapped softly

on the open door. He looked up from the papers and his Bible spread across his desk. "I didn't expect you today. I thought you were helping Josie."

"We're finished with the laundry. I even had some time to go off by myself and think."

"You don't do that often enough."

"I probably need to, don't I?" She sat on one of the chairs in front of his desk. Sometimes she sat there when they discussed sermon topics and on occasion she stopped to visit, but today she felt like one of his parishioners who'd come for counsel.

He rested his ink pen in its holder and flattened both hands on his paperwork. "What's on your mind, daughter?"

Chapter Nineteen

"Were you disappointed when you learned what Gabe had done before coming here?"

"I wasn't awfully surprised," he replied. "Not after hearing how he handled those train robbers and seeing how he walked right up to that man who was holding Donetta Barnes. I can't really say I was disappointed. The elements simply fell into place and made sense." He studied her. "I take it you were disappointed?"

She admitted she was. "I understand that plenty of men carry guns," she said. "But you carry yours for protection. You don't set out in the morning to shoot someone."

"What about Gil?" he mentioned. "His gun is for protection, but also to uphold the law if need be. He doesn't go to work in the morning planning to shoot someone. And I doubt that's how Gabe set out to bring in criminals."

"I'm sure you're right."

He studied her a moment longer. "He wasn't judging the people he tracked down. Either they'd already been judged by a court and found guilty or he planned to turn them over to the law and a judge once they were in his custody."

"But he did shoot men. And kill them."

"Yes."

She'd probably thought about this too much, but she couldn't let it go. "Couldn't he just shoot them in the knee or something?"

"Have you asked him that?"

She shook her head. "No."

"How effective do you think that would have been with Mrs. Barnes's life at stake?"

"That was different."

"They were probably all different," he suggested. "Each one an individual case with its own degrees of danger and difficulty. Ask him if a shot in the knee was ever good enough."

"All right."

"David was the apple of God's eyes, and he killed men in battle. However unpleasant Gabe's work was, he did a service to protect law-abiding citizens. Someone has to do that job or the country would be overrun with outlaws."

She begrudgingly acknowledged the truth of his statement with a nod.

"You asked me how I feel about him. I can only guess how you feel about him, but ask yourself this— What does God feel toward Mr. Taggart?"

She looked at her father with surprise.

"Well?" he asked.

"God loves him," she answered.

"And places great value on him," he added.

And with that, Elisabeth had even more to consider.

She got up and skirted around the desk to give her father a peck on the cheek. "Thank you."

"Who's coming for dinner tonight?" he asked.

"No one that I know of."

"Ah, an intimate family dinner." He chuckled. "See you then."

Out of doors, she strolled toward the corner. Irene called to her, "Wait, Elisabeth! I need to ask you something."

She paused and waited for Irene to join her near the curb.

"I'm planning to take the train to Denver and shop for a wedding dress. Would you like to come with me?"

Elisabeth could think of half a dozen reasons not to accompany her, but knowing how important the trip was to Irene, she said, "I'd love to go with you."

Irene beamed and hugged her. "Oh, thank you. We'll have such fun. Maybe we'll go to the theater while we're there."

That evening after supper while the family was occupied with their individual activities, Elisabeth again made the trip down the hill. She knocked on the door of the parsonage, relieved when Gabe opened the door.

"Irene isn't here."

"I suspected as much. I was hoping to speak with you."

He glanced over his shoulder, and then stepped outside. "Want to walk?"

"All right."

He went back in and returned wearing his vest, so she knew he'd gone back for his ever-present holster. They walked slowly toward the central portion of town, passing home after home with lights glowing behind windows.

"What's on your mind?" he asked.

"I've been doing a lot of thinking," she answered.

"Today I spoke with my father, and he had more insight into some of the things that have been troubling me."

"He's a wise person."

"Yes, he is."

"Good listener," he added.

That remark had her wondering. "Have you…talked to him about personal things?"

"Some."

She couldn't fathom it. But of course her father wouldn't speak of it to her. Neither would he share their private conversations with Gabe or anyone else. "You surprise me at every turn."

"What's so surprising?"

Every time they had a conversation, it got off track, and she wasn't going to let that happen this time. "Nothing. What I wanted to mention to you was that he suggested I ask you about some of the things I was wondering, rather than just letting my thoughts run rampant."

"What do you want to ask?"

"It's about your occupation. Regarding what you did before you came here."

"Hunting for bounty, Elisabeth. Go ahead and say it."

"Bounty hunting," she punctuated with a nod. "Where did you travel?"

"Wherever an outlaw's trail led me. I've sought men everywhere from the Dakota Territories to the lower half of Texas."

"How did you know who to look for and where they'd be?"

"Well…there are a couple of agencies who send out papers on wanted men. They pay higher bounties than local towns or state law enforcement agencies. Most every town has a marshal or a sheriff's office, and the bigger ones keep the up-to-date papers.

"As for where to look, well, knowin' that takes a lot of footwork and talking to the right people. Nobody can disappear, though, it's a fact. And people like to talk."

"I'm sure you had to be careful, because once the person you were seeking found out you were after him, he would try to kill you before you got to him."

"That's the truth."

"And when you did find a man…say for example he'd changed his name and his ways and settled down, perhaps even had a family. What did you do then?"

"I didn't go busting into their house and shoot 'im at the dinner table if that's what you're asking. I waited to find him alone, got the jump on him and handcuffed him. Most fellas like that went along peaceable like."

"And the others? The ones who were still robbing trains and what have you?"

"I still got the jump on them and tried to take them in without a fight."

"I guess some fought back. Or ran."

"Some." He paused just as they reached the trumpet-vine-covered arbor that led into the midtown park. "If you want to know how many men I killed, I can't tell you that. I didn't keep a log or notch my belt. Sometimes it happened, just like it happened that day in front of the doc's place."

"Did you…did you ever aim so as not to kill them if you could help it?"

"Yes."

They entered the park, which was lit only by two gas lamps at the entrance. Elisabeth knew the layout, so she led the way to a center area with stone benches.

They sat. The stones under them were still warm from the day's sun, and the heat felt good since the night air had cooled.

"If it makes you feel any better, Irene asked me some of the same questions."

That did make her feel a little better.

"Did you learn all you wanted to know?"

"Thank you, Gabe. Yes."

"Since we're talking, I have a question for you."

"All right."

"Weeks ago, when we first spoke about Gil and Irene, and I asked if you had feelings for him. Then I asked you about Rhys and you said—I can't remember your exact words—but you said you weren't in the market for a husband, unless God sent you one."

"That's still true," she said.

"I asked then how you would know. You said we'd talk about it later, but you never answered my question. So I'm asking again. How will you know if God sends you a husband?"

She had to think about it. How *would* she know? "If I even suspected, I would pray about it," she began.

"And what would you ask God for?"

"I'd ask Him to give me wisdom." She'd done that actually. "And I'd ask Him to point me in the direction He'd have me to go. And I'd ask for my will to become His."

"Pray for wisdom," he repeated. "How would you know if you got it?"

"There's a book of the Bible called James, and James says if any of us lacks wisdom, we should ask God and He'll give it to us. So we only have to ask, and wisdom is ours."

"I know who James is," he said. "And I know his book is toward the back."

She stared in surprise. "Yes!"

"I started reading Irene's Bible one night. A day or so later she bought me my own."

"She never said anything."

His shrug was barely perceptible in the semi-darkness. "And after those prayers, then what?"

"Then I'd be open to direction. It's not easy to explain."

"Try."

"For me, when I question whether or not something is right for me...if I have doubt, that's probably a sign to back off. When it's right—for example the job I took as the notary, I was at peace with the idea from the start."

"I've tracked a lot of outlaws who were probably at peace, but doing wrong."

"I doubt they truly had any peace, and if they weren't convicted of their wrongdoing, it was because they had neglected the little voice inside for so long that they'd become immune to a sense of right and wrong. The Bible talks about hardened hearts."

"You were right not to answer me that night, even if you didn't know it," he told her. "I wouldn't have understood your replies."

"That wasn't why I avoided the question." She wanted to see him more clearly, so she scooted closer to where he sat. "And now you do understand?"

"I think so. Irene prayed for me all the years I was gone. Your father prayed for me when I was shot. I wonder...have you ever prayed for me?"

"Yes," she replied. "The day you walked out there

in front of that man with the gun. I prayed for God to keep you safe so that one day you'd know Him as Lord."

"And He kept me safe."

"Yes."

"What else have you prayed about?"

"I've been confused a lot, so I've prayed for wisdom."

"I guess you got it since it was promised to you."

"I guess I did. I did figure out some of the questions I had. And I was wise enough to listen to my father and ask you about my concerns."

"There's a lot about me that bothers you. I scare you."

Yes, admittedly he did. Or perhaps it was more her reactions to him that frightened her.

"I make you feel things you don't want to feel."

Maybe that was so.

"If you let go of all the anger and disapproval and let yourself feel, that would frighten you, too. If you felt anything for me—or for anyone—it would challenge your thinking."

"I'm working on letting go, Gabe."

"Maybe you're afraid of losing your freedom."

"I don't believe that thought scares me," she told him. "I'm seeing how Irene and Gil are handling that, and as long as a husband was open to me keeping my notary job and still helping my father, marriage wouldn't inhibit me."

"You don't want children. That might hold you back."

"I didn't say never. I just said not right away."

"It's just me then. I scare you."

"I'm not afraid of you."

"But you're afraid of loving me."

Chapter Twenty

Her heart stopped. Discussing anything with him became impossible because he was so deliberately challenging. "Why do you have to do that?"

"What?"

"I'm trying to work through things in my head, hold
civil conversations, and you add more confusion."

"You came looking for me this time." He got up and
paced a few feet away. "You wanted to talk."

"I do want to talk."

"Maybe you do too much talking and too much
thinking and not enough feeling," he said. "Our dis-
cussions never end well." He walked back to stand in
front of her and reached for her hand.

She offered it and he pulled her to her feet and into
his arms. She steadied herself with a hand on his solid
arm. Standing so close she could smell the starch in his
shirt and the soap he'd used.

"Here's something we agree on." He lowered his
head and pressed his lips to hers.

If only life and relationships were as simple as a few
nice kisses, she thought. If kissing him was the only

thing she had to concern herself with, he was right—
they could get along.

He released her, took her hand, and led her back in
the direction from which they'd come. "I hear you're
going to Denver with Irene," he said.

"Yes. We're staying over at least one night. Maybe
two."

"I was hoping you'd agree to do some shopping for
me while you're there."

"What is it you need?"

"A stove, table and things for the kitchen. Do you
know how to select things like that?"

"I could figure it out," she replied.

"And furniture," he added. "At least three beds and
bureaus, and a few chairs and whatever else a house
needs."

That was a lot of responsibility. "Are you sure you
don't want to choose those things yourself?"

"I'd grab whatever I saw first. You, on the other
hand, will compare prices and sizes and concern yourself with colors and the like. You'll do a much better
job."

She found it noteworthy that he had her pegged so
accurately. "Do you have a budget?"

"I've had money wired to the bank there. I'll give
you the papers, and you can withdraw it as you need
it. I trust you to be frugal and yet purchase things of
quality."

"I'd enjoy shopping for those things. But I need you
to be a little more specific. Do you have a floor plan
of the house?"

"I could bring it up tomorrow evening so we could
go over the rooms."

"All right. I'd feel more confident with better knowledge of what it is you need."

"One more thing I'm indebted to you for."

"You're not indebted to me."

"I have no way of repaying how you and Josie took care of me when I was laid up, or for all the meals…or for taking Irene under your wings."

"There's no tally for kindness, Gabe. If a person expects something in return for a good deed, he shouldn't do it."

They'd reached the street and walked past darkened buildings into the neighborhood until they reached the church. "I'll walk you up the hill," he told her.

"It never crossed our minds how many times we'd be walking up this hill when we picked out our house," she told him. "Josie bought it as a surprise for my father."

"I'll bet he was really surprised."

"Yes." She looked up at him. "Especially because she'd never mentioned she was wealthy before they were married, and he had no idea."

"There are definitely worse things to learn about the person you married."

They laughed together. The moment felt right. She was glad she'd come right out and asked the things she'd been wondering about. He'd been straightforward about all if it, even asked her about something he'd had on his mind. Elisabeth felt as though they had shared something special as only friends could do. Maybe she'd been wrong. Maybe she and Gabe could be friends.

The Jacksons were their guests for supper the following evening. Beatrice told Sam how much she was looking forward to fall and the cooler temperatures.

"The nights have been perfect for sleeping," Sam mentioned.

"Perhaps I'll find that out sometime soon," Josie added.

Sam gave his wife an apologetic look. "Little Rachel would rather be awake during the night than during the day."

"I remember Rhys went though that stage, too," Beatrice said. "And his father slept right through the racket."

Rhys gave his mother a sidelong glance. "I'm sure he had to get up and go to work at the bank in the morning."

"You're right, he did," she answered. "And there's nothing the father can do when that little one is hungry."

Rhys kept his eyes on his plate.

Eventually, the meal was over and Elisabeth sent Josie to join their guests while she and her sisters did the dishes. She was drying a stack of plates when Gabe showed up in the kitchen doorway.

"Your father offered me a seat in the great room, but I told him I'd come to see you."

"Did you have supper?" she asked.

He nodded, but his gaze slid to the peach cobbler at the end of the work table.

Elisabeth spooned out a generous serving, poured cream over the top and sat it along with a spoon on the table. "The coffee is nearly ready. I'll pour you a cup when it's done."

He sat. "Did you make this?"

"Abigail did. She's the best baker of the three of us."

Gabe tasted a spoonful. "This is the best peach cobbler I've ever tasted," he told Elisabeth's sister.

Abigail gave him a warm smile. "Thank you, Mr. Taggart."

"How old are you? Twenty? Thirty-five?"

She giggled. "I'm seventeen."

"Well, I envy the people you'll be cooking for when you're twenty-five."

"That will be my husband and all of my children," she said. "I'm going to have a big family, just like Papa and Josie. And a house like this one, with lots of room for guests."

"That's a good plan," Gabe told her with a wink. "Is there anyone special you have your eye on now?"

"I used to like Lester Quinn, but he has poor table manners. James Finley was sweet on me in elementary school, but his family moved to Idaho."

"I guess you'll know when God brings you a man to be your husband, won't you?" Gabe suggested.

"I guess I will." Abigail got a cup and poured him coffee. "I just hope he has good table manners."

Gabe and Elisabeth exchanged an amused look while she mulled the fact that he'd just mentioned God in a matter-of-fact way. As though he'd changed his thinking on the subject. She'd noticed he was a good listener, and he asked questions as though he was genuinely interested in others. He had the uncanny ability to draw things from them that she'd never heard before. "God knows your heart," Elisabeth said to her sister. "And He'll send you a husband who is right for you. If the fellow has poor manners, you'll just have to overlook that or give him lessons in etiquette."

"I won't be overlooking it," Abigail assured her.

"What if he's as handsome as a prince?" Gabe asked.

"Charm is deceptive, and beauty is fleeting," she replied.

"Proverbs?" he questioned.

She nodded.

"What if he's as rich as a king?"

"Better that he's wise," Abigail replied. "Solomon asked for wisdom, and because he didn't ask God for riches, he got wisdom, plus riches and honor. He was the wisest man who ever lived, you know."

"No one's ever going to best a Hart sister in a battle of wits," he said with a shake of his head. "You have a good plan. Don't let anything shake you from it. Are you sure you're not thirty-five?"

Abigail laughed.

"As long as I eat with good manners, will you keep making these delicious cobblers? I will even plant fruit trees on my land just for you."

Her smile lit up her face. "You will? Can I come pick fruit? What? Cherries and peaches?"

"Whatever you like. And you're welcome anytime. You can bring all of your children, too, and I'll teach them to ride."

Abigail glanced at her older sister. "What about Elisabeth and her children?"

"They're welcome, too. What shall I plant for you, Elisabeth?"

She hung a towel to dry and removed her apron. "How long does it take chestnut trees to mature and produce nuts? I do enjoy chestnuts in stuffing at Thanksgiving."

"I'll look into that."

She sat at the table. "Did you bring a floor plan?"

He reached into his vest pocket and withdrew a paper

that he unfolded and spread on the table. "I drew this for you. The measurements are pretty accurate. You can get an idea of room sizes and what we'll need."

"Is this a dining room?"

"It is."

"Do you want furniture for that right away?"

"It can wait if you don't want to bother, but if you see something like what's in your parents' home, buy it."

"A table and chairs, a sideboard…even a china cabinet?"

"I guess I'll need dishes, right?"

She looked at the sketch. "The kitchen seems plenty big enough for a table. You'll be feeding ranch hands every night, right?"

He nodded.

"I'd get a long narrow table for the kitchen. That way they can wash up outside and come in through the rear door—here—and it would be a lot easier for Mrs. Barnes to serve and clean up from there than carrying it all into another room.

"You will want to furnish your dining room, but I'd wait on that until you have the rest of the house serviceable and ready for work."

"You got that wisdom already," he said.

She met his eyes, and he was smiling at her in that way that lifted one side of his mouth and curled her toes. "I'm inordinately practical," she informed him. "Always have been."

"That's why I trust you to do this."

"I'll do the best I can."

"I know you will."

Abigail had left the room while they were talking, leaving them alone.

He covered her hand with his, his calluses grazing her knuckles and sending a shiver up her arm. "What you feel for me isn't practical, is it?"

"Not in the least."

"Your father and Josie, they have a practical marriage?"

"He needed a wife. She was widowed and wanted a family. That was practical."

"I guess it worked out well for them," he said.

"I guess it did."

"Not everything in life is practical," he suggested.

He glanced at her as though assessing her. Her hair was in a practical braid so it didn't get in the way during the day. Her clothing was plain and unremarkable. What was he thinking when he studied her?

He reached for the chain above her collar and gently extricated the wedding ring from under the top of her shirtwaist so that it hung atop her clothing. "That's not practical."

"It's sentimental," she replied.

"Do you own anything that's just for fun?"

After thinking, she shook her head.

"You wore ribbons in your hair to church," he said. "And your straw hat has little painted cherries with paper leaves."

She widened her eyes. He remembered the details of her clothing and accessories?

"They're not necessary. But do they make you happy?"

"I suppose so."

"I could make you happy if you'd let me."

His words set her nerves on edge.

"Remember how much fun we had together on Independence Day?"

"Life isn't all ice cream and fireworks," she told him.

"Isn't life whatever you make it?" he asked.

"We need to talk about the furniture," she insisted. "If I'm going to do this, I need to be completely knowledgeable about your needs."

He released her hand. "Yes. Let's talk about the shopping trip."

She had to force herself to listen, because his insistent flirting knocked her off-kilter, as usual. The man was full of surprises. She'd been pretty sure she had him figured out, but the more she learned, the more she realized she didn't know him at all.

He'd teased Abigail in a brotherly manner, while at the same time encouraging her dreams of the future. He'd been responding knowledgeably to Biblical references, indicating he'd been reading the Bible Irene had given him. Elisabeth tried to picture it, but couldn't.

Nursing her sense of betrayal regarding him not telling her he was a bounty hunter was making her feel smaller and smaller. He hadn't lied, though not being forthright was the same. He'd explained himself whenever asked. His job had been to uphold the law, and he'd done it the only way that worked out here in this part of the country.

She remembered her father's comment about society needing men like Gabe or else the country would be overrun with outlaws, and she supposed that was true.

But even if she could set all that aside, he still didn't meet the standards that she'd already set for a husband. He was nothing like her father. He'd never been to church before he got here…never read a Bible. He didn't even have a basic knowledge or know about people in the scriptures.

Maybe she did have cherries on her hat, but she'd have a different hat come winter.

* * *

Shopping for her wedding dress in Denver, Irene wore Elisabeth to a frazzle. Nothing suited her, but finally on the second day they stumbled upon a seamstress with stunning dresses on display. The woman agreed to make her a dress just the way she wanted it and took numerous measurements.

"What about you, miss?" the woman said to Elisabeth. "You'll need a dress for the wedding, won't you?"

"Oh, goodness, yes!" Irene's eyes shone with excitement. "You'll stand up with me, won't you?"

"Me?"

"Who else? You're my dearest friend. Any friends I had at the academy have been scattered to the winds. Besides, those weren't friendships like ours. Say you will, Elisabeth."

"Of course," she agreed.

"What color?" the seamstress asked.

"I'd love it if she wore pale blue," Irene said. "Don't you think it would be a good color for her? And I will add pale blue ribbons to my bouquet and to the flower arrangements at the church."

"I have just the fabric," the woman said and rushed toward her store room, returning with a bolt of the most beautiful cloudlike blue chiffon Elisabeth had ever seen. "Will this be too insubstantial for a fall wedding?"

"The days are warm," Elisabeth assured her. "But the nights are considerably cooler."

"We'll make you a white fur wrap for evening," the woman suggested. "Like this one." She showed the two young women a soft white rabbit fur stole.

"Do you like it?" Irene asked.

"I like it a lot actually."

The seamstress measured Elisabeth. "I can make a hair bob with matching white fur, rhinestones and pieces of the dress fabric." She turned to Irene. "Can you ladies come back in two weeks for an initial fitting? I want to make certain the basic dresses are perfect before we start adding lace and beads and trim."

"Will you be able to return with me?" Irene asked Elisabeth.

"Yes, of course. I'll probably need to finish your brother's shopping anyway."

Irene accompanied her on a hunt for a stove. Once that was selected and purchased, Elisabeth had a driver take them to each one of the furniture makers so that she'd seen every last available piece before making a decision.

"Help me choose bedroom furniture," she said to Irene. "The less ornate pieces appeal to me, but perhaps your brother would like something fancier."

"I agree on the more simple pieces. The other parts of the rooms, like curtains and coverlets, can always be added and changed."

"We didn't talk about this, but each room needs a rug. Floors are awfully cold come December and January."

Irene pointed across the street. "I saw carpets in the window over there."

With Irene's help, Elisabeth selected three sets of bedroom furniture and six room-size rugs. They made a trip to the bank, and she returned to each store to pay for all the items and plan their delivery.

"The other things are going to have to wait until tomorrow," she told Irene. "We have plans for the theater tonight."

Relieved, Irene smiled and hugged her. "Let's start getting ready and have an early dinner."

Two hours later, as the carriage they'd hired drew closer to an enormous two-story brick building, Elisabeth noted that the entire front was larger and square, a facade for the slant-roofed long narrow building behind it.

As they pulled directly in front, light spilled from the windows on the first floor and loud music met their ears. Both women stared out the windows in confusion.

The carriage jostled as the driver climbed down. He opened the door.

Elisabeth accepted his assistance and climbed to the ground. "Are you sure this is the right place?"

"You wanted the Denver Theater, didn't you, miss?"

"Yes, but this…this doesn't look like a theater."

"The performances actually take place on the second story. The entrance is on the side over there. This first floor here is a saloon and gambling hall. You can try your luck at any number of games. Faro, poker, roulette, monte, chuck-a-luck…and you don't have to worry about your play getting over too late. The place is open twenty-four hours a day, seven days a week."

Dubious about the wisdom of being left in front of this establishment, Elisabeth turned to Irene, who now stood beside her. The other young woman wore a concerned frown.

"Need a hand, ladies?" A burly fellow in wrinkled trousers with suspenders over his flannel shirt called to them. "I'd be glad to show you around. Appears to me you're new to the gaming tables."

"We were just leaving, thank you." Elisabeth turned. "Back in," she said to Irene. "Please return us to our hotel."

"Elisabeth," Irene whispered and grabbed her arm. She was staring over Elisabeth's shoulder toward the noisy gambling hall. "Isn't that...?"

Elisabeth followed her gaze. At the corner of the building, a gas lamp shone down on a gathering of well-dressed men. "Rhys?"

Chapter Twenty-One

"That's what I thought."

"Maybe he's here for the theater." Once they were back inside, before the driver shut the door, she asked, "Wait just a few minutes, please. Until that group of gentlemen over there moves along." She leaned back to stay out of view and still be able to see.

The driver climbed back atop the carriage.

One of the men shook hands with Rhys before turning and leaving. The rest of them, Rhys included, walked to the front door and entered the hall.

Apparently the driver had been watching, because the carriage pulled away from the curb.

"Sorry about our evening plans being spoiled," Irene said.

"We'll go to the music hall tomorrow evening," Elisabeth suggested. "I've been there before, and it's not located over a saloon."

They laughed together.

"Will you tell your father?" Irene asked. "That you saw Mr. Jackson there?"

"I'm not sure what I should do." And she didn't. The

Jacksons had been guests at their table for the past seven years. Elisabeth perceived that Rhys would have welcomed her interest and, because he was such a close friend of the family, she had considered the idea of courting. She wanted to give the man the benefit of the doubt, but seeing him at that place didn't really leave much doubt.

"Yes, I'll mention it to my father," she decided. "Then he'll have as much information as I do and can form his own opinion."

The following morning they finished shopping for furniture and household wares. Most of the afternoon was spent looking for slippers and underclothing. Elisabeth let Irene know she'd need boots and a warm coat in the coming months, so that was next on their list of errands. Elisabeth sent telegrams to her father and Gabe informing them the two of them would be staying a second night.

They enjoyed a leisurely supper and attended the music hall before spending their last night at the hotel.

Gabe and Gil met them at the train station the following day.

Gil swept Irene up in a hug and spun her in a circle. "I sure missed you."

Standing right there on the platform with passengers moving around them, she tipped her head back and kissed him.

Elisabeth glanced at Gabe just as he looked at her. He gave her a grin.

"Did you notice I was gone?" she asked.

"Life was hardly worth living without you."

She laughed and smacked his arm playfully. "What *did* you do?"

"Plastered walls."

"I have a lot to tell you. I made a few sketches and I have your receipts in my satchel."

"You can clean up and rest, then tell me later."

"This evening," she said. "Come to the house for supper."

That evening Kathryn DeSmet, the schoolteacher, had been invited for supper, along with Donetta Barnes.

Irene chattered about their trip, about their dresses and the seamstress, and then launched into the tale of how they'd changed their mind about the theater once they'd seen the location.

"That was using wisdom," Sam told his oldest daughter.

Somehow it didn't seem like the right time to mention seeing Rhys there.

Later, after cleaning up, when Elisabeth and Gabe were alone in the dining room, she spread out the receipts and her drawings and proceeded to describe everything they'd purchased.

"What your father said about using wisdom," Gabe inquired. "Would some people call that common sense?"

"There is common sense, as well," she answered. "But do you remember when I said I knew inside whether something was wrong or right?" At his nod, she continued. "I knew it would be a mistake to go in there. I didn't see lightning bolts or hear an audible voice from above, but I just *knew*. In here." She touched her bodice.

He listened attentively.

"I can't say for sure something bad would have happened, but I think it might have. This way I may never know, but I probably avoided something I'd have been sorry for later—if I hadn't heeded the warning."

She showed him her drawings and described the furniture. "I'm not much of an artist. I didn't do these pieces justice."

"You bought 'most everything the house needs," he told her.

"I hope you're going to be pleased."

"You need to come out and see how the house is coming along. It's nearly finished, and you haven't seen it. I should have taken you before."

"I'd love to see it now."

"Let me know when you have a free morning, and I'll rent a rig. Or you can ride."

"I'm not much of a rider."

"Once things are more settled, you and Abigail can come for riding lessons."

She never thought she'd think it or say it, but after considering learning to ride and thinking about having Gabe as an instructor, she said, "I'd like that."

A person would've thought she'd given him the deed to a diamond mine, the way pleasure lit his features. "All right then."

The following morning, he arrived with a buggy pulled by a single black horse.

"Isn't Irene coming with us?"

"I asked her, but she had something she wanted to do."

He helped her up to the seat.

"I took the liberty of buyin' a lunch to bring along in case we get hungry."

She couldn't picture the two of them sharing a cozy

picnic lunch without finding something to argue about, but she supposed it could happen. Last time they'd ridden out here they'd had Phillip along as a buffer.

Already, there was a road of sorts, where before there'd been only grass and fields. She remarked on the difference.

"All those wagons filled with supplies and all the workers coming and going have fashioned a path right to my house," he said. "Ought to make it easier on the horses when there's snow on the ground."

Up ahead, Elisabeth spotted something that surprised her and made her heart leap. In the place where they'd crossed the stream previously, a bridge had been built. Just wide enough for a wagon, but solid and well above the water.

"You built a bridge!"

"Made it easier to get the full wagons across," he told her. "And this way if Anna comes out to the ranch, it won't be as hard for her."

She turned to look at him.

"Your father mentioned that Anna was afraid of water. You didn't like crossing the stream much, either." He didn't meet her eyes. "A bridge was practical."

"Indeed."

She was grateful for the ease of crossing. *If Anna comes to the ranch,* he'd said. Interesting how he thought of her family coming to visit him. He'd probably invited Anna to come ride horses, too.

The entire clearing looked so different; the sight caught her by surprise. She'd expected a house, yes, but this was beginning to look like a ranch. A stable had been constructed, a long low building, painted white with a red roof.

A tall fellow in a faded blue shirt and a dun-colored hat was setting a fence post into the ground as they pulled up. Elisabeth didn't recognize him. Another man exited the stable and caught sight of them.

Gabe motioned him forward and called to the other, "John!"

Both men approached and removed their hats in deference to Elisabeth's company.

"This is Miss Hart. Elisabeth, this is Ward Dodd and John McEndree."

John, the one who'd been putting up the corral fence, gave her a toothy smile. "Pleasure to meet you, miss."

"These are my first two hands," Gabe told her. "They already think I'm workin' 'em hard, and the horses don't even arrive 'til next week."

John laughed. "I'll be glad when it's horses we're dealing with, and not fence posts."

The men went back to work, and Gabe ushered her toward the house. It was a long one-story home. The exterior wood siding hadn't been painted yet, but there was a door and plenty of windows.

The dooryard was dirt, of course. A walkway of boards had been fashioned, and she supposed the wood came in handy when it rained.

The door opened into a foyer. Not as grand or as large as the Harts', but adequate. Doorways led to rooms on either side, and a hallway led back to a wood-paneled hallway on the left and a smaller hall on the right.

The smells of new wood and fresh plaster permeated the air. "I've never been inside a brand-new house before."

The first two rooms were large with floor-to-ceiling

windows. "A sitting room?" she asked about the one on the left with the fireplace.

"Yep. And across the entryway is the dining room. I thought about having a cabinetmaker build storage right into this wall. What do you think?"

"It sounds perfect."

"He led her through a doorway into a small room with shelves all the way to the ceiling. "I did these myself, because they're simply functional. This area is for dishes and storing food," he explained. "And the kitchen's right through here. You can get to it this way, or by continuing on down that front hall where we came in—or of course by the back door."

The kitchen was as big as the Harts', with work spaces built along the walls and a long, waist-high table about four feet away from the stove. There was even room aside from that for a long table for eating.

"Donetta is going to love working in here," she told him. "The stove I ordered is perfect. I was concerned it might be a little big, but I see now this room called for it."

Again, there were floor-to-ceiling windows, and the view of the stables with the mountains behind was spectacular.

She remembered the diagrams he'd drawn for her and pointed. "This must be for Donetta?" None of the rooms had doors yet, so she simply walked in. The space was more than adequate, and even had a small dressing room area. "You've given her such a nice big space. And two windows. She'll like this."

"I hope so. It's going to be a big adjustment. I want to give her privacy, but don't want her to feel alone."

They walked back out to the kitchen. "I'll dig a root cellar next summer."

"It looks as though you've thought of everything."

"Come on. I'll show you the rest."

"Each one of these rooms will have a small heating stove," he said. "I ordered them from a catalogue at Larken's. They should be here in another week or so."

"You'll need them when the snow and wind blow."

The hallway was wide and long with doors opening off each side. His wasn't a traditional home like those that lined the streets in Jackson Springs, but it was practical and plenty adequate for even a large family.

She supposed two and three stories atop each other saved lot space in the city. Out here he hadn't needed to concern himself with that and constructed a sprawling dwelling.

He showed her one large empty bedroom and five smaller ones. "You didn't plaster all of this yourself?"

"I'd have been here all winter," he replied. "No, I've had help throughout the entire process. I don't know how happy the people in town are now, though. They've had to find someone else to run their errands. Junie Pruitt was in the telegraph office one day when I was there and expressed an interest in coming out to see the work going on. Turns out he's pretty handy with a saw and hammer. He's been here every day since."

"Where is everyone today?"

"While the plaster's hardening this morning, we're finishing the inside of the stable, and you saw the fencing going up."

She suspected the diversion of workers may have had something to do with her visit, too.

"I'll show you where the bunkhouse is going to be."

Chapter Twenty-Two

"You already hired a couple men to work the horses with you, didn't you? Where are they staying?"

"Stables. Cook their meals over a fire for now. They're counting on that situation changing real soon." He guided her back through the house and out the front door. "As soon as the floors are varnished and there's furniture, I'll bring Donetta and Irene."

"It's really nice that there will be another woman for Irene."

"For the short time that Irene is here," he said, "yes."

Gabe helped her back into the buggy, got in and guided the horse to take them around behind the house. With this view it was plain just how long the structure was. He had chosen the level piece of ground well.

"I plan to go up in those hills and dig the largest trees I can manage," he said. "Plant several along the side of the house there. He slanted her a grin. "Can't forget to order Abigail's fruit trees, either."

"You're kind to my sisters."

"Surprised that I'm not all bad?"

"I never thought you were all bad. Or bad at all."

"When I see how they thrive in your family…how different it all seems from anything I ever knew…well, I see how I let Irene grow up without that. I don't know that I could have given it to her the same, being just a brother and only one person, but I'll never know now."

"She turned out just fine, Gabe."

He deliberately looked away, and their ride was silent for several minutes. The land sloped upward and the horse slowed. "I'm going to bring water from up there," he said. "There are springs farther up. Gravity will carry it."

"How will that work?"

"We'll build a sturdy trough, and it'll bring water right down to the house. Can even water a garden with it."

"What about in winter when it freezes?"

"In winter we'll melt snow. Are you up to walking?"

"Sure."

After finding shade for the horse, he unharnessed the animal so it could graze. He reached for her hand, and together they made their way up the hillside. They came across a deer trail, and followed the path upward. The trail reminded her of the one Josie had told her about behind their home, though this was farther from Gabe's house.

It had turned into a warm morning, and perspiration cooled her face before they reached the first spring. Water poured from crevices in rocks and spilled into a sparkling clear pond.

"This is beautiful," she breathed.

They found a place to perch and settled to catch their breath, enjoying the peaceful sound of the water. The loamy scent of the earth and pine needles enveloped them. In the stillness, a raccoon emerged from the undergrowth and carried a twig laden with berries to the water's edge.

Elisabeth glanced at Gabe. He'd seen the animal, too. Reaching for her hand, he met her eyes. She turned her attention back just as three baby raccoons joined the first and sat on their haunches waiting for her to wash their meal.

She drank from the stream, and the babies followed her example. Minutes later, she turned and nature's parade disappeared back into the foliage.

"If a person sat here long enough, he'd see deer and all manner of creatures," Gabe said. "The entire area is covered with tracks."

"What about something dangerous, like a mountain lion?" she asked.

"Wouldn't do to come up here without a gun," he advised.

Her gaze slid to his vest, where the bump of his holster was visible.

At the water's edge, they cupped their hands and drank the cold clear water until they'd had their fill.

Gabe wiped his chin with the back of his hand and studied her in the sunlight. The sparkling reflection from the water cast darts of light across her face and hair. Maybe it was this place or maybe it was because she'd softened toward him however minutely, but she seemed more at ease. Her whole demeanor was less rigid, and her enjoyment genuine.

Knowing he didn't stand a chance with her didn't prevent him from imagining how it would be if she married him and this became their home.

He didn't even want to admit the fact to himself,

but during his hours of work, whether it was sawing and planing logs or pounding shingles on the roof, he pictured her living here. He imagined the two of them sitting in front of the fireplace. He imagined sharing a room and a bed. He imagined children.

She'd run for the hills if she had an inkling of his thoughts. But the seeds were planted in his mind's eye and he watered them daily.

Her family could come for Sunday dinners. Irene and Gil would join them. Their children and Irene's children would grow up part of a family.

His throat got tight at the wistful thought. He reached for her hand. "Come on."

He harnessed the horse and they took the buggy even farther from the ranch house, exploring the sights and enjoying the day. "There's another deer trail," she said, spotting one heading into the brush on a hillside.

"Want to follow it?" he asked.

"Let's."

"I'm getting hungry. I'll grab the food this time." He took the small crate from the rear of the buggy.

The trail led them higher and deeper into the woods than before. "Will we find our way back out?" she asked.

"We head downhill, right?"

"We should have left breadcrumbs."

"What good would that do? The birds would eat them."

She'd been leading, and she turned to look back at him. "I was kidding. That's what Hansel and Gretel did."

"Who are they?"

"It's a children's fairy tale."

"Oh."

Here the smell of the forest changed. The verdant scent of pine needles was masked by a sulfurous smell. The air seemed more humid, and Gabe broke out in a sweat.

It wasn't long before the trail leveled out and brought them to a long steaming pool. At first he thought the vapor was a phenomenon caused by warm air and cold water, but the humidity and the smell said otherwise. There was no sound of running water here. The water seemed to move with an inner life.

Gabe set down the crate and walked straight to the rocks lining the pool, where he knelt and plunged his hand into the water. Even though he'd expected the temperature, the warmth shocked him. He plunged in his other hand. "It's *hot*."

Elisabeth drew up beside him and knelt, the hem of her skirt falling into the water. She dabbled her fingers and then her hand, and her eyes widened. She raised a questioning gaze up to him.

"A mineral spring," he said in amazement.

"I've read about them," she said. "Some think they have restorative healing abilities."

He nodded.

"There are places you can go to bathe in mineral springs. Wealthy people do it."

He nodded again. "And pay a lot of money for the privilege." His mind rolled back over the incidents he'd questioned at the time, but dismissed. "This could be why Rhys Jackson keeps offering me twice what my land is worth—or what I thought it was worth."

"Do you think he knows this is here?"

"There's probably more than one spot where the

water seeps," he said. "It's being fed from underground. Probably bubbling up wherever it finds an exit."

"Do you suppose he's known about this for a long time?"

"And kept it under his hat. He said he'd looked for the property owner, and now we know why. He wanted to buy the land and make himself rich."

"*You* could be rich, Gabe."

"It's a tempting thought after all I've spent on building my ranch." He took off his hat and ran his wet hands through his hair. "I don't know that I'd want a lot of people traipsing across my land to get here though."

"You can think about it," she suggested.

"I don't know that I want to eat here," he said. "It's warm."

"I'm getting rather used to it," she said. "And I'm hungry."

He agreed and unpacked the food.

Elisabeth unwrapped a turkey sandwich. "This is a treat."

"I wasn't sure what you like or don't like."

"I like everything." She paused before taking a bite. "Except olives."

"Half the crate is olives," he teased. "Guess I'll have to eat them myself.

"Guess you will."

After they'd finished their sandwiches, he washed shiny red apples. To finish off the meal, he uncovered slices of cake, which they had to eat with their fingers because there were no forks.

She laughed and washed her hands in the warm water. "Cleanup's not a problem, but we can't drink this."

With a flourish, he produced a single jar of buttermilk and no cups, so they took turns drinking from the jar.

"I still want some water," she said, once they'd finished.

"I'll find you some cold water," he promised.

"I haven't been on a picnic for a long time. Of course we ate out of doors on Independence Day, but other than that."

"I ate half my meals over a campfire when I was on the trail," he said. "Ate a lot of hardtack and biscuits. Shot an occasional rabbit or squirrel. Nothing too big to eat in one sitting."

"We ate a lot of rabbits on our way west," she said. "I don't remember having squirrel."

"It's not prairie game." He gazed across the water, again envisioning a family. "Do you think your sisters would like to swim here?"

"I think they would. It's not frightening in any way. In fact it's rather like a big washtub. We'll have to buy bathing wear first. We have none."

"If it involves shopping, Irene will join you." He chuckled.

They moved to sit comfortably on a bank of grass and pine needles. "You speak differently when you talk about Irene today," she said.

He nodded and took the stone from his pocket. "I can't change the past. That's what you told me."

"I also said you'd done the very best you could for her."

"How many stones are in *your* pocket today?"

She reached into her skirt and produced three on her open palm.

"What is it they symbolize?"

"Sacrifice. Dedication."

"Seems like I remember you said they remind you of the choices you've made and the results of those choices."

She looked away. "Yes. That, too."

"Which is it?"

She glanced back at him. "What do you mean?"

"Well, I've thought a lot since you gave mine to me. I stopped blaming myself for things I couldn't change. I regret missing those years with my sister, but I can't change it. You helped me look at my plans for Irene honestly. I can only move forward and be glad for her because she's in love and very happy."

"That's good, Gabe."

"I'm having trouble with the logic of the stone, however."

"Why's that?"

"Because when I hold it every day, it reminds me of the past, not the future."

Elisabeth studied his hand, now loosely holding the rock and opened her palm to look at her collection.

"You said we can't change the past or the poor decisions we've made," he said.

"That's right."

"But you carry around those rocks that remind you of something you feel guilty about. I was reading in Philippians…"

Her head shot up and she raised her eyebrows.

"Can't remember all those words like you can, but the gist of it was that Paul said we should forget those things that are behind us and just look toward the goal out in front."

Elisabeth knew exactly which scripture he referred to. She could have quoted it perfectly. *I count not myself to have apprehended: but this one thing I do, forgetting those things which are behind, and reaching forth unto those things which are before...*

Before her sat a man who'd never read a Bible until he'd met their family. Now he spoke about truths of God's Word. He hadn't quoted scripture the way she could, but he'd obviously interpreted the verses and understood their meaning in a way she never had.

At first she wanted to be angry with him for questioning her thinking or for believing he had a better understanding than she...but she really wanted to get mad because he'd forced her to think about something she'd clung to for a long time.

The stones did remind her of sacrifice. And choices. And her mother.

Her eyes smarted and her nostrils stung. But the memories the symbols provoked were not happy memories of her childhood or of her mother as a sweet-natured, pretty blonde woman. They were memories of a woman floating facedown in the water, fair hair snagged in the brush along the shore. The reminders evoked memories of an ashen-faced person being wrapped in her parents' wedding quilt and lowered into a grave.

All the memories made her regret her fear and behavior that fateful day. The mementos reminded her she couldn't go back and fix what had happened. And when she thought about her regrets logically, she believed just as Gabe had said weeks ago that she'd been a frightened girl and had done what anyone else would have done in the same situation. She'd had no way of knowing that she would have been saved—or even that her mother could have been rescued in time.

She couldn't live those hours over to change the outcome, but she relived what she perceived as her mistake every time she looked at or touched one of these stones.

The stones were her past. She didn't know what her future held, but she couldn't let it be filled with regret. From here on out changes had to be made.

Elisabeth got to her feet. One at a time, she threw the rocks into the steaming pond. Each stone made a satisfying plunk and created circles on the surface before the water swallowed it into its depths.

"What have you done?" Gabe now stood beside her.

"I put the past behind me." She stared at the water.

Another rock sailed through the air and landed with a watery plunk where hers had disappeared. She turned to find Gabe staring at the spot where he'd thrown his stone. "Hope that was okay," he said. "It bein' a gift and all."

"It was perfectly okay. I'll give you another gift to replace it."

"Not necessary."

"I know. Thank you, Gabe."

"For what?"

"For opening my eyes to the fact that I was punishing myself."

"Wasn't me," he said. "That Paul fella said it."

She laughed then, a laugh that came from deep in her belly and echoed across the water and off the rocks. She laughed until she wore herself out and had to stop to breathe.

Gabe shook his head. "As long as you're laughing, I have something else to say that you might find amusing."

She composed herself in preparation. "I'm ready."

For a moment she thought he'd changed his mind about sharing whatever it was he wanted to say, but then he pursed his lips and took a deep breath. "I don't expect you to do anything with this. I don't expect anything. I just want to say it, and then I'll have it off my chest."

"Oh, my goodness. Is this something serious and not funny at all?"

"I guess that depends how you look at it."

"All right. What is it?"

"It won't change anything. You're still you and I'm still me."

"Gabe," she said impatiently.

"I just want to be honest."

This time she sighed. "Now you're starting to scare me because you won't just come out with—"

"I love you."

Chapter Twenty-Three

Hᵢₛ words stopped the sentence she'd been forming—
and her brain—for about thirty seconds. Had she heard
correctly?

"I realize I can't measure up to the standards you've
set for your future husband. I'm not going to regret that
fact or bemoan it, because I can't change who I am. I
can't change that I wasn't raised in a family like yours
or that I never really knew about Jesus until you spoke
of Him. Until your father taught me. Now I'm inspired
to be a better man. And that's the future.

"I've lived a life you can't condone, and that's just
a fact. So that's why I'm sayin' you don't have to do
anything with the information. You don't even have to
respond. It's okay. I just wanted to say it. Just once."

He turned and picked up the crate.

It took her a moment to get herself oriented and follow him. He led the way down the hillside, and the
whole time she thought over his pronouncement. She
was thankful he hadn't expected her to say anything,
because she didn't know what she would have said. She
felt as though she was a pebble rolling down a hill to

spin off a cliff into midair. Her rational thoughts were suspended while she processed Gabe's startling proclamation.

They arrived at the buggy and Gabe guided the horse back to the house. He dipped water from a barrel with a dented tin cup and handed it to her. The liquid was warm and nothing like the cold-water spring they'd visited, but it was wet and she thanked him.

"Well, you've seen it all," he told her.

She took a last look at the house. "You've done an amazing job."

"The first horses will be here in a couple of weeks."

"Were you serious about bringing my family here? To the mineral springs?"

"Yes, of course."

She nodded. "Good. When I return, I'm going to bring the rest of the stones and throw them in."

"How many more are there?"

"Maybe twenty or so."

"You're welcome here anytime. Not just with an invite or with your family."

She blushed, unable to prevent the rush of embarrassment. The last thing she wanted was for their friendship to get uncomfortable.

As though her high color had signaled him, he said, "I don't want things to get awkward between us, Elisabeth. We'd just settled into something manageable."

"I don't want that, either."

"All right. We're friends?"

"Yes. Friends."

He helped her aboard the buggy one last time and headed toward Jackson Springs.

* * *

Midafternoon, Gabe left Elisabeth in the shade on the boardwalk and pushed open the door on which gold letters spelled out the name of the bank above the name of the man he'd come to see.

The teller recognized him, and the man greeted him warmly. "What transaction can we help you with today, Mr. Taggart?"

"I've come to see Mr. Jackson."

"He's in his office." The man turned as though to exit the caged area. "I'll let him know you're here."

"No need," Gabe interrupted. "The one with the big bold letters that spell his name, right?"

"Mr. Jackson doesn't like to be interrupted without an appointment, sir."

Gabe strode past the lobby and down a short hallway, where he opened the office door without a pause.

Startled, Rhys looked up from a ledger on his desk. "Mr. Taggart?"

He stood and reached behind him for his jacket.

"Don't bother to dress for me," Gabe said.

It was obvious the man was uncomfortable at not having had time to prepare for a visit or don his jacket. He gestured for Gabe to take one of the plush chairs that faced his desk. "Please have a seat."

"This won't take long."

"What can I help you with today?"

"It's about my land."

His expression lightened, and his eyebrows rose. "Have you had a change of heart about selling?"

"It's funny you should ask."

With an eager step, Rhys came around the corner

of the desk. "I'm prepared to sign a cashier's check over to you."

"No need to pay."

Rhys stopped in his tracks. "What?"

"What are friends for, right? I just came to tell you to let your mother know she might want to buy a bathing costume."

"What?"

"I recall her saying she has a touch of lumbago. Perhaps a nice hot mineral bath will relieve those symptoms for a spell. Bring her out, why don't you?"

Rhys's face turned as red as a ripe tomato. It was warm in the room, but Gabe detected his color had nothing to do with the temperature, but rather the anger and embarrassment of his deceit being discovered. He stiffened, straightened his tie unnecessarily and walked back to his chair where he dropped before mopping his face with a handkerchief. "A mineral bath, you say?"

"Yes. Who'd have known there were hot springs bubbling from those rocks up there? Isn't that a wonder?"

"Yes, indeed." Rhys folded the handkerchief. "Should you change your mind, I might be able to facilitate a sale. There are rumors that former President Grant is looking for a vacation spot."

"What a coincidence." Gabe flattened a palm on the desk and leaned forward. "I won't be selling. Not to you, not to the former president, not to the king of England should he come lookin'." Gabe straightened. "What do you say we never talk about this again?"

Rhys's expression eased a measure. "Not to anyone else, either?"

"I won't say a word. Miss Hart will likely tell her father, however."

Rhys sighed and dabbed his face again.

"But it'll blow over. We all make mistakes, don't we? I couldn't let this go, you understand that, without letting you know I was aware of what you did. Now we're all wiser." He headed for the door. "And I hope smarter."

Rhys gave a sheepish nod and Gabe exited the room.

Ten minutes later, Elisabeth knocked on the open door to her father's office.

Sam looked up and spotted them both. "How was your ride?"

"Gabe's house is almost finished. It's going to be an excellent home."

"We learned something today," Gabe added. He went on to explain how Rhys had been making offers on his land and then explained how they'd discovered the mineral springs.

"I don't want to think he was doing something underhanded," Sam said. "But it sounds as though he knew all along, doesn't it?"

"There's something I haven't mentioned to either of you," Elisabeth brought up. "The time didn't seem right until now."

"What is it, daughter?" Sam asked.

"When Irene and I took the carriage to the theater in Denver and learned it was above a gaming hall, we saw Rhys with a group of men. He went inside that place."

Sam shook his head. "That surprises me."

Gabe didn't appear to share his feelings.

"I take it you're not surprised?" Sam asked.

"In my experience, most people don't have the same...*convictions* your family does. Rhys strikes me as a greedy fellow."

"Since he comes to my church, I suppose I'll have to talk to him."

"Before we came here, I let him know I was on to him."

"His mother probably isn't aware of his behavior, and there's no need to draw her into it," Sam said.

"It was okay that I told you?" Elisabeth said.

"Yes, of course," Sam answered. "Just because something's uncomfortable doesn't mean we don't need to address it and handle it. Now finish telling me your reactions to Gabe's ranch."

"There aren't any horses or cows yet."

Sam and Gabe chuckled and Elisabeth finished her descriptions.

That night Elisabeth went to her room shortly after supper and read her Bible. Finding the verses Gabe had called to her attention, she read the chapter in Philippians. Those words had never been as real to her as they became at that moment. It had taken a man who'd only seen those verses for the first time and spoken about them to bring them to life.

Glancing around, she got up and gathered the individual piles of stones and placed them inside a drawstring bag. No longer was she going to look at the symbols every day and regret a past that had been out of her control. She set the bag in her armoire to await her next trip to the mineral springs.

After she'd turned down the wick and plunged the room into darkness, she got comfortable on her bed and closed her eyes. Words and images swirled in her head like colors in a kaleidoscope.

What was she supposed to do with the news Gabe had delivered that day? He'd told her he wasn't expecting an answer or anything in return. He'd just wanted to say the words. But she had to lock her mind around them some way.

He loved her?

I just wanted to say it. Just once. Those words told her he wasn't going to bring it up again.

But the knowledge was there. Like a heart beating beneath a breast. He loved her. He loved her. He loved her.

She and Gil had been friends a long time, and while they did share a friendly affection, neither had ever had the inclination to express love. Yes, God's children are commanded to love one another, but this love was something else entirely.

How was she supposed to sleep?

I've lived a life you can't condone.

I can't measure up to the standards you've set.

He'd been taking sole responsibility for her inability to accept him.

I can't change who I am. I can't change that I wasn't raised in a family like yours or that I never really knew about Jesus until you spoke of Him...until your father taught me.

But he was changing who he was. At that point, she'd been too stunned to say that. Too stunned to say anything.

I'm inspired to be a better man. That's the future.

She'd seen changes in him since his arrival. She believed his inspiration wasn't created by anything she'd said or done, but fueled by the examples he was reading about in the Bible.

He'd gone to great lengths to provide for and educate his sister. He'd wanted to make a home for her...

and he wanted her to have a good husband. More importantly, he'd been willing to forfeit some of his plans for them because he wanted her to be happy. Irene may have complained a bit about his overprotectiveness at the beginning, but Elisabeth suspected she truly appreciated his concern.

If she was really honest with herself, Elisabeth had to admit she'd been a little jealous of how easily he made friends and how quickly he'd acclimated himself into a new community. People liked him and some even admired him.

As though glossing over his ability to make friends, he'd said he was good at reading people. Understanding people was a gift, however, and he had the gift.

He'd undeniably saved Donetta Barnes's life. That had been an amazing feat of skill and bravery, but the thing that stuck out the most to Elisabeth was the fact that he'd consequently found ways to take care of her now that she was widowed.

The congregation had taken her food, but Gabe had given her a job. That was an act of mercy and kindness, but also one conceived in wisdom.

He wasn't the person she'd first thought. He wasn't callused or heartless. Just the opposite in fact.

And she enjoyed kissing him.

How was she supposed to sleep now?

The following week, sooner than expected, Gabe moved Irene and Donetta out to the ranch house. He gathered them and Elisabeth instructed them how to manage a horse and buggy.

"Once you know this you won't have to rely on me or

one of the hands to get you back and forth from town. And you're going to need to learn one more thing."

He led them behind the house where hay bales had been stacked and bottles set atop them. He presented each of them with a rifle.

Irene accepted hers. "You're going to show us how to shoot these?"

"Yep. Never know when a coyote or mountain lion or even a two-legged critter will turn mean."

Elisabeth wanted to protect herself, but she didn't believe she could shoot another person. "Will you show us how to aim for a place that won't kill a human?"

"Yes, I will, Elisabeth."

He first taught them how to load the chamber and how to keep the barrel lowered for safety. Eventually the lessons progressed to target practice.

Donetta had experience, so right away she was the best shot. Irene jerked and jumped back each time she fired, so she didn't hit much. But Elisabeth was as precise and efficient about aiming and shooting as she was about everything. Within an hour, the bottles she aimed for shattered nearly every shot.

"I might have known you'd be my prize pupil," Gabe said to her later. "The one who hates guns."

"If I'm going to learn, I'm going to learn to do it well," she replied.

That week and the next were filled with normal activities in addition to shooting practice and Irene's wedding plans. Elisabeth stayed busier than ever.

Irene invited her for dinner one evening, and they sat at the long table in the new kitchen. "How do you like that stove?" she asked Donetta.

"It's a dream," the older woman replied.

Gabe entered the back door. "I saw the buggy and knew it was you. Is your rifle under the seat?"

"Irene invited me. And yes, it is."

"Told you you're welcome anytime even without an invitation." His hair was damp and his tanned face ruddy as though he'd recently washed. "The hands take their meals with us."

"I remember."

As Irene helped set the last few bowls on the table, John and Ward entered and hung their hats on pegs.

"How do, Mizz Hart," Ward said and John, too, greeted her, giving her a broad smile that showed all his teeth. Both of them were freshly scrubbed and wearing clean shirts. They seated themselves across from each other in about the middle of the table.

Gabe held out Mrs. Barnes's chair before taking a seat at the head. Everyone quieted, with heads lowered.

"Thank You for this food, Lord," Gabe said.

Elisabeth was so surprised she looked at him from the corner of her eye.

"Thank You that we have plenty of work to keep us busy. Keep us safe and well. In Jesus's name, amen."

The prayer hadn't been particularly eloquent or lengthy, but the fact that he'd said a prayer at all threw her thoughts askew.

Donetta picked up a heaping bowl of mashed potatoes and handed it to John. The food was simple fare of sliced roast, potatoes and carrots, but there was plenty of it and the men ate more than Elisabeth had ever seen anyone pile on their plate. They worked long, strenuous hours out of doors, and obviously worked up an appetite.

Irene met her eyes and grinned, obviously not a newcomer to this dinner table. "We pick up our dresses in Denver day after tomorrow."

"After supper show Elisabeth the beds and rugs and bureaus," Gabe said. "So she can see what her choices look like in the house."

After they'd finished the meal and eaten rice pudding, they drank hot cups of dark sweetened coffee. Donetta stacked dishes. Elisabeth carried bowls to the sink and the woman took them from her. "Not here, you don't. This is my job. You run along with your friend."

Irene showed her all the pieces of furniture they'd shopped for, and Elisabeth was pleased with how they looked in the rooms.

Irene excused herself for a few minutes, and Elisabeth stepped out the back door. She appreciated that Gabe had built a covered porch on the back of the house, and she stood in the shade of the roof, gazing toward the hillsides with their variegated shades of green.

Gabe spotted her and strode over. He didn't climb the stairs, but stood below her. "While you're in Denver, take Irene to a few of those furniture makers and see what she likes best. If you can somehow manage it without her knowing, I'd like it if you ordered a bedroom set or maybe a dining table or whatever takes her fancy."

"Without her knowledge?"

He nodded. "As a wedding gift. They're going to have that house and will need things to fill it. I don't figure Gil can buy it all on his lawman's wages."

She wanted to run down the stairs and hug him. Kiss him maybe. His thoughtful gesture touched her. "I already have somewhat of an idea what she likes from our previous trip, but I'll ask questions." She studied him in the fading daylight. "If I had an older brother, I couldn't ask for a better one than you."

He returned her perusal, letting his gaze take in her hair and fall on her dress. "I don't think of you as a sister, Elisabeth."

"I know."

The sound of hoofbeats reached them, and Gabe's attention shifted. Gil galloped toward them, then reined the horse to a walk and stopped several feet from the porch.

"Evenin', Deputy. Is Irene expecting you?"

Gil climbed down and used his hat to swat dust from his pant legs. "No. I thought I'd be working this evening, but Dan was feeling better and took his own shift back." He glanced up. "What kind of trouble are you finding here, Lis?"

"I'm well, thanks."

He grinned. "You're always well." He turned back to Gabe. "Is she inside?"

"She'll be out in a minute," Elisabeth replied.

"Have a seat on the porch there," Gabe said. "Elisabeth and I are taking a walk. Join me?"

She gathered her skirts and descended the steps.

A long low building had been framed with a stone fireplace at one end. The structure was a new addition since her last visit. "The bunkhouse?" she guessed.

"The men are lookin' forward to moving from the stable," he said. "I talked with a rancher who runs a spread up by Pagosa Springs. He told me he'd placed sod in between two layers of wood on the roof. Before the shingles went on his bunkhouse and barn. Holds in the heat, he says. I'm gonna try it."

Elisabeth considered how their relationship had

evolved from that first day on the train until this moment as he spoke to her about the development of his ranch and day-to-day happenings.

She trusted God for her provision and her safety, and in doing so she had to believe He'd had a hand in how they'd met. "Have you ever thought," she asked, "that you and I could have taken diffcrent trains? But we were aboard the same one."

"That's a fact."

"Those bandits could have held up a different train and hurt innocent people, but they chose the train the two of us were on."

"I've thought a lot about people and the choices they make. The choices we all make. Remember the day Doc Barnes was killed?"

"Clearly."

"I asked you how God could have let that happen."

"I remember."

"You told me God has given each of us free will to make choices."

"That's right."

"If I believe that—and I do now—then God didn't put those bandits on that train. They had free will to do as they chose. They chose to do wrong. Ours was the train they picked." Their walk took them to the stream that ran behind the clearing where the house and outbuildings sat. It was a narrow rivulet of water, only about five feet wide, but flourishing trees grew along the banks. "You and I have free will, too. How can God use us?"

"Because we listen to that still small voice on the inside," she reminded him. "God doesn't have to manipulate us. He simply speaks to us, and we respond."

She studied the branches of a huge oak tree that towered over them. "I've never told you this. I was planning to stay in Morning Creek another day, but when I woke up that morning, I felt very strongly that I should go home. I packed my bag and bought my ticket."

Gabe bent to pick up a stick. "I read in the Psalms that God knows everything about us. He knew us before we were born. He knew you'd take that particular train."

"Nothing is a surprise to God. He wasn't up in heaven wringing His hands when He saw those robbers get on board. I'm sure it breaks His heart when people do sinful things, but He made a plan to rescue innocent people by sending you."

"You're saying God worked through me?"

"You were willing. That's all He needs. You're important to Him. He had a plan for you, too, just as He created a plan for all mankind by sending Jesus."

"It took me a while to grasp that when Sam told me, but I understand how big God's love is now. I've accepted His love for me."

Elisabeth got a lump in her throat. She walked several feet away and stood looking out over the water. The sight and sound no longer had the hold over her it once had. She had released her guilt and her grief. Gabe had helped her do that. One more reason she knew God's hand was at work in bringing him here.

Tears welled in her eyes and blurred the sparkling stream in her vision. Why this man, Lord? Why not the man she had believed for—the one just like her father?

She composed herself and turned. He squatted a few feet from the edge of the water, breaking a stick into pieces and tossing bits in. He'd left his hat back at the house, and she studied the way his dark hair curled over his collar and around his ears. A lock fell forward over his forehead.

He was pleasing to look upon, no doubt about that. And he was smart and enterprising, with a plan for a ranch and the tenacity and grit to make it happen.

Her father had taken their family west because he had a vision of a new life, and he'd faced adversities to make it happen—continuing on even after the death of his beloved wife. He'd loved his daughters enough to marry a woman he wasn't sure he could love, but who would be there for them.

Gabe loved his sister like that. Enough to sacrifice and do what he'd believed was best for her.

Her father loved God with all his heart and served Him in all his ways. He taught people about God's love by example and through his preaching.

Elisabeth thought of that simple prayer Gabe had spoken at the supper table. He had once said he couldn't change who he was, but he had been changing ever since Elisabeth had met him. *I can't change that I wasn't raised in a family like yours or that I never really knew about Jesus until you spoke of Him. Until your father taught me. Now I'm inspired to be a better man. And that's the future.*

Her father had been raised in a Christian home, taught of the Lord his entire life, so of course he had more experience and eloquence. But maybe the important thing was what a person did with the knowledge they had. Gabe's hired hands saw the example of a man who sat down to pray at the supper table. Maybe he was their only link to hear about God's love for them.

Sam Hart loved people and went out of his way to help them. Gabe had provided a job—a good job and a home—for a widow. How could a person show more compassion than that?

It had been easy to set a lofty expectation, knowing there wasn't another man like her father and thereby conveniently keeping herself out of the marriage market.

She'd been so afraid of losing herself that she hadn't been open to love. She'd envied Irene's ability to make herself vulnerable. Love made a person transparent, and for a long time Elisabeth hadn't wanted anyone seeing through her.

No, there wasn't another Sam Hart.

But there was only one Gabe Taggart, as well.

And she loved him.

Chapter Twenty-Four

The sun had dropped low in the sky, casting her long shadow across the grass as she walked toward him. At her approach he threw the stick in the water and turned to sit on the bank and face her. One side of his mouth turned up in the teasing grin that had once provoked her, but now turned her insides to jelly.

"I recognize that determined look." He reached for her hand. "Come sit beside me. Should I be scared?"

She took his hand, but instead of sitting on the ground, she plopped herself into his lap so hard, he released a surprised, "Ooof."

"I'm sorry. Did I hurt your ribs?"

"What are you doing?" He steadied her with one hand on her elbow.

"Putting an end to a big mistake."

"What do you mean?"

"I'm pigheaded and a perfectionist. I like things orderly."

"Is there a surprise coming?"

"And I'm a coward."

"Not that I ever noticed."

She placed her hands on his shoulders. "You changed your whole life, Gabe. You moved right into a town where you'd never lived before and you made friends. You embraced something completely foreign to you—the concept of God's love and His will for your life. You move forward and you don't look back. You abandoned your past for a fresh start."

"How does that make you a coward?"

"It doesn't. I was making a comparison."

"To you? You don't have a past to bury."

"I did. I hung on to those stones so I could nurse my guilt. You opened my eyes to that. I held everyone at arm's length by expecting so much of them that they could never live up to my model of perfection.

"But I wasn't perfect. Far from it. I was afraid. Afraid of loving…of being loved…afraid I'd let someone down or that I'd be let down. Afraid of so many things. That's how I've been cowardly."

"I believe you're a brave woman who stands up for what she believes and for the people she loves."

"I wanted a husband just like my father."

"There's nothing wrong with that standard, Elisabeth."

"Except that there isn't another man like him. And if there was, I wouldn't want him."

"Why not?"

"Because I already love a man."

His expression flickered with uncertainty. Overhead the leaves of the oak tree rustled in the breeze. Crickets chirped in the underbrush. "You do?"

"I've fallen for a man who's generous and compassionate and brave. He shares my faith, and he has a good plan for the future. A future I want to be part of."

"Elisabeth, if there's a surprise coming, out with it. If you tell me this man is Junie Pruitt or Lester Quinn, I'm going to dump you right out of my lap into that water."

"It's not Junie Pruitt or Lester Quinn." She placed a hand on either side of his face and brushed her palms over the warm rough texture of his lean cheeks.

He brought his hands up her back to hold her more closely and stared into her eyes.

"This man has already said he loves me. And I'm praying he means it."

He threaded the fingers of one hand into her hair. "He means it with all his heart."

"He told me he would only say it once, so I can't be sure."

"That was before he thought there was a hope of having his love returned."

"And now?" Her breath caught in her throat as she waited.

"I love you, Elisabeth. I've been in love with you since the moment you looked me in the eye and challenged me to get out my gun and do something about those train robbers."

Her heart was already pounding, but at his words it raced harder. "I *what?*"

"I was content to sit there minding my own business, let them take their watches and baubles and be gone. You on the other hand, insisted you'd seen my gun and challenged me to stop them."

"I did no such thing."

"You did."

She thought back over those moments, fraught with tension and fear. She'd done precisely as he'd said. "I did."

They looked into each other's eyes. He grinned.

She leaned forward and kissed him, and he met her eagerly. She put every apology, every regret, every hope into that kiss, then leaned back, still framing his head in her hands. "I love you."

"Enough to marry me?"

Her eyes stung. "Enough to marry you tomorrow."

He kissed her soundly. "We'd better wait until after Gil and Irene are married or we'll steal their thunder."

"But no longer than that," she insisted.

"No longer than that."

Epilogue

On a sunny morning mid-September Gabe stood beside Samuel Hart at the front of the church. Constance Graham played the wedding march and the notes from the old organ made his heart skip a beat.

The front pews were filled with family—and people who would soon be family after this ceremony. His sister held baby Rachel, who slept soundly. Her new husband, Gil, stood beside her, his expression soft as he looked down at his new wife.

Clasping hands, Abigail and Anna, dressed in frilly pale blue dresses, gave him broad and encouraging smiles. They turned every few seconds to peer over heads to the back of the church in anticipation of their sister's entrance.

Josie gave Gabe a nod and a smile. The service hadn't even started yet, and she took a white hankie from her sleeve and dabbed the corners of her eyes. Beside her were John and Peter, and directly behind them stood Kalli with Phillip.

The doors opened and she stood haloed in sunlight, a vision in white satin and layers of lace and pearls.

She'd spent numerous hours on the details of the dress and the veil, but all he saw was Elisabeth. The woman he wanted as his wife from this day forward.

Instead of a practical braid, her blond hair had been fashioned into loops fastened to the back of her head, while long curls hung down her back. The veil wasn't long or cumbersome, but a small stylish embellishment that barely covered her eyes.

Since Sam was the father of the bride as well as the preacher, he waited until she'd come halfway forward and then went to accompany her the rest of the way. He folded the veil back from her eyes and gazed into them, then took her hand and kissed her fingers.

He then turned to Gabe and offered Elisabeth's hand. With emotion thick in his voice, he said, "I give my daughter to you to marry."

Gabe accepted her hand. When her shining blue eyes turned to him, his heart stopped altogether. For those moments no one else existed. She was the most beautiful woman he'd ever set eyes upon. And she was looking at him with such love, she took his breath away.

His heart started beating again. He took a breath. *Thank You, Lord, for giving me this woman and a whole new beginning.*

"We are gathered here in front of these witnesses, and in the name of our Lord God…"

Gabe Taggart was marrying the preacher's daughter.

* * * * *

WE HOPE YOU ENJOYED
THIS BOOK FROM

LOVE INSPIRED
INSPIRATIONAL ROMANCE

Uplifting stories of faith, forgiveness and hope.

Fall in love with stories where faith helps
guide you through life's challenges, and discover
the promise of a new beginning.

6 NEW BOOKS AVAILABLE EVERY MONTH!

SPECIAL EXCERPT FROM

LOVE INSPIRED
INSPIRATIONAL ROMANCE

Temporarily in her Amish community to help with her sick brother's business, nurse Rachel Blank can't wait to get back to the Englisch *world...and far away from Arden Esh. Her brother's headstrong carpentry partner challenges her at every turn. But when a family crisis redefines their relationship, will Rachel realize the life she really wants is right here...with Arden?*

Read on for a sneak preview of
The Amish Nurse's Suitor *by Carrie Lighte,*
available April 2020 from Love Inspired.

The soup scalded Arden's tongue and gave him something to distract himself from the topsy-turvy way he was feeling. As he chugged down half a glass of milk, Rachel remarked how tired Ivan still seemed.

"*Jah*, he practically dozed off midsentence in his room."

"I'll have to wake him soon for his medication. And to check for a fever. They said to watch for that. A relapse of pneumonia can be even worse than the initial bout."

"You're going to need endurance, too."

"What?"

"You prayed I'd have endurance. You're going to need it, too," Arden explained. "There were a lot of nurses in the hospital, but here you're on your own."

"Don't you think I'm qualified to take care of him by myself?"

That wasn't what he'd meant at all. Arden was surprised by the plea for reassurance in Rachel's question. Usually, she seemed so confident. "I can't think of anyone better qualified to take care of him. But he's got a long road to recovery ahead, and you're going to need help so you don't wear yourself out."

"I told Hadassah I'd *wilkom* her help, but I don't think I can count on her. Joyce and Albert won't return from Canada for a couple more weeks, according to Ivan."

"In addition to Grace, there are others in the community who will be *hallich* to help."

"I don't know about that. I'm worried they'll stay away because of my presence. Maybe Ivan would have been better off without me here. Maybe my coming here was a mistake."

"*Neh.* It wasn't a mistake." Upon seeing the fragile vulnerability in Rachel's eyes, Arden's heart ballooned with compassion. "Trust me, the community will *kumme* to help."

"In that case, I'd better keep dessert and tea on hand," Rachel said, smiling once again.

"Does that mean we can't have a slice of that pie over there?"

"Of course it doesn't. And since Ivan has no appetite, you and I might as well have large pieces."

Supping with Rachel after a hard day's work, encouraging her and discussing Ivan's care as if he were…not a child, but *like* a child, felt… Well, it felt like how Arden always imagined it would feel if he had a family of his own. Which was probably why, half an hour later as he directed his horse toward home, Arden's stomach was full, but he couldn't shake the aching emptiness he felt inside.

She is going back, so I'd better not get too accustomed to her company, as pleasant as it's turning out to be.

Don't miss
The Amish Nurse's Suitor *by Carrie Lighte,*
available April 2020 wherever
Love Inspired books and ebooks are sold.

LoveInspired.com